Shoot

Black & Blue # 4

Shoot (Black & Blue #4)
By
Melyssa Winchester

To the one and only, Tyler Breeze. Thank you for being so god damned gorgeous. This is all your fault.

A shoot in professional wrestling is any unplanned, unscripted, or real-life occurrence within a wrestling event.

Chapter One

Dawson

A degree in broadcasting, ten years reporting on celebrities for LiveWire as their most popular on-air personality, and this is what I've been reduced to.

Maybe reduced isn't the right word, but really, what word can be used to describe where I'm currently located?

Sitting across from my cousin and his partner Bryan, in what apparently passes for an office these days, but in reality, is just a trailer around the back of their training facility. Watching the latter tap his leg impatiently as he waits for Reese (who would be my cousin) to get on with this whole thing.

Oh, how the mighty have fallen.

Okay, I'm being a tad bit dramatic.

I didn't fall anywhere. I wasn't tossed overboard.

I jumped off the boat myself.

That's what people who have lost the drive for what they used to love, do, right? They get off the boat before it capsizes and sinks to the bottom of the ocean?

At any rate, it's what I did.

Contrary to what you might think, reporting on celebrities was surprisingly fun. It wasn't what I imagined doing for the rest of my life, but since I was on the air, and basically a local celebrity because of it, I wasn't about to knock it.

After ten years, though?

Well, Owen Hart said it best. And considering the company I'm currently keeping, he's the best person to explain it.

Enough is enough and it's time for a change.

Which brings me to this newest development, or rather, opportunity.

Shuffling some papers, Reese taps them against the desk before laying them down and sliding them over.

A man of few words, his actions now, what I see is the three-year contract we spoke about over the phone, tell me everything I need to know.

He wants me here and he's making it official.

Even if I've got a three-month probation period to get through before the real money comes in.

"Everything we discussed is there, Daws. You'll also see, as per your instruction, I made sure to draw up an alternate contract for the announcing we'll require once Lauren steps down next month."

I suppose if we're going to get into the second contract, we should probably go over exactly what the first one contains, huh?

Having just secured a television deal a few months prior, it appears as though my cousin and Bryan are in need of an on-air personality they can trust. Someone who knows the basics of the business—in this case, professional wrestling—and is capable of handling a backstage interview.

Now, this is *exactly* what I aspired to do.

Interview a bunch of apes in spandex.

Life's ambition achieved.

Harsh? Maybe. But, come on. How seriously am I supposed to take a show that by design is scripted beforehand? Where there are giants, monsters, and men running around in capes around every corner. I mean, if I wanted that, I should have studied acting instead.

Based on looks alone, and the scowl I'm sure has become a permanent fixture on my face, I could easily be cast in a *Revenge* revival.

Can anyone say new Emily Thorne?

Clearing his throat again, I shake myself and tip my head.

I really don't need to look this over. If there's one thing I've learned over the years, it's that no one has a head for a business like my cousin. Everything we discussed, I trust it's here, and honestly, even if it's not, I need to start looking at this like the opportunity it is. Grab the bull by the horns and own it like every other job I've had over the years.

Use it to find my smile again.

Shawn Michaels reference aside.

See? I'm fitting in already.

"When's the first taping?"

"Next week. It's all detailed in the contract, but we'll be needing you twice a week. Maybe more, depending on how smoothly things go." I part and wet my lips, ready to speak but the continuing of his dry monotone stops me. "Look, Daws. I know this isn't exactly the job you were looking for, but its exposure, right? I think we can make it work. This can be a good thing."

Of course, it can. With Reese's business acumen, and Bryan's love and desire for the sport, they've built quite the promotion over the last five years. Securing a television deal is just the tip of their iceberg.

Add me to the mix, especially with the knowledge I can bring to the table pertaining to the on-air aspects, and there's only one direction this can go.

Up.

Also, the direction I need to go in now that he's finally laid out the contract. Snagging a pen from the holder barely hanging on in the corner, I click it and scribble my John Hancock on the dotted line.

Sliding them back, I stand from the desk and leaning over, shake Bryan's waiting hand before doing the same with Reese.

"Dawson, wait," Reese calls out as I begin making my way toward the trailer door. "There's one more thing we need to discuss."

Resting my hand on the knob, I turn back to face both men and that's when I see it. Reese's expression changing. Hardening. Whatever he's about to tell me, something he takes even more seriously than he does the contract I just signed.

Skirting a look between him and Bryan, and seeing the other man giving nothing away, I raise an eyebrow and motion with my hand for my cousin to get on with it.

"We've got one rule I didn't go over."

"And the rule is?"

"The talent."

Consider my interest peaked.

"What about them?"

"They're hands off."

I can't help it. Between the serious expression he's sporting and how ludicrous his rule is, I laugh. A lot.

What only seems to embed the frown he's wearing deeper into his face.

Reese isn't a stranger. We've spent quite a bit of time together over the years, being so close in age and all. I also know a whole hell of a lot more than I want to about the men he employs. He has to know how pointless it is even bringing this up.

Like I'm going to go for a wrestler. *Please.* It's laughable.

"No screwing the talent. Got it, boss." I wink before bringing my hand to my forehead and saluting him. What as I turn my back and begin to head out the trailer door, earns Bryan's laughter as he calls out.

"Welcome to HFWA!"

Welcome indeed.

Chapter Two

Gavin

Contrary to what you've heard, I'm not infallible. I can be hurt. Wounded even.

I just don't broadcast it.

All anyone wants to hear about me anyway, is what random, panty dropping chick I'm banging this week.

It's the one thing that hasn't changed since I dropped the title and left CPW for the supposed greener pastures of HFWA. I might not be a champion—the honor going to my adversary, Matthias Kemper—but when it comes to women, I hold the damn title.

I just don't fucking want it anymore.

Not after her.

Kimberlee Parker.

Wycked, to anyone with eyes, a television set, or tickets to an event in the last three years. A sinful body with an equally damning mouth to match it.

To me, she's the first girl in years to see the real me. Make me want to be someone other than the persona I've created and mastered over the last ten years.

Also, the girl who spent the entire time with me, in love with another man.

Guess I should have seen it coming, huh?

After all, I'm the one who mastered the art of messing around with taken women years before Kimber even landed her ass in CPW.

She wounded me, the wicked one did.

Whooping my ass at the showcase at her first match in, and not letting up the entire time we were together.

Half a year might not seem like a long time to most, but for a serial deviant like me, it was a record.

Making Kimberlee the one chick on the planet with the power to tame the beast.

Only these days, the only beast she's taming is Kemper.

It's that bitter pill finding me at Johnny's tonight.

Whenever I've been in need of a glorious distraction, this is where I know to find it. The girls, some fans of what I do, others just in need of shedding their own labels for a night, looking for the same thing I am.

Excitement. Something different. A few hours of pleasure.

A pleasure I'm more than happy to oblige and give. Especially when as I'm going down on them, they're freeing me of my own bullshit.

Freeing me of Kimber.

"The reason you can't do this is him, isn't it?" I demand when after spending an inordinate amount of time outside, I catch her slinking back in through the side door of the building.

"Can we not do this now?" she whispers, dejected. Her eyes are unable to meet my own. Guilt and shame written all over her.

I'm right. Kemper is causing this.

"When would you like to do this? When would be a more convenient time for my girlfriend to admit she's in love with another guy?"

"You have no idea what you're talking about." She seemingly finds her fight as she meets my eyes, hissing before flicking her eyes down and around the hall.

"Matthias is gone, you find out about it, and suddenly you're done with me and you vanish. You wanna try and sell me on not knowing what I'm talking about again?" I laugh, despite finding nothing about this funny.

What is it with me? She was supposed to be another fuck and forget, the way I do with the rest of the girls. She puts me in my place a few times, and suddenly I feel an unfamiliar ache starting to form.

I care about her.

A lot, if the way I'm torn between pulling her sad body into mine and reaming her out is any indication.

I'm the king of screwing around for Christ sakes. It's not like I've got room to judge, but here I am doing it because this time, I'm the one on the receiving end.

"We have history, Gavin. I wouldn't expect you to understand."

"So, basically you're telling me you fucked the choir boy."

"Right." she snaps. "That's exactly what I'm saying."

I need to cut my losses. Walk away from this girl and the boatload of drama she's clearly dragging around with her, but I don't.

I can't.

She's different, and something about the way her eyes begin to sink as they lower, and she genuinely looks as though she just experienced a grenade leveling everything in her path, makes my next move clear. Effortless and easy.

"Come here,"

"What?" she asks as her confusion in my change filters its way through her eyes.

"You heard me."

"I did. I'm just not sure I understand."

That makes two of us.

"Let me spell it out. Whatever was going on or is still going on with you and Kemper, I don't care. You're here. He's not. It's obvious that whatever happened out there, didn't go the way you wanted it to. So, come here. Let me hold you. Nothing else. You obviously need someone. Let me be that someone."

What the hell has gotten into me? Since when did I become the sympathetic one? This girl has clearly gotten under my skin more than I thought. Not having my first thought be about how quickly I can get her out of those tights is unheard of.

But is the right move because right before my eyes, her feet begin to move until she's the one waiting for my arms to open and give her entrance to what I offered.

"I'm sorry, Gavin."

"I know, baby." I hush softly. "It's gonna be okay. I'll make sure of it."

There it goes again, my mind.

When I give it free rein, it always comes back to her and the pseudo-relationship we entered into after that day in the hall. The relationship on paper only, but unbeknownst to her, I put a hell of a lot more stock into.

I'm sick of this shit.

I need to get laid. Repeatedly. Ridden so hard, and so god damned often, it obliterates her from my head and heart altogether. It's the only way I'll survive going back to work and seeing them together.

Happy.

A first for Kemper.

All I ever wanted for my wicked one.

"Another one, Gav?" Johnny interrupts with a tap to the rim of the bottle. "You've been staring through this one for a while."

"Yeah, s—" I begin, as a hand slapping down a bill on top of the bar stops us both cold.

"I want three of something harder than what he's having, and while you're at it because he clearly needs another, throw in his next one too."

It only takes a second, but once I hone in on the fact that the voice attempting to buy my drink is female, I waste no time giving her a quick perusal, liking what I see and easily gifting her the look.

The one Kimber hated, but what has served me well over the years. Gotten me all of those perks she bitched at me about the night I met her.

Also, the one with the way her curvaceous body is now turning toward mine, is gonna score me another win tonight. My dick springing to life at the thought of having it—and my face—buried between this girls' thighs later.

Long, cascading, sun-kissed blonde hair falls away from her perky oval-shaped face, revealing perfectly pursed lips curving into a half smirk that has my dick tightening with need.

Her chest is covered, leaving every-fucking-thing to the imagination, which is more than okay. Half the fun for me is imagining just what it is I'm going to uncover when I push her down later and strip her of it. The barely there jutting out of her tits already telling me she's on the smaller end.

Good. I need something natural after all the silicone I've been pretending to enjoy.

Hers weren't. The damn vessel that needs to keep its thoughts to itself pipes up.

In an effort to squash it, I turn my attention to my partner at the bar again, flashing a smile of my own. One I'm hoping will relay genuine interest, and not just my perverted thoughts on her body. Only leaning back more comfortably in the seat when she returns it.

Her smirk lifting into a full smile.

Waiting until Johnny places three shot glasses of amber liquid in front of her and honing in on her throat as one after the other, she downs them all, I clear my throat and get down to business.

"Don't you think three is a little excessive?"

"In normal circumstances, yes." She winks. "But if you had the day I did, you'd need to drown yourself in these beautiful babies too."

I'm not a small talk guy. I'm the one who will sit down beside you once I've staked you out, hit on you in the way guaranteed to get me what we both want, and pull you away. With this one, though, there's something about the way she describes her day, and the way it sounds eerily similar to my life of late that has me switching things up.

"What's so funny?" she asks, and that's when I realize I'm laughing.

"Not a damn thing, princess."

Snorting, she signals to Johnny for another three shots, and this time when I laugh, it's deliberate.

"You're gonna need to tell me what was so bad you're about to drink your body weight in booze. There's a story. There has to be. You've already put more back than half the guys I work with."

Slugging shot after shot back and slamming them down on the bar top, she releases a laugh of her own. A beautiful evenly pitched melody which seems to go along with the rest of her.

Man, this dry spell must have been longer than I thought if I'm this caught up in the sound of some random chicks laugh.

A dry spell I desperately need to fix. Stat.

Leaning across the bar at the exact moment I pick up my own newly placed bottle and take a long draw of my own, she taps the bar and giggles.

Should have seen this coming.

She's already blasted.

I'm capable of fucking just about anyone, but I draw the line at inebriated girls. Their consent isn't real. They don't even know their own names half the time. How the hell can they have the wherewithal to tell me it's okay for me to go down on them? Or worse, fuck them into next week?

They can't. Which means I need to scour the place for someone who can hold their liquor.

"Stupid ass men. Family. God," she drawls, slamming her hand down on the bar. "Fucking family. They always get you."

She doesn't have a clue, and I know I'm taking her words out of their intended context but she's right in her assessment. Not about men—well, wait, maybe them too with the need I still have to get her underneath me—but her family comment.

They do get you.

In my case, they get me better than anyone else.

My family is the one set of people—the one place—I don't have to be Gavin Fortune, the former champion. I can just be Gavin.

Son of a bitch. Getting the warm fuzzies at a bar used primarily for hooking up isn't the way I intended to spend my night. This girl, whoever she is, has got me all sorts of screwed up.

"Aww, did your daddy cut you off?"

Snorting again, she shakes her head before gathering her wits and leaning back in the seat. The distance she's putting between us with her move, leaving me with an unfamiliar and unwanted sense of emptiness.

Yeah, I really need to get on with locking this shit down. I'm not sure how much longer I can keep this weird back and forth shit I'm doing up.

"My *daddy* would have to know what I'm doing in order to cut me off," she announces. "So no, pretty boy. I wasn't cut off. I wish it were that simple."

So much for the joke.

"So, your issues are with someone else. Let me guess. Mom? Older brother, maybe? Am I getting warmer at least?"

"Oh, you're hot as hell, but something tells me you, pretty boy, already know this. But no, you're actually ice cold."

Hot as hell, huh?

Game back on.

Except it's not at all what happens when I speak again.

"Who made you come here of all places to drink your day away?" I probe instead, finding myself interested. This place is only for deviants like me. A bar brat she's not.

"My cousin," She admits easily. "But it's not his fault. He only offered me a job."

"Doesn't seem so bad. Seems like a pretty stand-up guy if he's looking out for his family."

"It's just not what I pictured myself doing." She continues to ramble. "I spent half the ride from there to here wondering if I dreamed it. I can't possibly be what he needs me to be."

God help me. I should be turned the fuck off with the number of words pouring out of this chick's mouth, but I'm not. I'm intrigued. My interest, not the only thing piqued by the information dump she's giving.

Kimber clearly did more of a number on me than I thought.

Picture her naked, Gav. Just strip her down and imagine playing with everything underneath.

I can't do it, though. I can't picture this girl without her clothes, or what I could spend hours doing with the canvas she has to work with.

Not when I'm more interested in what she's going to blurt out next.

"What exactly does he need you to be?" I press, and she doesn't waste time, though I'm not at all prepared for the laugh escaping.

"You wouldn't believe me if I told you. I'm not even sure I believe it, and I'm the one currently living it."

She obviously doesn't know a thing about professional wrestling. There isn't much I wouldn't believe. I've pretty much seen it all, and have the mental scars to prove it.

"Try me."

"For real?"

"Yeah, for real. Did you take a job as a mascot or something?"

Real bright there, Fortune. There are worse jobs than having to wear a costume around for hours at a time. You're living it, remember?

"I wish. There's respect there. No, this is far worse."

"Then let me have it, or I'll have Johnny cut you off." I teasingly threaten, laughing when her eyes widen to the size of golf balls as she flicks her gaze over to where Johnny is serving a couple at the other end of the bar.

"You wouldn't dare."

"Try me," I repeat, smirking, and that's when she does it.

She tries me.

"I'm the new backstage personality for Harbour Front Wrestling Alliance."

Well, I got what I came for. It didn't happen the way I wanted it to, but there's no denying with just those seven little words, she's done it.

I've been fucked.

Dawson

You know when you drop heavy news on someone and their entire being changes in a way you can only describe as turning white as a sheet?

Until I sat down in this dive, dropped my choice of employment on the random, yet too gorgeous for his own good stranger, I didn't realize just how true the meaning behind it is.

He pales, and by pale, I mean, his coloring has drained away so much he's got to be seconds away from becoming one of those resulting white sheets.

It's not the coloring that gets me, though. It's the widened eyes first, then his posture changing, going from what had seemed to be pretty lax when I sat down, to hard. If I've got to compare it to something, it's as though he's readying himself for battle.

I just haven't the faintest idea why.

Is it possible he knows HFWA? Maybe has had some run-ins with some of the people who work for my cousin and it left a sour taste in his mouth?

Or could it be more?

Could this stranger be a co-worker?

He's pretty enough to be one, but something tells me with what he's wearing, the cut off at the arms shirt and the shorts giving me access to enough of his body to make a determination, he's not.

I might not spend the majority of my time knee deep in professional wrestling, but I do know when most of these guys walk away from a show, they're doing it sporting war wounds. Scars or marks from their battle that take the whole fake argument and toss it right out the window where it belongs.

Whoa, Daws. Just because you work for them now doesn't mean you've gotta get defensive on their behalf.

"Backstage personality, huh?" he finally manages to choke out, turning toward me and actively attempting to appear as though my admission hasn't phased him.

"Yeah, whatever *backstage personality* means," I say, nailing him with air quotes. "So, now that you know my reason for drowning in drinks tonight, what brings you here?"

His face contorts, and again, his body straightens, doing away with the small attempt he'd made at appearing relaxed and putting me on edge again.

What is his deal?

"You seemed surprised I would choose here to get my drink on earlier, could it have something to do with that?"

I'm expecting more silence given the way things have gone over the last several minutes, but it's not at all what I get.

Instead, he's meeting my eyes, smirk firmly back in place, and after a slight shake of his body, he leans over into my personal space and answers.

"Kind of, yeah."

My earlier verbal diarrhea comes back to haunt me as he encroaches on my space, making it almost impossible to put a thought together, much less take a breath. I thought with the crap hand I've been dealt with in the love department as of late, I was immune to reacting.

Apparently not.

My breath is physically lodged in my throat and my head is swimming. I'd like to blame it on the shots I repeatedly slammed down, but I know different. It's the company.

The hint of cologne wafting its way over me, soft and subtle, which judging from the look of him, he is anything but. The lines in his face as his lips curve up and his eyes seem to twinkle playfully, like he knows the effect he's having and isn't above exploiting it.

Oh yeah. It's *definitely not* the alcohol.

"You shouldn't...well, you shouldn't leave a lady in suspense."

Tapping the bar, his eyes pulling from mine to one of my newly filled shot glasses, he turns back, only this time, his eyes are sheepish and he's blushing.

"Looks like I'm not the only one who needs this." I motion to the shots before picking one up and holding it out to him. "So, drink up, stop acting like your reason for being here is more embarrassing than mine, and let's have it."

Brushing his hand against mine as his fingers slide around in order to take the offering, he brings it to his lips, draining it and placing it down on the bar before doing as I ask.

"I came here to get laid."

Oh. My.

Clearly, someone's turned the temperature up in the place with the way I can actually feel the sweat begin to prickle and set on my skin. It's taking everything in me not to fold the napkin on the bar and pat myself down.

If it wouldn't bring more attention my way, I'd reach up and undo the first couple of buttons on my blouse just to let the air in.

I went from comfortable, albeit a little embarrassed, to crawling out of my skin in the time it takes to blink.

As it is, the puddle of heat seeming to explode inside of me with his admission is so intense, I'm almost willing to risk the innuendo of it all just to solve the problem.

Almost.

Get yourself together, Traymore.

"Surely there are better places than here," I say, finding my voice again as I do a quick scan of the place. And being confronted by couples in varying degrees of undress. One lady even taking things to the next level and straddling some guys lap.

With what we're surrounded by, maybe he's in the right place after all.

How did I not see this when I walked in earlier?

"Out of the two of us, you're the one who doesn't fit here."

Whistling low, I laugh. He's not kidding. I definitely don't fit.

"I'm not having sex with you." I feel the need to state, and it's his turn to laugh.

"Trashed girls aren't really my thing, but even if they were, it was the furthest thing from my mind with you, princess."

"Hey, you could have just said I wasn't your type. No need to be a jackass." I mumble, lifting another shot from the bar and downing it before he has a chance to see how much the small statement did affect me.

Jesus. I must really be messed up if some stupid comment from a guy who trolls bars to get laid is getting to me.

My earlier statement was true. Stupid men.

Reaching out at the exact moment my hand goes for the third and final shot, he snags it, grinning when I level him with a scowl.

"Hand it over," I demand with a flick of my hand.

"No thanks. I think I'll take this one. Seems I need it more than you anyway. My asshole appears to be showing."

"Well, in that case, have at it." I nod toward the shot. "You definitely need it more than I do."

Reaching over for my purse, having more than stayed my welcome, I turn back toward my companion just in time to witness him downing the shot. My eyes are drawn to his throat and the way it bobs as he swallows. Not quickly the way I expect with as fast as he'd put the glass to his lips, but slow.

Achingly so.

Caught in the rise and fall of it, the heat from before creeps up on me again and no longer caring how it looks, I reach for the napkin and do what I should have earlier.

Bringing it to my brow, I wipe at the sweat, making sure to wipe it clean before moving on to my blouse.

What seems to capture the stranger the second my fingers connect to the plastic of the buttons as I slip the first one out and quickly move on to the second.

Meeting his eyes when after clearing his throat, he looks up from my chest, I bite into my lip, and the way his tongue slides out and over his own seductively, I know what's going to happen now.

I'm going to give him what he came for.

For one night, I'm going to forget I'm the responsible one in my family. I'm going to embrace my new position in HFWA, becoming like one of their larger than life stars. Adopting a new persona that's a far cry from the woman with a plan who doesn't let distractions get in the way that I normally am.

I'm going to let this stranger take me for a ride.

One where I learn if his tongue will be as hot running over the contours of my body as it is running over his lips now.

"Johnny," he calls out, slamming a hand down hard onto the bar and pulling me from the pool of desire I've fallen into. "Another shot."

"Didn't you get enough stealing mine?"

The wrong choice of words clearly as he moves in close, tongue slipping out over his lips, so near that one small dip of my head could have me tasting him.

"Something tells me that with you, one taste wouldn't be enough. I'm going to need the drinks to keep coming so I don't steal anything else from you tonight."

Groaning, when after he's dropped his latest rejection and he goes to move back into his own territory, he pauses and studying me, I see the trace of something, desire maybe, as it passes through his eyes right before time seems to stop.

I hear the sound of the shot glass being placed on the bar. I can even hear the music from the jukeboxes stationed throughout the place still playing, though they're infinitely lower. But nothing else moves. I can't even feel my own breath.

The only thing I'm acutely aware of, the way his body slips from the chair until he's standing directly beside mine. His hands grabbing a hold of the back of it and spinning it around until our bodies are aligned.

We're face to gorgeous face.

No more invading each other's space across the bar as we commiserate about our day.

Oh, no. This is something else entirely.

A fire ignited as his hand reaches out and cups my face, bringing it forward at the same time he leans in until it erupts and the flames climb until they're out of control as his lips descend down on mine.

The liquor we've both imbibed, flavoring what has to be the smoothest pair of lips I've ever had the pleasure of touching. Tasting.

Drowning in.

A sound, unexpected and unfamiliar, rises from the depths of my chest, and as the vibration of it touches his lips, he releases a moan of his own before probing deeper. Taking a longer, deliciously slow taste of everything my lowered inhibitions want him to have.

What I'm freely giving.

"I was...right," he admits in a breathless pant, all traces of his earlier smirk wiped clean and nothing but raw hunger remaining. "One taste is definitely not enough."

"Take as much as you want." I bravely tell him, resisting the urge to wrap my fingers up in his own shirt and pull him back until we're connected again.

I'm dripping with need, drowning in the all-encompassing warmth that continues to flood me, and God help me, I don't want to do it alone.

Downing the shot and shaking his head, his entire face scrunching as the sour taste of the liquid meets his throat, he clears it, righting his shirt before turning and facing me down.

"Don't say things you don't mean."

"Who says I don't mean it?"

Moving back into my space, my voice and all the courage I'd managed to muster falls away, as his nose brushes mine before he captures my lips again. Teasing me with his tongue, making deliciously slow love to my mouth with his own until he's pulling back again with a low hiss.

"Do you know how easy it would be for me to pull you off that stool, bend you over the bar, and fuck you?" Sucking in sharply, words failing, he grazes my ear with his teeth and makes the dampening taking place between my legs harder to contain. "That's what I came here for tonight. I wanted to bury myself inside some wet and willing pussy."

"So, do it."

"You want me to break my rule, princess?"

Oh God, yes. I want to break all the rules with you.

"Jesus Christ." He curses and that's when I realize my thoughts are no longer mine. "Johnny, your office free?"

Grunting out something to the effect of the room is free, with no attempt to hide his disgust, it's all my stranger needs to hear.

Turning his attention back, and wrapping an arm around my back, he hoists me up with an ease that given his size, I should have expected, but am still taken aback by. Throwing my legs around his back, he stares me down before taking another step, searching my eyes for any sign I've changed my mind. A silent question I give him the answer to as I lock my legs in tighter and bring my body flush to his.

I want this.

And with how quickly we end up crossing the room and entering a private office in the back of the place, buried out of sight, I'm not the only one.

Pressing me up against the door after we've crossed the threshold of the room and he's kicked it shut, he breaks our kiss to drop a name before pushing his body back into mine, rubbing and grinding against me as I push back with more of the same.

Gavin.

"Dawson." I practically purr when his hand drops away from its place against the door and moves in between our friction, slipping easily into the dampness he's created. Both of us moaning on impact.

Devouring my lips again, his fingers pick up speed between my legs as he assaults my every sense with the feel of him. Nipping my lips with his teeth before pulling me back off the door and making his way briskly across the room, spreading me out across Johnny's desk.

"Last chance."

Shifting on the desk and lifting, I fist his shirt the way I wanted to at the bar, and after yanking it—him—to me so close our lips actually brush, I swallow the out he's offering and give in instead.

Lifting the fabric up until he's pulling it over his head and tossing it to the floor, his lips are finding mine again, the free hand now wrapped securely around my back, reaching for the buttons on my shirt.

His voice, when he's unfastened the final button and pushed it back from my skin and proceeded to tease me with his tongue, lapping at my skin and dragging his teeth across the edges of my bra, etching the rest of the evening in stone.

"I'm going to fuck you now, Dawson. But because I can't trust myself not to shoot my load, it's going to be fast and hard. Your legs in the air and me buried balls deep until I'm filling every god damned inch of you with what you do to me."

He's saying it like it's a bad thing, the way he wants this to play out, and if I could find my voice, I'd tell him it's not. I want it the same way.

Want *him* that way.

"It won't be enough, though." He continues, his ravenous eyes penetrating mine long before his body does the same. "Like your kiss, I'm going to want more, so I hope you don't have plans for the rest of the night."

Chapter Three

Gavin

Lowering the shades over my eyes after exiting the car, and lifting my hand to block the effects of the sun as it zeroes straight in on me, I groan.

I'm not in the mood for this today.

After the beer, and what felt like an endless supply of shots, all I want to do is crawl back to the car, drive to the hotel, and hole up in my room until this shitty feeling passes.

This isn't normal. I don't drink to excess. A few beers here or there with the boys, and I'm good to go.

This nauseated feeling, the dizzying sway that almost took me off my feet when I finally dragged my ass out of the bar this morning, is unfamiliar.

I'm not used to it, and after dealing with it and the headache that started presenting on the drive here, I'm sick of it.

I am *never* drinking again.

For more than one reason.

The hangover is the least of my worries after the shit that went down last night. Or rather, who it went down with.

Dawson Traymore.

Otherwise known as my boss's cousin and the newest acquisition to the HFWA family.

Also, the one who brought every damn fantasy I've ever had about getting my fuck on in Johnny's office to life as she went round for round with me for three solid hours before we finally passed out sated in each other's arms.

The girl not at all as trashed as I assumed when I told her my stupid rule. Also, the girl that if Reese gets wind of me screwing with, is going to get me out on my ass.

Pushing down thoughts of Dawson, I shove my way through the gym doors and run straight into the last thing I want to see with the mood I'm in.

Kimber.

More specifically, Kimber and Matthias.

Great. I should have stayed at Johnny's.

And just the thought of his office, and the way Dawson looked as I had her bent over the desk taking her from behind, is enough to rouse my dick awake. More than ready to go another few rounds.

Ugh. I really should have stayed in bed.

Shuffling my way around the lovebirds, hoping to get by without having to stop and attempt small talk, especially with the sledgehammers being driven into every part of my skull all at once, I make it about two feet away before she's calling out.

Damnit.

I know we're supposed to be friends. She is my friend. I care about her. But with Kemper bending to her will, shouldn't it mean she leaves me the hell alone?

"Hey." She pops up beside me, hand resting on my shoulder. "Did you not hear me calling you?"

"I heard. Just not feeling in the mood to talk."

Pulling the glasses up and over my head, getting my wayward hair out of my face, her eyes widen as her mouth drops open.

"What?"

"You look like crap."

"Aww, Kimber, thank you! You always know how to make a guy feel good."

"What?! You've got serious baggage going on under your eyes. They're bloodshot, Gav. What else am I supposed to say?"

"I don't know. Nothing, maybe?"

Damn. I'm biting her head off and she's done nothing to deserve it.

"What happened last night?"

Now, this I can work with. She's used to me screwing around. Telling her I had a hot and willing girl under me should end this conversation easily.

"I got laid."

"Not likely." She scoffs. "You forget I know you. When you get laid, you're even cockier than usual, and you definitely aren't wearing those dark ass circles under your eyes."

"We were up all night."

"Right. Try again. How many all-nighters did we have, and you still came out smelling like a rose?"

"Kimber," I sigh in defeat. "Is there a reason you're over here instead of back there with Kemper the way you should be?"

It wasn't all that long ago I thought if we just stayed together long enough, I could make her forget all about Matthias and the hold he seemed to have over her.

Take what was fake and turn it into something real.

I underestimated their connection *and* my ability to be something other than a one-man fucking machine, obviously.

Nothing short of a nuclear blast would tear those two from each other, and I have serious doubts even that would have done it. It's like they were made that way.

For each other only.

Strange how I used to wish the same could be said for me. That I could finally shut down the Fortune persona and just be Gavin.

"Is checking in with my best friend not allowed anymore?"

Do you see?

This is why I need to keep my distance. She's my best friend too. The only damn person on HFWA's roster who actually gives me the time of day, and seems to have fun doing it.

Feelings are bullshit.

I should have just stuck to screwing my way through the talent. Things were so much easier. Damn her and her blunt ass, knock you on your ass attitude. She'd made me want to change.

Be me.

"That's not it. It's allowed. Of course, it is. It's just...I can feel his eyes staring a hole through my back. I think you should go over to him. We can catch up later."

There's no love lost between me and Matthias. He knows more than Kimber does. It's not exactly like I did a bang-up job hiding it. She got to me the same damn way she did him, which should honestly make us buddies, but instead, it's turned into something more adversarial.

"You're being ridiculous."

"And you're blind." Shifting around and letting my gaze fall on Matthias, I see I'm right and when Kimber catches it, she laughs.

"Okay, fine. You're right. I'm blind. But you're still reading too much into it. He's just looking at us."

"Maybe we should give him a show?" I joke, even though it pains me. Enough time clearly not having passed yet for it to sound like something other than me being a disrespectful tool.

"Gav..."

"Don't do that."

"Do what?" she asks, genuinely surprised.

"Say my name all pathetic. Go. Go back with him before Bryan and Reese get here and pull you away to separate corners. You know you want to."

The grin lighting up her face tells me everything I need to know. She'd come over with the best of intentions, and deep down, I appreciate her for it, but her place really is with Matthias these days. Our time, fake or otherwise, has passed.

"Stick around after the meeting, okay? Matty is going on some scouting trip with Reese and Bry, and it's been too long since we hung out."

She's killing me here.

"No can do, sweetheart. I've got a hot date after this."

Visions of Dawson's loose hair shifting back and forth as my hands cupped her tits as I fucked her over the desk invade my senses, and it takes everything in me not to reach down and adjust myself.

This is not the god damned time.

Forcing a laugh while I swallow down the reminder of the night before, I place both hands on her shoulders and turn her around to face Matthias, grinning when I'm met with his familiar scowl.

"Go, Kimber. If you don't do it, I won't be responsible for what happens when I smack your ass in order to make you."

Lifting my hands up and rubbing them together, I slap one across the other before lowering it down towards her ass. A move that has her laughter spilling over as she flies herself back across the room to her boyfriends' side.

Congratulating myself with a mental pat on the back, I turn and head over to the weights. Tossing my bag on the floor and laying down on the bench, I prepare to do a few reps at the exact moment Bryan and Reese make their entrance.

"Gather round, ladies and germs. We've got an announcement to make."

As lame as Bryan's greeting is, I have a feeling I know what's coming, and he doesn't have to say another word.

It's her.

Dawson's here.

Let the games begin.

Dawson

"That's right, princess. Spread those legs of yours and show me what you want me to taste next."

It's been like this all morning. Gavin and his dirty talk on an endlessly repeating loop. This latest one, of course, one of my personal favorites, since up until that point, he'd been so focused on my chest, he hadn't even realized he was the one preventing me from spreading my legs sooner.

My stranger turned dirty talking, sensual gift giver. A man whose last name I'd conveniently forgotten to get before we parted ways. A fact if I was into facing them this morning, I'd realize, was because it was never meant to be more than it was.

A one-night stand.

I actually did the unthinkable.

But it was *so* worth it.

The way he felt under my hand when after our third round, I turned the tables and pushed him down into Johnny's chair. Straddling his lap and letting my hands roam over the contours of his chest. The definition alone, enough to drive me straight into another orgasm.

His hands in my hair, fisting it while I rode him, slow and teasing at first, but faster and harder the longer his lips devoured mine until we were both spiraling into the abyss of pleasure together.

I should have known when he told me, once wouldn't be enough, it really wouldn't be. That even after we passed out in each other's arms on the shag carpeting, we'd wake and want to do it again.

Under his hand, a new Dawson had been born. An insatiable, wanton one, where every touch, every caress, only made me crave more.

And with the searing kiss he planted on me after we were done getting dressed, I wasn't alone in it.

I want to do it again.

Which has me both kicking and chastising myself as I follow behind Bryan and Reese as they enter the gym to meet with everyone. Kicking myself for not getting his number, or hell, even his last name. And embarrassed that of all the times for this to become an issue, it's now.

Right when I'm about to meet everyone who works for HFWA.

Who am I kidding?

Even if I wanted to see the mysterious Gavin again, there's no way in hell my new job would allow me the chance to.

Let alone Reese.

God, if he knew how I spent the night after leaving him, I'd never hear the end of it. The idea of me fraternizing with any of his superstars outside of the ring is enough to disgust him. I can only imagine what admitting to a sexual encounter with a stranger would do.

Thank God we're not that type of family.

"Gather round, ladies and germs. We've got an announcement to make." Bryan announces when we've made our way far enough in for the door to shut and when everyone's attention turns to us, Reese steps back, letting me move forward as his partner continues.

"You know we've been on the lookout for someone to do our ring announcing, backstage interviews, and promo spots. Reese and I wanted you here this morning so we could let you know we found her, and we hope you'll make her feel welcome." *Somehow, I doubt that's gonna happen.* "So, everyone, meet Dawson. Dawson, meet everyone."

Lifting my hand with a weak smile and an even weaker wave, I take in the sea of faces around me, all of them varying in size from midget and puny, all the way down the line to a monstrous behemoth. Their faces all masks. None of them, but maybe one or two of the guys nearest us, showing their true feelings at all.

It's only when I catch movement from the corner of the room, my breath catches, and the night before, along with all the naughty thoughts that come along with it, slams straight into me.

Making his way around a couple of the other guys, weaving around others until he's front and center, is none other than the man who brought my deepest fantasies to life the night before and has been non-stop starring in newer ones this morning.

Gavin. *My stranger.* He's here.

Oh no.

No. No. No. It can't be. He can't be.

There's no way the man I met last night can be one of them.

Except with the pained expression he's wearing, his eyes quickly pulling from mine and landing on Bryan, along with the defeated slump to his body, there's no denying it.

It's true.

Gavin is one of them.

A professional wrestler.

"The talent."

"What about them?"

"They're hands off."

It's not even my first official day, and one thing is abundantly clear.

I'm screwed.

Chapter Four

Gavin

I was wrong last night when I said I was fucked finding out who she is.

I may have gotten fucked in the most literal sense of the word. Hell, I was fucked repeatedly last night, but standing here and meeting her eyes as she's introduced to the rest of the roster, this is what being truly fucked looks like.

The second she saw me, the confusion became apparent as her brow furrowed and she repeatedly blinked, as if in doing so, she could unsee the reality of our situation. Then, as it seemed to kick in, I saw the hurt filter through. Her eyes watered—what I had to look away from—at least until she blinked it away and put on what I have to assume is her game face.

A face I'm familiar with as I've been wearing the same one for well over a year now.

Having to lie will do that to you.

It just never should have happened to her.

And it wouldn't have if I had just told her the truth before I let my dick do the talking.

This is all my fault.

"Daws—" I call out as she turns toward Bryan, but the rest pulled from my lungs as a hand slams down hard on my shoulder blade.

"Rethink what you're about to do, Fortune."

Reese.

"Rethink what? Introducing myself to the new girl?"

"Exactly."

"Didn't Bryan say he wanted us to make her feel welcome?"

Tightening his grip on my shoulder, making it damn near impossible with the weight he's shoving down to shift, much less break the hold without actually getting into an all-out scuffle, he wastes no time letting me know what he thinks.

"You damn well know how he meant it. Everyone here is well aware of your reputation. Being warned shouldn't be a surprise."

He acts like I wasn't the one living it. *Jesus.* I know what a whore I am. I don't need the reminder.

"I was one of the biggest and loudest advocates for bringing you in, you'll recall. Bryan didn't want to take the chance, knowing exactly the kind of bullshit you'd bring with you if you ever came here." Motioning to where Matthias and Kimber are, away from the rest of the group and huddled together, I get the message loud and clear. "Don't go through with whatever you're planning and make me regret it. She's hands off."

My hands are the least of your problems, Harrison. It's my mouth and my cock you should be warning off considering where and with who they were buried in last night.

"I got it. The new girl is Fortune free."

"Good. Glad we're on the same page."

We're not even in the same damn book, but if it means he screws off and leaves me alone so I can figure out a way to get to Dawson and attempt to explain, I'll tell him whatever he wants to hear.

"We are. I did just want to say hello, though."

"It's never just hello with you, Fortune."

Touché.

"For once, just do what you're told. Stay away from her, Gavin."

There's no denying their family connection. Even though they look nothing alike and don't even share the same last name, there's no mistaking he cares. The need to repeatedly warn me, speaking to his need to protect her.

Little does he know that after last night, Dawson isn't the one who needs it.

I am.

"Gonna be hard to do that if she's interviewing me, boss," I smirk. "But, don't worry. I'll keep my distance. Now if you don't mind, I've got someplace to be."

The only place I really want to be is back in Johnny's office where the rest of the world and all of the judgment can't get to me. The office where I wasn't Gavin Fortune, resident man whore.

I was just Gavin.

A man tasked with giving pleasure to a woman who to her credit, was determined to do the same in return. Giving back just as much, if not more, than she was getting.

Giving me one of the best nights of my life.

I would give anything to go back to that moment because, this one? Where I have to stay away, when all I've wanted to do since she walked in is steal her away again, is for the fucking birds.

What a mess.

Dawson

"You need to be careful with him."

Turning toward the voice, I take in the woman standing beside me and following her gaze, I see it on Gavin, the same way mine was before she interrupted.

"Excuse me?"

"Gavin. The guy over there lifting who you haven't been able to tear your eyes away from."

"I don't know what you're talking about."

Patting me on the shoulder, obviously seeing through my lame attempt at feigning stupidity, she smiles softly.

"Keep telling yourself that."

Bringing her hands to her side, she smiles again before turning to go, making it a whole two feet away before curiosity gets the better of me, and I'm calling her back.

"Why do I need to be careful?"

Grinning when she turns around again, she skips back, and when she stops, she motions around the room with a sweep of her hand.

"I'm guessing you don't know much about what we do."

"You'd be right."

"So, what do you know? I mean, don't take this the wrong way, but if Bryan and Reese brought you in, there had to be a reason. And not knowing anything about the roster is a black mark if you catch my drift."

"I have a degree in broadcasting. I've spent the last ten years interviewing celebrities and reporting on stories. It's my background and experience landing me here."

"Well, sure, but you're also related to the boss. I'm sure that one didn't hurt either."

Scowling at her insinuation, she laughs, holding her hands up in surrender.

"I'm sorry, Dawson. What I should have said is, I know better than anyone what it's like being related to someone in the business. Forgive me?"

"Who are you?"

"Kimberlee Parker. Otherwise known as Wycked when I'm in the ring. But you can call me your current Women's Champion. I find that one's much easier. Plus, I happen to like it a lot more than the others."

"Well, Kimberlee Parker, you're forgiven. I know how it looks. Hell, how it is. I don't really fit here."

"No, no. You wouldn't be here if they didn't think you belonged here. It really was just me being too blunt. Though, according to him," she pauses, pointing to Gavin again. "It was me being blunt that made him pull his head out of his ass."

There's an affection when she looks at Gavin, and the way she smiles at the memory has my insides twisting. A feeling so foreign it's got me rubbing at my chest in order to rid myself of it.

Why the hell would their relationship set me off? It's not like what happened last night was some life-altering event. It was a night filled with meaningless, yet passionate sex. Two people giving in to the urge for release.

Nothing more, nothing less.

"Are you two together?"

"Ha!" she laughs, slapping me in the arm. "You're funny. No. We're most definitely *not* together."

There's more to this then she's saying. Her finding the entire thing humorous, mixing with the affectionate look on her face whenever she looks his way, lends to it.

I'm just not sure I can handle knowing what the story is with the rising need I have to tell her to stop looking at him the way she is.

"So, why do I need to be careful with him?"

"Gavin has a reputation. A not so good one."

"And?"

Someone needs to tell this girl we all have a reputation. All it takes is one jilted or pissed off person, and none of what we did before or after will matter. All that will define us is the one horrible mistake we may have made.

Like the mistake I made last night.

"And a lot of nice girls fall victim to it."

Now I get it. She's warning me off him. Little does she know she has nothing to worry about. With the guilty look on his face when he made his way to the front of the group, it's clear he was holding a whole lot more than just his last name back last night.

Not that it would have made much difference.

"You don't need to worry about me falling victim to Gavin, Kimberlee. No offense, but wrestlers don't exactly do it for me."

At least, they didn't until last night.

"None taken." She laughs, her hand coming out and pointing across to where I see Reese talking with another guy. "It means I've got nothing to worry about with him."

"My cousin?" I'm so lost. A few seconds ago, I thought there was something with her and Gavin. Now I have no idea what's going on. All I do know is that whoever elicits the look transforming her entire face, is probably the luckiest guy in the world.

There's no denying she's in love.

"The guy beside him. Matthias."

"Matthias...Kemper?" I ask as his name sparks a memory of a story I covered before leaving LiveWire.

"Yeah. You know him?"

"Of him. When he had his accident, I reported on it. Celebrity news." I offer up in lame explanation.

"Ahh, okay. Makes sense now. It was all over the place when it happened. We didn't realize just how big he'd gotten until then."

"I'm sorry."

"What for? Were you one of the reporters camped out on our front lawn waiting to shove a microphone in our faces?"

"No, but I know how it goes. I've lived it."

"Why did you leave?"

"I needed a change. It was growing stale, I guess. I didn't exactly set out to report on celebrities for the rest of my life."

"You figured you could go a little faker?"

Slapping a hand over my mouth when the laugh falls so loud it garners the attention of a few of the people around us, I just nod until it subsides.

"That's exactly it."

Falling into a comfortable silence, both of us standing and taking everyone in, I'm startled when she breaks it.

"He's a good guy, you know? Even if he does everything in his power to sabotage it before anyone catches on. If you're interested," she leans in whispering, catching me in the act again. "You should go over and say hey."

If she only knew.

Gavin got a pretty big *hello* last night.

"I'm good, but thanks for the info."

"Alright. I better go catch up with Matty before Reese and Bryan steal him away for the weekend. It was nice to meet you, Dawson."

"Same here, Madame Women's Champion."

"Now you're getting it." She grins, leaning over and giving me a half hug before setting off, taking a few steps away before calling back over her shoulder. "Next time, if you don't want anyone to know you're looking, try not squinting. Dead giveaway, newbie."

Chapter Five

Gavin

"You lied to me."

Resting the weight back, I shift to who's talking, cursing when a hand impacts hard with the back of my head.

"Ow!" I exclaim, bringing a hand over my hair and rubbing the spot she attacked. "No, I didn't."

"You said you had a hot date once the meeting was over. Yet, here you are lifting an insane amount of weight for fun. Want to tell me again you didn't lie?"

"I wanted to get in a workout before I go. Any more questions, officer?"

After another thwack to the back of my head has my jaw locking and her laughing uncontrollably, I give up the game.

There's no sense lying to Kimber. She always sees right through it, and on the rare chance she doesn't, she'll browbeat me until she gets the answer she's after. Might as well just fess up.

"I'm lame, and I suck. I didn't have anywhere else to be. I just didn't wanna start something with Kemper. I know he's still touchy about us."

"You guys, I swear." She sighs exasperatedly. "You need to talk to each other because your heads are so far up your own asses, you don't see the truth for shit."

"That truth being?"

"He knows what happened between us. And as much as he hates that he pushed me away, and drove me to that extreme, he's not upset about it."

"Says you. Do you really think he's going to come up and tell you he doesn't like me? Kimber, guys, we just grunt, stare, and throw our weight around."

"You forgot the growling."

"See?! You do get it."

"You make it sound bad. Sometimes a little grunting and growling, mixed with a hardened, sex on stick look as they stare at you staking their claim, can be hot."

Gagging and jamming my finger down my throat, she lifts her hand threatening another whack and making me laugh.

"Sorry. I read a lot when Matty goes out of town."

I like to think with the number of women I've been intimate with over the years, I know a thing or two about what they find attractive. But this, a guy acting like a possessive jackass, doesn't compute.

Is it really a turn on?

"The look on your face right now! Oh my god, Gav. It's priceless."

"What look? The disgusted one?"

"I was thinking more along the lines of curious, but sure, we can go with disgusted."

"There is nothing curious about this face." I circle it. "But I'm almost all the way to grossed the fuck out."

"Yes!" she fists the air. "Mission accomplished. I win."

"Obviously. Since when does Parker lose?"

"Annnd this," she says, throwing her arm around my neck and squeezing her body into my side. "Is why you're my best friend."

Returning her squeeze and bringing my head down on top of hers, I sense movement to the left of us and flicking my attention to it, I see just what—or who—is behind it.

Dawson.

Of course, this is how she finds me. Because you know, after the warning shot fired by her cousin—who doubles as my boss—it couldn't possibly get any more awkward.

Kimber is my friend. She's happy with Matthias. There's really nothing going on I need to feel even the smallest sliver of guilt about, yet that's exactly what happens when our eyes meet, and I swallow. The taste in my mouth uncomfortable, bordering on acidic.

I don't want her to see me like this.

Get the wrong idea.

I know I perpetuated the damn idea, whoring myself out to any and all comers, but shit. I haven't done it in months. I don't want to do it anymore.

"Kimber, I need a favor."

Pulling back with a raised eyebrow, I resist the urge to crack a joke and just spill what I need.

"I need to talk to Dawson."

"What does that have to do with me? Better yet, why would you need to talk to the new girl? Did you do something you shouldn't have?"

When I don't so much as dignify any of her questions with answers, her eyes go wider, and she slaps the shit out of my arm.

"You, stupid jackass! You did do something with her, didn't you? That's why you're not answering. Please tell me you didn't screw her. Anything but that."

What the hell am I supposed to say here? It's either I lie, resulting in me lying about Dawson, which for some unexplainable reason I don't want to do, or I tell her the truth and she beats on me for being 'Asshole Gavin'.

I'm damned either way.

"Are you going to beat me for telling the truth?"

"No. Yes. Maybe. I don't know." she laughs. "How about you start by telling me first and then I'll decide."

"Where's the benefit for me?"

"There isn't one no matter what way this goes, Gav. I thought you knew by now."

"We hooked up last night."

There. It's out.

Bringing my arms up in a defensive position around my face and head, I wait her out, only lowering them when I've gotten what I'm after and she's laughing.

"So, you weren't lying about that earlier."

"Nope, and it really did go most of the night."

"Gross, Gav. TMI."

"Says the girl who gets wet thinking about Matthias growling."

"Touché."

"You know the kind of mood I'm in if I go to Johnny's, Kimber. I'm looking to score ass. I need the release. I wasn't prepared for her to be the one to sit down beside me."

"Dawson was at Johnny's?"

"See? She's as out of place there as she's going to be here. I could tell she wasn't like the regular crowd, and with the way she came in downing shots, I wasn't going to touch her anyway."

"But?" Kimber probes once I finally shut my big mouth. "There's gotta be a but. It can't end there."

"It doesn't since I already admitted we had sex."

"So, get the rest of it out, and then tell me why you need my help to cross the room and talk to her because I'm lost. You're one of the cockiest guys I know. If you can't talk to a girl, the world really *is* screwed."

"She turned me on when she talked."

"You don't go for girls who talk?" she covers her mouth, muffling her laughter, and I roll my eyes.

"That's not what I meant."

"Okay, I'm done making jokes. Explain please."

"There's a way the guys are at Johnny's. They're the ones buying the drinks for the chicks they're gonna end up banging. This girl storms in, throws her body down onto the stool, and before I can even get a good look at her, she's slamming money on the bar asking for shots *and* to pay for my drink. It was different. Kind of hot."

"We seriously need to talk about the girls you nail when we're done with this. God, Gavin. If a girl ordering drinks for herself is such a rare occurrence for you that it's a turn on, something is wrong."

"Maybe we like a little bit of ballsy in our women. Ever think of that, huh?"

"You're such a child."

"Yes, yes I am. Anyway, I started talking to her, and it just got worse. I wanted her. And before you throw up, let me finish. I'm not gonna detail shit, but God. She might have been the best kiss

I've ever had. I don't kiss when I fuck, but her, I could have spent the entire night just kissing her, and it would have been the sexiest night I've had in ages. If ever."

"Umm...okay. Wow."

"Too much?"

"No. It's just, we've talked a bunch about some of the girls you were screwing around with last year, and none of them ever made you talk like this."

She's right. I know how I sound right now. How unlike myself I'm acting.

But last night, again this morning, and for a third time when she walked into the gym and we saw each other again, there's been an unexplainable pull to her that has me wanting to shed the old Gavin altogether. Adopt a new model.

A better one.

"How can I help?"

"Reese swore me off her. I'm not even allowed to say hello. I need to talk to her. Explain."

"Of course, he did. She's family and you're..."

"I'm me. Yeah, I know."

"What do you need to explain?"

"Last night, she told me she was going to be working here. I could have told her who I was, and I didn't."

"You knew who she was before you had sex with her? Jesus Christ, Gavin! So, you willingly did something you knew would end up coming back to bite you? Do you really want to end up out on your ass?"

"It's a risk I'm gonna have to take because I don't regret it. It wasn't a mistake. The only mistake is me not telling her who I was and letting her find out like this."

"She's probably feeling pretty uncomfortable and embarrassed, huh? Must be why she lied to me when I called her out on staring at you earlier."

"You did what?"

"She was standing off alone watching you. She looked sad. So, I went to talk to her. Called her out on looking at you, and making it so damn obvious."

"You see why I have to talk to her, right?"

Nodding, she grins. "I do, but if I do this for you, you owe me big."

"Anything."

"You need to have dinner with me and Matthias when he gets back."

"Anything but that." I groan, and she laughs.

"Take it or leave it."

Following Dawson, as she moves across the room, and swallowing down the bile threatening to lift over having to break bread with my adversary both in and out of the ring, I make my choice.

"Fine. You give us a chance to talk, and I'll come for dinner. I'll even make something."

"Deal. Now listen carefully, because this is my plan." Leaning in and bringing her hand up to my ear in a lame attempt to keep her next words private, she lays her grand plan on me. "You get up, march over, and talk to her, because Gavin, Reese left right before I came over to see you."

"I'm out of town for two days tops, maybe three. I know it means I won't be here to guide you through your first day, but I'm only a phone call away."

This sounds suspiciously like a father-daughter chat, and considering how close we are in age, it's bordering on uncomfortable.

"Got it, Dad."

"Daws, I'm serious. I know this is new to you. If you need me, call."

"If I promise to call you, will you stop sounding like my father?"

Smirking, he pulls me into a quick embrace.

"Never. If he's not here, he'd want someone picking up the slack. You know Uncle Eric. He'd kill me if he thought I left you vulnerable."

He's right. I do know my dad. I just figured turning thirty meant I was old enough for the protective detail to slack off, at least a little.

"If I need help, I'll reach out to someone, and if that doesn't work, I'll call. But it's gonna be fine, Reese. I'm a big girl, and I've handled heavier stuff than this."

Chewing on the inside of his mouth, I can tell he doesn't believe me. I just don't have the first clue how to make him see I don't need him hovering.

"Look, before I head out, there's one other thing I wanted to talk to you about."

"If this is about the show, we've already been over everything. You're just looking for excuses not to leave."

"It's not about the show."

"Okay, well, let's hear it."

"Gavin Fortune."

Stomach meet the floor.

Of all the names he could have dropped, that's the last one I'd been expecting, though, given his earlier warning about staying away from the talent, it shouldn't be.

Just walking around here for the last thirty minutes, I can see Gavin's reputation really does precede him. He's the talk of the room, even though none of it is being said to his face the way it should be.

I've gotten more than enough history of his time in both CPW and HFWA over the last few minutes here than I ever would have doing research on him.

This is such a mess.

"What about him?"

"I know I told you the talent was hands-off, and I meant it, but it's different with Gavin. If he approaches you, attempts to talk to you or fuck, flirts, I'm going to need you to step away. Don't engage with him."

Excuse me?

I'm expected to work with these people, getting to know them all on a more intimate basis so I can do my job correctly, but I'm not allowed to so much as a wave at one of them?

"So, you want me to let someone else do the work you hired me for?"

"No." he sighs, running a hand over his head and down over his face. "You obviously have to work with him, but I'm talking about when the cameras are off. I need you to stay away from him."

"Why?"

"He's a phenomenal performer. I mean, there's a reason he ran at the top of CPW for so long, but his downfall is in how he operates away from the ring. Dawson, I know I probably have nothing to worry about, but just do me this one favor and stay away."

If Reese thinks for a second, he's going to come over here and warn me off someone, not giving me reasons why, he's got another thing coming. I don't care if it delays his trip out of town with Bryan and Matthias. He's giving me answers.

"You're not making any sense. What is so bad about this Gavin guy that you're seconds away from making me pinky swear to stay away?"

"He uses girls. Screws them and dumps them. Fucks and forgets them. It's his MO. I knew it when I snagged him from Smith, but because of his relationship with Kimberlee at the time, I didn't think I had anything to worry about."

Kimberlee.

I knew there was more to the story than she was saying.

They *were* in a relationship.

"They dated?"

"If you can call it that. Whatever it was, Fortune seemed to be on his best behavior. There were no reports of his extracurricular activities outside of the ring like there were when I first showed interest. He was clean as a whistle. With Kimber and Matthias together now, it's left the door open for the Fortune of old to make a comeback. I don't want you anywhere near it."

Sorry, cousin. A little too late with your warning.

"Maybe he's changed. If you're saying he was good when he was with Kimberlee, and he hasn't given you any trouble since they split, maybe you're making something out of nothing."

"With Gavin, nothing is always something. Just stay clear of him."

"No."

"Excuse me?"

"I'm not going to actively go after him if that's what you're afraid of, but I work here now. You hired me to do a job, and in order to do the job effectively, I need to interact with everyone the same way. That includes Gavin. So no, Reese. I'm not going to stay away."

"Fuck me, Dawson. Do you have to choose *now* to be stubborn?"

"Nope. I'm always stubborn. It just doesn't suit your needs right now, so you're annoyed by it."

"He inserted himself into another wrestler's long-term relationship a few years ago. Picked up with his girl and had an ongoing affair. Are you hearing me now? An affair that culminated in one of the best performers CPW ever had turning into a wreck. He's nailed pretty much every girl there, and even a few we brought in here before the merge. He's bad news, Dawson. Even for someone as stubborn as you."

Sucking in a breath as I come to terms with what Reese is telling me, my stomach recoils.

Just who the hell did I sleep with?

He didn't seem like a homewrecking man whore last night, even with his blunt admission of being in the bar to get laid.

It's not a side I saw, and it's not because I was focused on his backside.

It was a nice backside, though.

Sighing and leaning into Reese, resting a hand on his shoulder, I give up the fight, pushing down Gavin and the night entirely, gifting Reese with what he wants.

Considering how easy it was for him to keep mum last night about the connection he had to the job I told him about, and everything I'm hearing now, it's an easy decision to make.

I might not believe Gavin is bad news, but I do know he's probably not the best guy for me, and that's enough.

"I'll stay away, Reese. If it doesn't pertain to my actual job, Gavin Fortune will be persona non grata."

"Thank you." He smiles lightly before bringing me into another embrace. "I know it seems like I'm being a prick, but I just want to keep you safe."

"I get it. It's okay. Now go. I know you've got to get on the road."

"You're sure you'll be alright until I get back?" he asks again, pulling back and looking from the door where Bryan waits, and back again.

"I'm gonna be great. Promise."

"Love you, Daws."

"Nice try, cousin." I laugh, shoving his shoulder, and motioning with my hand to the door. "I'm always going to love you more, and you know it. Now get out of here before I make Bryan leave you behind."

"Don't think he needs your help for that." He laughs, but listening, he turns and starts walking away, but pausing a few steps from the door where Bryan and Matthias now wait, he turns back to me.

"Before I forget. Call Uncle Eric. He knows."

Crap.

I was hoping I still had a few days before I had to go home and face the firing squad of my parents. The first time in years I held back a plan from them, but a decision that given the closeness of our family unit, was surprisingly freeing. But if I thought protective Reese was a pain in the ass, there's no telling how this conversation with my father is going to go.

Reese is a puppy compared to him.

Turning toward the side of the room where I left my purse, determined as Reese makes his way out of the building to handle this call so I can get it over with, I pause halfway across the room when the hairs on the back of my neck shift and stand on end.

Looking around for a reason for it, my eyes land on and meet his and everything is made clear.

Kimberlee attached to his side, the two of them comfortable, and exuding a closeness I've only dreamed of having, my mouth goes dry. Saliva sticking to the roof of my mouth as my stomach twists and recoils. My head swimming with pangs of regret and a little rage.

Slow your roll, Dawson. You're acting like a crazy person.

A jealous crazy person, if the way my fists clench at my sides is any indication.

I need to heed my cousin's warning. The history lesson on Gavin I was given. Taken with everything else I've seen since I realized he worked here, and the way he is with Kimber now, it's clear he really is bad news the way Reese said.

Bad news for my heart.

Chapter Six

Gavin

I've never held a woman before.

Okay, wait. That's not coming out right.

What I mean is, until last night, I've never stuck around long enough to really connect with someone I jammed my dick inside. It was almost always about the release or the craving I had to have a body underneath me.

I was a selfish piece of shit, what can I say?

All I did before was take what I needed from these nameless, faceless women. Never once thinking about how they might feel after it was over. I couldn't risk a connection even though; from the time I was old enough to understand what a real coupling meant—based mainly around my own parents' marriage—that's exactly what I wanted for my life.

Somewhere along the way, I drove off the road I was on and ended up straight in a dirty ditch.

One where I focused on what they could do for me, and not what in the end, I should have been doing for them.

Last night with Dawson was a game-changer.

I held her last night. Cradled her in my arms. Felt her slow breathing against my chest, once even over my heart when her face seemed to gravitate there.

The emptiness I felt the last time I indulged in a woman, the intense bottom feeding ache that remained long after the woman disappeared from my bed, wasn't there.

I was full.

The fullest I've ever been.

I know what my intent was in going to Johnny's. I even know what a cheap and dirty move it was, being like some of the other regulars there, and using the man's office to have her. She deserved better. I knew it then, and I'm well aware of it now.

But even the tawdry way it started doesn't take away from what happened. What I experienced for the first time in my life.

Genuine connection.

I can stand around here and act as I have in the past, putting a label on last night that speaks to it being just another case of me needing to bury myself inside someone, but it cheapens the moment.

Dawson, the way it felt having her resting so comfortably in my arms until the alarm on my phone sounded and pulled us apart, is so much more than a less than.

She's a greater than, and watching her now as she moves around the room, trying to appear as though she's not a deer caught in the headlights of what this business can be, all I want to do is cross the divide and tell her.

Introduce myself the way I should have last night, and showing her the respect she deserved then too. Making her understand she wasn't just another notch in an endless bedpost, but one that despite knowing next to nothing about her, someone I want to experience again.

This is so fucking foreign to me, even after Kimber.

There's a battle raging inside me with both sides fighting for ultimate supremacy.

In the one corner, you've got the halo-wearing hopeless romantic who used to go on trips with his dad twice a week to pick out presents for his mom, just because. The same guy who would sit down in the kitchen later, helping her bake, all the while listening to stories of how they met, fell in love, and managed to stay that way.

A guy who wanted the same thing they had.

A guy I haven't been in a *very long* time.

And in the opposite corner, there's the guy with the permanent smirk etched on his face who flaunts his accomplishments in and out of the ring and isn't against using them to get what he wants. Which, for those of you not keeping up, is the cocky son of a bitch who doesn't give two shits what other people think or see when they look at him.

It's easy to be the second guy. I've been him for the last ten years.

It's in the rearing of the first guy's head where everything gets muddled.

That boy has been dying to break free for a while, and after Kimber, and now with Dawson, it's becoming increasingly harder to rein him in, and let the pussy master prevail.

Sex is supposed to be just that. *Sex.* And last night should be as cut and dry as they come, yet it's not.

What is it about this girl, besides being Reese's cousin and damn near forbidden, that has me so fucking shredded?

Screw this.

I'm not going to get answers to this shit standing here like a chump. The character I've been portraying for years is a confident asshole, and right now, it's that confidence I'm going to rely on. If I want to know what it is about her, I can't seem to let go of, I need to face it head-on.

Willing myself across the room, breaking free of the group of hands trying to stop and pull me into their conversation, I don't stop until I'm standing directly behind her as she talks with Lauren, the current in-ring announcer.

Waiting them out patiently, I catch Lauren telling Dawson she needs to head out to pick up her husband, and it's then I make my move.

Tapping Dawson on the shoulder, I take it a step further when I actually let my hand rest and begin massaging her. Touching her, even innocently this way, enough to ignite the spark between us from the night before and make all of the blood in my body runs straight downstairs to the last place I need it to be.

For once, I'm not gonna think with my dick.

I want more.

Leaning into my move, she releases a soft moan. Lingering in the position for a second before reality seems to set in and she's reeling back quickly, spinning on her heel to face me. All traces of the obvious pleasure she was experiencing with my hands completely erased and a cool, hardened edge in its place.

You knew it was going to go down like this, Gav.

"Gavin." Her inner ice princess greets me. Her eyes never once breaking their hardened glare.

"Dawson."

Jesus, this is more awkward than I thought. I expected given the way she seemed to melt into my touch, this cold shoulder shit would break quickly, but as she tenses up in front of my eyes, pulling her gaze from mine and letting it linger anywhere but where I want it, I'm apparently stuck with it.

"Look, Dawson. About last night—"

"Don't worry about it."

Say what? Isn't that supposed to be my line?

It has been in the past. No way this girl is going to steal my gimmick.

"Don't do that."

"And what would *that* be exactly, Mr. Fortune?"

It's worse than I thought if she's resorting to last names.

"Knock it off. I know I should have told you who I was, but maybe you need a little reminder of why it didn't exactly go down that way."

"No thanks. I remember just fine."

"Dawson..."

"Gavin, I get what you're trying to do, I do, but here's the thing. You don't have to do it. I don't need any explanations. We met, we liked what we saw, and well, we spent the night together. Over and done."

No. Fucking. Way.

She really is trying to turn herself into me with the shit she's spewing. This same speech pretty much verbatim what I've had to give a few of the clingier girls in the past.

The *'it was just a bit of fun'* speech.

I'm the master of it, and there's no way she's taking it away from me, especially since it was more than just a bit of fun for me.

For both of us.

She can pretend all she wants, but she's not that great an actor.

Dawson was as affected by last night as I was, and it's evident in her arctic cold demeanor now.

"It was more than that."

"I know this is going to be hard for you to believe, given your reputation and all, but sometimes, you're not the only player in the room. I wanted you, so I had you. Not every girl you bang is going to follow you around like a lost puppy when it's over."

I take back what I said. She's a better actor than I thought, because the way she's selling this now, has me twisted.

This morning right after my alarm went off, and she stirred in my arms, she shifted her body on top of mine and kissed me. Not on the lips or some equally damning erogenous zone. No, she pressed her lips to the skin over my heart. The sweetest, albeit strangest given my lack of experience with it, move.

A move born out of something more than what she's trying to sell.

So, which one of these pictures is the wrong one?

The woman I woke up beside this morning, and who upon first look when our eyes met, I'd wanted to bury myself inside of again? Or is it the one trying to get me to believe that all I was, was a cheap alcohol-induced fuck?

My, how the roles have reversed. Jesus.

There's something more pressing to deal with now, though. Everything else is going to have to wait. I could have sworn she said something about my reputation.

What, up until she walked through those doors this morning, she didn't have the first clue about. So, who the hell talked?

My luck? It was Kemper.

Swallowing down the sting of having my own shit used on me, I harden myself the same way she has since I walked up, and ready myself for the battle about to ensue.

"My reputation, huh? And what would you know about it?"

Smirking in a way that's anything but friendly and open, I know I'm in for it.

"A whole lot, actually. It seems to be all anyone talks about around here. Three girls at once. Quite the feat. Did it really happen?"

It was four, and for half that time, I was drunk off my ass, but with my silence, she appears to make up her mind.

And there's not a damn thing I can do about it.

"What I really want to know is, if the rumors about you being the reason Melinda and Jackson split are true. Did you need to get laid so bad that a taken woman seemed like a good choice?"

Son of a bitch!

She really does know it all if she's bringing up that ancient history.

"Yeah, I did."

"So, the homewrecker moniker is true. Interesting."

Okay, I've heard enough. If she wants to throw around the labels I've been saddled with over the years, she might as well get the full list.

"Yeah, I'm a home wrecker. I'm also a man whore, slut, and a deviant. To hear some people tell it, I'm also a piece of shit who doesn't care about anyone's feelings but his own. You name it, I've been called it, earned it, or am working towards capturing it. But I'm also a whole lot more. Bet you didn't hear any of those names when you were making the rounds, though, huh?"

It's quick, there and gone really, but there's this split second after I call out every name I've been called, where the grip she's got on her anger slips. Her eyes softening before she realizes the error and rights herself.

The girl who placed her lips over my heart this morning is still in there.

Now I just have to figure out how I'm going to get her to embrace it, instead of this bullshit one she's forcing.

We're the actors. The ones paid to put on a show. Not her.

She's real. Tangible. The only real person in the place.

I've gotta keep her that way.

Even if it means embracing the Fortune of old in order to do it.

"You're good, princess. For a split second there, I actually believed you were using me for sex. Which, honestly? Would have been a first. It's just too bad your eyes aren't as easily controlled as the rest of you."

"You don't know what you're talking about." She stands her ground, cute as a button in her denial. Earning a genuine smile, as she stands a little taller in an effort to make me believe she means business.

"Oh, I disagree. I know exactly what I'm talking about. Like, for instance, I'm willing to bet the title, and any further shots I might have at the main event, you haven't been able to stop thinking about last night. That it's dominated your every damn thought the same way it has mine."

"You'd...lose."

Grinning at the momentary falter I hear, giving her true feelings away even faster than her eyes did earlier, I step in closer, bridging the divide between us and giving us what I'm damn sure we both want.

We both need.

Closeness. Connection.

Two things I know I need, anyway.

And with her. Only Dawson.

"Back...up." She stammers, and the grin on my face just grows as I lean in.

"You're a horrible liar, Dawson. It's cute. You're cute. All this effort to deny what's plain as day is just so incredibly cute."

"Jesus." She curses. "You really are full of yourself."

"Tell me I'm wrong."

"What exactly is it you want me to admit?" she hisses, eyes darting out around us before coming back to mine where they damn well belong.

"For starters, that you want me as badly as I want you. Admit all of those hours we spent together, were just the tip of an iceberg. In other words, not enough. I'm buried under your skin just as much as you are mine."

"I'm never going to admit those things because it's not true."

"There you go, lying again," I smirk, and bringing her hand out, she shoves it hard into my chest, pushing me back and putting distance between us. Leaving me off kilter and unprepared for what comes next.

"There's only one liar standing here, Gavin." She states her tone even, her angry mask slowly making its return. "And it's not me."

Pulling away, she takes a few steps out and beginning to laugh, her lips part and her voice raises as she takes our moment from private to public in the time it takes me to blink.

"Someone please give Gavin a mirror. He's in need of a serious reality check."

With those as her parting words, a series of low laughter fans out over the room as she walks away, and nothing, not even her name being called, first by Kimber and then by me, stops her.

There one minute, gone the next.

Leaving me right back where I started.

Alone.

Chapter Seven

Dawson

It's been surprisingly easy acclimating over from what had been my bread and butter in celebrity reporting, to this new climate.

The reality is, it's not so different. There had been multiple times in the years preceding my time in HFWA where I was given the opportunity to not just report on said celebrities, but sit down in a one on one style atmosphere and interview them.

Sure, what we spoke about was based heavily in reality, and not seeped in make-believe the way everything seems to be here, but the responses, facial expressions, and body language, they're all telling, and very much the same.

Take Brady Raines for instance.

I'd spent the time Reese was out of town delving into the backgrounds of each of HFWA's performers, accumulating a wealth of information about their careers, and even the odd snippet about their personal lives. Brady, though, he was different.

Most of the people on the roster aren't third generation superstars. They don't come from wrestling stock. They came into it in other ways, some of them even falling into it.

The same couldn't be said with Raines.

With a great uncle and a father who dominated the business during their heyday, he came in with a wealth of knowledge and understanding not a lot of others had. Taking that knowledge, and using it to his advantage to secure himself a spot in CPW, and now, gunning for the Heavyweight Title in HFWA.

But what the internet, old interviews, and even biographies can't tell you is, what really makes the man tick.

Only he can. Hence the reason for this sit-down today.

I'm supposed to stand in front of a camera for the second time this week, in a little over six hours, knowing my stuff. And while I think I've got a lot of the history of this man nailed down; I need more.

This two-minute interview, it's got to pop.

I demand nothing less.

"This better be good, darlin'." He announces his arrival, pulling out the wooden chair and throwing his body down into it with a huff before leaning over, eyes locked on mine. "I gave up the possibility of a quickie for this."

Another way Brady Raines differed from the others I spent the week researching.

Because of his legacy within the wrestling business, he was followed a lot more in online blogs, and in what I've heard the guys backstage complaining about, dirt sheets.

Shredded apart, move by move, look by look, in those, then sainted in some of the more prominent and well-known sports reporting sites. Everything about him was only a finger click away.

Especially his personal relationships.

More specifically, the one with his current wife, Emery.

"Something tells me there's nothing quick about you, Raines."

Winking, he lowers his arms to the table and leans back in the chair, making himself comfortable, and putting me even more at ease.

"You'd be right. Now, what was so important you had to pull me out of bed for it?"

"We're working together tonight."

"I'm aware. And I'm also aware that someone," he brings a hand over his mouth coughing, before whispering my name, and coughing again. "Did their homework already."

"I did, but if this is really going to get over, I need a more personal connection."

His laughter, loud and boisterous, is surprising. As unexpected as the slap of his hand as it lands on the table that follows.

"Please tell me I'm not the first person you've used that line on."

"You're not," I answer truthfully, confusion still swirling. "I tell everyone the same thing. I work better when we get on well."

"Something tells me you're not going to have a problem getting on with anyone, darlin'. One look from those innocent little doe eyes of yours, and you're going to take what we do here and spin it on its axis."

Shaking my head with a roll of my eyes, he chuckles.

"How so?"

"Well, for one, what we do out there in the ring, makes us storytellers. But, one interaction with you, and I guarantee, we'll be looking at a shoot in no time."

"A shoot?"

"Yes, darlin, a shoot. Because something tells me things are about to get very real up in HFWA now that you're here."

"I don't get what you mean…" And I really don't. I have no idea what this shoot thing he's going on about even is, and I've been knee-deep in wrestling research since I was hired.

"You're going to take what we do and make it real, sweetheart. All these other boys in the locker room are going to fall to their knees in order to do your bidding."

"Do you always turn innocent questions into something dirty?"

Winking again, he motions to the barista as she steps out from inside the café, and after ordering, focuses his attention back.

"Not always, but most of the time, yeah. Life's too short not to be a filthy pervert."

"Would Emery agree?"

"Who do you think made me this way?" he says with a sly smile. "So, now that we've established a rapport, or whatever it is you, reporter people call it, what do you wanna know?"

"You know what, Raines? I think I like you."

"Why's that?"

"You get straight to business."

"We've been over this, darlin. I've got a quickie to get back to. She's not gonna stay sleeping forever."

There's something past the playful way he admits to getting home and having sex with his wife that stops me cold.

It's not my first time seeing it, but there's something about it happening here, away from the lights and the energy of the ring, that sets it apart, and strips me of any quip I may have thought up to shoot his way.

He's in love.

Wholeheartedly, unabashedly, head over heels in love with the woman he's now teasing me about getting back to.

It shouldn't hit me this hard given everything I've managed to learn about him from my research, but it does.

Every belief I've had about professional athletes, all seems to become utter bullshit with how Brady is responding.

I've treated this business no better than the damn dirt sheets they hate so much.

"No way, darlin. No looking at me like that."

"Like what?' I shake myself free, asking.

"Looking like you're guilty of something. It's supposed to be you doing the interviewing here, not the other way around. So, knock it off, or you're in for more questions than I think you're ready for."

"Sorry. I noticed something, realized it, really. I guess I'm feeling a little guilty about it."

Slapping a hand on the table again, he lifts his cup to his lips, and after taking a long drag, he places it down and leans across the table, his voice when he speaks again a slow easy drawl.

"Tell Uncle Brady all about it. He's a great listener."

"Fine, I'll bite. I noticed you're in love."

"How's that some big bombshell? It's not like I'm quiet about it. Fuck, if Emery would do it, I'd have her coming to ringside with me. 'Course I'm in love."

"It's just odd."

Eyebrow-raising, he leans his face into his hand and motions with the other one in a rolling motion for me to continue.

"I don't have a lot of experience with wrestling, so I know it's weird I'm working here, but the little knowledge I do have, a lot of the guys aren't like you. They're notorious for being players. The bad boys. Users."

"You're not wrong."

"Really? I've only been here a week, and I've spoken to more guys in love than any other type. I looked guilty because after seeing it from you too, I was starting to think I'd judged too harshly. That I didn't know half of what I thought I did."

"You ever been in love, darlin?"

Ugh, no way. I don't want it to be about me. I'm insignificant.

"We're not going there."

"Figured you hadn't. You're too jaded by the way things have been portrayed, to have ever felt half of what two people in love do. Because of it, you've fallen into the trap of believing what the promotions want you to believe. You've bought into the work, not the shoot." Pausing and rubbing his chin, he smiles. "Are there guys we work with who aren't interested in settling down and want to see how many girls they can get before they hang up their boots? Sure. I can name off at least six of them just in HFWA. But the majority of us, darlin, we're like you. We want to settle down. Fall in love and make babies. Or like me, die trying."

He doesn't know what he's saying, because he doesn't know me. I've had the chance to settle down, more than once over the years. Yet, here I sit.

Holden was my last attempt.

No love lost or bad blood between us when it was over. An amicable breakup, much the same way the relationship itself was.

"Pretty sure this isn't the type of information you banked on getting when you called me out here, huh?"

"No," I admit, softly laughing. "I was actually going to ask you some questions about your time in CPW, and what led to your decision to come here."

"All well documented. If you really need more though, hand over your phone."

Pulling it out of my blazer and handing it across the table, he makes quick work of unlocking my screen, fingers flying over it as he does whatever he's doing. Eyes scanning the screen before handing it over and motioning to it with his head.

"Jackson Merrick? Why would you give me his info? Is there something going on with him, Reese, and Bryan?"

"Nah. He's out. Retired. I'm giving you his info because if there's anyone who can give you a real good look at the way things were during my time in CPW, it's him. Well, him or Emery, but now that we seem to be wrapping things up here, she's gonna be unavailable for a while."

Oh, no way. We're back to his sex life again. Gross.

"God," he claps his hands together. "I really love getting that reaction from people. Just do me a favor, would you?"

"Sure."

"Wait until I'm a couple of feet away before you throw up. No sense in both of us paying the price."

"Deal. It'll be hard, but I'll do my best to hold back the bile until you're gone."

Pushing the chair back from the table and standing, making sure to push it in when he's done, he makes his way around to my side of the circular table, and leans over, his thick shadow covering me.

"Don't feel bad about assuming we're all just a bunch of sluts. You're not the first. But do feel bad for the look you're wearing that says you're one of them. You're good people, Dawson Traymore. I knew it the other day when we met, and you've proven it again today. Your time will come."

With an annoying pat to the top of my head and a grin, he salutes me before turning and weaving his way around the other tables, taking off.

Leaving me pondering his final words, and just how confident he'd been in delivering them.

Could Brady be right? Could it really be my time?

Gavin

"Someone needs to say something to Reese, man. If I have to go out there and have that dumbass bitch fumble over shit one more time, I'm not gonna be responsible for what happens."

Tossing my bag on the bench and rooting around inside for my phone, determined to screw around for the few minutes I've gotta be here before heading out to the ring to run through the match with Zach, I perk up when Kyle's partner Mark chimes in with his two cents.

"It's like she doesn't know squat about us or what we're doing. I know they're related and all, but come on. If you're gonna bring someone on board, at least vet them, and make sure they know their shit first. She's a damn disgrace."

Hairs raising on my arms, knowing just who it is they're talking about, I slam my teeth down hard on my tongue. Wanting to go off, defend Dawson, but knowing I need more to go on first.

I want to hear whatever shit they're gonna let fly before putting them in their place. No matter how bad the urge is to pound their faces first, and ask questions later.

"You know who she is, right?" Kyle slaps Mark on the arm, snickering.

"Yeah. She's some reporter lady from the news."

Kyle shakes his head, and again I'm swallowing down the rage building, having to sit here listening to them attack someone they don't even know.

"Remember when we were riding through Newmarket, and we were holed up in that one dump off the highway? The show playing on the piece of shit TV with the bubbly little blonde?"

"Yeah, what about it?"

"You're a fucking idiot. Think about it! The bubbly blonde with the barely-there tits. She was reporting on who got caught with their pants down in some fancy fucking restaurant or something." Kyle gives up, detailing an episode of LiveWire, Dawson's old show.

"Shit." Mark whistles. "That was her?"

"Mmhmm." Kyle hums. "Must have been what? Two years ago? Looks like she's still waiting on the tit fairy or fuck, puberty to hit."

I've heard enough.

Having spent a night with her, hands firmly wrapped around the very pair of tits they're ripping on, I'm disgusted. There is absolutely nothing wrong with the way Dawson looks. She's fucking perfect, and anyone with two eyes and an actual brain knows it.

Even an OG dickhead like me.

"You wouldn't know what to do with a set of tits, Ronsen. Much less a set like hers."

There's only one way this is gonna go down now that I've spoken, much less said what I did. They're gonna turn, look at me like I've lost my damn mind, and we're gonna end up getting into it because I'm not acting the way I usually do.

The days of me sitting around with the guys shooting the shit, mainly about what chick I had under me, and how she faired on a rating scale of one to ten, are long gone.

"What do you know about her tits, Fortune? You already break her in?"

Don't play into this, Gav. You can't give away just how intimately you know her. They'll never let up on her if that happens.

And this, what I'm doing here in defending her, when I'm probably the last person she wants coming to her defense, is what it's about.

Keeping her safe.

"No, but I remember her from the show you two morons are ripping on. She was smoking. The little bounce she did with the mic? Fuck. Can you imagine how that would feel if she was doing it on your dick? Shit."

This is harder than I thought. Fortune is bleeding into a moment that doesn't require his presence. I sound like an asshole, sexualizing her this way.

"He's got a point, Kyle. There's more to her than the tits. I could ignore those as long as I got access to the peach she's hiding under her dress."

Fucking hell. That's not what I wanted.

I can visualize her *peach* just fine, even remember how it felt having it tightened around my dick every time I buried myself inside her. I don't need the help or hell, some other asshole thinking about her in the same way.

That's for me only.

She's for me.

"She still needs to be schooled on shit. I don't care how tight her body is. If she's dumb as rocks upstairs, she shouldn't be here."

I've got to get out of here. I've had my fill.

I'm done.

"Instead of sitting around here like a bunch of old bags gossiping, why don't you take your shit to Reese. If she's as bad as you claim, deal with it properly. You know...like a man."

Tossing my phone back in my bag, and slinging it over my shoulder, I stand, not even bothering to wait around for a response as I cross the room and make my way out the same way I came in.

Pausing to take a breath once the door closes and changing course. Heading off in the direction I should have when I arrived.

If Kyle wants to take his shit to Reese, maybe it's time I go to. The days of these guys ripping her apart are done.

It's just too bad fate seems to have other plans.

Chapter Eight

Dawson

Oomph.

The air rushes from my lungs as my body connects hard into what has to be the equivalent of a brick wall, even though, I know with the extra set of footsteps on the floor as we both react to the altercation, is a person.

A very *big* person.

"I'm sorry." I offer up softly, pushing my weight into the wall's chest as I attempt to right myself. Wiping down my dress, before looking up and meeting the eyes of the person I just mowed down.

The very last person I want it to be given how I've spent the last week managing to dodge him at every turn. His presence so vacant since the last time we spoke, I was starting to believe I imagined him working here.

"No, no. It was me." He shakes off my apology. "I was so focused on getting where I was going, I wasn't paying attention."

After a few beats where we just stand there, both of us shifting back and forth uncomfortably on our heels, he finally exhales and ends the torture.

"Are you okay?"

"Yeah. I'm just running late." *Because I was too busy dreaming about us screwing to wake up when my alarm went off.* "Are you? Okay, I mean."

"I'm fantastic."

"Good."

"Yeah."

Can this be any more awkward?

"I should really go meet up with Brady."

"Yeah," he seems to agree, even though his pinched brow and closed eyes tell me he wants to say different. "I need to get where I'm going too."

"Okay."

"I'm sorry, you know, for umm…almost taking you out."

"It's okay."

God, Dawson. You went to college. You know more words than this. Bigger ones. Sexier ones.

Pulling my hand off his chest, my cheeks flushing when our eyes connect, I move around him quickly, managing to get a few steps away before the softness of my name has me pausing in place.

"Daws?"

Stilling, I shift my head to the side. "Yes?"

"How are things? I mean, how has it been going since you started? Is everything working out okay? Are you comfortable?"

Who is this guy and what has he done with the confident Gavin of a week ago? The one who stepped into my space without any regard for how it would make me feel and demanded I admit to my attraction to him.

Is this how he is when he's not performing?

No, that can't be right. He wasn't performing in Johnny's office, and he was definitely full of himself then.

Hell, we both were.

Deciding to entertain his questions, I turn and head back to him, sure to keep at least a foot or two between us.

The reminder of what we shared at Johnny's mixing with the dreams I've been having non-stop since, demanding it. His ability to snare and own me even in my dreams and only after one night, off-putting, to say the least.

Also, what he can never find out about.

"I'm still nervous. I feel like a fish out of water here. It's strange, but thankfully, most of the people I've had to work with so far have been understanding."

His face morphs at my explanation, aloof and indifference twisting into what looks like anger and maybe annoyance, his lips shifting downward into a frown.

"There are people who haven't been nice?"

"Yeah, but I expected it. It's okay."

"Who?" he asks, completely ignoring my answer, and when I don't offer up any names after a few seconds of us staring each other down, he steps closer.

One step has my breath catching. The second step steals my breath entirely. And the third step, what puts him right in my face, as his head dips down and in, causing me to lose control altogether as heat pools between my legs, and my entire body begins to burn.

God, even after a week, there's no stopping the way I react whenever we're close. No matter how deep into work I threw myself, how far I pushed him and our night together out of my mind, it's all still there.

As potent and fiery as it was then. Challenging me to be different.

To be someone other than plain old Dawson Neveah Traymore.

He lied to me, holding something pretty huge back. The stories, all corroborated by him, speaking to it being the type of guy he is. Yet, when he's so close I can actually feel the warmth from his body capturing and filling mine, I seem to forget it all.

"Who's not treating you right, Dawson?" he asks, his tongue snaking out and running over his bottom lip, offering me another hard-earned lesson in self-control, as it takes everything in me not to step into him and snare it.

"No one. Everyone…everyone is great."

"Wrong answer."

"No, it's not. Gavin, everything is fine."

Reaching out and resting his hands on my shoulders, he controls the dance as he moves us away from the center of the hall and over to the right, not stopping until my back is pressed against the coolness of the wall.

"Everything is far from fine, princess."

He's right. It's not fine, but I'm not about to confirm it. Not with the shades of anger I caught earlier when I let it slip that not everyone was welcoming.

"I tried, Dawson. I really fucking tried to stay away from you. It's impossible. I'm done."

Snippets of my dream flash through my head as he speaks. Words like déjà vu as they're spoken just as raw and seductively as they were then. What he spoke before he carried me to the sofa and made love to me.

The images so vivid now, I'm transported from our place in the hall, the dream taking over until it becomes my reality.

Turning over in bed, I'm shaken from my slumber by a series of smashes emanating somewhere in the distance. Jolting up and hurriedly throwing my legs over the side, I clamor from the bed and making my way to the door, instinctively grab the baseball bat as I head to investigate what the hell is going on.

Dragging my padded feet through the room and raising the bat the closer I get to the door; the wooden structure is shaken again as what sounds like a battering ram connects. Once, twice, three times in succession before finally relenting.

Inching toward it, bat held high, I sneak a peek through the peephole, and that's when the breath I didn't even realize I was holding, releases.

Lowering my hand to the knob, I flip the lock before turning, opening it, and coming face to face with the person determined to take the door clean off its hinges.

"Gavin?" I question, rubbing at my eyes in an effort to wake up.

"I tried, princess. I really fucking tried staying away from you, but I'm done." He barks, shoving his way past me and heading deeper into the house.

Shutting the door after doing a quick scan for the battering ram I'm positive he was shoving into my door, I turn, readying myself for what I'm about to find, but find my body being shoved back against the door instead.

Lips crashing down on mine as his hands pull around me and hoist me in the air, forcing my legs against his back as he pushes himself on me so easily, my back is slamming roughly against the door.

"Fuck, I've waited weeks to taste you like this. I wonder if this," he says, slipping a hand effortlessly in between my legs, groaning when he's met with my very eager reaction to his presence. "Will taste as good as it did the first time."

Burying his face in my neck, nipping my skin with his teeth before clenching down and sucking so hard I feel the second the blood breaks the surface as he marks me, I lean into him, hands going around his neck before falling to his back as I react to him, nails at the ready.

What only seems to fuel him more as he grinds his pelvis into mine, driving my need to have him, higher.

"Does it, Dawson? Do you still taste as sweet?"

"Why..." I pant, sucking in a sharp breath when teasing me again, he grinds his body into mine, just the hard brush of his dick against my heat enough to make my eyes roll back. "Why don't you taste and find out?"

Lost in a flurry of movement, he pulls us away from the door and crosses to the sofa, laying me down before I hear the pop of the button on his jeans, followed by the sliding of his zipper, and the brush of his now bare leg against mine as he kicks them off. Focusing again on me once he's stripped himself bare, he lifts my legs in the air and rests them on his shoulders.

Slipping a hand between my legs, he runs a thumb over my lips before separating them and rubbing his thumb across my clit. Growling when my body shifts under the roughness in his touch on what is sensitive with nothing but eager, wanton lust and need.

"Fuck, princess. You've been holding out on me. If I had known you were this wet, I wouldn't have waited. I would have taken you weeks ago."

"Gavin..." I plead as he continues to thumb my clit as he positions his fingers at the entrance to my pussy and pushes inside. Hard and quick, he violates me, relentlessly teasing me, pushing in hard and pulling out agonizingly slow, making me cry out, begging him for more.

"Oh, Dawson. If you keep that up, I won't be able to hold back."

"So... don't."

That's all he needs to hear. In the time it takes me to suck in a breath, his fingers have pulled out, and he's filling me in a whole new way. Pushing himself deep inside, stretching me. Not relenting until he's positioned himself so deep inside, I can feel him brushing against my walls.

"Fuck me, Daws. You're so damn tight. Snug. You fit my cock like a glove. It feels…"

"Amazing." I finish for him, breathless.

"Better than." He adds, leaning down, filling me even more as his lips hungrily take hold of mine and devour, my own need fighting back to match his until we're both being swept away.

Our bodies finally moving, Gavin's curses breaking up our kiss as he pulls back, grabbing a hold of my leg and begins to push and pound relentlessly into me.

Ruining me.

Owning me.

"No one else, Dawson."

Unsure of what he means, I reach for him and lowering his hand to meet mine, letting his control of my legs go, our fingers come together and it pauses him.

"Promise me. Promise me no one else will ever have this. Tell me it's mine. That you're mine."

"Only yours, Gavin."

Moving again, but this time, at a much slower pace, he lowers himself to me, letting my legs fall loosely around his back, the precipice he's left me dangling on with his slow, methodical movements, stripping me of all my fight.

This, the ease at which he slowly moves in and out, we're not fucking anymore. It passed fucking a very long time ago.

Gavin is loving me.

His breath, even with the slower pace, becoming labored like mine, as my hand finds his ass and I bring him even deeper inside. His name falling as my heavy-lidded eyes finally flutter closed as my release rolls out in delicious waves.

Body clenching around him, causing him to curse as I flood him, the wet sound of his thighs as they slap against mine, deeper and faster as he climbs and reaches his own release, nothing short of perfection.

"Dawson..." he murmurs before collapsing on top of me, spent. "It's not enough...it'll never be enough."

"Gavin..." I murmur softly as I attempt to free myself from my position, finally freed of the memory of him, and ready to do the same with the reality.

"Jesus, Dawson." He regards me with hooded eyes, teeth biting down hard into the lip I'd wanted nothing more than to capture earlier. "That was the hottest thing I've ever seen."

"Wh...what do you mean?"

"You went somewhere in your head, but your body was still here. Pressing itself against mine, bucking into it. Princess, fuck. You called out to me, and then you...shit."

"Then I what?" As embarrassed as I am, I was reacting at all, I need to know how far I took it.

"You came apart."

Inwardly groaning, my head drops to the floor, the flood of embarrassment reaching my face quicker than I can move, and giving me away before I can hide it.

Moving his hand, he reaches out and cups my face, pausing me and lifting eyes until they're locked on his.

"Don't hide from me. Not with this. Please."

"Okay." I acquiesce, and not breaking eye contact, he finds my hands, locking them in his own before lifting them and pressing them above my head on the wall. His lips once he's licked them, descending forward and down onto mine.

The spark ignited when we connect again, draining me of my fight, and all arguments I had at the ready in order to break free and create some distance. The mint flavor intoxicating as he tugs on my bottom lip and sucks it into his mouth, grazing it with his teeth, growling like a ravenous animal that's just been given a taste he's been craving.

"When you pressed yourself against me, it took everything in me not to fuck you right here for the entire damn place to hear."

Furthering his point, he presses his body into mine, his arousal evident. A clear weapon he's willing to use as he rubs it against mine, eliciting a moan that after cursing and sucking in a breath, he swallows up as his mouth takes possession of mine.

Moving with his body as it continues to grind, his lips break away and begin a slow, sensual descent down across my jaw. Going lower and centering his attention on my neck, he softly kisses before creating enough suction to begin sucking, and not relenting until he's broken through the skin. What has me crying out as my hands grip his back and my nails dig in, my own teeth grazing his shoulder.

"Let it out, Dawson. Mark me up if you have to. Give me everything you've got. Let me feel what you feel."

An easy request to fulfill when his mouth shifts, dipping even lower and stretching my dress, he pulls it down and feeds on my breasts. One at a time, bringing them into his mouth and sucking, tasting, and devouring. When he bites down on one, my cries are again swallowed as I bite down hard into the flesh of his shoulder. Gavin increasing the speed of his body rubbing against mine showing me his approval.

The way we are, our bodies pressing and pushing as close as we can get—what is still not close enough—reminiscent of what it felt like to have a boy in my room and be touching each other so intimately without any clothing being removed as a teen. The rule-breaking mixing with the forbidden.

"I need you, Daws."

Surrendering to the way my heart swells with his impassioned admission and pushing down the fear of what will happen between us if I give him what he wants, I give him the truth.

"I need you too."

Vulnerability is not something I've ever allowed myself to show. Being so open with someone is usually the last place I would ever think of going, in the past and present, but with Gavin, it seems impossible not to.

Spending the last week cursing anything to do with him or his secrets and lies, while he continued to dominate my every thought—my every dream—is clearly not working.

I want to hate him and I can't.

I crave him too much.

This has got to be what an addict feels like. Even knowing what I do, still feeling the sting of how I learned who he really is, I can't pull away.

I can't stop this.

I don't want to stop this.

I want this man with every fiber of my being. I want to be with him. Experience everything there is to experience. Good and bad. Painful and pleasurable. I want it all.

Brady's earlier words coming back to haunt at the worst possible time.

"Your time will come."

Shuddering and melting into Gavin as his hand finds my skin, raising the hem of my dress up as he moves deeper, continuing to grind until his fingers brush against my outer core, I whimper.

"So damn needy." He observes, teasing me with a brush of his thumb over the outside of my panties. His lips swallowing mine as a cry falls and dulls as our tongues meet.

Nothing able to stop us now as his fingers slide under the lining of my panties and he buries one finger, then two, inside of me, his thumb massaging and driving my need higher.

As consciously aware as I am of where we are, it's not enough to stop me.

Stop this.

Reaching out and finding the belt loop of his pants, I use the friction he's created with his own arm between my legs and push into him rubbing until he releases a low sultry moan of his own.

Fingering the button of his jeans, I pop it, lowering the zipper as he shudders.

"Dawson..." he shakily pleads.

"Do you need me to stop?"

Running my fingers over the top of his tightly worn briefs, I slip my hand inside and revel in the warmth of his skin as I wrap my hand around his cock, lifting and springing it free. Gripping it hard and beginning to pull, hand moving up and down until his control begins to slip and his body begins to shake.

"Fuck no, princess. I need to be inside you."

I should stop things now. Tell him I can't do this. Not here, where just about anyone could happen upon us, but I don't because as bad as he wants to be free to bury himself inside me, I want it more.

Dragging his briefs down enough to free him, he moves, and lifting me up and throwing my legs around his back, he does it.

He penetrates me.

But before either of us can catch our collective breaths or move together, a throat clearing has me tightening around him, a groan falling from his lips as he uses his body to block me.

"Oh shit." The intruder backtracks. "I was looking for Dawson. I had no idea there was anyone back here."

Shit. Shit. Shit. Shit.

It just went from bad to worse.

The intruder to our loss of control—my loss of common sense—is the exact person I should have been halfway across the building with.

"Gavin…" I whisper, and when he turns from Brady, his expression blank, I swallow nervously.

"Yeah, princess?"

"You need to…we need to…" stammering over my thoughts brings a whole new expression over his face as his lips curve into the tiniest smile. "Can you please let me down?"

"Do I have to?"

"If you want Brady to go tell Reese where and who he found me with, then no."

This does it. The reality check of my cousin—our boss—moving us until I'm completely hidden away behind him, what for my feet, covering me, keeping me safe from the other man's eyes, he slips out of me and squeezing my legs together and swallowing down the whine threatening to escape at the loss of him, he lowers me to the floor.

Not moving until I've managed to not only right my panties but my dress. Looking as presentable as I did when I got here. As if I wasn't just caught about to fuck one of the stars.

What the hell has gotten into me?

"You okay?" he asks softly, cupping my chin and bringing my face up to meet his. His eyes growing more concerned when after a few brief seconds all I can manage is to stare back.

"Dawson, please. Are you okay?

"Yes." I push out in a rush. "No. Honestly, I don't know."

Pulling me into him, burying his head in my hair and inhaling, he pulls back and brushing his lips against my forehead, leaves me unsettled when he speaks.

"This isn't over, Dawson. This is just an interruption. So, whatever plan you have to run off and stay away, it's not going to work. I'm going to find you later, and we are going to finish this."

Gulping and swallowing the influx of saliva built up since Brady interrupted, all I can bring myself to do is a nod.

"You should go." He admits, his tone dejected. Pained. "Brady's already seen more of the both of us than I ever planned on."

"Yeah, okay." I agree, finally finding my voice again, and when he lets me go, I don't just walk casually away, I scurry. Not stopping until I'm standing beside Brady and under the scrutiny of another pair of eyes entirely.

"You and I clearly need to have another conversation." He states, furious. Turning his attention to the hall, I track his gaze and follow it, as we both watch Gavin begin walking back in the direction he was originally attempting to go.

His back to us, body straight, without so much as a head twitch in our direction, I just hold my breath as I watch him walk away. Rubbing at my chest when after he begins to become nothing but a shadow in the distance, an uncontrollable ache appears.

Why does his walking away bother me? It had to happen, both of us have things to do and places to be. So, why does it hurt so bad?

It's only when Brady speaks that it hits me.

"When I said your time would come, it wasn't supposed to be with Fortune."

It's because I want him to stay. Not Fortune the way Brady says. Not the wrestler at all.

Just him.

Gavin.

Chapter Nine

Gavin

Son of a bitch.

How could I have been so fucking reckless?

Even when I was at my worst, I never took advantage of them in public. It was too much of a risk.

My reputation was already solidified but there were aspects to it I didn't give into. Whatever happened between me and the women I chose to have under me, it always happened behind closed doors.

Okay, so maybe a secluded vehicle and a paused elevator a few times too. The point is, it always happened when there was no one else around to witness it.

The foreplay, the teasing, whether it be dirty dancing at a club or teasing and tasting over drinks at Johnny's, those were public. Everyone was well versed in me putting the moves on girls. I didn't hide it.

But the final act. That was **always** private.

Until now. Until her.

Fucking Dawson Traymore.

Walking around the place in a dress begging to be ripped off, with her hair falling loose down her back, calling to have hands in it, gripping and tugging. Her bra pushing those gorgeous tits of hers up, making them pop, and calling for my mouth to be on them. Pleasing them while I slide that thin piece of fabric known as her panties to the side and bury myself deep and pleasure her.

Shaking off the visuals with an audible groan, I raise my fist and let my knuckles do their job, rapping them against Reese and Bryan's door.

Moving back and forth on my feet as I wait for one or both men to respond, I find myself having to swallow down the encroaching hard-on threatening to reignite as the smell of Dawson's perfume wafts its way over my nose.

Even when she's nowhere near, she's with me.

Damnit. This is not the fucking time for this to be happening.

"What the fuck you waiting for? Get your ass in here!" Bryan's voice carries, and swallowing the last few minutes down, and praying my dick follows suit, I enter. Wasting no time when both men's attention lands on me and getting straight down to business.

The faster I deal with this, the faster I can head back to the locker room and tug one out before my match.

"I need to talk to Reese."

"Does this have anything to do with the show?"

"Yes, and no."

"In that case, if you need to talk to him, you need to talk to me. So, sit down and tell us what's going on."

I didn't wanna get into this with Bryan. For some reason, even though he's Matthias's best friend, he's always been decent to me. The last thing I wanna do is drop this at his feet, especially with Reese's earlier warning. What I have to assume Bryan knows nothing about. It's drama none of us need.

Doing what he said and lowering into the chair, I lean back and cross my arms over my chest.

"The last couple of days, there's been talk amongst the boys. A lot of it, and before it turns into something worse, I think you need to be made aware of it."

I'm not a narc. I don't hear things and spread them around. I've played a lot of games, but this wasn't one of them. Anything I did, began and ended with the use of my body, and I was a willing participant in it. This is unfamiliar territory.

It feels like I'm turning a page. Burning a bridge.

"What kind of talk?"

"It's about Dawson," I say, focusing my response on the man who needs to hear it. "And none of it is good."

God, with the way they were talking about her tits, and I threw in shit about burying myself in her while she bounces on top of me, bad is an understatement.

We're disgusting. The epitome of tools in the workplace.

Setting the women's movement, especially in this business, back about twenty years.

"What's being said?" Reese barks, sharing a look with Bryan before hardening his eyes and shooting them my way.

Great. He probably assumes I'm the ringleader.

"She's got a method to the way she does things; I think. I mean, I haven't worked with her yet, but I assume, given her background. It's not meshing with the guys. They're pissed off because it's like she doesn't know shit about them. They don't want her here and feel she shouldn't be here, without the knowledge."

"That it?"

"No."

"What else?" Reese demands, his jaw ticking.

"There's been some talk about her physically."

"Thank you for telling us, Gav," Bryan says, slipping off the edge of the desk and making his way over to where I'm seated. Waiting until I've stood before thrusting a hand out and shaking when I've done the same.

"We're not done here." Reese cuts in, and turning along with Bryan, jaw still set, eyes ablaze, it's easy to see it's not over by a long shot.

Reese Harrison doesn't get riled up about much, but apparently, when it comes to his family—to Dawson—all bets are off.

"Who said what, exactly?"

"Reese," Bryan interrupts before I can respond. "We don't need to know who said what. We knew this was inevitable when we brought her in, so now we've got to nip it in the ass."

More like beat it into their asses. I add silently. Bryan's laid-back approach obviously not sitting well with Reese either, as he shoves his chair back from his desk and jumps to his feet, fists firmly in place and ready.

"Like fuck, we don't need to know what was said. She's fucking family."

Reese and I don't have a whole lot in common. He never wrestled, staying strictly on the business ends of things, so I never expect to see eye to eye with him. But here and now in this office?

We've never been more alike.

"She's an employee." Bryan reiterates, and the speed at which Reese's head snaps around and levels him with a glare has my blood running cold.

If he's this pissed at his partner, there's no telling what he'll do if he's unleashed on the guys. Maybe coming here was a mistake.

No, it wasn't. You did the right thing. She deserves to be treated better.

"Kyle and Mark were ripping on the size of her tits. There was some talk about getting inside her. Most of it was just complaints about her job performance, though. A bunch of bitching about the only reason she's here being her connection to you."

I'm not helping. I can easily see that as my admission does nothing to settle Reese down, but again I'm being thanked by Bryan, this time with a hearty pat on the back while he motions for me to head to the door.

A place I'm glad to go given the way I can see things about to explode.

But before I can make it past the threshold after opening it, Reese is calling out again.

"Why'd you do it, Fortune?"

"Why did I do what?"

"Come in here. I gotta know. Why did you turn your back on the boys to come to tell me this?"

Because I can't stop feeling whatever the hell I'm feeling for your cousin. I silently admit, but thankfully don't say. Though what I do, is just as truthful as the first part.

"Because it's the right thing to do."

Dawson

"There's another reason I wanted you to call Jackson," Brady admits when after spending the entire time silent as we walked across the building to where we'd be filming, he finally speaks.

"You think?"

"I guess it would have helped if I just said that before, huh?"

"Just a little."

"I've known Gavin a long time, Dawson. We go way back. I was there when Melinda screwed around on Jackson with him. I saw how he handled himself. Handled the entire thing. Even after the entire thing came out, they finally split, and she and Gavin became a legitimate thing. I was there for it all."

"Why are you telling me this?"

"Because someone has to. What I just saw..." he fades off, running a hand roughly through his hair. "What you're getting involved in, it's not going to end well. It never does with him."

What is with these guys?

Can they not see I'm an independent woman? One who has spent the better part of the last fifteen years fending for herself? With as stubborn and set in my ways as I've been, it's probably been even longer.

"I can handle it."

"Can you?" he cocks an eyebrow. "Because I've been there when Gavin puts the moves on a girl. How enamored she becomes. Like she's been put under some kind of spell. He has a way about him. It takes even the strongest person and turns them sideways."

"That's a bit over the top, don't you think? I mean, you could have easily just said, he knows how to play women."

"If I thought it would work with you, I would have said it that way, but you're not like the usual girls he picks up. You've got a solid head on your shoulders based on everything I've heard and witnessed myself. So, for you, I've gotta change things up. Tell you how it really is."

"Okay, well, answer me something."

"Shoot."

"Were you always the same guy standing here today?"

"No, but—"

"Then you have no idea who Gavin really is. None of us do. Maybe the guy you knew then, isn't who he is now."

"Daws—"

"No, Brady. I know what you're trying to do, and it's sweet. That you'd care enough about some random girl you barely know to wanna keep her heart safe, makes you one of the good guys. But, I'm a big girl. I've managed to handle my business this long, so I'd appreciate it if you kept your opinions to yourself and let me keep doing it."

Leaning over and picking up one of the blank white cards off a chair to his right he lifts it in the air and waves it back and forth, signaling a truce.

"Just be careful, alright? Mind your heart."

"Why do I get the feeling there's more to your warning than you're letting on?"

"Emery had a crush on him."

"Did he hurt her?"

"No. He never got the chance. I messed him up before he could."

I can actually see that. Brady, with the protective streak he's already displayed, must be hell on wheels for his wife. I get the feeling if a guy so much as looked at her sideways, he'd finish them.

"If I promise to keep my eyes open, can we get down to business?"

"Mmhmm."

"Then hear this. My eyes are wide open. Now forget whatever you saw and let's get to work."

Flipping the switch on the mic and placing it on the chair, I'm not at all prepared for the bear hug I'm pulled into when I go to turn around.

Arms crushing me into a warm body as the faint sound of clapping resonates from across the hall.

"That was phenomenal!" Reese exclaims when he finally lets me go, and taking in my surroundings after righting my clothes, I see Bryan off the side, grinning from ear to ear.

"I second what Reese said." He says, stepping forward, his smile never wavering.

"Has he always been this easy to work with, or is it just something he saves for me?"

Bryan snickers and Reese reaches across the divide and slugs him in the arm.

"Your cousin, he's an abusive son of a bitch, Dawson. You're my witness."

Smiling at Bryan, I turn to Reese, and all pretense is gone. I wasn't going to mention it when he finally released me from the hug, but I've spent enough time with him over the years to be able to tell when he's on edge.

I just can't understand why.

"What's wrong?"

"Nothing."

"Ahh yes, because you're always this clipped when you answer questions."

"Reese," Brady comes up, interrupting, throwing an arm around my cousin's neck. "You'd best answer her question. She'll put you in your place if you don't."

"You sound like you're speaking from experience." Reese practically seethes, his upset not even attempting to be hidden.

"I am." Brady throws a wink my way. "She put me in my place before we taped the spot."

"What did you do to her?" He shrugs off Brady's arm and spins, glaring through him.

"Nothing, Reese. Brady didn't do anything. He's joking around. God."

Putting myself between both men, I silently apologize to Brady before turning my full attention back to the man who any second, looks like he's about to combust.

What I'm sure a lot of the guys around here don't know is, my cousin had a lot of struggles growing up. Behavioral issues mostly. And because of it, ended up in a lot of fights and altercations he probably could have avoided had cooler heads prevailed. I'd seen the change as adults, though. He's settled down considerably from the boy I knew. This is a side of him I never thought I'd bear witness to again.

"Guys, can you give us a second? We need to have a family meeting."

With a quick nod from Brady, and after a stare down with Bryan which I win, he backs away before turning and heading down the hall, leaving us alone.

"What's really going on, Reese?"

"I saw what you did with Brady. Watched the entire thing. It was clean."

"Yeah, it was great. So, why does that piss you off?"

"It doesn't." he snaps, fists clenching and unclenching at his sides.

"Then what is pissing you off because honestly, I get the feeling it's me but I have no idea what it could be."

"Has anyone been giving you issues since you started?"

No way.

There's only one person who knew some of the guys here were less than accepting of me. The one person that given our history, I would have assumed would have avoided having to talk to Reese about anything, but apparently not.

Gavin talked.

"Don't even think about it, Dawson."

"Think about what?"

"Lying to me. I can already see there is someone. Just tell me who it is so I can handle it."

How he plans on handling it is what I wanna know because with the side of him I'm seeing now, the protector out in full force and the businessman shelved, there's no way in hell I'm dropping names.

And I'm pissed I even have to do it in the first place.

Gavin Fortune can screw himself.

"I'm not saying a word until you calm down."

"Dawson, now is not the time for you to pull this."

"Then chill out so I don't have to."

Stalking over to the chair and shoving the mic and papers to the ground he throws his body down onto the seat and sighs heavily before leaning back and banging his head off the wall.

"I'm acting like a Neanderthal, aren't I?"

"Just a little," I say, slipping into the chair beside him and patting his leg. "I know why, though."

"You belong here. You're good. You know it, I know it. I just wish everyone else could get on board too."

"But you get where they're coming from, right?" I ask, giving him a little to go on, but making sure to keep the names under wraps. "Lauren has been their go-to since you opened your doors, and Hannah before she got sick, was practically the same way. They were family. Some new girl gets dumped on them, and because she's so out of her element, she's playing catch up. It's bound to piss them off."

"So, there are people giving you a hard time?"

"One or two, yeah."

"Tell me who it is, Dawson."

"No, Reese. I'm sorry, but I can't do that. Not yet. Maybe not ever."

"Why the fuck not?"

There it is again. The edge in his voice. All the more reason for me to keep my lips firmly in the shut position.

"Because I'm determined to earn their respect. Not have it beat into them by their boss."

"I'm not going to touch anyone."

"You say that, but you forget I know you. I also know you're fierce when you care about something. I can't trust that you won't go above and beyond in an effort to do right by me. So, no. I'm not telling you squat. And if you've got any respect for me, you'll let me handle it."

"Fine." He concedes reluctantly, complete with a pout.

Hauling off and punching him in the arm, laughing when he flinches and moves back, his hand immediately coming up and rubbing, I'm drawn away when I hear the scuffing of boots across the floor.

"Sorry to interrupt."

Yeah, I'm sure you are. You tattling little tool.

"What do you want, Fortune?" Reese snaps, and for once, I just let him go. His feelings on the intrusion at the moment mirroring my own.

"Bryan said I needed to get my ass out here. Supposed to be meeting up with her." He points to me, his face neutral. Like we hadn't had a moment almost an hour before.

I've got to hand it to him, he's a phenomenal actor.

Maybe Brady was right after all.

"Yeah, okay. I need to deal with a problem anyway." Hauling his butt off the seat he watches Gavin for a minute, maybe two, before moving over to me. After pulling me to my feet and bringing me in for another embrace, he pulls away but instead of walking away, he issues a warning.

"Be careful, Daws. Remember what I told you."

Looking from my cousin to Gavin and lingering, suspended in time as our eyes meet, I smile weakly before turning away.

"Like I could ever forget," I inform Reese before turning my attention back on the microphone.

Shaking his head, he turns and shoving into Gavin as he passes by, I react. Flinching with the impact and wishing that for once, Gavin and I weren't the people we are.

That we were strangers.

Sighing, I turn the mic back on and turning back toward him, thankful for my cousin's absence, I pull on my confidence earlier with Brady and shoot straight.

"Did you tell Reese people were screwing with me?"

"No."

Shaking my head, I move toward him and shove the microphone under his face.

"Did you tell Reese anything today?"

"Yes." He surprises me, answering honestly.

"And what did you tell him?"

"Dawson, come on." He sighs, pushing the microphone away from his face. "Why are you being like this?"

"Reese knows, Gavin, and you're the only one I told. So, tell me, why'd you do it?"

Shoving the microphone back his way, I miscalculate the speed of my arm and before I realize it, it bounces hard off his lips.

"Gavin, shit. I'm sorry."

Plucking the mic from my hands, he tosses it away and moving in close, he stares me down and does exactly what I want him to.

He gives it to me straight.

"I told your cousin about the two pieces of shit who were ripping on your body earlier. It's not the first time they've done or said shit like it. They learned from the best."

Holy shit. He's upset, and damnit if he doesn't have every right to be. I let my mind run away with me and I judged him. Again.

"Gavin..."

"Save it, Dawson. I don't want you feeling bad for me. I earned this." He motions between us. "I've been earning it for years. It's not exactly surprising you'd think I betrayed your confidence."

"I shouldn't have."

"Maybe not, but if we're gonna keep doing whatever this is, there's something you need to know. Even when I was the biggest piece of shit walking, I never betrayed a confidence. What you told me in the hall before things got complicated, it's ours. I wouldn't tell anyone, least of all the guy with a serious pole up his ass when it comes to me even looking at you."

It's ours.

Damn him for knowing exactly what to say. He's making it extremely hard to hate him.

"I'm sorry," I repeat, and shaking his head, his hand lifts and he rests a finger against my lips.

"I don't ever want you to apologize for believing the worst. Like I told you, I earned it. I can handle whatever you've got, princess."

"W—what should I say then?" I stammer when after a few seconds, he pulls his finger down, running it softly over my jaw.

"I lied to Reese earlier, Dawson. I don't have to be here with you tonight. I just needed to be around you, especially after what happened earlier. So, now that you know I'm a liar when it comes to getting what I want, I suppose all I want from you is an answer."

"What's the question?"

"Will you go out with me?"

Chapter Ten

Gavin

I'm flying by the seat of my pants with this plan, but since I've secured her agreement, gotten her in my car, and we're now sitting outside the place, there's no going back.

When I asked Dawson out, I did it for a couple of reasons.

One, I need to make this girl like me. I've already moved at the speed of light with her, taking her in Johnny's office the way I did. But where she differs from everyone else is, this time, I wanna go deeper. See if what I've been experiencing since that night is real, and not just more of the same.

Not just curiosity.

I never thought in a million years with the way she came at me with the god damned microphone, red hot anger filling her blue irises, she'd agree. Truth is, I was ready to be laid out on the arena floor with the gumption I had asking in the first place.

But here we are. Uncomfortably seated in what is a pretty damn comfortable car. Radio turned off, windows up, and engine powered down. The only sound to be heard the sound of our collective breathing.

A moment I've now got to break because the second reason I did this is waiting on the other side of the front door a few feet away. A moment she beats me too.

"Do you always bring girls home when you ask them out?"

Fuck no. There's never been a girl in my home.

That's what I want to say. I just don't because she needs to know this isn't my place. She needs to know what I'm about to walk her into.

Another first for me.

"This isn't my place."

"If it's not yours," she questions, slipping her belt off before turning to me. "Then whose is it?"

And this is where things are about to become uncomfortable.

There's no way with all the dirt she's managed to dig up or hear about me, she doesn't know about Kimber. I mean, there's not a whole lot to say about my relationship with the current Women's Champion because it was fake, even if for a while I had feelings which felt very real, but I'm sure she doesn't know that.

To this day there's still not many who know it was all a play. *Us doing business. A work.*

How the hell is it going to look when of all the places I could have brought her to, I happened to drop her at my pseudo-ex-girlfriends?

"Kimber's."

As soon as the scowl presents, I know I've done it. I drove myself into the ditch.

Instead of saying Matthias, I've made the wheels turn. Wheels that given the scowl and the way her body tenses, give away what I thought before.

There is more going on here than she admitted to.

She feels it too. Maybe even wants it.

An issue I'm damn well going to deal with. Just not right now. Bigger issues at play here need to be handled first.

Like clearing the damn scowl off her face and telling her the reason we're both here.

"It's not what you think."

"I wasn't thinking anything, Gavin."

"The scowl says differently, princess."

"I don't know what you're talking about."

Of course, she doesn't. She wasn't going to admit to feeling anything for me the day I confronted her at the gym, so she's definitely not going to do it sitting here in my car.

She'll keep wearing her mask the same way I have been.

Only, I think I'm ready to take mine off.

"Sure, you don't."

Pulling her eyes away from my smirk, they fall to the door first before looking out to whatever waits beyond the window. Moving around until she's looking straight down the back and trailing back over me as she looks past me out my side.

What she's doing plain as day.

Calculating how to get out of here, and back where she belongs.

I'm really mucking this whole thing up and I haven't even told her the truth yet.

"Dawson, it's really not what you're thinking."

Releasing a resigned sigh when she must realize we're pretty far from home, she leans back in the seat, flashing her annoyance my way.

"Then what is it?"

"I had to make a deal the other day in order to talk to you. Reese, you know the way he's been. I'm not allowed within a few feet of you unless its work related. I got Kimber to help. I had to agree to something in order to get it."

Waiting for a few beats, and rubbing at her forehead, she finally ends the torture.

"And this is what you agreed to? Bringing me here?"

"No. I was supposed to bring myself here, you're just a bonus." Allowing myself to chill when I see the miniscule lift to her face, I give her the rest. "Matthias and me, we don't have the best history."

"I heard."

This gets me. I know people talk. For a long time, I fed off all the talk, giving them shit to sling. But this, Matthias and Kimber, the relationship we have, or lack of one in Kemper's case, I never said shit about it.

"What have you heard?"

"Mainly that you and Kimber were a thing before. With the way I saw Matthias looking at her the day I met all of you, and the way she looked back, I figured it didn't sit too well with him, your past."

Expelling the breath I'd been holding, it's my turn to lean back in the seat. Thank God the real story is under wraps.

"Dawson, contrary to the way we started, I want to get to know you. Explore this. I know we can't do it openly with the rules, but tonight, away from work, I'm hoping we can."

I've been screwing around with girls since junior high, and never once have I ever said anything remotely close to what I have to her. It really has been all about the physical connection.

But here and now, nothing but what I said does.

This matters.

Dawson matters.

"I know how you feel about me. After everything you've heard, and what I've been showing you from the moment we met, it would shock me if you didn't. But what you see, it's not real."

"You're not Gavin Fortune, former CPW champion, and pussy master extraordinaire?" she asks seriously, lasting a few seconds before scoffing and snorting at what after hearing her say it, has to be the absurdity of it all.

"No. At least, not tonight."

"Then who are you tonight?"

"Just Gavin." Pausing, gauging her reaction to my very real admission, hoping like hell she'll see it for the honesty it is, and not another play I would have been famous for before, I wait until the half smile is back before leaning over and resting my hand on hers, finishing this.

"So, just Dawson, will you help just Gavin grab the pie out of the backseat, come inside, and have dinner with me?"

Silence falls over us again as she looks out the windshield to the door, biting down on her lip nervously before turning and flashing her gorgeous baby blues my way. The smile etched into her skin, making my heart spring to life as her fingers slip around my own, squeezing.

"Just Dawson would love to."

God help me. I like just Gavin.

From the way he ran around after I did as he asked and grabbed the pie off the backseat, opening my door for me, to the way he slipped his arm through mine all the way up the walk to the door. I was hooked.

It was the smile that did me in, though.

The genuineness of it as we stood on the porch waiting for the door to be opened. Capturing and lighting his entire face up.

The knowledge that for whatever reason, being here with me makes him genuinely happy.

And it's only gotten worse since Kimber opened the door. Matthias hovering behind her, his expression clear on what he thought seeing me standing here, but Kimber's the opposite.

He never broke a sweat. Never giving into the steely expression he was dealt from the current HFWA champion as they locked eyes. He just smiled bigger, and when Kimber had taken the pie from my hands and thanked me for baking it, he'd only furthered the butterflies fluttering their way through my body when he pulled me to him and admitted it was him.

Gavin, *the Gavin Fortune*, baked the pie.

Jaw meet the floor.

This self-proclaimed playboy bakes pies when he's not out there beating the hell out of people for entertainment.

"Fortune," Matthias grunts, stepping around his girlfriend and hovering over us. "You got a minute?"

Call it the steely expression he's worn since we got here, the scowl on his face now, or the way he stands so rigidly over Gavin, almost begging him to act like a smart ass so he can pummel him, but I can feel in my bones this isn't going to be good.

If Gavin goes off with him, leaving me with Kimber, I just know the night is going to get off on the wrong foot.

I may have scouted the best escape route in the car before he explained what was really going on, and I still feel out of place, but with as honest as he seemed, asking me to be here with just him, I don't want it to end yet.

I'm too curious to see what else he has up his sleeve.

Speaking of sleeves, I gently grab onto his and tug, getting what I want when almost instantly, his attention is being pulled from Matthias and he's leaning into me.

Smile still in place, though dimmed in comparison to the way he'd been on the porch, he tilts his head to the side, questioningly.

"Don't do it," I whisper, skirting my eyes around to make sure I've kept it between us. "I have a bad feeling."

Lifting his hand and pushing a few stray tendrils of my hair back behind my ear, his fingers move down over the side of my face until they land on my jaw, halting position. Leaning in even closer, I watch as his lips quirk up, the smile again meeting his eyes before he speaks again, just as quietly.

"Careful, Daws. All this caring might make people think you like me."

I do. I admit silently as my heart hammers against my chest in agreement. *I just wish I didn't.*

Switching gears, not wanting him to catch on to just how right he is, I roll my eyes and it only serves to make his own twinkle more.

Shit. This is not going the way I need it to. Maybe if I say something to match, he'll stop looking at me like he can see everything. All of my secrets. My truths.

"It has nothing to do with like. He looks like a dog ready to rip apart a bone. I wouldn't wish that on my worst enemy."

Taking my time, lifting my eyes in order to see his, its not his response that comes, but the booming sound of Matthias's as he laughs.

"Don't worry, Dawson. When it comes to Fortune, this dog is allergic to meat."

See? His eyes tell me when I finally catch them, and I settle. Realizing just how crazy I must look with the way I took up for him. My entire plan falling apart the same way my expressions did.

All his fault.

It's not like he made it easy.

God, where is the guy I met at the bar a week ago? It would be so much easier if he was the one standing here now. I could find things to hate about that guy. His hair, the confident way he carried himself, the ballsy way he admitted to wanting to get laid. Hell, even what I thought had been his rejection at first.

This guy, this version of him, it's impossible.

He's...*nice*.

"I just wanna talk to him. Shop talk. Shit that bores the hell out of this one." Matthias speaks, bringing Kimber to his side in an intimate way that matches what Gavin had done earlier, but differs because it's deeper. All it takes is seeing the way her eyes closed and her body practically melts into the move, to know.

Gavin's was intimate, but also for show.

I'm his showpiece tonight.

There it is. *Finally.* I'm out from under the Fortune spell and firmly planted back in reality. I can't believe I didn't see this until now.

Of course, this was the plan.

Bring the new girl to dinner and make it look like you're into her, so having to spend the night watching your ex get it on with her new man isn't as uncomfortable as it's guaranteed to be.

I'm an idiot.

I can't believe I fell for that shit in the car.

Brady was right. He has a way about him. He's turning level headed Dawson into a putty filled version I don't even recognize. The one who left her brains back at her place before coming to work today.

No way. It's not going down this way.

"Come on, Dawson." Kimber interrupts, slipping her arm through mine and pulling me with ease away from Gavin in the direction of what I have to assume is the kitchen. "Let's leave them to it."

"Gladly," I tell her, not even bothering to lower my tone or look back and see just how my date for the night feels about it.

But what I really want to do is more than just leave them to it.

As Kimber pulls me into the kitchen, and motions for me to take a seat at the table as she pulls out and occupies the one across from me, all I want to is act on what I should have done when I was in the car earlier.

Leave. Getting myself as far away from Gavin and the obnoxious fluttering still attacking me, altogether.

This is gonna be a long night.

Gavin

My eyes never left hers when Matthias pulled Kimber into him. I saw how she reacted to their closeness. Felt the halt to her breath, the catch as Kimber melted into Matthias's side the way she's been doing since they finally worked through their shit.

I also felt the change taking place immediately after it.

Gone was the Dawson from the car. The one open to giving me a chance. It was so quick, part of me is starting to think I imagined that version of her.

Damned if I know what caused the shift.

What the hell was it about seeing Kimber and Matthias that turned things around so drastically, and what the hell will it take to turn it around? Get things back in my favor?

Have her pressed closely, letting me touch her that tenderly.

"What's your game, Fortune?"

Damn. In my attempt to dissect what the hell just went down with Dawson, I forgot I still had this jackoff to deal with. The one my best friend wants me to believe actually wants to bury the hatchet.

Right. Like that's ever gonna happen.

It's buried in his DNA to hate me. The same way it seems it is for Reese.

"No clue what you're getting at."

"So, Melinda, Cassidy, Rosa, and Michelle. Not to mention Lauren before she finally wised up, and Amanda. You forgot about those, huh?"

Well, I would have if you didn't insist on bringing them up.

"What's your point?" I ask when it's not even close to what I want to say. My respect for Kimber keeping me from really letting this piece of shit have it.

He forgets what I lived through back when he kept running like the pussy he was. What I saw the love of his life go through, and just how many times she had to lean on me in order to survive it.

This guy can spare me.

What I really want to tell him, though, is his definition of a game and mine, are vastly different. What I see as nights of pure unadulterated sex, he sees as me playing women. Making them expect more than what I clearly laid out on the table beforehand.

He needs a reality check.

So do you, idiot.

"You've always got shit planned out. Three steps ahead of the rest of us. You've been that way for years. In the ring, out of it. With the girls. So, what's your plan here, huh?"

He knows nothing about me. Especially tonight. Shit, other than knowing I wanted to be near her, have her with me, I don't know what the fuck comes next.

They call it flying by the seat of your pants for a reason.

I plan matches. That's it. At least it is these days.

"Don't know what you're getting at, but there's no plan."

"So, you're not trying to get fired?"

Dawson. Reese's cousin. Family. Do not touch order.

Right.

"Contrary to what I know you're hoping for, no. I'm not trying to get thrown out on my ass. At least not until I take the title from you."

Normally, when two guys are booked together, most of their rivalry is for show. The alpha male show they put on, getting in each other's faces and laying shit down, it's all for the cameras and the crowd.

That's not at all how this is with us.

It's been gearing up to go this way from the second I stood in the damn hallway and learned that my girl, the one I thought legitimately wanted to be with me, was in love with him. It's only because of her and Smith, and then Bryan knowing the money it could generate, it hasn't hit the fan yet.

That and Kimber.

This isn't about butthurt. It's not about me losing her to him.

I never had her to begin with, and I'm not so lost in my own shit, I don't know that.

No, the reason I haven't hauled off and knocked his ass out is that I respect her. What she wants to happen here. Her home. The family she's going to one day make with this guy even if I don't trust him as far as I can throw him. Respect our friendship.

"This isn't about the title, Fortune. The world doesn't revolve around what we do."

"Funny," I laugh in his face. "Coming from the guy the world claims *is* wrestling."

"Things change."

"Yeah, I know. So do people." This dig feels good. Because if there's anyone on the planet who should understand what the hell I'm trying to do here, it's Kemper.

He changed. More than once. Became the pussy whipped fucker he is now of his own accord. He shouldn't be the one looking down on someone else for trying to get a piece of the same action.

Least of all me.

From where I'm sitting, he owes me.

"You should know better than anyone."

"I do. I also know that guys like you don't." *Guys like me. Right. Because we're so god damned different.* "I'm gonna ask you again, what are you doing here? What's the play? You trying to hurt Reese, or is there something about this girl you wanna play with and break?"

The urge to hit him dissipates with the way he words his last question.

It's there. Miniscule still, but there's no denying it exists. There damn well is something about this girl, and I'm not gonna walk away, give up, or go back to my different girl every night policy, while it's here and staring me in the face.

This is my chance. A chance to be someone other than Gavin fucking Fortune.

I have to see it through. Even if it costs me everything.

"It's none of your business."

And here's the thing. It's really not.

We're done here.

"If you're planning on taking another girl on this roster, and ruining her so Bryan and Reese have no other alternative but to let her go, that's where you're wrong. It damn well is my business. I won't let you do it."

There he is. The choir boy. I wondered how long it was going to take for him to make an appearance. Protector to everyone. Matthias "the Saint" Kemper has arrived.

"Did it ever occur to you," I snap, closing the distance between us until I'm in his face, looking him square in the eyes—the growled threat of backing up falling on deaf ears. "We're not so different? That, maybe I'm sick and fucking tired of being what everyone wants me to be, and I just want to be myself instead? Or are you so far gone into your hero persona, you're blind to the reality staring you right in the face?"

"I'm not gonna tell you again, Fortune. Step back."

"Why, Matty?" I sneer, egging him on. "What are you gonna do if I don't?"

"Nothing." He states his voice calm, his body language anything but. On edge, ready for the fight just as much as I am. "I made Little One a promise when we moved here. No violence. Of any kind. And unlike you, and the empty promises you've given the thousand plus girls you've screwed with over the years, mine actually means something. It matters."

Well, fuck.

I don't know a lot about this guy's demons, but something tells me if he made a promise to Kimber, it's for a reason. One that even with as pissed as I am, I'm not willing to exploit.

Backing up, I halt when I hear him exhale a strangled thank you.

"You're welcome."

"Why'd you do it, Gavin? Was it for her?"

God knows how many years we've spent working together, and this might be the first time I've ever heard him call me by my first name. Damn. But first things first, time for me to set the record straight.

"No, man. I didn't do it for her. I did it for you."

Stepping back with his admission, the way he knows I felt about Kimber before, I'm not at all surprised he asked me this. We haven't so much as said two words to each other since everything went down back in CPW, so it's only natural when we finally do, it comes.

"She's yours, Kemper. She always has been."

"Then what's your play with Dawson?"

"Still trying to figure it out myself."

It's barely there, but there's no mistaking the angry growl that follows my attempt at the truth, or the groan I let escape when I realize this is the kind of shit Kimber meant last week.

What turns her on.

Gross.

"I know we don't exactly like each other, but you mind doing me a favor?"

"Guess it depends on what you're after."

"Save the growling for the bedroom. Please. For the love of God, I was actually looking forward to eating dinner tonight."

It's not much, but when he laughs, his eyes turning toward the kitchen before his hand reaches up and finds his forehead, I realize what's taking place. The neutral ground Kimber was talking about before, us needing to get past things. It's happening. And what Kemper says next only confirms it.

"She told you?"

"She did."

"Fucking books, man." He admits and when he shakes his head, I laugh.

Fucking books indeed.

Do you think it's too early to ask Dawson not to read?

"I'll do you the favor, but only if you do me one in return."

He's Kimber's boyfriend. No surprise they're shifty in the same way. Looks like I'm getting roped into something else now.

"Anything."

"Whatever this is, what you're still trying to figure out, I'll keep my mouth shut. Just be smart about it."

"Agree—"

"I'm not done."

"What else is there?" I ask, secure in my earlier attempt to answer knowing there won't be anything past what he said, I wouldn't be able to deliver on.

"Don't hurt her."

Shit. Anything but that.

Because something tells me with the way she acted before heading off into the kitchen with Kimber, that's exactly what I did.

I hurt her.

Chapter Eleven

With the way the night started, I'm genuinely surprised by how comfortable everything is once we all sat down, the food was served, and we dived in.

A lot of which is because of Kimber and her incessant need to keep the conversation flowing. Every short lull of silence not sitting well as she quickly switched from one topic to another.

Story after story coming out about her start in the business, where I learned not only how old she was, and how long she's been working to be where she is now, but also how long she and Matthias have known each other.

Been in love.

If she wasn't going out of her way to be one of the sweetest people on the planet, I would have found it nauseating the number of times she had to pause in what she was saying to touch him in some way.

Kisses. Soft brushes of their hands. Both of them leaning in and their foreheads touching. The look of longing and even desire in their eyes whenever they did come up for air, focusing back on the other two people in the room.

It was clear how deep their connection ran, and not just to me.

But where I expected some kind of reaction from Gavin, a giveaway to his feelings on the subject, there was nothing. No anger in his eyes or tense body language. If anything, he was the opposite. His body leaning back, relaxed. His posture open. Engaged in what was going on, and throwing himself into every conversation, especially the ones centering on their time in CPW.

Smiles leading into laughter lines on his face, making his eyes crinkle.

He was happy to be here.

The opposite of what I expected with the history lesson I'd received, both in my research, and talking with a few of the other superstars.

All of it, Gavin's reaction included, being the opposite of anything I'd been a part of in the past.

This isn't my first dinner party. Holden and I hosted a few of them when we were together. Mainly ones he would throw in order to as he said *get my name out there*. Networking, he said, because you never know when I would need to make a career move, and he wanted me prepared.

The only way I ended up prepared on the nights where I had to perform as his dutiful girlfriend being when I had a glass of red wine in hand, possibly even more than one.

You can't be uncomfortable when you're halfway to drunk off your ass.

Which is the opposite of the way this is tonight.

There's no alcohol here, what Matthias explained was his fault. What I don't seem to miss with the amount of laughter and genuine conversation flowing around the table. The conversation I'm now going have to be a part of as the question was aimed directly at me.

The last thing I want to talk about.

I'm more interested in hearing more stories about them. *About him.*

The man who for the better part of the last hour has had his arm slung around the back of my chair, trying to appear innocent as he brushes his fingers gingerly over my shoulder. Grazing and exciting me. Once even driving me so crazy I'd slapped his hand away and earned a round of laughter from Kimber and Matthias.

It was nice. Refreshing. I didn't need to put on a show for anyone. I was just Dawson and accepted easily.

At least, that's how it's been.

Now it's like the spotlight they live under is shining on me and I'm under the microscope. Kimber's question about if I was born and raised here, and if I still have family in the area, demanding a response.

"I was born here. And other than a few months in Los Angeles, I've never left."

God, Daws. Can you be any more clipped and less forthcoming? You sound like you're reading off a cue card.

"What about family? Are your parents still here, or is it just Reese?" Kimber presses, arms settling in on the tabletop, clearly eager to learn more about me than I feel comfortable giving.

"They're all still here. My sisters live in Barrie, but my parents are still in the city."

"Oh, you have sisters!" she practically squeals slapping her hands together.

"Don't mind her, Dawson." Matthias laughs shaking his head. "She got stuck with an older brother."

"Are they older?" Kimber jumps in again after smacking Matthias on the arm. "Younger? Twins or triplets?"

"Janine's older by five years, and Hanna is younger by five." I laugh softly.

"You guys are so lucky." Kimber sighs, and looking from her to Matthias, chancing a glance at Gavin, he doesn't waste any time explaining why.

"I've got a younger brother. His name's Evan. Don't ask me why it means I'm lucky, but she's been telling me I am for two years."

"I think I know why."

"You do?" his brow quirks up, and I'll be damned if it's not another thing about him I find attractive.

"Yes. It's because he's younger. I'm guessing," I pause, looking to Kimber for confirmation. "Growing up with an older brother is a lot like growing up with Janine. Doesn't matter how big you get or how old, they always think they're superior."

"Yes!" Kimber claps. "That's exactly it. See?! Dawson gets it."

Laughing when she nudges Matthias and glares at Gavin, it hits me.

The fear I have about opening myself up and letting people see beyond the parts of me they've gotten to see on air isn't a bad thing.

Sitting here, surrounded by these three—even if the jury is still out on one of them—it's okay. They're not judging. They're not giving it much focus at all. They're just making conversation. Enjoying time.

It's like I walked away from my life with Holden and LiveWire and walked straight into an episode of the Twilight Zone.

Kimber's reaction is trivial, but it makes me like her more. As far as exes go, it looks like Gavin lucked out with this one. It's no wonder Matthias is in love with her.

I get the feeling she has a lot of people who feel that way.

"Okay, enough of the interview. I'm gonna get the pie." She announces, but before she can even push her chair back to stand, Gavin's on his feet.

"Actually, I figured you two could save it for later."

"But it'll only take a minute. Just need to slice it."

Motioning to the counter where I watched her put it earlier, she stares him down, but Gavin doesn't budge. Instead of accepting with the look she's giving him, he just makes a motion of his own with his head.

To me.

A motion that once it's done, changes everything.

Gone is Kimber's stubborn stance, and in its place, softer understanding. What her boyfriend seems to second when his attention falls to me and he's offering up a weak shrug and smile.

No way. This isn't happening.

I was finally unwinding. The last thing I want is to be ripped away from it in favor of dealing with Gavin alone. It was bad enough how easily I gave in to him in the car when I thought he was being genuine.

I don't think I've got it in me to go another round.

But another round it appears I'm going to have because as I'm sitting here driving myself crazy, I can faintly hear them saying their goodbyes. What's quickly followed up by his hands finding my shoulders again and rubbing as he leans his head down, breath hot against my ear.

"You ready to go?"

"I wanted pie." I pout sadly, the nicest way possible I can say no. I'm definitely not ready to go and be left to my own devices with this man again.

"You bake a pie, and you don't let your girl have any," Kimber says, punching Gavin in the arm. "You're a lousy date, Fortune."

"I know." he agrees, and that's when I catch it.

The belief in his eyes. I saw it a few times over dinner when I'd catch his attention on me. His eyes studying while I was eating. I put it out of my mind, but there's no ignoring it now.

He believes he's a bad date, and it's got nothing to do with the damn pie.

His wanting to leave. His eagerness to do it, even bringing me into it with his touch in an attempt to get me moving, it's all about that. Where I was sitting here thinking this was one of the better nights, he was just praying for it to be over.

"He's right. We should probably get going. I forgot I had to stop by and see Reese before heading home. I'm sorry, Kimber. We'll totally do pie next time."

The lies fall so easily, it's like no time has passed at all. I'm right back in my apartment with Holden, giving the people what they need to hear.

Yeah, it's definitely time to go. I've overstayed my welcome.

With Gavin *and* with them.

"Yes," she agrees, making her way around Gavin and wrapping her arms around me, pulling me in for a tight hug. "We're definitely doing pie next time. One even better than this jackass can make."

Moving back, she backs up her words with an elbow to his side and Matthias, who until now has just been quiet and watching, busts out laughing.

Everything moves quickly then. My chair coming out, Gavin moving back, rubbing at his side, but not speaking as he turns and heads for the door once I've stood up.

A silence Kimber fills as she throws her arm around me and walks me to the door.

"I know it doesn't feel like it right now, but this isn't about you."

Like hell, it isn't. Who else could it be about?

There's only one person he's looking to unload.

"It doesn't matter."

"But it does." She argues, pointing to my eyes. "They give you away, same as mine."

"It doesn't matter," I repeat. "I know what tonight was."

Pausing mid-step, I fall back with her, eyes slanted toward the door for any sign of Gavin and finding none.

"What do you think this was?"

"He didn't want to come alone. I'm a stand-in. It's okay. It was stupid of me to think it was something more."

Except it wasn't. Not with the things he said before we even got out of the car.

He made me believe it was more.

That *he* was more.

"You're wrong, Dawson. Gavin, even before I got him to agree to this, never brought anyone around. I never met any of the girls he was involved with, apart from the ones I worked with. But even then, it was never in this way. You're the first."

Matthias, having made his way past us and catching what Kimber says, adds his own two cents in.

"Judging from the way he's out there unloading on his tires; I figure you're the last too."

Gavin

"King of stupid—" Kick. "Idiotic—" Another kick. "Moves." Delivering a final kick to the tire and leaning back against the car as I attempt to catch my breath, I hear the door open a few feet away and await what's coming.

A *very* pissed off Dawson.

I don't know what I was thinking about coming here, and worse, bringing her into it. I mean, who in their right mind has their first date at their fake girlfriends' house?

Even more preposterous?

My belief I can be someone other than *Gavin fucking Fortune* for five damn minutes. What's worse, realizing what a stupid move this was at the worst possible moment, and proceeding to make an ass of myself after it.

She's going to kill me.

And she's going to have every right.

I'd do it myself but I'd feel bad leaving Kimber with the cleanup.

Pushing off the car and turning my attention back to the tires, ready for another wailing, I'm midway through my first kick when I hear my name being called. Ignoring it with a quick shake of my head, loose hair falling across my face, I continue to wail—this time silently—on the tire until the voice becomes louder.

Impossible to ignore.

"Gavin, stop!"

Whirling around until our eyes are deadlocked on one another, I catch sight of the shock first, the rigidness of her stance next, which once she realizes I'm no longer wailing on the tires but instead throwing my wild eyes her way, results in a shiver of fear.

A completely valid reaction to how I'm sure I appear, but the opposite of what I want.

I don't want her to fear me.

Blinking once, and shoving down my feelings, I easily slip back into character. The very thing I asked her to put aside for the night, is now going to be all she gets.

I can't believe I thought I could have it any other way.

"Why Dawson? You want a go?"

Stepping toward me, letting her eyes fall to the tires before rising again to mine, I'm frozen when without so much as a blink to break connection, she takes another even step forward, followed by another until she's standing so close, I can feel the warmth of her shaken breath against my face.

"Your question doesn't make sense."

No, I suppose with the way she found me, it doesn't. I wasn't asking if she wanted to wail on the car. I wanted to know if she wanted to wail on *me*.

Making my attempt at normalcy tonight, even more ridiculous.

I'm never going to be normal.

"Get in the car, Dawson."

Annoyed when she shakes her head, instead, moving to my side and leaning back against the car, I release an uneven breath of my own as I'm given access to the house *and* the two occupants standing on the porch watching.

Great. We've got an audience.

"Hey, guys!" I call out, with all the false bravado I can manage. "You wanna join the party?"

"Gavin…" she says softly, reaching her hand out until its covering mine.

"No, Dawson. If they want a show, maybe they should come down here and be a part of the one we're putting on."

"What happened inside, Gavin? Where is this coming from?" she asks instead of reacting in the way I expect. Obviously not having any part of my act.

There's no way I can tell her when I can still feel both pairs of eyes watching me from the doorway. Waiting for whatever mistake it is they know I'm going to make next. Every step I'm taking now all the ammunition Matthias needs, despite how he acted over dinner.

"Get in the car, Dawson." This time, before she can argue, I sweeten the pot. "Please."

Both sides of me at war again.

What the hell it is about this girl? Why is it so damn hard to keep the persona going with her?

"I've got a better idea."

Swinging my attention to her, releasing the fist my hands have balled into and exhaling, I wait.

Motioning with her head down the street, and turning her gaze toward the very two people still standing on the porch, she smiles weakly at me.

"It's a nice night. Go for a walk with me."

If I wasn't seeing it with my own eyes, I wouldn't believe it.

She knows, and the only showtime she wants to allow is ours.

Privately.

"Kimber was right about you, Dawson. You've got a horrible poker face. I'm sure the last thing you want to do is take a walk with me."

Leaning in close at the same time her hand slips down and through mine, her weak smile from before turns into a full-on grin.

"You're right." She admits easily. "What I wanted was the chance to meet the real Gavin. He was what I was promised, after all. But all I've gotten since you came back from talking with Matthias is more of the same." When I don't so much as blink, she laughs softly to herself. "Not even going to try and deny it?"

"I'm a lot of things, Dawson, but a liar isn't one of them."

Applying pressure with her hand locked in mine, she graces me with yet another smile, as she again flicks her head to the sidewalk.

"I figured as much. So, stop wailing on the poor car and walk with me. Give me what I was promised. After you've done that, you can drive me home and forget this night ever happened."

Slipping her other hand out between us and looking from it to me, it's obvious what she wants, but it's also painfully obvious to me, she's not going to get it.

"I'm not shaking your hand. No deal, Dawson."

"Why not?"

"Because of all the things I want to do tonight, forgetting it exists, isn't one of them."

I'm not sure he's aware, but being around him is like being on a tilt-a-whirl.

It starts off slow, you're going around and around, the speed picking up with every roundabout it makes. Reaching a plateau when you're at your most nauseated. Your head spinning and your stomach bottoming out. It being a miracle at the end when you step off the ride and you're able to walk at all.

One could also liken it to the whiplash one experiences after a car crash. I'm just not that morbid. Definitely not ready to go there with this guy this soon.

He switches between who I think is the real Gavin, and the performer, quicker than most do flipping a light switch. It's definitely taking me off my game.

"Considering the way you've been acting all night, I'm going to have to disagree." I open up, admitting once he's indulged me and we've started walking down the street.

"I refer you to what I said before. I don't lie, Dawson."

"And I'll refer to the conversation we had before we went inside." I snap, reacting to his cold inflection. "You wanted me to see you, Gavin. The real you. At least it's what you led me to believe. Only, after you went off with Matthias, it's been the opposite. You've been cold. Aloof. Well, other than the times you engaged with Kimber. How am I supposed to see it when that's what you're giving me to work with?"

The worst part about this is, I don't even know why I'm trying so hard to get to the bottom of this. Yeah, sure, I like having all the facts. I'm huge on understanding what's going on because I hate being confused. What's happening tonight with Gavin, though, it's something else entirely.

And honestly, it's off-putting.

If this was anyone else, by now I would have cut my losses. Made good on what I told him when I realized who he is, and who it was he works for. Chalked it up to a one-night stand and mild curiosity.

But this isn't anyone else, and I can't walk away.

It's like Brady said. He's put some kind of spell on me.

Huffing in frustration, making him have to keep up with me as the steam threatening to blow from my ears pushes me forward so fast, I'm damn near power walking, I keep going.

"For part of the time tonight, I thought I had you figured out. You brought me here to pay back Kimber for what you think she did for you, but also to show her you'd moved on. I was a stand-in. Sure, it went against the way you were in the car, but it made sense. I hated it but went along with it. Then over dinner, it was like the Gavin from the car was in the room. You were different, so I started to think I was wrong. Shows what an idiot I am, because, with the way you bolted out of there, it's pretty obvious you were done. You wanted the night over with."

Catching up to me, gripping my arm and tugging, he spins me around to face him.

"Is that really what you think tonight was about?" He practically seethes, his body like stone and his eyes filled with fire.

"You've given me no other reason to believe otherwise, so, yes."

"Jesus Christ." He curses, dragging a hand roughly through his hair and quickly looking away. "If that's what you think, I've really botched this entire thing."

Say what?

"You've got it all wrong, Dawson."

An admission I might believe if I didn't have the entire nights actions backing my position up.

"I don't see how."

"No, of course, you don't, because despite me asking you to forget about the guy I am when the cameras are on, you're still seeing him. I'm not exactly making it easy for you to see otherwise, though, so this is as much my fault as it is yours."

Oh, hell no. I'm not taking the blame for this. I was enjoying myself before he up and turned the tables on me. This isn't on me.

"I didn't cause this, Gavin. The only thing I did wrong was agreeing to go out with you in the first place."

Flinching from the impact of my words, he releases the hold he has around my wrist and takes a few steps back.

"At least you're honest." He whispers, his gaze falling back to his car before turning to meet mine again. This time, the look I'm met with, not one of indignation or upset, but sadness. Defeat.

I've hurt him.

"I think this is a good time to call it a night. This was a mistake."

Something I might believe in if his voice didn't crack midway through. His attempt at flipping the switch and being the cocky guy failing.

Motioning with his head back the way we came, he turns away but doesn't start walking.

"For what its worth, being around them is hard for me, so I slip on this mask in order to get through it. It's not like Kemper hides the way he feels. I know what he thinks about me. What everyone thinks. So, I just give them what they want. That's what you were getting from me tonight, Dawson. Not me bringing you there as some sort of doll to parade around. As for what happened over dinner, I wanted to get you alone. I'd fulfilled my obligation and wanted you to myself before having to bring you home. Seems I did a bang-up job there, huh?"

He laughs roughly. Everything about it as fake as the persona he displays in the ring. The persona I went in expecting instead of giving him the chance he deserved.

Gavin was right before.

This is my fault.

"Gavin—"

"No." he interrupts. "It's all good. I had a feeling the night would end this way. So. let's just go back to the car, I'll drive you home, and we can both do like you said and forget it ever happened."

Not bothering to wait for my response, he starts to move, showing me up close and personal how it looks when someone truly wants to get away from you. Not slowing until he's reached his destination, unlocking the car door and slipping into the drivers' seat.

Only when I'm safely tucked away beside him does he put the key in the ignition and start the car, pulling away as quickly as possible from the curb. The sound of the tires on the asphalt the perfect crescendo for the night that's just taken place.

The night I've officially ruined.

Chapter Twelve

Gavin

After the disaster of my first date with Dawson—my first real date in fourteen years—the last thing I'm expecting to be met with when I land at the building for our show, is the grinning face of her cousin.

Hell, with the way we left things, waking up to a pink slip would have been more appropriate.

Just what the hell is he grinning for? Better yet, why isn't his partner in crime displaying the same enthusiasm? Bryan's face is decidedly more serious in comparison to Reese, which only serves to scare me more.

I haven't known Bryan as long as Matthias has, not even as long as Kimber has, but what I do know about the guy just from the short time we've been working together is, he's never serious unless given a damn good reason.

That's always left to the man to his left. The one currently grinning like a Cheshire cat.

Something tells me, the trickle of fear I'm experiencing as this plays out, Reese's grin gaining momentum and actually growing bigger the closer I get, shouldn't be ignored.

It means something.

Which, when I get close enough and his arm is coming out, throwing itself around my own and bringing me in closer for one hell of a pat on a back, he doesn't waste time dropping on me.

"Just the man we were waiting for!" he exclaims and shooting Bryan a look that I hope displays just how thrown off I am, I focus again on Reese and what the hell is going on.

"You wanna tell me what this is about?"

Last we spoke, he wanted nothing to do with me. I can't see how his attitude, especially as it pertains to me being anywhere near his cousin has changed.

I'm the king of switching gears, changing faces, and even I can't flip that fast.

"Last we spoke you wanted me nowhere near you. Let alone near Dawson. What changed?"

"That was family shit, Fortune. Nothing personal."

Nothing personal, my ass. He called me out on my history before I landed here. It doesn't get more personal.

Before I have the chance to call him out on it, though, our party of three turns into one of four as Kemper saunters up, coming to a stop closest to Bryan, the same grin Reese is sporting, clear as day on his face too.

What the fuck is this?

"Not for nothing, guys, but you all standing around smiling like this is starting to give me a complex. Someone wanna fill me in?"

"We've been doing some thinking." Kemper steps forward, offering up more with just those five words than either of our bosses have in the short time I've been standing here. "With Brady's run finally coming to end, these two are looking for the next big draw."

"Okay," I acknowledge, finally starting to make the pieces fit. The smiles now making a bit more sense. "I guess it means it's finally going to be you and me?"

With a quick nod, he's smiling again, and I'm stuck on how to respond.

On the one hand, I'm thrilled, because this program has been a long time coming. It would have happened two years ago if Kemper hadn't gotten his panties in a knot over having to work with Kimber. It's about damn time they're looking at it again. But on the other hand, I'm confused about why now.

And what, if anything, it has to do with the disastrous dinner a few nights ago.

Is this the reoccurrence of Saint Kemper? Did he run to Reese and Bryan and request this so as he said at the house, he could make my personal shit his business?

Jesus. Thinking this hard is giving me a damn headache.

"Was this your idea?" I question Kemper, knowing in my gut it is, but completely thrown off when instead of nodding, he shakes his head and Reese cuts in.

"It was mine, actually. Bryan has been telling me for months that I need to take a more active role with the matches. I'll admit, I don't have the amount of knowledge he does, but he's right. I do have to do more than scour over the books. This is my chance."

"You wanna put us in a feud?"

"I do. A long term one, if the two of you can manage to put your differences aside and do what's best for business."

"Already done, boss." Matthias interrupts and shooting a scowl his way, his smile just grows and it takes everything in me not to reach out and knock it off his face.

What is Kemper's game here?

"My personal shit never touches what I do in the ring," I state.

Never once in the ten years I've been doing this have I ever let a personal beef, relationship or otherwise private situation enter into the ring.

I came close once when I was involved with Melinda Richardson, but even then, with as much as Merrick and I hated each other, we never let it change the way we did things in the ring. Our years-long program still one of the top-selling draws for Smith before he packed it in.

Kemper and I? With as long as we worked together, other than knowing how he really feels about my screwing around, and us having the same ball busting girl in common, have never had beef at all. We've just done what the other boys have and tolerated the existence of each other since we both had the same damn goal.

Ruling the business.

This is gonna be a breeze.

"How does this play out?" I ask, curious if it's going to end the way I want. Making me a three-time champion. "If you want this to play out in a long-term way, am I going over at the end of it?"

It's Bryan's turn to enter the conversation now, albeit silently. He nods before turning toward his best friend, a look passing between them that if I hadn't spent so much time around them over the last year, I wouldn't recognize, but do now with ease.

The lightening of their eyes as they look at each other all the answer I need, but what Kemper wastes no time proving me right on when he ends the silence.

"You're going over, Gav."

There it is again. Him calling me by my first name.

Jesus, I don't know what to do with this. It's weird. *Am I being punked?*

"When?"

"We don't have a date locked in because we wanted to discuss it with both of you first, but we were thinking a best of three matches."

With us working practically every day, with what he's saying, I could be going over this Friday. That can't be right.

"What do you mean three matches?"

"He means, we face each other once a month, for three months. We'll be involved in each other's shit in other ways during that time, but it will all be the lead-in for these three matches. The man with the most wins at the end, well, he holds the crown."

The crown.

Otherwise known as the HFWA Heavyweight Championship.

The belt that when I landed here and Kemper won it off Raines, I figured would never come my way because Bryan and Reese would want to keep it on the clear favorite.

Seems I was wrong.

I'm screwing up everywhere, apparently. Not just with Dawson.

I judged these three. Even after spending the last ten years working with Kemper, I still believed his friendship with Michaelchuk would win out, and he'd ride it for all it's worth. I've been shown otherwise, but my stupid brain wouldn't let me see past it.

I really am the asshole everyone claims I am.

"Sounds good." I manage when after a few seconds of being stared down by all three, I realize they're waiting on my acceptance. "But what happens at the end?"

"I'm pretty sure you know already, Fortune."

He retires.

The look I saw between him and Bryan, and even the one he's wearing now, no matter how peaceful it appears on the surface, it all lends to it.

Matthias Kemper is ready to hang up his boots.

Kemper leaving, wanting to go off and live his life with Kimber, it should make me happy. With him out of the way, I'll have everything I wanted when I landed here. I'll be back at the top of the heap and carrying a company again, much as I did with Smith. I'll be given any match I want, along with all of the perks that come along with being named the champ.

So, why do I feel like puking?

Maybe it's because I know what being the man around here means. Or maybe, the thought of Kemper getting to go off and live the real dream, settling down and making babies, has me twisted in knots.

I mean, isn't that what I wanted before Smith handed me the brass ring?

A life outside of wrestling? Someone special to come home to instead of the empty as fuck house I have now?

"You okay, man?" Kemper cuts through the barrage of my subconscious, bringing me back. "You don't look so hot."

"Are you really gonna pack it in?"

"Yeah."

"Why?"

I know it's none of my business, but I'll be damned. I care. I need to know why this seems so fucking easy for him. To hear the rest of the locker room, the dirt sheets, and even the media talk, Matthias *is* wrestling.

How can the so-called God of the squared circle give it all up and walk away?

Better yet, why is it him, and not me? What's so special about Kemper?

"It's time. When the doctors cleared me, they did it reluctantly. They knew they couldn't hold me back, but they also knew that any shot to my head could be my last. Coming back, I told Bryan I wanted to do it on my terms. End it the same way. This is me delivering on it."

"Did you always plan on dropping it to me?"

It's such a prick thing to ask but no taking it back now.

"Yeah, Gavin. It was always going to be you."

Son of a bitch! Maybe Kimber was on to something after all.

"Why?" I choke out, weighed down by the heaviness that comes from knowing you were the only choice for a guy who for the better part of ten years, you thought hated your guts.

"Who better?"

"Sniper, for one. He's been pissed ever since he dropped it to you the first time. Raines, for another. I know he wasn't exactly ready when you put the title on him, but he made one hell of a champion. Jesus, you could probably coax Merrick back in and put it on him."

"None of those guys are you, Fortune. And for my last run, I want the one I've never had. I want the best. It's about damn time we put the past in the past and give the people what they want."

"Don't you mean, give them the chance to see you finally kick my ass for stealing your girl out from under you?"

Where I expect Kemper to react, for his chest to rise, his expression to harden, or worse, to come at me the way he would have in the past when I'm goading him this way, he just smirks.

"That too." He laughs. "So, what do you say, Fortune? You game?"

Looking from Reese to Bryan, and then over to Matthias, seeing the sincerity staring back at me through their eyes, my decision is made.

"I'm in. Let's tear the house down."

Chapter Thirteen

Dawson

My, how times have changed.

When I accepted the job from Reese, signed the contract, and showed up here ready to put my all into this position, I'd done so wanting to avoid any and all contact with the superstar known the world over as Gavin Fortune.

The name I called him the night of our first date, wasn't one I came up with on my own. It's what it seems like the entirety of the internet refers to him as.

A name he's done nothing but own from the moment I learned who he was.

Yet, here I am a week after our disastrous first date, hunting him down. Becoming more annoyed with each passing second when each place I look turns up nothing.

He's due in the ring in a little less than thirty minutes for a face to face showdown with Matthias. I've managed to come across *him* five times so far in my travels to locate Gavin, yet the man I'm looking for continues to elude me.

"Hey, pretty lady." a voice calls out as I round the corner where the last set of male locker rooms reside. "Just the woman we were coming to see."

Finally looking over toward what I see now are the two bodies standing directly in front of the room I need access to; I plaster on the fakest smile I can and pretend I just wandered here.

Reese's rules from the day I signed the contract flashing like neon lights.

Admitting I'm looking for Gavin, especially with the looks these two are bestowing on me, is only going to add fuel to what is already a very lit fire.

"What'd you need me for?"

The older guy, River, looks from his partner quickly then back to me, confusion written all over his face when neither one of us responds.

"Our match is after this one, and we're supposed to be talking to you before we head out." River easily fills me in, and as it all comes crawling back, my hand easily finds my forehead and I slap it.

"Duh! Of course. Sorry guys."

Sharing another look, the other guy, Ross, smiles, the setting of it on his face as awkward there as I feel where I'm standing.

"You weren't coming to find us?"

Okay, Dawson. You've been around these guys for weeks. Time to spin a story, and sell it better than these guys do in the ring.

"Actually, no. I ran into Bryan earlier and he couldn't find Gavin. Since I'm supposed to be filming a spot with him later, I offered to come to find him."

Please let this work.

After another quick look between them, River slams his fist down on the locker room door, the sound reverberating off, harsh and more violent than I'd been expecting, causing my body to jolt backward from the force.

"Hey, Fortune. New girls looking for ya!" Ross chimes in when River steps toward me, concern laced in his eyes.

"Sorry. Sometimes I don't know my own strength." Looking me up and down he grimaces. "You alright?"

"Yeah, of course," I tell him, playing it off.

As he takes a step toward me, the door to the locker room opens and hovering there, almost flanking it, is the very man I've spent the last half hour looking everywhere for. Looking less than pleased at my appearance.

"What do you want, Dawson?" he grunts angrily, and again like before with River, the surprise has me taking a step back as a cold shiver drives straight down my spine.

I've seen Gavin a lot of different ways since I came to HFWA, but this is a new one.

Who did this to him?

Too bad River and Ross don't give me a chance to answer before they're on him. His tone obviously setting off alarm bells for them too.

"Didn't your mama ever teach you not to speak like that to a lady?"

Rolling his eyes and smirking, Gavin pushes back, stepping toward River, while keeping his eyes trained on Ross's every move. Aware of the situation he's presented with.

"Didn't anyone ever teach you to mind your own fucking business?"

"Gavin…" I interrupt, cutting this off before it becomes something none of these men are going to be able to come back from. "Bryan sent me to find you."

"Well, you found me."

Standing my ground, refusing to take him or this attitude he's determined to spew at me seriously, I look from River to Ross and back again. It's time for me to get these guys out of the way so we can talk.

Not the bullshit attempt at talking and failing we did a week ago. This time, we're really going to talk. I need to get to the bottom of just what it is about Gavin Fortune I can't seem to walk away from.

"Why don't you guys head over and get ready for the match. I'll be there in a minute and we can work the spot."

Ross, seemingly okay with the idea, starts heading off. River, on the other hand, holds back, shifting as close to me as he can get before leaning in and whispering.

"You sure?"

"I'm good, River, thanks. I'll see you two in a sec."

Waiting until both men have walked away and turned the corner, I steel myself then turn on my heel to face him. The look I'm met with when our eyes finally do meet, not at all the one I'd been witness to before.

There's no anger to be found, and when he takes hold of my hand and pulls me to him, chest to chest and then walks me back against the wall, his lips crushing themselves to mine and stealing my breath, he tells me without words exactly what he wants.

"I've been dying to kiss you for days." He admits when after leaving me sufficiently spun he pulls back with a softened grin. "I was beginning to think I'd never see you again after last week."

In the few minutes since he opened the door and very loudly announced his presence, I've been struck by whiplash. His moods all over the map, unable to be kept up with.

Is this the final version of Gavin for today, or is he going to bless me with another one in the next two minutes?

"I didn't come here to kiss you, Gavin."

"Since I know for a fact Bryan isn't looking for me, it means you were, princess."

Shying away from the knowledge in his eyes, he laughs.

"I knew it. So, if you're due to interview River and Ross, what the hell are you doing here, Daws?"

A shortened version of my name sounding like sugar on his tongue aside, I'm in awe at his cockiness. He may have seemed genuine when he said he didn't expect to see me again, but in the same breath, he's treating me like every other woman he's been with before. Easy to read and disposable.

I'm not having it.

"I can assure you, it's not for what you're thinking. And honestly, I now realize I've made a mistake, so if you'll excuse me, I need to get back to the real reason I'm here."

Spinning on my heel, more than ready to get out of here and away from this nauseating back and forth we're doing, I barely make it a few steps away before I feel his touch around my wrist, my entire body moving into his as he swings me back around.

This time though, continuing to move with me until we're buried away inside the locker room and out of the hall.

"I've learned my lesson about getting into things with you in public places, Dawson. So, since it appears as though we're going to do this now, might as well do it here."

Do what? Huh?

"I'm not going to screw you if that's what you're thinking I came here for."

"Never crossed my mind, princess."

Where I expect him to grin, wink or raise an eyebrow, giving me some kind of indication, he is, in fact, lying to me, I'm met with the opposite. His expression is clear of all humor.

He means it.

"Then why'd you say all the other stuff before?"

"Because I enjoy getting a rise out of you. Plus, I had to do something to keep from wanting to tear River and Ross's heads off for being so close to you."

If I wasn't confused before, I'm sure it's evident now.

Why in the world would he have such an issue with River and Ross? It's not like he opened the door and caught us making out. And besides, even if we were, he'd made his position clear the night of our first date. What I do and who I do it with are none of his concern.

Except, like before, I can tell he's as serious as a heart attack.

"Nothing happened."

"Oh, I know. River won't touch any woman, and Ross is on his way to becoming the next Gavin Fortune, at least as far as the barflies go."

"Then why would it bother you?"

"Easy," he starts, bridging the gap me taking a step back once inside the room has put between us. "Because you're you, Dawson. You're sweet. This is the wrong place to be with that level of sweetness."

Is this guy for real? Is he actually jealous?

"You were jealous," I state and after a few seconds, where I can see the internal struggle he's having admitting it, he finally breaks.

"Yeah, okay? Is that what you want to hear? The great pussy master extraordinaire, Gavin Fortune, turns into a jealous as shit fuckboy when anyone so much as breathes in your direction."

Woah.

There's an edge to his admission but an understandable one. Just hearing the name I'd picked up in my research coming out of his own mouth, is enough to make me sick inside. I can't imagine how disgusted Gavin must have been saying it.

Sighing, he drifts from our place in the center of the room, heading over to the benches, throwing himself down hard. Sighing before leaning his back and resting it against the wall behind him.

It's as though this admission was so huge; it took everything out of him.

"Why did you really come, Daws?"

Now it's my turn. No more secrecy and lies for the other people around us. If he can be honest and admit, as much as it obviously kills him to, that seeing me with other people makes him jealous, I can easily admit I came to find him because for some reason I can't explain, I can't walk away.

I miss him.

The way we talk, the playful banter, even the sex.

I want more.

"I need an answer."

"What's the question?" he fires back just as swiftly.

"Will you go out with me?"

Sitting forward, leaning his elbows into his knees, he looks me dead in the eyes. "Are you serious?"

"Yeah, I'm serious. But before you answer, there are ground rules."

"I'd expect nothing less, but yes, to all of them."

"You haven't even heard what they are."

"I don't care. It's a yes regardless, but okay. What are the rules, princess?"

"No sex."

"Done. I don't want to fuck you."

Ignoring the sting of rejection rearing its head despite it being my own rule, I keep going. "I choose the place and time."

"Deal. Clearly, my dating skills need work." He laughs and I can't help but smile. "What else is there?"

"You've got to be yourself. Not the guy you are when you're here, but the guy from Johnny's. The guy I met in the car before we went to dinner with Matthias and Kimber. I want him or nothing."

It takes a little longer for him to answer this time, the conflict obvious given how long I'm sure he's been living as the other version of himself, but when he does, he seals both our fates.

"You've got yourself a deal, Dawson."

Crossing the room at record speed, he plants another kiss on me, breaking it and the connection before he has the ability to sweep me off my feet.

"I'll be seeing you soon."

"I don't want to fuck you."
Like hell, I don't.

I don't pride myself on lying, but I knew it was going to be a condition. Screwing around all those years came in handy, in my ability to read women.

Dawson is one of the easiest ones.

Practically all we've done since the first day we met is screw. It stands to reason if she wants to have a real date, the same way I wanted to when I brought her to Kimber's, sex can't be a part of it.

Chemistry is definitely not an issue for us.

Like her, though, I want more. There's something about this girl. She makes me feel things and actually, enjoy feeling them. Physically my body stirs whenever I'm near her, but that's not all it does. My mind fires on all cylinders, I'm consciously aware of every answer I give, and more to the point, I'm aware of all her responses, both physical and not.

I'm inherently better when she's around, and unlike the last time I felt this way, Dawson wants me back. She's here and in it as much as I am.

Allowing me to see Kimber for what she really was.

Preparation.

My only goal now is keeping the Fortune of old at bay. It's so easy to revert back to the character I built. I mean, I did it a few minutes ago in the hallway. In an effort to curb my feelings seeing River and Ross so close to Dawson, I just flipped the character switch.

Using earlier as an example probably isn't the best road to take considering after the way I was acting; River almost didn't walk away.

If his tag team partner Ross is the second coming of me, I'm sure River is the second coming of Kemper. Their sole aim in life is to protect the people around them. Which is another reason jealousy made me its bitch.

I want to be that guy for Dawson.

Me and no one else.

I just have to make sure when I do, I'm not being a Neanderthal or she's definitely going to walk away again, and this time, she won't be coming back to find me when I'm hidden away from the world.

She'll just be gone.

Something I can't and won't let happen.

Gavin Fortune the wrestler, tonight is his last performance.

If Dawson wants just Gavin, then just Gavin is what she'll get.

I just hope she's ready.

Chapter Fourteen

Dawson

Growing up, this was my favorite place to come when I wanted to be alone.

The sheer amount of walking you've got to do in order to get here made it ideal, but the view is what really sold it.

Back when I found it, I wasn't what you'd call popular, but I wasn't exactly a pariah either. I just preferred being alone. It was a running gag with a lot of the people I ended up working with at LiveWire when they heard how I was, because how does a loner end up in front of the camera? How does a girl who absolutely loathed everything about her high school drama class, end up in broadcasting?

I was an enigma.

It's one of the reasons I wanted to bring Gavin here for our date. To this exact spot. He can't exactly flip the performer switch off when we're at work, and since I was serious when I told him I wanted the version of him he lets me see whenever we're alone, I figure taking him here, where I loved to be because I was always alone, is a great place to make sure it happens.

Give him the freedom to be himself.

When he pulls the car into the parking lot, though, finally taking notice of where I've brought him, it brings about a whole other topic of conversation. Starting with, why I would bring him here of all places.

My old high school.

"I'm starting to think you're as bad at planning dates as I am, Daws."

"Maybe so," I concede. "But at least I didn't bring you to my ex's place for dinner."

Gripping his chest as though I've wounded him, I laugh as I slip myself out of the seatbelt and step out of the car.

Waiting as he does the same and hits the button for the auto lock on his keys, I make my way over, taking a risk and slipping my hand through his and pointing out to the front of the school, where unbeknownst to him, our journey for the night begins.

"You want to show me a bus shelter?"

"No, idiot. I don't want to show you the shelter. I want to show you something beside it." Gripping his hand tightly in mine, I start moving, practically pulling him along until we're standing right where I want us. Looking from me to the ground and back again, he questions me with his eyes and I merely smile. "Look down again, and this time, Gavin, really look."

I might have been a loner growing up, may even still be one now, but it didn't mean I didn't want to make a mark in the world or at the very least, with what it is I'm wanting him to see, leave my mark behind when I changed direction.

Which, after a few minutes of staring at the ground, even squatting down in order to see better, he seems to get when his breath catches and his head turns, our eyes meeting again. This time, his widened in surprise.

"When did you do this?"

Lowering to the cement, I give him a little insight into the Dawson before HFWA.

Before adulthood, really.

"The year I graduated was rough. There were so many decisions I had to make. For the guidance counselors at school, for my parents, for any adult with any sort of authority. It felt as though I had to have my whole life mapped out in that very moment. So, in an effort to maintain some form of control, I skipped class one day, came out here and found signs warning me away with the threat of wet cement."

"Which you obviously listened to." He comments with a point to the ground and a soft laugh. "I had no idea you were such a rule breaker, Daws."

"Yeah, that's me. Dawson Traymore, resident bad girl."

Moving into me, he nuzzles his face into my neck, his next words hot against my skin.

"You definitely were the night we met."

Oh boy.

If just the feel of him being this close is making the need rise, there's no way with the rest of the night I'll be able to stay true to my own rules.

Whenever I'm near him, everything else fades away, and it's just us. We're in Johnny's office again and losing control.

Shaking it off, I put us back on track.

"I needed something just for me. Something I could control, if only for a few brief moments. So, when the coast was clear, I sat down and placing my hand in the middle of the freshly laid cement, I left my mark. Adding my name to it a few seconds later for added effect."

"Dawson was here." He says, whisper quiet and in his understanding of how I felt then, I confirm it.

"Exactly."

Pulling my face up to his, he smiles. "I take back what I said in the car."

"What do you mean?"

"This, you showing me parts of yourself and being so open about it. I take back what I said about you being horrible at this."

Heart sufficiently swelling at the sentiment behind the words, I bravely reach out, even knowing what the touch will do, and cup his face, brushing my fingers along his cheek and down his jaw before leaning in and pressing my lips ever so softly to his.

The only sound the beat of my own heart like a drum in perfect rhythm for the brief seconds we are here and enjoy each other.

"There's more." I breathlessly inform him when we both pull away.

"I can't," he pauses, brushing his nose against mine. "I can't wait."

Gavin

This time when she slips her hand in mine, I'm ready for it, and I'm the one holding on for dear life. Wanting the connection we have to grow instead of fade. Never once letting up on the pressure as she walks us through a hole in the fence, through a lot of trees and brush, all the way into what appears to be a forest.

A walk that eventually leads us to a pathway with large boulders on what appears to be a cliff overlooking the lake spread out expansively before us. Water glistening under the appearance of the moon above.

I was right earlier. She is definitely better at planning a date than I am.

This is incredible.

"Is there a story about this particular spot?" I ask when after looking down and over the cliff below, I take a few tentative steps backward and lower myself to one of the flat boulders behind us.

"Not specifically no." Taking a seat beside me, never once attempting to slip her hand from mine, she continues. "This was just my spot."

"I'm not sure I follow."

That's not entirely true, but just like at Johnny's, it's happening again. I'm invested in hearing her speak. Hung on every word she utters, almost desperate to find ways to keep her talking so this feeling never has to fade.

What had been unfamiliar that night, all I want from this moment now.

I understand what she means about having a spot. I had one myself back home before jumping into wrestling. I spent a lot of time like her. Displaced. Drowning in responsibilities I was in no way prepared for, the older I became, and needing a place where none of it could touch me.

Sure, wrestling eventually became my outlet, and I grew into the person I am now the more I put myself out there, but there's no denying it all started with my own little spot away from the rest of the world, same as Dawson.

Maybe that's why I can't seem to walk away from her. Why my body gravitates to hers. Because we're more alike than either of us realize.

"Something tells me you do, Gavin."

Part of me wondered if she'd call me out on the lie. She seems to realize, the same as I do, how similar we are.

"You're right. I do get it. I have a place, though, not like this one, back home. My little hideaway. Not even my brother knows about it, and he spent years following me everywhere."

Woah, Gav. Slow down.

"What were you like growing up?" she asks, her eyes lighting up with curiosity.

"I'm gonna go out on a limb and say, probably a lot like you."

"How do you mean?"

"I've watched you backstage a few times when no one else was around. You're a lot like me in that when the camera turns on, you morph into this energetic, bouncy, upbeat personality. And when the camera shuts down and eyes are pulled away, you go quiet, lose the bouncy, and become more reserved. You also spend a lot of those moments alone."

"Wow." She mutters softly, and there's something about the way she says it that causes me to start up again. Make her understand what I'm really trying to say.

"It's not a bad thing, Dawson. In fact, it's one of the reasons I can't seem to stay away from you. When I'm not putting on a show for everyone else, I'm the same way. I would rather be alone. It's probably why you're the first real date I've had in fourteen years. Why it's always been fucking and leaving for me. I couldn't handle people sticking around."

"But with me?"

"It's entirely different," I admit easily. "This is going to sound fucking bad, but when I go to Johnny's, I go there to pick up a chick to get laid. Period. I'm not there for idle chit-chat or getting to know you. All I wanted the night we met was to drown my sorrows by burying myself in some random stranger."

I was right. As soon as I admit the truth of our first encounter, the real truth, her eyes lose their sparkle. The very light I'm mesmerized by. My way of being before I met her, it hurts her. And I'll be damned if it doesn't make me sick inside because the last thing I want to do is hurt this woman.

"Well, you got what you wanted."

"No, Daws, I didn't."

Head lifting, eyes finding their way to mine, she studies me. "What do you mean? I was there, Gavin. All night, I was there. We both got what we wanted."

"This isn't coming out right. Let me start again." When she nods, I don't waste time. "When you sat down and bought my drink, pounding back those shots of yours, everything changed. I was curious. I wanted to know what made you want to drink so heavily. Who hurt you so badly it brought you there of all places to unwind? I wasn't lying when I said you didn't fit in there. You opened your mouth and started spilling your guts, and I was hooked. Even believing you were inebriated and I wasn't going to get what I wanted with you because of it, I couldn't walk away. I didn't want to. So, whatever my reasons were for going there before, you changed it. You changed me."

"Wow."

This time, her inflection is different. She's no longer hurt by what I'm admitting. It's more like surprised.

"I brought you here because you spend so much time living as the character you created, it's hard to tell where he ends and you begin. I've seen sides of you, just in the last couple of weeks that speak to there being more to you than what is said by others. What I've heard in the locker room or from the women you've been with before I arrived. If there was a place I felt I could see the real you, even for a moment, it would be here. Because this is where I come when I need to remember the real me."

Given everything I've admitted since we got here, how close I feel to her on a purely emotional level, apart from the attraction we both know is there between us, I'm pretty sure she got what she was after.

I've never been this honest with anyone. Kimber included.

Dawson is making me venture into new territory.

"It's a fight, Daws. A daily struggle."

"What is?"

"Being who they want and expect me to be, and who I want to be. Who I am."

Squeezing my hand, words no longer needed to display her understanding, she brings herself closer and leans her head on my shoulder. Welcoming her warmth for a few seconds, basking in it, I slip my arm around her back and pull her fully into my side.

Wanting her as close as possible for whatever comes next.

"Why can't you be both? Why the struggle?"

This is both the easiest and hardest question I've ever had to answer, but with her, I let the words fall because I know deep down, she'll get it.

"Just Gavin doesn't sell tickets."

What I don't expect is her quick reply.

"Just Dawson doesn't get ratings."

If I didn't already know we were alike, this would seal it.

We're opposite sides of the same coin.

Her admission brings up a slew of questions I have, but the peacefulness of this moment, the water rolling into the rocks below, and the sound of crickets brushing in the background, stops me from asking them.

Why she really ended up in HFWA can be a story for another day.

What can't wait is my need to tell this girl another truth.

"This is the best date I've ever had."

It's quick, barely there really, but there's no missing the soft snort she lets escape.

"What? You don't believe me?"

"You've been traveling for years, Gavin. Something tells me in all that time, there had to be one date, one experience with a woman, better than this."

Oh, Dawson. You have no idea the power you wield.

"And you'd be wrong. I've seen a lot of different places in my travels, but I've never met a woman, much less had a moment like the one I'm having with you tonight."

"Oh, Gavin…" she sighs and it's in the sound of utter contentment, I find the strength I always seem to lack when in this woman's presence and do what it takes to make her mine.

"Does this mean you like me now?"

Laughing softly, she rests her hand against my heart, a subtle reminder again of our night together at Johnny's, raising her head just enough again to be able to meet my gaze.

"You know, I think it does."

"Then, say it."

"Excuse me?"

"This would go down so much better if I had a microphone, but since I'm fresh out of those, just pretend I'm the one interviewing you and say it."

"You're ridiculous."

"I know," I admit grinning. "So, if you want me to stop, just admit you like me."

Burying her face in my chest in an attempt to hide her laughter, I don't let her have it, pulling back and putting distance between us, coming face to face with her flushed cheeks as I do.

"What's in it for me if I admit it? I mean, I enjoy you being ridiculous."

Enjoying the moment but done with the teasing, I give the only answer I can.

"You get it all, Daws. Whatever your heart desires. It's yours."

Eyes softening as they glisten under the light of the moon, head dipping to the side, she smiles before leaning in and brushing her lips against mine. Her answer quickly following.

"What if my heart desires you, Gavin?"

"Then what your heart wants, your heart gets."

Meeting her gentle kiss with a more passionate and needy one, especially with the knowledge that what she wants is me, here on this rock, I do it.

I go all in.

Chapter Fifteen

Gavin

"As much," I say, returning her kiss with one of my own. "as I would love to continue this…" I pull away with a pained grimace upon seeing her lips pull downward in a playful pout. "we can't."

I want nothing more than to lean the seats back and have my way with Dawson, but with the rules we're currently breaking even being in the same car together, and how dangerously close to the building we're parked, there's no way we can.

Not to mention the title match against Matthias I'm supposed to be inside readying for.

The first of what will be three matches with me eventually coming away with two wins and the very thing Matthias has coveted almost as much as I have since we started in this business.

The Heavyweight Title.

"Five more minutes."

Capturing her lips when she moves in, a wicked grin lighting up her face, I give in to her demands and spend the next five minutes losing myself in her. The feel of her hair brushing against my shoulders, her breath, hot when we separate long enough to take in air, and the deep guttural sound of her moan as it falls when we come back together again.

I could spend forever with Dawson this way.

"Daws," I finally croak when I declare victory over the inner war taking place inside me. "I've gotta get ready for my match and *you* need to be backstage."

Catching her scowl when she shifts back in the passenger seat, releasing a heavy sigh, I reach across and slip my hand over hers.

"This isn't done, baby."

It still shocks me, every time the term of endearment falls. Taking me a few seconds after to realize it was indeed me saying the words, and not some other poor schmuck.

For whatever reason, I'm the schmuck this woman wants.

"Matthias goes over tonight, right?" she asks, thankfully changing the subject and giving me a chance to release the tight noose my briefs have become since I got in the car and she pressed her lips to mine.

"Yeah."

"Any special stipulations?"

"No, not for the first match. We're gonna meet up later this week and come up with a plan for the final two matches. I figure we're going to want to do something bigger for those."

"That's probably why Kimber asked me to hang out."

"Might be a part of it, yeah." I agree easily. Kimber has been talking to me a lot lately about Dawson, and what I plan to do about us. Her and Matthias, of course, being the only two people on the planet who know about the rules we're breaking under her cousins' nose.

Dawson must have done the same as she'd done with me the first night we met, with Kimber, because even though she might want to get together because Matthias will otherwise be engaged, she also wants the two of them to get closer.

Kimber sees what I do when she looks at Dawson.

She sees perfection.

Okay, well maybe not what I see. But she sees a friend, which is basically the same thing.

"What other reason could there be?"

"Besides how amazing you are?" I admit which earns me a light slap to my arm. "She likes you, Daws. She wants to hang out because she wants to be friends."

"Hmm..."

Giving her a minute to ponder but turning my attention to movement outside the car and seeing a few of the guys heading in, I'm thrown right back into the reality of the situation we find ourselves in.

"You should head in. I'll hang out here for a few."

Thankful again for the tint I added to the windows of my car, I press my lips to hers one more time as she leans over, swallowing the ache of her leaving, when she does as I suggest and exits.

Not letting my eyes stray until she makes her way across the parking lot and inside the building, I let the countdown begin.

All the while wishing for the day to come where we don't have to hide this anymore and when we enter the building, we're doing it together.

Time to put on a show.

With Dawson having made her way to the ring and announced both Matthias and myself, and Wade Roberts, our ref for the night stepping up between us, the bell rings and everything else gets tuned out.

Matthias taking the lead, advances toward me, hand halfway held in the air, ready to lock up. My hand meeting it, our dance begins as he pushes into me, walking me back into the corner. My back mildly tapping the turnbuckle until Matthias uses his body to put more pressure on me, causing the ref to break us apart.

Smacking his face and laughing, taunting me to come and get him, he steps backward, and that's when I take my moment. Advancing on him, and finally out of the corner the both of us finally lock up, before Matthias spins his way out.

Twisting around, he maneuvers me into an armbar, quickly turning it around and into a headlock, but before he can get it fully locked in, I slip out, taking hold of him and swinging him toward the ropes. Seemingly unprepared as a few seconds later, he bounces off the rope as I move forward and damn near takes my head off with a clothesline.

Wasting time, he picks up momentum as I'm laid out flat in the center of the ring, running from one end of the ring to the other, but caught as he tries to go through the motion a second time as I jump to my feet and catch him as he takes a swing at me. Ducking under and causing him to stumble as I slide through the rope, my move causing yet another break, and the ref to step between the both of us in an effort to separate.

Sliding back through the ropes, we lock up again, this time, with me as the aggressor and landing, not one, but two knees to his chest. Quickly following it up with a punch to the face, knocking him into the far corner turnbuckle. Grabbing him by the arm, I swing him from one side of the ring to the other, the way he'd taunted me with earlier, and before I know it, I'm greeted again by another clothesline, which knocks me harder to the mat than expected.

Kemper proving why he's one of the best.

As my head bounces off the mat with a resounding thud, I see stars in my eyes before I close them and just take in the rush around me. The sound of the crowd as their interest begins to peak, along with the sound of my opponent's boots as he stalks around the ring.

Matthias, capitalizing on the move, grabs me and lifts me again to my feet, knocking me back into the center of the rope and flipping me over to the unforgiving floor below.

Looking from one side of the building, and the fans in attendance, to the other, he continues his ownership of the match by taking a run back at the ropes, running forward and springing forward off of them, making a beeline straight for me.

Having gotten unsteadily to my feet, I shift out of the way at the perfect moment as Matthias comes diving through the ropes straight to the floor, collapsing, as I fall to my knees, still experiencing the stun of the earlier clothesline.

As both of us get our bearings, I slip in under the bottom rope from one side of the ring, getting to my feet at the moment Matthias slides his way back in, both of us on each other again, this time with Matthias swinging me over the ropes, determined to get off his move from before, knocking me to the ground. Only this time, not wasting a second as he follows after me, diving through the middle rope and taking me off my feet again as our bodies collide.

Landing on his knees, he quickly rises and leans back against the barricade, smiling maniacally as his shoulders and chest are quickly covered by the fans closest to him, all of them clearly enjoying what has so far been his annihilation of the one everyone loves to hate.

Pulling away from the crowd continuing to build around him, he goes on the attack again, stalking toward me. Grabbing me by the hair and hoisting me up before dragging me toward the apron, tossing me under the bottom rope back to the inside. Making quick work of the steps and climbing from them to the top rope, readying himself with a quick glance to me and my position in order to dive off.

A move that as planned, I catch and prevent. Getting to my feet and diving across the ring, hoisting Matthias up on my shoulders and power slamming him down hard in the very center of the ring. Taking the opportunity given to me, and climbing to the top rope myself, I land a cross body as Matthias stands, but the tables turn as he rolls on top, hooking my leg for a count of 1, then kicking out right at the beat of the ref's hand hitting the mat for 2.

Getting to his feet and moving around, Matthias walks straight into a superkick to the face, knocking him to the canvas hard, at which time I take my opportunity to pin him, the ref slapping the mat for a count of 2 before he kicks out and rolls over to his side.

Raising a hand to my face, cracking my jaw in frustration, my eyes lock on Kemper's, and I slam my hands down hard on the mat, my face quickly morphing into the anger I feel at not being able to put him away. My now loose and unkempt hair falling into my face only serving to frustrate me more as I shove a hand through it and push it away, readying myself for my next attack.

Stalking Matthias, coming at him from behind, I grab him and pull him over to the left turnbuckle, smashing him off of it, and as he turns, I level him first with a kick that knocks him on his ass in the corner, then follow it up with repeated and swift kicks to his chest. Stomping a hole straight through him, he reacts by flinching in proposed agony while hunching over, his body going limp against the rope as the ref finally steps in between the middle, breaking the kicks, the count at ten, and pushing me back using all of his strength.

Matthias doing his best with the reprieve he's being given to both sell the kicks to the crowd, appearing weary and tired, and gather his breath as he shifts in his position in the corner.

Again capitalizing, I make quick work of grabbing him again by the back of his neck, bringing him to his feet. Moving across the ring, I throw him through the middle ropes on the right side, his body collapsing to the mats below. His hands immediately reaching to the back of his head as he lands.

Turning my attention to the ref as he jumps down to the outside, I curse at him before putting my focus back on my opponent, who has somehow gotten to his feet. Pulling energy from the rush I get being in this atmosphere, I springboard him into the barricade, his hands immediately finding his back as he falls to the ground again, pain etched over every part of his face as I go at him, relentless in my pursuit.

Realizing I need to get him into the ring to pick up the win, I cross to where Matthias is laid out and pick him up, sliding him back into the ring and easily following, leading into another pin attempt, one this time going to two and a half before he kicks out. The force of the kick out propelling him into a sitting position, as his hands find his face.

Adding insult to injury, I smack him twice in the back of the head, making him stumble in his positioning before I move around and grab a fistful of his hair, landing another punch to the face before bouncing back against the ropes and flying forward, hitting with another hard fist.

Taunting him, I bounce off the middle of the ropes landing another punch as he continues to struggle to an upright position. Each subsequent punch not taking him out completely, but making him stumble in his attempt to get up and keep fighting.

"You're not better than me, Kemper!" I yell across the ring. "Just give up!"

Not falling in line with what I've told him to do, I move backward again to the ropes, ready and willing to deliver yet another blow to his face, but having finally gotten his bearings, he's ready for me, as he ducks under as I come ready to strike, and lands a hard fist of his own, following it up with a series of hard slaps to the chest. Using the ropes to his advantage much as I had before, and taking their momentum to bounce off and shove me to the canvas.

Getting quickly to my feet, I'm again taken back with another shove to the face by Matthias, and knocked to the ground, our little dance repeating two more times before I finally find my way to the right corner, and Matthias, using the far bottom rope for leverage, runs at me. Hitting me dead on with a body splash before pulling me out of the corner and into a running bulldog.

Falling to the ground, and with a quick run of the ropes, Matthias delivers a hard elbow before making his way to the corner, slowly climbing to the top rope, diving off and leveling me hard with a flying elbow.

Picking me off the mat, whispering his next move as he pulls my head under his arm, he plants me face first hard into the mat with his patented headlock driver. Falling back against me, clearly worn, he lazily hooks his hand through my leg as the ref hits the three count.

Making the match we'd put together on the fly, come off just the way we wanted it to, and giving Matthias the leg up in our best two out of three falls.

Matthias is your winner.

Only, with the smirk I caught when he pulled himself off me, it's more than just a win for him.

When we leave here tonight, we're both winners.

Chapter Sixteen

Dawson

"Gavin," I call out, cordless microphone in hand, speeding up as he crashes his way through the backstage curtain.

The act of loss, the show he'd put on after being pinned, and eventually, after Matthias had made his way out of the ring and back behind the curtain, the struggle to get back to his feet to do much the same, still seeping from every pore.

All for my benefit. This spot set up hours before.

"Gavin," I repeat when I finally catch up, my hand resting on a shoulder slick with sweat. "Can I get a word?"

Spinning around to face me, familiar smirk in place just like we planned, his eyes harden as he takes me in, devouring me with his eyes and winking for added effect.

"Sure, I've got a few words for you, princess."

Lowering my head in faux embarrassment—another plan—I force my mind to go back to the night at Johnny's, what we'd done with and to each other, and as predicted, the heat rises to my cheeks so when I look up again, I'm full on blushing.

I can't believe how easy this is coming together.

"What are your thoughts on the loss to Matthias tonight?"

Stepping into me, so close the hairs on my arms rise to attention with his presence, he grins. "Now, now, Dawson, you know that's not the real question you want to ask."

Narrowing my eyes, pretending to be more annoyed than taken aback, I continue playing along. "And what pre-tell do you think the real question is?"

"It's the one all of you at one time or another ask. You know the one because, despite your every attempt at being disgusted, you're thinking it right now. What would it take to get me alone?"

"Oh, I'm sure you're quite familiar with that question, Gavin, but let me be the bearer of bad news. With the loss you suffered at the hands of Matthias tonight, I don't think you'll be hearing it again for a very long time. If ever."

Turning away, he waits for a total of three beats before grabbing me and spinning me around to face him. Gifting me famously with his self-entitled sneer.

"Oh, really? Well, maybe when you hear what I've got planned for our second match, you won't be so quick to make assumptions. You do know what they say about people who do that."

"Let's pretend I don't. How does the pretty boy, Gavin Fortune, plan to turn this best of three matches around?"

As close to my face as he can get, his breath running like lava from a volcano across my skin, he lifts the microphone between us, his chest brushing against mine as he delivers what is his final blow.

"A Ladder Match, of course." Releasing his hold on the mic, he smirks in my direction before stalking away. This time, the weight of the match faded away, and all of the self-confidence of a man on a mission for the title in its place.

His next words, his parting shot, both scaring and exciting me at the same time.

"I'll be seeing you, Dawson. Real soon."

Gavin

"Man, I wasn't going to say anything, but what you and the new girl just did out there was straight fire. Shit, I could feel the heat from here."

I'm damn pleased the spot went over as well as we hoped it would, but the aftermath of being so close to Dawson and not being able to wrap her legs around me, kiss her senseless or otherwise have my way with her very willing body, is enough to put a damper on the whole thing.

One of the dangers of working with the person you're involved with is keeping your head straight. Not letting the very real way you feel, invade the moment you're in. Not giving yourself away to anyone backstage watching.

And trust me, I'm aware I'm being watched.

Ever since our date and us becoming an item, I swear there's even more of a bullseye on my back. I can feel Reese's eyes even from behind the closed door of his office. Bryan's too, though, of the two of them, he's the more understanding. They don't have a clue what's really going on, but with the sheer amount of looks I'm getting, it's as though they do.

They know it all.

"Not so quick to give the girl shit now, are ya, Mark?"

Holding his hands up in the air in mock surrender, I laugh before making my way across the room, snagging the towel and soap on my way and heading into the showers. His response called out easily before I've turned the water on.

"You win, Fortune! I was wrong."

Damn right you were. I think but don't say. Content just knowing my girl showed these guys what she's really made of, making them eat their words.

Washing away the events of the night, but still riding high off the buzz from not only the match but the aftermath, I'm unprepared for the solemn face of Kemper when I step back out. The room now empty but for the two of us.

"Where'd everyone go?"

"I asked for the room," Matthias explains with a glance toward the door.

Nothing about this feels right. The high from before, quickly about to drop if he doesn't fill me in.

Did something happen to Kimber? Dawson?

"What's wrong?"

"Nothings wrong, Fortune. Relax. I just wanted to continue our conversation from dinner awhile back. See if you'd come to any conclusions about what we discussed. Figured you'd be more apt to do it if I cleared the room."

Reaching out, I slug him hard in the shoulder, while at the same time breathing a sigh of relief. The guy's a bastard for letting it play out the way he did, but I'm also thankful for it.

Talking openly about Dawson is a definite no go.

"Kimber hits harder." Matthias laughs and I just roll my eyes. "So, what you two just did…" I had a feeling it was going to come sooner rather than later. Especially with the way I brought her to his house. "You figure out the play yet?"

"Told you before, there is no play."

"Humor me here, man. I don't keep shit from Bryan, so if I'm going to start, I need to know the truth."

"We're seeing each other, okay? There's not much else to say right now. We're keeping it secret, making sure Reese doesn't catch wind. For what it's worth, though, I like her."

"Word of advice?" Eager to roll my eyes again, knowing this is the moment he flips back into his Saint Kemper role, I nod instead of answering. "Get better at hiding it. What I caught on playback was a hell of a lot more than the two of you acting."

Well, shit. If Matthias caught it, it won't be long until Bryan does too. Or worse, Reese.

"That it?"

"For now. But what I told you before still stands. Don't hurt her and we're not gonna have any problems."

"No worries. Don't plan on it. You might want to think about letting Reese in on that little tidbit, though. He's taking the family ties thing a little too far."

Merely nodding, proving again he's a man of few words, he turns to the door.

"For what it's worth, Fortune, I think she's good for you."

As he heads out, the words—my response to him—which has been on the tip of my tongue all night, finally comes out.

"She's the best."

Pulling the car into her drive and turning off the ignition, I lean over the steering wheel and watch the scene unfolding through the windshield.

Her curtains being pulled back, I'm given a clear view of my girl, moving around the living room without any knowledge of the creepy stalking tendencies I'm displaying a few feet away.

Her attention is pulled from the organizing of the table she appears to be doing, to the phone call she takes when she puts the cell phone to her ear.

Curiosity killing me, wondering who's on the other end of the call. The person making her smile so bright and also making her laugh as her head rolls back, and her entire body seems to shake.

The scene unfolding, one I could easily find myself getting used to.

From coming home to her to just watching her go about her day. Every expression, every feeling. Being privy to them all, while the force of all of them together makes me fall even harder.

What my parents have, this is it. I'm sure of it.

A realization so profound it makes the real reason I asked to see her tonight, even more important.

Since Dawson arrived in HFWA and I've had a lot of my past slammed to the forefront of everyone's minds again, I've had a lot of time to think. Go over my actions from CPW, the horrendous choices I made which resulted in a lot of pain that honestly should have, and could have, been avoided.

The biggest lapse in judgment, what I put Jackson Merrick through.

What even to this day I have never apologized for. Well, apologized and meant, anyway. I did what I had to do to create peace in the locker room.

Basically, the bare fucking minimum.

Being with Dawson, experiencing what it feels like to be so into someone you can barely think straight when you're around them, I'm starting to see just how much damage I did all those years ago with Merrick. What I took from him.

I'm guiltier than Melinda in this case because, every step of the way I knew what I was getting into. I knew what they were to each other. I exploited a weakness in Merrick's armor and took his girl from him, even enjoyed doing it, because of what it got me.

The championship, the perks, and the attention. I wanted it all and wanted to leave Merrick with nothing. I took a business driven by fiction, an angle we were set to perform, making it anything but.

I played games with his life.

If wanting to be real with Dawson is going to happen, if she's going to get the best of me, and not the guy I was in CPW or the guy I became in HFWA, it begins with him.

Merrick.

I've got to go back and make things right.

We may not work together anymore, but it's not even about the job. It's about growing up. Owning my craptastic behavior and proving my apology is real. To him, and everyone else.

Proving to Dawson I'm the man she believes I am.

The difference between then and now is, I don't want to go to Merrick alone.

I want her with me.

Pulling back and turning to the window when I hear the sound of knuckles on glass, I'm met by the grin of the exact person I'm here to see.

Stepping back when I motion from her to the door, her lips only raise higher when I step out. Catching her right when she jumps into my arms, smashing her lips to mine.

"I missed you." She admits, her cheeks flushing when I place her back down.

"I missed you too, princess. Sorry, it took so long for me to get here. Got caught up with Kemper before I could leave."

Eyebrow-raising fast, her eyes do a deep scan over my face before she relaxes.

"I told you before, it's all good with us, Daws. I don't expect us to be best friends, but we're tolerating each other, which is good enough."

"What did he want to talk about?"

"Besides the amazing set up we did for the next match tonight?"

Addicted to the glow of her face when she smiles, I make no effort to stop the way my lips raise to match it. Her beauty even weeks later taking me off center.

"We were pretty awesome, weren't we?"

"It was all you, princess."

Slipping my arm around her back, I bring her close and start making my way toward the house. Following her into the kitchen when she slips out of my arms and heads that way, I take a seat at the table and graciously accept the beer she passes over before grabbing one of her own and sitting beside me.

"So, was tonight all you two talked about?"

"You know it's not, Daws. He asked me about us, and I explained things."

"I know how close Matthias is with Bryan, are you sure that was the right move?"

"He called me on my shit when I took you there for dinner. He's known for weeks now. If he was going to say something, he would have already done it. We can trust him."

And surprisingly enough, admitting it to her, there's not a hint of doubt.

Maybe there's hope for me and Kemper yet.

"There's something else I wanted to talk to you about, though. Something I wanted your help with if you think you can get away."

Taking a swig from the bottle, she swallows, placing it down on the table and turning my way. "What do you need?"

"Since my next booked match is with Cameron, and it's not until next week, I'm not really needed here. I was going to use the time and head out of town. Catch up with an old buddy from CPW." I'm using the term buddy as loose as possible. There's nothing friendly at all about my relationship with Merrick, but I'm hoping when this is all said and done, there can be.

"What buddy?"

Shit. Figures she'd be curious.

"Jackson Merrick."

Awareness flashes through those bright blue eyes, and I know I've been had. She knows all about my history with

Merrick. What she doesn't get, but will soon enough, is how eager I am to change it.

"Gavin, what are you thinking?"

"Truthfully?" I ask, taking a long pull from the bottle before doing as she did and placing it down. "I'm thinking I made a huge mistake, and if I want to do right by you, do right by myself, I've got to make amends. Most everyone else I hurt works with me in HFWA these days, but Merrick? He's out."

"You're serious? You want to go to California and see Jackson?"

"Yes, but this is where you come in. I don't want to do it alone. It's already been proven I'm better when I'm with you, so if you can pull it off, I'm hoping you'll join me."

Tapping her fingers on the table, looking from me to her beer and taking another swallow, she makes me suffer through another few minutes of utter silence before finally giving me an answer.

"Let me talk to Reese. If he doesn't need me this weekend, I'm all yours."

Turning in my seat and pulling her chair closer, I reach across and pull her into my arms. Words never going to able to express how I feel here in this moment, knowing she not only trusts and believes me, but has my back.

What she's doing is absolutely impossible to fight.

She's making me fall in love.

Chapter Seventeen

Dawson,

Having been in the air for well over an hour, Gavin having pressed his lips to my forehead before making himself comfortable and falling asleep, I'm left to my own devices. Only our interwoven fingers, still so tightly bound, and the quietness of the moment, my only company

Allowing me more than enough time to think about my last encounter with my cousin.

Where I'd almost had to give away everything.

"You want to do what?" He asks again, the second time in as many minutes.

"Come on, Reese. You heard me the first two times."

"Yeah, maybe, but I can't have heard you right. Why the hell would you want to take time off and go see Jackson Merrick? He's been out since CPW folded."

"Right, but you know how I operate. I want more information on the guys who came from there. Get to know more about them, so when I'm working with them, it comes across natural. Authentic. Brady said if I wanted the real scoop on what went down in CPW before Smith sold it, to talk to Jackson."

Whispering something under his breath, making sure I'm aware he's doing it but not speaking loud enough for me to catch, I reach across his desk and smack him in the chest. Hard.

"Stop talking like I'm not here. Then, tell me what you just said."

Rubbing the spot where I left my mark, he scowls but ultimately concedes.

"What the hell is it about Merrick this week? Am I going to have to take a trip down there myself and hire the guy back to keep the rest of the roster away from him?"

Hmm, now this I can work with.

I'm already aware Gavin is heading that way, but with him having the time off, I'm positive it wasn't him in here talking to my cousin about Jackson. So, who else was?

"Who else wanted to go to see Jackson?"

"Brady for one, then Cameron. Since I know Merrick and Cam don't exactly have the best track record, it made me curious as to why he'd want to talk to the guy. Kemper brought him up yesterday in passing, and well, now there's you."

Wow. Jackson Merrick is making the rounds.

"Well, I just told you why I want to go meet with him."

"And you could easily do it over the phone, Dawson. You've done so with other guys before. Why is it so important for you to meet with the guy now?"

I had a feeling it wasn't going to be easy getting Reese to agree to let me out of his sight, but geez. It wasn't supposed to be this hard.

"There's no hidden agenda here, Dad. I just want to follow up with something Brady told me to do."

Calling him dad hits him right where it hurts because the adversarial cousin I've been meeting with for the last several minutes fades away as his face softens, and he leans back in the chair with an exasperated sigh.

"I'm sorry, Daws. I keep doing it and you deserve better. I guess I'm just on edge."

Color me even more curious.

"On edge about what?"

Shaking off whatever concerns he obviously has, he shakes his hands at the same time as his head follows in kind. "Nothing you need to worry about. Forget I brought it up."

"Brought what up? All you said was you were on edge. And if you're going through something, as your family it's my job to worry."

Massaging his hand into his forehead, the struggle clear, I try again to get him to talk. Whatever it is, it's got to do with me if he's trying to talk me out of worrying.

"Reese, come on. You can tell me anything."

Slamming his hand down onto the desk, he curses.

"Gavin is going to be in California. He told me yesterday. With the way you two are carrying on backstage lately, it's made me think I need to call another meeting."

Another meeting? What does he mean? When was there a first meeting?

"Reese, what are you talking about?"

Cursing again under this breath, he finally stops pussyfooting around and gives me the answers I'm after.

"The day you signed the contract, you remember what I told you, right?"

"Yeah. So?"

"Well, I had the same meeting with the entire roster. Not everyone was there at the time, but I made sure they knew the score, same as you. Bryan wasn't aware of it; I didn't tell him. I just let him think the day we introduced you was the first time you'd been mentioned."

Oh my God. I knew fraternizing with the guys was a sore spot for Reese, but I didn't think he would take it this far. Warning the locker room off before I even got here? What the hell has gotten into my cousin?

"Reese, what the hell does this have to do with Gavin?"

"He wasn't there the day I warned everyone. I figured he was off looking for his next conquest, especially after everything that went down with Kimber. Seeing you two working together, Bryan showing me how easily you play off one another for the camera, it's got me on edge."

He's not the only one on edge. If I wasn't trying so hard to hide how close he is to the truth, my cousin would be seeing a whole other side of me right now. I've never been more disappointed.

"What you did was wrong, Reese."

Flicking his head up, stone cold eyes so similar to my own staring hard at me, he doesn't even hesitate. "Don't you think I know that?"

"You specifically hired me for this position because of my experience. My ability to work with others professionally. I've delivered since I showed up. I haven't crossed any lines."

Well, none you know about anyway.

"I know, Daws. I trust you."

"But you don't trust your own guy?"

Sighing, he shakes his head. "You don't know Fortune."

Yes, I do!! *I want to shout. It would be so easy to just admit the truth, no matter where it lands me. But I'm not the only person who this would fall on, and it's that knowledge keeping me silent.*

"I have a feeling no matter what I say, it's not going to make a bit of difference. So just tell me if I can go to California or not so I can get out of here."

"Dawson—"

"No, Reese. I think you've said enough."

"You can go."

"Good." Turning my back on him and everything I've learned about the man since I stepped into the room, I've almost made it through to the safety of the hallway when he calls out, his final words souring me more.

"Have a safe trip."

"Earth to Dawson. Are you in there?"

Popping my eyes open and turning to my right where I find Gavin's hand on my arm, shaking me, I begin to relax.

I'm here, safely on the plane with him, on our way to see Jackson. Not stuck in the office with Reese, learning just how many lines he crossed before even bringing me in.

"I'm sorry. I must have dozed off."

Barely cracking a smile at my excuse, confirming my weak lying abilities, he squeezes the hand still locked in his.

"Try again, princess. Where were you just now?"

His touch soothing, allowing me for a moment to forget the clusterfuck of a situation I left waiting for me when I get back, I bring him up to speed.

"I learned some things when I went to ask Reese for the weekend off. Some not so great things. It's making me look at him in a completely different light. I'm not sure what I'm going to do about it, or even what I should feel."

"Wait," he pauses as realization sets in. "You told me he okayed you going out of town. You never said anything else happened."

"Honestly," I admit with a defeated sigh. "I wasn't sure how to tell you."

"Well, you might as well fill me in now. It's not like I can make the pilot turn the plane around so I can go back and kick his teeth in. What did he say to you?"

What Gavin just alluded to in the light-hearted way he did, is exactly why I didn't tell him about this the night it happened. I didn't want him to feel the need to defend me or go off half-cocked in some bullshit attempt at protecting me. If he had, it wouldn't have ended well for either of us.

The last thing I need being another Reese.

But since I've already told him there was more, there's no sense shying away from it now.

"The day before Reese and Bryan brought me in, and you all met me, Reese held a secret meeting of his own. One, his own partner doesn't know about."

I can see him trying to place it, even the moment where he wants to argue it because he wasn't there, and has no knowledge of it.

"You weren't there. I guess you weren't important enough to be invited. Who knows? With the number of times he's warned me away from you specifically, maybe he assumed his warnings would be enough of a deterrent."

"He obviously didn't think that one through." Gavin offers, and I can't help smiling. He's right. I don't think given everything I know of the man beside me, anything could have kept me away.

"Gavin, he used the meeting to warn the rest of the roster to stay away from me. Not to develop any form of personal relationship. I'd already agreed to his damn rules, so there was no need for any of it, but I guess he figured there was."

"Is this where you tell me wrestlers aren't really your type?"

Laughing at how accurate he is, especially with what I told both Reese and Kimber when I first arrived, he lifts his arm, and the minute I see the opening, I fall into it. Into him. Soothed again by the vibration from his own laughter.

"In my defense, I said it before I knew the exception was pretty boys named Gavin."

Pressing his lips to the top of my head, he whispers. "I'll forgive it this time, princess. Just make sure it doesn't happen again."

"Oh, please. Like you'd ever let it."

Closing my eyes and listening to the low rumble of his laughter mixing with the steady even beat of his heart, the last thing I hear before the rest of the world fades away is the voice of the man I'm quickly falling for, softly telling me to rest.

And with the comfort of his arms around me, I give up the fight.

I fall asleep.

Gavin

I've been on edge since before we even boarded the flight, but having landed and picked up the rental car, the time for closing my eyes and pushing it down is over.

We're here, and in about two minutes when I finally work up the courage to get out of this godforsaken vehicle, this is really going to happen.

The one saving grace in all of this being the woman beside me.

Well, her and the fact that even with the evolution of the internet in the last ten years, no one seems to have picked up on my being here. If they knew, I've got no doubt the dirt sheets and internet rumor sites would have a field day.

Not to mention how easily my relationship with Dawson would be exposed.

Looks like all those backdoors I used in an effort to keep this visit off the radar paid off.

Now if only I could will my legs to work the same way, I'd be set.

"Tell me what you're thinking."

Besides wondering if it's too late to pull out of the driveway and head to our hotel, there's not much else to tell her. I'm sure she's aware given what I've told her about my history, exactly where my head is at right now.

How monumental and unheard of this is.

For some guys, it takes a Hall of Fame induction and twenty years to pass before things are made right.

Right now, I'm an anomaly.

"For what it's worth, what you're doing is the right thing, Gavin. Even if Jackson doesn't see it the same way."

She's right. I know it deep down, but it doesn't stop the nerves from rearing their ugly head despite it.

"Would it be easier if I went to the door?"

"No," I tell her, even though the truth is, some of the pressure would be relieved if she did. "I need to be the one to do this. Answering the door to you, accepting you, it's a no brainer. You'll charm the shit out of them both. He'll forgive me but I'll always wonder if it was genuine."

"Fair enough, but you might want to think about getting a move on since the door just opened."

Pointing out through the windshield, my eyes follow her hand and sure enough, both Merrick and his wife are standing on the front steps. Both of them squinting to get a look at what intruder awaits them on the other side.

"Well, I guess it's showtime."

With a final squeeze to Dawson's hand, we both go our separate ways and exit the car. My nerves keeping me planted until she makes her way around to where I am and slips her hand again through mine. The connection to her the one thing keeping me going when the fear begs me to turn and run back where I came from.

"Gavin Fortune?!" Avery, Jackson's wife calls out in surprise. "Of all the people I expected to get out of the car, you weren't one of them."

Finally making our way to where they're standing, I clear my throat and look directly to her husband, while Dawson moves easily, gravitating toward his wife.

"What do you want?" he asks, studying me, his eyes wary.

"A few minutes of your time for something long overdue."

I can hear myself saying the words but as they fall, I'm amazed at how calm I am. Sure, I could easily just throw myself into the persona again, but just like having Dawson fight my battles for me wouldn't make things better, this won't either.

Motioning over to where Avery is standing with Dawson, Jackson asks the inevitable question. "Who's the girl?"

"Dawson Traymore, she's a co-worker."

No. No way I'm putting her in a box this way.

She's way more than just someone I work with. But before I can retract the statement and change it up and tell the truth, Jackson throws out a question of his own.

"Have you screwed her yet?"

A valid question given our history.

"None of your business, Merrick."

Opening the door and motioning me to step through it, he grins smugly as I follow him in. "Based on that answer, it's yes."

"Again, not what I'm here to talk about, but for the record, she's more than just someone I work with. She's my girlfriend."

I wasn't coming here with the sole purpose of surprising Merrick. My only intent is to finally make right the mess I made years ago. But, not gonna lie, the surprise he levels me with once I've said my peace feels pretty damn great.

"You're serious? You, the ultimate bachelor, have a girlfriend?"

"Yeah, man."

"Well, I'll be damned. Can't say I saw that ever happening. I mean, not unless it was another one you stole from someone else."

Direct hit, which judging by the smirk he's still sporting, was exactly what he was after.

"Speaking on that, it's kind of why I'm here."

Both of us turning at the sound of the front door opening, I take in Jackson's expression when he catches sight of his wife. The softening of his eyes and the relaxed nature of his posture. A reaction I'm starting to become intimately familiar with as mine seems to always do the same when Dawson is anywhere near. Which, a few seconds later, she proves as she steps through the door and beams a bright smile my way.

"Wow," Jackson mutters, clearing his throat before turning his attention to me. "You really *do* have a girlfriend."

"Huh?"

"The way you look at her. Even now, you're choosing not to look my way because she's moving and you're following." Laughing, he slaps me on the shoulder, effectively pulling my attention away from Dawson and motions to the kitchen. "Unbelievable."

Heading to the fridge when we've entered the spacious room, he holds up a beer and when I nod my acceptance, he hands it over before grabbing a water bottle and pulling out a chair at the table. Waiting as I do the same before speaking again.

"So, since I never thought I'd see you gracing my doorstep, and I'm not sure I should be trusting any bit of this now that you are, you mind filling me on what you're doing here?"

"Melinda."

Choking on the water he'd just taken a swig of, he coughs, pounding on his chest a few times before staring me down.

"Ancient history. Figured you'd have gotten the memo."

"Oh, I did. Congratulations on the twins, by the way. Would have told you that when it happened but, well, you know."

"We aren't exactly friends."

"Exactly."

"The last thing I want to talk about is Melinda, so why the hell are you here bringing it up?"

Okay, Fortune here's your shot. Don't mess it up, or worse, lie.

"I've been doing a lot of thinking lately about those days. CPW and everything that went down there, both between us and everything after. I know it'll be hard to believe, but I'm not exactly thrilled about how I handled it. Any of it."

"You mean going behind my back and stealing my girl?"

"No...yes. More than just that, though."

"What else was there?"

"The underhanded way I was with Smith, how I let my ego get the best of me. The list could go on, but those are the big ones."

After taking another drink, he repeats his earlier sentiment.

"It's ancient history, Fortune. Haven't exactly made a point of lingering on it these days, if you get what I mean." With a quick motion to the living room, and then to the stairway off to the side, where I'm sure his babies are, it's easy to get what he means. "I left all the drama behind when I retired."

If only it could be the same way for me.

"Well, I'm here because I want the same thing. I want what you've got, and dealing with the past, I've learned, is the only way I'm truly going to get it."

"Your girl doesn't like you much, does she?" he asks, smirking again.

"Depends which version of me you're getting at."

Scoffing in response, he slaps his chest again.

"There's only one version of you I've had the pleasure of seeing, Gavin, so if it's the one you're showing her, it's a miracle she's here with you at all."

A point I'm not going to argue with because I know it's true.

"You're right. But you saw, the same way everyone else did, what I wanted you to see. I've been doing this same shtick for years now. I became what I had to become in order to get to where I wanted to be."

"So, let me get this straight." He mulls over as he takes another swig from the water bottle. "You're sitting here telling me your entire life has been one long work."

"Yeah."

Vince McMahon, back when he put his daughter and now son-in-law in a story where they were to end up being married, penned the name for when an unscripted and very real event takes place in an event. It was a shoot. In his case, it was when his daughter ultimately fell in love and began dating the man she was scripted to be married to.

What Jackson is getting at, calling what I did a work, is the opposite. I worked the guys and girls in the locker room, the same way I work the crowd now.

Why it matters, is because what Dawson and I have, it's a shoot.

Making this entire thing one conflict I'm determined to beat.

"Jesus, man. I thought I took things seriously and threw myself into it hard. What you did is on a whole other level."

"You believe me?"

"Yeah. I mean, I wouldn't on word alone but just in the few minutes you've been here, you're not the same guy I knew when we were on the road. From the way you look at the girl in there, to how easily you admit things instead of bullshitting the way you would have in the past, it's clear you're being honest."

Alright, I've got one half of what I wanted when I showed up here. Now it's time to all in on the rest.

"Right, so trusting your own view of me, the reason I'm here now is that I don't want to keep doing it anymore. I'm tired of working everyone around me. I want something more. But I won't get it until I own up to what I put you through all those years ago. I'm sorry, Jackson. I am. I took what I wanted without so much as a thought of what doing it would cause, and even though in the end, we made some great matches out of it, it never should have gotten to that point, to begin with."

Parting his lips, mouth open and ready to reply, we're both taken off guard as footsteps interrupt the moment and both women make their way into the room. Avery easily finding her way over to Jackson and wrapping her arms around him, and Dawson finding her way into the chair beside mine, connecting to me again as her hand easily slips into mine.

Looking from the women, back to each other again, it's in that second, where both of us are at our most relaxed, Jackson gives me what I came for.

"We're good, man. Do what you gotta do."

And with his forgiveness—acceptance—a clear end game is formed.

Step one was getting the girl to like me, and seeing as she's beside me now, holding on as tightly as I am to what we have, it appears the step is complete. Jackson giving me the second step in his forgiveness means there's only one left to go.

Coming out of the shadows, away from the work, and showing the world the truth.

The real Gavin, and how he feels about Dawson.

Finding a way to go public.

Chapter Eighteen

Dawson

Watching the cameramen as they move around me, adjusting my eyes to the brightness now shining down from above, I slip easily into the mask I've been wearing every time the red-light flashes and quirk my lips up into a smile. Though, what the others around me don't know is, this smile, even with it being a part of my mask, is genuine.

The man now coming into view as I introduce him, all I've been thinking about for days.

"Ladies and gentleman, Gavin Fortune."

Stepping into view, his body so close I can feel the heat radiating from him, he shifts his feet ever so slowly until the heat is hitting its mark as he's brushing his body against mine.

Breathe, Dawson. I remind myself, ignoring the tingle of warmth as it begins to rise with his closeness. Instead, doing everything in my power to focus on the task at hand.

Getting through this interview segment without letting on how badly I want him to push me to the wall and have his way with me.

Whispering as his eyes fall to mine, he smirks, before giving my body a quick once over. What won't look like anything to the people watching, but a scathing look I feel deep in my bones.

"What's up, baby?"

Alarm bells go off in my head with the term of endearment he just used. Knowing full well given what we're here to film and speak about, he's going off script. Ad-libbing. Not unheard of from any of the performers since I've been here, but putting me in one hell of an uncomfortable position now.

Shaking off the rising heat but making sure not to have my body move in kind and ruin the take, I do my best to focus again on getting through the interview regarding his second match with Matthias.

A match he's going to have to win if he wants to have the title at the end of this best two out of three tournament.

"Next week, you're set to face Matthias Kemper in the second of your best 2 of 3 falls tournament for the HFWA Heavyweight Title. With the loss to Kemper three weeks ago still fresh in your mind, what's your game plan going into the match?"

"Dawson, Dawson, Dawson. You should know by now, there is no plan. I'll give Kemper his due. He got the better of me in the first match. I was off my game. But it's time for a change in HFWA. Out with the old and in with the new. So, the only plan I've got is making sure that at the end of these matches, I'm retiring Saint Kemper."

We've been doing these spots for weeks, and it never ceases to amaze me just how easily Gavin steps into his character. Having seen this man in different settings away from what we both do here, it's like witnessing night and day.

What I can't deny though, is how good at his job Gavin is.

"Cut."

Lights fading out as each one around us shuts down, and the guys behind the cameras turning their attention to each other and away from us, I lean a little closer into Gavin, stealing a second to inhale his scent, sweat mixed with adrenaline, and one hundred percent masculinity. My own temperature rising, and what Gavin seems to notice as his smile widens as he begins to bridge the remaining gap between our bodies.

Both of us so enamored in one another, we forget we're not alone.

A sharp clearing of a throat bringing us back to reality in a flash.

"You guys nailed it!" Bryan says, stepping out from the shadows and slapping Gavin across the shoulders. "I was a little concerned when I saw how you went off script, Fortune, but man, it was hot."

Yeah, Bryan. You have no idea how hot.

"Thanks," I turn and tell him. Taking the moment that's been given to give me a little separation from what our boss almost caught between us. "It's all this guy, though. He's phenomenal on the mic."

Nodding, Bryan looks from me to Gavin and back again, the smile he was displaying when he stepped forward now grown so high into his face, he's completely transformed.

"This isn't the first time I've caught Fortune's promos or the interviews between you two. It seems like you've got a really good thing going here. And honestly, with the way you light up when he steps toward you, Dawson, it's the most engaged I've seen you since you arrived."

Not sure what he's getting at but in no way wanting to deny the effect working with Gavin has had on me during my time here, I just smile weakly and thank him again.

"Seeing the two of you together really has my mind going a mile a minute. I think we can use this chemistry."

Use us? For what?

Other than a few brief appearances in the ring announcing the competitors before they make their way down to the ring, and the work I've been doing backstage, there's really no chemistry at all to be found.

We've both made sure of it.

"What are you getting at?" Gavin asks, warily.

"I'm going to clear it with Reese, but I think I just found a new wrench for your feud with Kemper."

It doesn't take a brain surgeon to understand what he's getting at, and it's only made even more apparent by the scowl now beginning to appear on Gavin's face.

This isn't going to be something good at all.

"I want you two to work together. Gavin, meet your new valet."

Gavin

"You want us to do what?"

It's not unheard of, what Bryan is asking Dawson and me to do. Hell, it's not even my first rodeo working with a valet since I started in the indies all those years ago.

What is new, is who it is I'm going to be working with.

Putting a backstage personality on commentary during a broadcast or pay per view, all for it. In fact, it's one of the best ways this business is evolving, but turning her into a valet?

Just what the hell has gotten into Bryan?

"This is the third time I've watched you cut promos with Dawson, Fortune. Every single time, there's this glint in your eye when you're talking to her. It's chemistry. I want to use it."

Clearly, this guys history with Smith has turned him into the old bastard.

I know the companies merged, but I didn't think I'd witness Bryan becoming the very thing he fought against when he formed HFWA.

"No way. Not doing it."

I can sense Dawson's flinch before I see it, and as much as it pains me reacting this way, especially with how far we've come since the night we met in Johnny's, she hasn't been in this business long enough to see this for what it really is.

What Bryan is doing.

He's basically demoting her.

"Fortune—" Bryan starts in, and I waste no time shutting him down. Pleading as I turn to Dawson and her eyes meet mine, for her to understand that what I'm about to do has nothing to do with us.

"No, Bryan. One of the reasons I wanted to come here before Smith even folded CPW, was because you and Reese were running a different program than him. A better product. Everyone I reached out to before making the move, told me how much better you treat the guys. This, what you're trying to do, it's the opposite. You're pulling a Smith move, and I want no part of it."

Looking from him quickly to her and back again, I wait for the moment where Bryan finally sees this for what it is. Cracks up, says it was all a joke and gives us the real plan.

"So, what you're saying is, you're breaching your contract?"

Well, so much for him seeing the light.

This is a bad idea.

I'm willing to play ball with just about anything. I mean, I am the guy who took things a step too far in my feud with Merrick and turned it into a very real thing when I had a fling with Melinda. It's pretty clear when it comes to this business, I'm a team player.

But I do have a line, and it's one Bryan's about to cross.

This nonsense should have died when CPW did.

Dawson deserves better.

"If that's the way you want to play it."

"Gavin…" Dawson interrupts and turning my attention to her, within seconds the fire building in my veins over what Bryan is suggesting, starts to fade. Her voice, the softness of it— the absolute innocence—doing what it's been for weeks now and surrounding me with calm.

"Yeah, Daws?"

Ignoring Bryan's brow raise at the intimate use of her shortened name, I keep my focus on her and whatever she's about to say next. What I hope is her backing me up without me pulling her aside and having to explain why we can't do this.

"I want to do it."

No way. No-fucking-way!

Bryan's rising grin turns me inside out. I can feel the bile rising in my throat at the idea of this actually becoming an angle. What'll happen to me when Bryan finally gets around to telling Reese about his plans.

"You don't know what you're agreeing to, Daws. You wouldn't agree at all if you did."

Looking from me to Bryan, her eyes questioning, as if somehow the truth of the situation is going to be easily readable on Bryan's face, I choke on a laugh.

The Gavin of old rearing his ugly head at the best possible moment.

"All she does is stand around backstage when the camera is trained on her, and ask scripted questions. How do you think she's going to translate her ability to hold a microphone to actually speaking into one in the ring?"

Her intake of breath, along with the outward full-body flinch as she steps back from the blast I've put to her insecurities, lays ruin to everything we've been building in our time together the last several weeks.

The way I've come to feel about her.

With one statement, I've taken a big shit on all of it.

Might as well go for broke.

"You really want to put me in an angle with a female, Bry? How about you get me one who actually knows what the fuck she's doing. Otherwise, no dice. I'm going to become the HFWA Heavyweight Champion. I deserve better than some wannabe riding her cousins' coattails."

"Gavin, that's enough!" Bryan warns, stepping between me and pulling Dawson completely out of my line of sight.

"You saw chemistry because it's what I wanted you to see. It was fun, but we agree. It is enough. I'm done."

The tightness in my chest, the ache strictly on my heart as I turn my back and walk away, becomes more excruciating the further away I go from the two of them. The damage I did by turning into the very person I've come to despise, giving me exactly what I'm sure every girl who tried to be with me over the last ten years felt when I treated them like trash.

Waves of their agony and pain ripping at my chest, claws out, digging into my flesh and shredding my heart. Each step I take, another slice until I'm around the corner, heading toward the door getting me out of this building, and the freedom that comes when I finally hit the outside world and collapse against the wall.

My breath is hard to come by and lets me know in no uncertain terms, what a real broken heart feels like.

Wake up, Dawson. This is a bad dream.

Except it's not. It's really happening, and it's not a dream, it's a nightmare.

"I'm sorry, Dawson. I've been watching you for a while now. The way you light up whenever it's you and Fortune...I just assumed this would be something you'd both be into."

The way he's looking at me, all sad eyes and sympathy, it's like he knows.

He's fully aware of how I feel about Gavin, how deep those feelings go, and just how long it's been going on. How long we've been seeing each other behind everyone's backs.

But there's no way, right? I mean, we've both been the picture of discretion, even going so far as to meet at establishments towns away in order to keep it from the prying eyes of both my cousin and every other nosy person in the locker room.

"Why did he react that way, Bryan? From what Reese told me about him, he's usually the one suggesting ideas like this. Not the one turning them down."

"Your guess is as good as mine."

What could possibly be true if I even had a guess.

All I do have, though, is the vitriol he spewed, taking every fear and worry I have about being here and exploiting them.

The only clear reason for it, if you're trying to push someone away.

Is that what I'm missing?

Was Gavin's little show less for Bryan and more for me?

Just who the hell have I been sharing a bed with for the last three weeks? Who have I given my heart to?

"So, uh—what happens now?"

"This is just a tantrum, Dawson. Gavin will come around. He's just got to sell himself on how good this could be. So, for now, we keep things going the way we have been and wait until it happens."

"You sound so sure. Has he done this before?"

For as much as we've talked and gotten to know one another, learned things about each other we've never told another soul, there's still so much I don't know about the Gavin he was before I got here.

The Fortune he's been running from.

"No. At least not with this much ferocity. He's put his foot down about some stupid plans before, most of them when he worked for Smith, but nothing like this. I'm only pretending to sound sure, though. Hoping, I guess. With the way Gavin's been acting the last couple of months, I don't know what's going to happen."

It's miniscule, but it's still there.

The acknowledgment of Gavin's being different than they've all known him to be. Proving, even with the sting of his earlier words, he's still the man I believe him to be.

Even if he's at war with the other version.

He's still my Gavin.

"Since we're done for the night, I'm going to pack up and head out. Is that alright?"

"Yeah, of course." He says with a quick nod of his head. "For what it's worth, Dawson...I'm sorry things went down like this."

"Me too, Bryan. Me too."

As my boss stalks away in whatever direction he came from earlier, I make quick work of packing up the microphone and other equipment. Grabbing my purse off the stool where I placed it, and slinging it around my shoulder.

I am sorry it happened this way, but if Gavin thinks for a second that his little outburst is going to keep me away, he's got another thing coming.

It's time for Dawson Traymore to go off script.

Chapter Nineteen

Gavin

"I've gotta say, out of all the rejections I've dealt with over the years, yours may have been my favorite."

Jolted from my position, surprised over being found, I take a tentative step back at the moment she takes one closer.

The weight of my own words, the way I'd left things inside, had been too heavy to make it across the parking lot, let alone to my car. I knew my meltdown would soon become public knowledge with how long I've been out here doubled over on myself, but the last person I expected to catch it was the very person I'd turned on.

Even more out of the norm, the smirk across her face.

I've been claiming to know women for years, but the way Dawson's staring me down right now, it's as though everything I think I know is in actuality, nothing at all.

"Daws—"

"For both our sakes, this conversation can't happen here. I'm heading home. When you pull your head out of your ass, meet me there."

Righting her purse on her shoulder, she stalks past me, picking up speed and crossing the lot to where her car waits. Not so much as looking back in my direction after her parting words. Her invitation after the stunt I pulled, both making me sick and giving me hope.

Maybe I can fix the mess I created. Explain my reasoning for my tantrum. Make her see how wrong us working together is, and what a backward step this would be.

Revving the engine and backing out, I wait until she's pulled out of the lot entirely before collecting myself and doing the same. Taking my time crossing the lot, my words from earlier mixing with hers from just a few minutes ago and overloading my brain.

It's only when I hit the automatic starter and the doors click unlocked, I hear my name being called from the back.

Expecting to come face to face with Bryan when I finally do turn around, the last person I expect to have to confront is the very man we've spent weeks hiding from.

What the hell does he want?

"I just had a little chat with Bryan."

Yeah, I bet you did.

"Did he mention what he wants to do with your cousin?"

"Yeah." He grunts. "And I told him it's not happening. What I didn't expect was what else he told me." Raising a brow, knowing what he's about to tell me but not for a second willing to give it away, I wait him out. "You threatened to quit if Bryan forced your hand. Is that true?"

Not even willing to dignify it with words given the way I'd gone about it; I merely nod and am taken aback when the man smiles.

The guy who basically threatened me away from Dawson when she got here, made sure she knew all about my history before she became one of us, and has made no secret of his hatred for the way I am known, is actually smiling.

I'll be damned.

"Why'd you do it?" he asks, his disbelief in me evident as his eyes harden. "What would possess you to say no to this?"

"Besides the rules?"

"It's not a real relationship, Fortune. Rules don't apply. Try again, and this time, don't answer a question with a question."

Might as well go for broke and tell him the truth.

"Figure it would be pretty obvious, Reese. Your cousin was hired for a specific position. Sure, she's a performer like the rest of us, but a wrestler she isn't. Not to mention, having her parade out to the ring with me, not saying a word, and just leaning on me like arm candy…" I pause, my teeth grinding down hard just thinking about it. "It would be a demotion."

Eyebrows raised, eyes widening, it's obvious I've taken him by surprise. Not sure why.

Even if I didn't feel what I do for his cousin, I'm sure this is the expected response. Someone not looking at the next angle or a money-making tactic anyway.

"I told him the same, but since he's gotten Dawson's agreement, and he's determined to change your mind, he didn't want to hear it."

"You're his partner. I'm not a business guy, but something tells me in this case, he's got no other choice but listen."

Eyeing me down, like it's the first time he's seeing me, I hold back my need to laugh when his scowl finally fades and the muscles in his face relax.

Reese Harrison is wound even tighter than Kemper was, and that's saying something.

"If I said I was cool with you doing an angle with my cousin, would it sway you?"

"No offense, Reese, I respect the hell out of what you and Bryan have built here and I'm thankful, and honestly happy, with the steady paycheck, but no. It wouldn't change anything. I don't want any part of an angle that makes Dawson into something she isn't."

"Jesus, Fortune. What the hell has gotten into you?"

Well, Reese, for starters you've got it wrong. It's actually me getting into your cousin.

Shit. I'm all messed up. Standing here sticking up for Dawson in one breath, and in the next, turning it into something dirty.

"Nothing. I guess I'm just tired of the same old."

There it is. The quirk to his brow indicating he's still skeptical. I can't exactly blame him. With as much as he's seen since I got here, and god knows what else he's gotten wind of before he took me on, I'd be skeptical about me too.

It's not like I can tell him the change is because of Dawson. Something tells me, he wouldn't hesitate to relieve me of my balls.

"Despite what Bryan thinks, I'm not going to change my mind. So, if you came over here to warn me off, save your breath. For once, we're on the same page." Looking from him to the car and back again, I put an end to whatever this is. "I've got an early date with the gym in the morning, so if we're done here, I'm gonna head home."

"Yeah." He acquiesces, turning just slightly but not making any motion to leave. It's only after I open the driver's side door and go to slip in, he speaks again. "For what it's worth, Fortune, thanks for having Dawson's back."

"Always." I let slip, and before I can kick myself for the response and whatever Reese might read into it, he's turned and is making his way back toward the building.

With one last look out through the windshield, I turn the key in the ignition, bringing the car to life, and after flipping the radio on, I let my mind focus on one thing and one thing only as I pull quickly out of the lot.

Getting to my girl and making sure she stays that way.

Pacing back and forth, deviating between wondering what's taking him so long, and thankful he's not here for fear of what I would do to him if he was, I sneak a peek out through the curtain again.

Distressed at seeing the driveway empty.

Pulling back, more than ready to call this night done, the living room is bathed in light as a pair of headlights shine directly through the curtains.

So much for that idea.

Making my way quickly to the door, I pull it open and wait as he powers down and steps from the car. Pausing in place as he closes the door, eyes locked on mine just as mine is on his.

I've gone over this a billion times during the drive home. Struggling to find a reason for Gavin's very public outburst at the idea of us working together, and nothing seems to make sense.

If anything, this plan of Bryan's is ideal for us.

We can hide in plain sight.

The one rule Reese has had no issues holding over my head since I arrived, is not to involve myself in personal relationships with the superstars he employs. Becoming one of those same superstars never even occurred to him. As far as I can tell, especially with Matthias and Kimber, those relationships aren't frowned upon.

Sure, they may not be liked, but no one is going around firing anyone for being in one.

This, what Bryan wants, it's less about wanting to do it, and more about needing to.

Weeks we've been hiding now. Pretending we're just colleagues and nothing more, yet we're spending each night together, alternating between his place and mine. Waking up together. Hell, we're even carpooling together, though it's definitely been riskier pulling that off.

To be able to do all of these same things but right under their nose? I can't see it any other way but as a gift.

We don't have to hide anymore.

I only wish, with the sullen look he's wearing as he makes his way up the drive to the porch to where I'm standing, I could make him see it too.

Working together is exactly what we need.

"On a scale of one to ten, how pissed at me are you?" he asks, smirking ever so slightly.

"If you'd asked me an hour ago, it was an eight. Now, I'm thinking five and a half, maybe six."

Stepping back into the house, I motion silently for him to enter, making sure when he's through the threshold, to close and lock the door behind me.

There's no way given the events of this evening, and the bond I have with my cousin, I'm taking the chance of him doing a random drop in. Tonight, needs to be between us.

"I'm just glad you opened the door."

"Gavin," I sigh before turning to face him. "As much as the things you said bothered me, they didn't break me. I knew there was a reason for them. You haven't been that way with me in weeks. What I don't get is what it is about the idea you loathe so much."

Brow raising, he makes no move in my direction. Instead, he just stares at me, or what feels like through me the longer he does it without so much as a breath being taken.

"You really don't know why?"

"Not a clue. Feel like filling a girl in?"

Eliminating the distance, he moves into me, pressing his lips to my cheek before slipping his hand through mine, entwining our fingers and leading me over to the sofa.

"If you had been hired to be a valet when you first arrived here, we'd be having a whole other conversation right now, Daws. But you weren't. You were hired to be a backstage interviewer. A stand-in announcer for matches. And now, since I got wind of it from a few guys over the last couple of days, a scriptwriter."

He's not wrong. When Reese and Bryan called me into their office last week and asked what I thought about becoming more involved in the writing aspect, I'd jumped at the chance. If for no other reason than to learn more about this business that fell into my lap.

The only reason Gavin didn't know about it is that I was still getting my feet wet. I wasn't ready to share what might not work out long term.

What any of this has to do with his tantrum earlier, though, I have no idea.

"If you become my valet...if we become partners of any sort on screen, Dawson..." he pauses, clearing his throat quickly, but not quick enough for me to miss the wavering in his voice when he said my name. "It would feel like you were being demoted. Being punished. It would appear as though what those assholes in the locker room said about you made Bryan and Reese change their minds. You would become less than."

"Less than what?"

"Less than what you are."

Come on, pretty boy. You can give me more than that.
"And what am I?"

"Amazing. The best. Since you're going to think I'm saying all of this because I'm bias, let me give you some other words. You're insightful. Thorough. Detailed to a fault, and you're genuine. It's why all of these backstage spots we're doing, work so well. You feed into every single person you work with. Brady has seen it and admitted to it. I have. River and Ross even. You even put one of those douchebags Mark in his place too. He's eating his own words these days."

"Gavin…"

His determination when he speaks, the sincerity in his tone, but also in the words themselves, they speak directly to my soul, each and every time he does something like this. I hang off every word, and not like one of his ring rats or fans, but as someone who genuinely believes she knows him.

He may be a lot of the things he's been called in the past, but he's also more.

Honest. Sincere. Sweet. Appreciative. The list could go on.

This is the Gavin the world should be seeing, but I'm just thankful I'm lucky enough to.

"If working with me takes away from you being the amazing person you are, I don't want any part of it."

As content as I am knowing everything about what happened earlier, it's my turn to let him see the other side. How working with him isn't a demotion the way he thinks.

It's a promotion.

"Why did you agree to it, Daws?"

Here goes nothing.

"Well, part of the reason is in what you mentioned before. I've been taking on different responsibilities as of late. Learning new things, expanding my horizons in this business. Working with you, with anyone really, it would be an extension of the same idea."

Acknowledgment with the nod of his head aside, I can see he knows there's more. His eyes aren't all there in their belief.

"The other reason I said yes, is because of the doors it opens for us. You and me. If you really think about it, we're going to have to spend a lot of time together, especially if you're going to have to walk me through what we've got to do in order for this to work. You said it yourself, I don't know what I'm doing. Who better to teach me than you?"

"So, let me get this straight. You said yes to Bryan because you want to spend more time with me?"

"Yes...and no."

"Daws..."

"Gavin..." I repeat with a grin.

"Explain why it's both, please."

Turning to him, slipping my hand over his and locking my smile in place, I attempt to spell it out.

"What's the one issue we've had since we started whatever this is?"

Slipping his hand out from under mine, he lifts both to my face, holding me tightly in place, his eyes like a stone as he stares straight at me. Not allowing me with the intensity of his gaze to look anywhere but at him.

"Do you really not get what's happening here, Dawson?"

"What—What do you mean?" I stammer, desperate now to pull away, look anywhere but at him, unsure of when the mood changed, but hating that it did.

"Us. This isn't some whatever thing, princess. We're together. Dating. In a serious relationship. I have no plans on changing it either. So, unless you're about to tell me you're not on the same page, you really need to change up how you refer to us."

Oh. Wow. Okay. Now I get it.

Making light of our relationship, not wanting to read to much into it despite the way we've spent the last several weeks together, has upset him.

"We're on the same page, Gavin. I just didn't want to make assumptions. Seems like you've had enough people doing it to last a lifetime."

Softening his grip on my face, he strokes my cheek before pulling back altogether and leaning back into the sofa.

"You're right, I have. But, to answer your question, the one issue we've had is needing to hide the way we feel from the rest of the locker room."

"Right, so what better way to be together, not have to worry about people talking or running and telling my cousin what they saw us doing together, then for us to work together?"

It doesn't happen right away but after a few minutes of him sitting in silence, when he does meet my eyes again, I can see the wheels turning in his head. His understanding of why I said yes now becoming crystal clear.

The proverbial lightbulb has gone off.

"Since I'm not intimately familiar with the workings of a story like this, how close are a valet and a wrestler allowed to get?"

"Depends on what Bryan is going for, but usually pretty close. I haven't worked an angle like this in HFWA, but in CPW, when we did it, Smith used to want to film spots of us being as close as two people can get. His whole argument being sex sells."

"So," I begin, shifting my weight on the sofa and feeling brave when his eyes follow me, I straddle his lap and run my hands down over his shirt. "We could be this close."

"Mmhmm..." he hums as his own hands find their way to my arms and begin to rub.

Moving closer, his eyes closing as my breath hits his face and sucking in a sharp intake of air, I push it even further.

"How about this?" I whispered right before I press my lips to his, a muffled growl escaping from his throat as his arm finds the back of my head and he brings us even closer, our kiss becoming more passionate. Sufficiently stealing both of our breaths before we come up for air. "Would this be allowed?"

"If it's not..." he pauses, sucking in some air. "I'll fight until it is."

Slipping my hands down to the ends of his t-shirt, I grip it hard before bringing it up and over his head. My brave attempt at finding what's allowed, now turning into a whole different game.

"And this?" I ask, tossing his shirt to the floor and letting my hands roam over his bared skin. "Can we do this together?"

"Fuck yes, Dawson." He says, the tight grip he's had on his control finally snapping as he lifts me as if I'm as light as a feather, and flips us around until I'm flat on my back on the sofa and he's hovering over me, his eyes hooded and needy. "We can do it all, baby."

His lips meet mine and after losing ourselves in the moment, hands exploring, lips devouring, he pauses, hovering on top of me, our noses just barely touching, but his eyes seeing straight into my soul. All traces of the passion we'd created, at a standstill.

"Do you really want to do this, Daws?"

"This, as in right now? Or working together?"

"Both, really. I meant working together, though."

"Yes, Gavin. I do."

Pressing a soft kiss to my nose, before following it up with more of the same to my lips, he finds me again and he smiles. Giving me exactly what I'm after.

"Then let's do it."

Chapter Twenty

Gavin

When Bryan gets an idea, he really goes hard with it. I think to myself, watching him running from one part of the room to the other, involved actively in all aspects of what we're doing here.

It should have been a clue, when after getting on board with the idea of working with Dawson, he'd immediately thrown her to the wolves and had her out near ringside for my match with one half of the tag champs, Ross. This, what we're doing now, though, this is way above what I'd signed on for.

Contracting us out to have a professional photo shoot, goes above even the most underhanded tactics Smith used to use on us in CPW.

It's not Bryan or the photoshoot that's got me in edge most, though. The honor goes to Reese, as again he's calling out, halting the photographer from doing her job and prolonging this even more.

I've been doing everything in my power to swallow down the urge to strip Dawson where she stands since we got here and she pranced into the room wearing skin-tight black wrestling tights, and a top damn near resembling a bra to match it.

If I was any kind of betting man, I'd think Bryan was on to us, and he planned it this way. His sole intent to drive me crazy and have us dropping the illusion we're just colleagues.

Reese dragging this shit out, it's just another form of the continuous torture.

"Do you really need to have them so close together?"

Leave it to Reese to react like a rabid dog.

The man has had over a week to get used to this, for this exact reason.

Even if I wasn't like a dog in heat where Dawson is concerned, we'd still have to stand this close if we really want to sell our supposed relationship. I know the guy is basically a glorified number cruncher, but even he's got to understand the way this all works.

"Knock it off, Reese. They're doing what I told them to do."

"Which I still don't get," Reese growls back at his business partner, and Bryan shrugs. "What is the point of putting these two together? It's not like Kemper would care."

I'm seconds away from pulling away from Dawson entirely in an effort to explain this business to the bastard, but Bryan thankfully beats me to the punch, pulling Reese away and finally letting the photographer do her job.

"As soon as Bryan said he was going to be here, I knew he'd act like this," Dawson whispers under her breath, all the while following instructions, bringing her body even tighter to mine and driving the temperature up a thousand degrees in the confined space. "He always does this."

So, I've heard.

Not only from her since we officially became an item, but also in passing from his business partner. It seems as though even Bryan has had enough of the way Reese has been acting since they hired Dawson.

She doesn't need another father. I'm pretty sure one is enough. Not to mention that if anyone is going to have her back these days, it's going to be me.

Family ties or not.

I am interested in finding out how given his thoughts on Dawson working with anyone, least of all me, they'd gotten Reese to agree to all of this. Even with the flippant remark when we spoke in the parking lot, his actions today are proving he's still not entirely behind this idea.

"How did you get your cousin on board with this?" I ask, being sure as I do, to not break position.

"I didn't. Reese is as stubborn as I am, there's no way in hell I was going to get through to him, especially not about this. That honor goes to his business partner."

Flicking her head in the direction of where both men are deep in conversation, their bodies in an adversarial position, my interest is piqued further.

"How did he manage to pull it off?"

"If I had to guess, Bryan threatened him with something."

There's more to the story, I can tell by the way her eyes flick from mine after she's spoken, but I'm not exactly in a position to find out more, especially when after following yet another directional shout out from the lady behind the camera, we're on the move again.

"You guys are doing great." She calls out to us and switching up our positions again, this time, Dawson's arms wrapped around my neck and her fingers grazing my cheek, she sings more praises right before Reese hollers out again.

So much for Bryan distracting the guy.

"Erin," Dawson calls. "Give me five minutes, please."

Getting the approval of the photographer, whose name I now finally know, she pulls away from me and stomps her way over to where her cousin stands with Bryan. And with no attempt to hide her contempt, or even lower her voice, she lets him have it.

"Reese, I've had it! This shoot was only supposed to take at the most an hour. We've been here for three. So, if you can't get your head around the fact that I'm doing this, and I'm going to be working with Gavin, you can turn around and leave. Now. You may have all day to sit here and cause trouble, but the rest of us don't."

Not sticking around to hear whatever his response is going to be, she moves back my way, pausing when she reaches Erin and leaning in close, whispering something to her, she backs away a few seconds later grinning.

"What was that about?"

"You'll see." She grins brighter, and a few seconds later when Erin calls out for her to get into position, she stands by her statement.

She grabs my shirt and yanking me to her, plants a kiss on my lips.

Giving her cousin the world's biggest *fuck you* in the process.

Dawson

This week has been a whirlwind of nonstop activity.

From collaborating with Gavin on a new titantron video package for his entrance, and deciding on the best ramp walk for the times I would be accompanying him to the ring, to the countless hours we've spent together going over suggestions from the writers as well as ad-libbing our own stuff to make it more authentic.

The energy has been high, and after leaving the photo shoot, our last stop for the day, it's beginning to make my head spin.

Before experiencing a lot of this myself, I had no clue the lengths these people in the back go through in order to make the show what it is, both when it's televised, and otherwise.

Now, being home and away from the insanity, Gavin curled up on my sofa and me standing around waiting on the microwave in the kitchen, eager to get on with the popcorn so we can unwind and lose ourselves in a movie, I'm caught up in what all of this means.

The ease at which I stepped into this role of on-air personality, apart from my work backstage and the ring announcing. The joy I get working with Gavin through all of it, feeling like part of a real team, something I'd been seriously lacking toward the end of my time at LiveWire, and then the way it feels having him here, in my space.

How comfortable I am and how right it is.

My mind willing to believe, for the first time since I was hired, that this is where I belong.

"Daws, the popcorn done yet?" Gavin calls from his place on the sofa at the exact moment the microwave begins beeping.

"Just finished. Be there in a sec!"

Pulling out the bag and dumping it in the large bowl resting on the table top, I toss the empty bag in the trash, grab the bowl on my way past and head into the room. Pausing as I pass through the threshold and am given a full view of the man now sitting up with his focus on the television.

He even fits perfectly there.

Sucking in a sharp breath at just now natural it is having him here; the sound has him turning until his eyes lock on mine with concern.

"Everything okay, princess?"

"Yeah," I make light of what he heard. "Just placed my hand a little too close to the edge of the bowl and felt the burn." With a shrug, I head around the sofa and plop down beside him, passing him the bowl.

Taking it easily from my hands and resting it on the table, he focuses on my hand, and bringing my fingers to his lips, he kisses them. Bringing everything I've been feeling, especially over the last week, back to the surface.

I can't believe I've fallen in love with the biggest player in the industry.

Wait. What?

"Daws, are you sure you're okay? Your eyes are as wide as saucers right now."

Oh, pretty boy, you have no idea. I'm so far from okay it's ridiculous.

"I…" I begin, ready to blurt out my feelings, but he interrupts me.

"You're beginning to regret saying yes to all of this, aren't you?"

This, what he's asking, officially has my lips clamping down hard on what I was mere seconds away from admitting. Of course, I'd misread the expression on his face. He doesn't feel the same. He's just concerned about how I'm handling this new angle.

"No, of course not."

"For what it's worth," he continues, ignoring what I've said. "After the kiss, you laid on me at the photo shoot, come Monday,

I don't think we'll have to worry about working together ever again."

"What do you mean? Why wouldn't we be working together?"

"You were there, princess. I'm pretty sure you saw your cousin burst a couple of blood vessels in his head."

What is happening right now? Why is he so focused on Reese and what the fallout from today will be?

"Gavin, do you regret agreeing to work with me?"

"You're kidding, right?" he snorts and with a shake of his head, slips his hand over mine. "Not even for a second. You were right the other day. Getting to be this close to you at work every day, not needing to hide as much, it's been a fucking dream come true."

"Then why are you so adamant about us not working together on Monday?"

"I'm not. I just thought maybe all of your silence, the looks you're giving me, were about that."

Oh, God.

Unless I admit the truth and also use a word I haven't so much as spoken outside of my family in years, there's no way to make him see that while this is about us, it's not about us working together.

We're on the same page. As much of a whirlwind as it's all been this week, I wouldn't change a second of it.

"I'm sorry. I was just thinking about this week. How comfortable it's been, despite me being new. How right it feels working with you."

Smiling softly, he pulls me into him and releases a contented sigh.

"It's never been as easy to work with a woman, as it is with you, Dawson. It's so natural. Organic. I don't have to put much effort in at all."

As thankful as I am that we're on the same page, I'm also curious.

I know over the years he's worked with women, both in CPW and in HFWA, but no one could tell me how it felt working with them but Gavin. I could have reached out during those first few weeks where I was getting to know the roster, and spoken to the other halves of the pairs, but it never even crossed my mind.

When it comes to Gavin, I only want to get the info from him. Especially knowing what the rest of the roster seems to think about him.

"What was so hard about it before?"

"When I first started in CPW, and I do mean, right when I started, Smith wanted to use my look more than my talent. I was what they seem to enjoy calling me here these days. Pretty. There was a girl named Candace, and since back then I was still getting my bearings on the mic, he paired me with her. There wasn't anything remotely wrong with her, but we just didn't click. It was like pulling teeth to get me to open up. I was robotic."

"Maybe because you were nervous?"

Shaking his head, he opens up and gives me a little more to go on.

"I had already developed the Fortune cockiness then, Daws. I had it in me to pull out all the stops and create some really great moments, and eventually, we did, but they were all as fake as Candace's breasts were. And they took so many takes, it's a miracle they happened at all. After that, Smith kept me off women...until Melinda."

Melinda Richardson.

Now there's a name I know quite a lot about. Before we'd left California, I'd done as Brady asked and spoken to Jackson all about her and the past she shared with both men. With everything I'd learned about their history, or at least, Jackson's perception of their history, I could see why Brady was afraid when he caught me with Gavin backstage.

"Was it easier with her?"

"Daws," he says, rubbing at his head, his face resigned. "Are you sure you want to know about her?"

"Yes. She was a part of your history, whether good or bad. You wouldn't be where you are without her, so as much as I'm sure I'll hate it, I need to hear about it. I want to."

Bringing his lips to my head, he kisses me softly before squeezing me to him.

"I won the lottery when Reese and Bryan hired you, you know that?"

Lifting my head enough for him to see me, I smile before pressing my own lips to his softly. "You're damn right, Fortune. And don't you forget it." Winking, I slide back down into his arms and after a few seconds of silence, he takes me back in time.

"What Melinda and I had; was purely physical. We didn't go out on dates; we didn't meet the family. None of the stuff you do when you're serious about someone. All we did was put on a show for the locker room, the fans, and then the world. Behind closed doors all we did was screw."

Swallowing down the burn hearing him talk about his relationship with Melinda, I take him off in a different, hopefully, safer, direction.

"Was it easier to work with her than it was with Candace?"

"Yeah, but only because of the intimacy part. We had chemistry in bed. She fed my ego, among other appendages, and honestly made it incredibly easy to be the guy you see on television. Hell, part of me thinks the evolution of Fortune, from CPW all the way here, was because of her. She brought out my inner asshole."

He can spout all he wants about them being purely sexual, and I already know the reason he did what he did in stealing her from Jackson, but the way he's sitting here and basically thanking her for making him into the man he became in order to sell tickets, well, it speaks to something else.

And I don't stay silent about it either.

"You did care for her, Gavin, even if you wish you didn't. It's right there in what you're saying."

Biting down on his lip, looking out over the room, his mind deep in thought, I reach up with a hand, stroking the side of his face and bring him back to me.

"You're right, but I do know what it wasn't. It wasn't loving, Dawson. I don't think I've ever been in love."

Well, Dawson. There's an admission you didn't see coming.

"Why do you think you've never been in love?"

"Easy. Don't you have to be able to love yourself before you can love anyone else?"

Oh, Gavin.

"I've spent so long being this larger than life guy, I forgot what it was like to be me. That's why I said what I did earlier, princess. It's so organic, so damn easy to work with you because it's just so damn easy to be with you, period. There's no expectation. You're not wanting and taking from me. All you do is give."

Yeah, it's official. I'm in love with this man.

"Gavin—"

"No, Dawson. Before you say anything, let me finish." His eyes find mine, pleading silently with me to give him this moment and without so much as a blink, I nod. He can take as long as he wants if this is the kind of stuff he's going to say.

"You remind me of the real me. Every single day, waking up to you in the morning, falling asleep beside you at night, no matter where we're doing it, I'm not acting. I'm the real me. Thank you, Dawson. Thank you for helping me find myself again."

Chapter Twenty-One

Gavin

Walking down the ramp, followed closely by Dawson, I pause when I'm ringside. Taking in the sight of it all. The monstrosity in the ring as intimidating today, as it was the last time I saw it.

An opinion Dawson also shares as she stops beside me, releasing a heavy breath. "Are you sure there's no way we can change the style of the match?"

"Afraid not, princess. With the promo we did where I announced the match, I sealed my fate."

Turning to me, her eyes questioning, she asks the inevitable. "How many ladder matches have you had in your career?"

"One."

"Who won?" she continues, and my response is immediate. "My opponent. Merrick."

Shortly before I'd had the CPW title placed around my waist and run with it, this is the program Merrick and I were placed in. Our final showdown before we met again for the Heavyweight belt, being a ladder match for the title Kemper eventually owned, in the Middleweight.

My first sight of the ladder is seared in my memory. My ego at an all-time high, not even the sight of the hardened metal able to phase me. The unforgiving nature of it, what I now know all too intimately, what breeds the intimidation now.

If I'm not careful or we don't plan this match out perfectly, it could go a whole other way tonight when we face off in the ring. A situation made even worse because it won't just be Matthias and myself experiencing it, but Dawson too.

An innocent to this business, and the oftentimes brutal nature of it is going to be thrown to the wolves coming down to the ring with me. Her reactions what Bryan is banking on, especially with the way we've built ourselves as the 'it' couple, but what I also know for the woman beside me, will be all too real.

There is no way with the attacks we plan to dish out, Dawson is going to be able to keep her feelings for me, the true nature of our relationship, a secret.

After tonight, everything could blow up in our faces, and I'm not sure how I feel about it.

I'm ready for us to be out. All we need to do now, especially with Dawson's new position within the company, is out ourselves to Bryan and Reese. We're like Kimber and Matthias.

Except we're not them. We can never be them.

Because of Reese-fucking-Harrison.

"How bad is it?" she asks softly, bringing my attention back.

"No matter what way we play this, we're both leaving pretty damn broken. Which is another reason Kemper and Bryan asked for the time between matches."

"Can you get seriously hurt?"

"Yes." I don't even bother lying to her. "So, if even for a second, you think you can't handle it, you can accompany me out and then head back at the top of the ramp. You don't have to be there."

Moving in as close as we can, given the number of eyes I know are around the auditorium, her voice lowers even more.

"I won't let you go through this alone, Gavin. I want to be in your corner."

Oh, princess. You have no idea how good it makes me feel hearing those words.

"Be careful, Daws. Saying things like that is dangerous." I tell her instead.

"How so?"

"I could kiss you after what you said, but there are eyes everywhere, meaning I can't. You know I don't do so well with holding out."

"I wouldn't stop you kissing me." She admits, moving into the curve of my body and pressing her lips to the bare skin of my shoulder. A move that to anyone watching will look as innocent as they come, but for me is anything but.

"Nicely played, princess," I say, stepping away and moving to the ring steps. Taking the slow walk up them and turning at the top to her, and holding my hand out for her to join me.

"Why do you want me here, Gavin?" she asks once I've held the rope open and let her slip through, meeting her in the middle. Directly beside the monstrosity, I'll use as a weapon later tonight.

"So far in working together, your role has been easy. The matches have been standard. No special stipulations or other surprises. Though, you at ringside is a surprise for most of the guys I've faced. This is a whole other beast. I guess I want to be sure you can handle it."

I know without question this woman can handle anything thrown at her. My concern isn't to do with her ability to do her job. It's more about whether or not she can handle it from a personal place. I need to know she can handle watching me get hurt.

What she obviously catches onto with the next question.

"You and Matthias have worked out the high spots for this match I'm sure, what you won't call out to one another during it, so what's the worst thing that'll happen to you?"

"I'm going to get trapped in between two ladders and he's going to land a shooting star press from the top rope."

In other words, I'm going to feel hard metal front and back.

"Gavin…"

Here it is. The reality of the situation. It's already appearing as her eyes go wide in shock, and even begin to shine with a gloss of tears.

She's afraid for me.

"Dawson," I say softly, my chest aching at not being able to bring her to me the way I want. "I'm going to ask you again. Are you sure you can handle this?"

Wiping at her eyes, she raises them to meet mine and she steps forward, caution in the wind as she reaches out and touches my lips with her fingers. Both of us again on the same page, but her bravery on display where mine is hidden. Hyper-aware.

"I already told you I wasn't going to let you come out alone. I stand by what I said. I'm always going to be in your corner."

The air shifts under the weight of my feet then, and much like the step she's taken in reaching out to me, breaking the rules of this game we're playing and making a public stand, I do the same. Pulling her the rest of the way to me and embracing her, I press my lips to hers.

Whoever sees be damned.

I'm in love with this woman, and I'm tired of hiding it.

Jolted apart by the clearing of a throat, both of us, Dawson's flushed cheeks matching what I'm sure is my own, turn to the interloper of our moment.

Kemper.

"Uh guys, not for nothing, but Reese and Bryan are heading this way. They want to see us go over the spot, Gav. Whatever is happening here, you gotta shelve it."

Thankful for the heads up while at the same time, filled with anger at having to hide any of this at all, we both take heed of what Matthias is saying and pull apart. Dawson the first to the ropes, sliding through them and down the stairs, finding herself beside my opponent.

"I'll see you in a few," I call down to her, and she nods, leaning in and saying something to Matthias before heading back up the ramp and disappearing behind the curtain.

Matthias now getting into the ring himself, looks from me to where Dawson disappeared and back again before moving closer as the two men of the hour step through and head toward us. His whispered final words bringing a sense of foreboding I'm not in the least bit prepared for.

"You're so screwed."

Dawson

What did Brady call this during one of our sit-downs?

A scripted event turning real.

Was it a shoot?

I'm shooting hard right now with what I've had to endure, witness, and act like doesn't bother me for the last twenty minutes.

The move Matthias did on top of the two ladders, not even the worst of it. Some of the shots Gavin has delivered with the ladder, to both Matthias's ribs and back, making me feel like I'm stuck in this flinching position permanently.

If either of these two men can walk after this, it'll be a miracle.

The crowd is erupting in chants around me, half of the place calling out for Matthias while the rest are just screaming *holy shit* in rapid succession. All of what I expect given what these two guys have done in the ring tonight, with and without the ladder, but what's just making the overwhelmingly nauseous feeling I'm experiencing, worse.

Don't these people see the damage being done here? Long term damage? What is all in the name of entertainment and enjoyment? Better question, don't they care?

Burying my face in my hands and using one to wipe at the other, to wash away the very real tears streaming down my face over Gavin lying defeated and damn near broken in the ring, I focus again on my job. What I was told to do.

React in the most over the top way possible.

All of which I pull off masterfully because buried underneath the fake is a whole lot of very real and strong emotions. My voice almost louder in comparison to the crowd as they still continue hollering out at the two men in the ring.

Matthias now lifting the ladder from the far end of the ring, and pulling it to the center. Lifting it and setting it up, wasting no time climbing on it and beginning the rise to the top.

What, if he succeeds, will result in the end of Gavin's hopes at the title, giving Matthias two wins, but what I know Gavin, now stirring on the ground, is scripted to stop.

Well, he would be if he could move.

Snails are putting him to shame with as slow as he is to slip over to the where the ladder stands. His hand hitting the bottom step hard as he uses it to raise his body up.

As both men are climbing, Matthias at least three steps ahead of his opponent, Gavin realizes his place and, in a move so swift it almost seems surreal, he's jumping a step, as Matthias claims another. Both men repeating the cycle until they meet on either side of the ladder, staring each other down.

Gavin the first to swing, hits his mark and stuns Matthias, shaking his position on the ladder, and gears up to do again at the exact moment his opponent hits back, leaving Gavin the one to sway.

If either of these men in their need to put on the best performance of the night, fall off this ladder, it's not going to end well. Their bodies are already full of signs of abuse. Red angry marks cut deep into Gavin's back, while Matthias's chest bears the brunt of his.

When Gavin comes back, gripping the next step of the ladder and hoists himself up, I'm back in the acting game again, screaming and clapping as he reaches for the next step. A move Matthias is called to and attempts to stop by reaching out much like Gavin had before and hitting him in an attempt to break his momentum.

Counting down the seconds, I close my eyes and pray it turns out right as I watch both men battling it out at the top of the ladder. And when I've reached five, I'm sliding under the bottom rope, doing just like we planned. Running over to Matthias's side and getting my footing, climbing up until I'm pulling on his jeans. My hands hooked in his waistband as I pull with every bit of strength I have, until in an attempt to force me off, he kicks his leg out, hitting my body with a force I knew was coming but am unprepared for the magnitude of, and I'm knocked back, falling to the mat.

Gavin using the distraction as Matthias's gaze falls to my position and landing another hit. This time, the move costing his opponent as one of his feet slips off the ladder stair and he's wobbling again.

With one last collision, I feel the vibration as Matthias's body comes to find itself bouncing off the ring mat below, about a foot or two from mine. His face a mask of both agony and the faintest trace of happiness as I see the corner of his lips raised.

A response strictly for me, as I listen to the crowd lose their minds as Gavin reaches the top of the ladder, grabbing the title, and from my vantage point as I begin to turn, holding it high above his head.

The bell rings as Gavin makes his way down, and the ref ready and waiting, holding his hand high in the air as he declares Gavin Fortune the winner of the second match.

With a smile crossing my own lips watching him take his rightful place as the winner, I close my eyes and before I know it, everything goes black.

Gavin

I knew I should have put my foot down when Bryan brought up the idea of getting Dawson physically involved.

Judging by the rage on Reese's face, it's obvious I'm not alone in it either.

The impact from Matthias's kick doing far more than it should have, and knocking her out. The team of trainers looking her over now in the back, all coming to the same conclusion almost immediately.

"I'm sorry, man," Kemper says as he makes his way into the room and over to where I'm standing. His eyes, much like every other pair in the room, right on her.

"It's not your fault."

"Maybe not, but it was my shot that did it."

Moving away from him and toward Dawson, not caring what anyone else in the room thinks, I lean over, willing her silently to wake up, to come back to us so I can take her home and we can finally do what we should have already been doing.

Celebrating the win.

Celebrating us.

"Please wake up, baby," I whisper, my voice so low I'm basically mouthing the words. "You're scaring me."

Feeling the heat from behind before being bathed in the shadow, my body hardens as I turn and I'm face to face with Reese, with Bryan directly behind him.

My anger at seeing the man who put all of this in motion causing me to flip my position from the softness with Dawson to immediate rage.

"You!" I yell, moving in on Bryan. "You did this!" Reaching out, ready to strangle the man, I find myself being held back by Reese and Matthias. My rage at having Dawson here this way so powerful, it's taking them both to keep me away.

"It was a mistake!" Bryan yells when after both men have me subdued, he's able to speak freely.

"More like a botch," Matthias interjects quietly, admitting his part in what happened. "But I'm with Fortune on this one."

"Matt—"

"No, Bry. I know what you're going to say. I know you didn't intend to send her out there to get hurt. You don't have it in you. It's the only reason I'm holding him back and not being the one gunning for you. But it still happened, and the only reason it did is that you let dollar signs override common sense."

Cursing his name under my breath, I agree before focusing my attention solely on Bryan.

"You've been doing it since you saw us working together. The whole point of putting us together was money for you. Look at her, Bryan!" I yell, anger getting the better of me. "Was it worth the cost?"

Shoving my way out of the hold of both men, I don't make a beeline for Bryan the way they expect as they shadow me.

Instead, with one more look back toward the woman I love laying on the gurney, I slam my way past everyone and out through the door.

Able to breathe once I'm out in the hall.

I need to chill. Not wanting the first thing she sees when she does open those gorgeous eyes, being the sight of rage in mine.

I've got to get myself under control.

After pacing the hall repeatedly, I pause mid-step when I hear the door to the room open and Matthias makes his way out a few minutes later.

"She's awake."

Chapter Twenty-Two

Dawson

Waking up to four pairs of eyes on me, their expressions tight, but clearly concerned, is quite possibly the most intimidating situation I've ever found myself in.

Gavin's face is front and center, thankfully, but if it's possible, his face is the most frightening. Whatever happened since the match, obviously doing a number on a guy who is normally known to be jovial.

"Not for nothing guys, but could you all just take a step back?" I ask, my voice rough but thankfully, otherwise no worse for wear.

Thank God.

The last thing I remember being Gavin holding his hand in the air, along with the belt, and Matthias's short smile. Both men are clearly pleased with how the match had gone down.

Leading us to now, where no one is happy.

"God, Dawson! Finally!" Gavin shoves toward me until I feel his rough hands encompassing my own. "I was starting to lose it."

"Well, settle yourself, pretty boy. I'm okay."

In an effort to prove just how truthful my claim is, I shift my body on the gurney and attempt to sit up.

"Yeah, that's not happening." He informs me quietly, focusing his attention solely on me, his eyes finally softening. "No matter how much of a badass you are."

"He's right, Dawson. Best to wait for the trainer to check you over." The familiar voice of the other man I shared the stage with tonight calls from his place in the corner of the room.

Right. I took a shot from Matthias. Fell back and hit the mat pretty hard. Maybe even did damage to my head. All of what I've seen as their fussing over me, finally making sense. I really *am* a badass.

"You won the match." I smile, remembering the moment Gavin ripped the belt down from the cord holding it at the top of the ladder.

"I did, princess." He responds with a small grin of his own. "Thanks to you."

Stomach sufficiently turned to jelly, I shift my head away from the man whose gaze I've been taken by for weeks and focus on the outskirts of the room, where I now see Reese and Bryan huddled together, their eyes focused on me.

"I'm okay, Reese's Pieces," I say to my cousin, calling him by his childhood nickname and earning quite a few snickers through the room. "I think I needed the hit. It cleared out the cobwebs."

My lame attempt at a joke falling on deaf ears, I turn again to Gavin, but before I can tell him to lighten up, remind him I'm here, and I'm all good, he's moving backward and Reese is stepping into his place.

"You're not going to ringside anymore, Dawson. What happened tonight, I'm not allowing a repeat performance."

Damn.

It only took a total of about ten minutes after waking up for Reese to go full dad mode. This might be a new record. Too bad I'm not going to be giving him what he wants.

I knew the risks.

"Back off, Reese. I was doing my job and I got hurt. You make the guys do this every day and don't bat an eye. Just because we're related, and you're doing a great impression of my dad right now, doesn't mean you're keeping me from what I'm paid to do."

"Dawson..." he growls, and I release a shaky and ragged laugh.

"Don't even finish the thought, Dad."

It's the same thought he has any time I exert any bit of authority against him. He wants me to toe the line, and even though he knows me better than most everyone in this room, he still forgets how I am.

"Maybe Reese is right." I hear the familiar lilt of Gavin's voice calling from his place from behind my cousin. "Most of us have been doing this for years. You've only been doing this a few weeks."

"Not you too, pretty boy," I grumble, using the last few minutes of rest in order to push myself up on the gurney until I'm sitting up fully, my brain a little foggy but otherwise, feeling like my usual self again. "I don't need another father. I'm content with the one I've got. And, you know, this one over here." I thumb over to Reese.

"Fine." Gavin easily concedes. "But I'm going to veto you getting involved."

Scoffing at him with what I think is the deepest eye roll I've ever done; I attempt to slip down to the floor and Reese catches me.

"Can you stop being stubborn for five damn minutes, Dawson? Shit."

"No can do, Reese's pieces. Get the trainer in here to clear me so I can get out of here."

Moving from his place against the wall, Matthias steps forward, commanding all our attention, my eyes unable to look away when he smirks at me and laughs as he points to the other guys.

"On that note, I'm going to head out. I've got to go and update Kimber. I'll leave you guys to deal with this."

Deal with this, is right.

Matthias Kemper might be the smartest guy in the room, getting out the way he is.

Watching as Gavin steps in his path and the two of them speak to one another, voices low, but a look of ease and relaxation on both of their faces as they speak, I focus my attention back on Reese, but not without smiling at the change taking place directly in front of me.

Looks like these two can coexist after all.

"I'll round up your stuff and when the trainer clears you, I'll bring you home." He states and I'm instantly shaking my head in defiance. There's no way in hell I'm going from one enclosed space with this guy, to being boxed inside a vehicle. One time a night is my limit for all of this hovering.

"Reese, you and Bryan still have a show going on. It's best you stick around for it. I'll just call a cab."

Clearing his throat, Gavin steps away as Matthias leaves the room and interjects himself. "I've got her, Reese."

Flashing me a look of distrust, his forehead pinching, he looks between us.

"I think it's best if I take her," Reese argues.

"She's got a point, man." Bryan cuts in. "We're still on out there, and since Gavin's done for the night, other than the spot he was supposed to have with Dawson, he can take her."

"Fine." Reese concedes, though his expression is still wary. Not liking the idea of Gavin and me alone together one bit.

"Okay, great. Now, if you don't mind, I'd like a few minutes alone."

Both men grunting in their acceptance, and Gavin meeting my eyes in question, I wink and wait as both bosses slip from the room, leaving us alone.

"They're going to expect me to join them, you know," Gavin says, crossing the room, but instead of taking my hand this time, he captures my lips instead. Needing, the same as I do, the comfort found there. "I was so fucking worried, princess."

"Right back at you, pretty boy."

My mind is flooded with every moment of fear I experienced watching Gavin and Matthias in the match. All of the spots they did, moves not typically seen in a regular one on one, all pooling in the bottom of my stomach.

"I'm better knowing you're okay." He admits and pressing his lips to mine again quickly he separates at the exact moment the door opens and the trainer steps in.

"I'll be outside when you're ready." He says and turning my attention to the man here to check me over, I merely nod, and he grins slyly. "See you soon, Bruiser."

Gavin

"Back off, pretty boy. I'm capable of getting out of a car on my own."

Ignoring her protest, I shove my body in and over the seat, unclipping the belt and doing just as I intended when I ran around and opened the door, to begin with, and bring her up and into my arms, lifting her out.

Thankfully away from prying eyes, I'm going out of my way to make up for every second I wasn't able to do what I wanted earlier. Take care of her.

The way she deserves.

Shoving against my chest as I make my way up the walk, I laugh. "Sorry to break it to you, princess, but if you're attempting to hurt me, you're failing."

Releasing a low growl, I place her back on her feet as I go about unlocking the door.

"Thank you." She huffs, relishing in what has been her first independent movement since she came out of the trainers' room. The memory of her flushed cheeks when I'd carried her out of the building earlier, raising eyebrows in the process, causing my face to rise.

"Stop looking so smug."

"Not smug, just happy."

Pushing the door open, I turn back in order to again sweep her off her feet, but she beats me to the punch, pushing her way quickly through the door, making a beeline straight for the stairs.

Good. At least I won't have to force her to rest.

Kicking the door shut behind me, I flip the lock and head after her, making it to the top of the stairs just as she slams the door to her room hard enough to shake the walls.

"Oh, come on, Daws! Don't be like this. I just wanted to be sure you were okay."

Raising my fist to the door, I rap my knuckles against the wood and when no response comes from inside, I repeat it. This time a little harder. What obviously annoys her even more, but grants me what I'm after when she pulls the door open and I'm face to face with her scowling face.

Batting my eyes, using what both Dawson and Kimber have called my superpower, she rolls her eyes, and despite knowing it's probably going to earn me an ass-kicking, I laugh.

"Can I come in?"

"Are you going to throw me over your shoulder and carry me around like a caveman again?"

Visions of Dawson wearing an outfit inspired by Wilma Flintstone flash through my head, and before I give my younger self's perversion away, let alone the visceral body response to the shortness of the white little getup, I clear my throat.

"No. I'll behave."

Eyeing me dubiously, not for a second believing I have the ability to behave, and not being wrong, she moves from the door, allowing me entrance. Which, once I'm in, has me wanting to test the waters to how much more she'll give me.

"Can I ask you for a small favor?"

"Depends. What do you want?"

Moving toward the bed and sitting, I pat the space beside me and make my intentions clear.

"Wow." She snorts. "Even you can't want that from me right now."

"Eww," I say, shaking my head vehemently. "I don't want to fuck you, Dawson. Jesus. I just want you to rest."

Easily finding her way to the bed beside me, her silent version of an apology, I pull back and shift over, and finally, on the same page, she follows suit. Finding her way to my arms and laying down, head directly over my heart.

A position I could maintain forever.

A moment reminiscent of the first night we were together.

"Mmm," she moans softly, snuggling her body even more into mine. "This is nice."

No, princess. This is much more than nice. It's perfect.

"Yes, it is," I tell her instead, squeezing her shoulder. "I'm glad I thought of it."

Snorting again, she playfully slaps my chest and I'm struck. A small moment with this woman causing my heart to feel full. Everything I need and want being right here in this room.

"We need to have a serious talk about that ego of yours." She laughs.

"Okay, but only after we talk about your complete lack of stroking it."

"You've never complained about my stroking abilities before."

You're damn right I haven't.

"Touché."

Running her fingers across my chest, we spend the next several minutes in silence, me enjoying the peace and the sound of her breathing when it evens out. So, swept up in her and this, I almost miss the soft words she's spoken.

"Thank you."

Stroking her hair, curious as to what she could be thanking me for, when all I want to do lately it seems is be the one thanking her, I probe deeper.

"For what?"

"Being here, I suppose. Taking care of me, even after I acted like a stubborn jerk and bit your head off."

"You don't have to thank me, Dawson. I wanted to do it, even knowing you weren't going to make it easy."

Lifting her head from its place on my chest and turning, she stares me down.

"Really?"

"Yes. There's nowhere else I'd rather be, then right where I am."

"Careful, Fortune. Saying things like that could be dangerous."

As she eases herself back into my arms again, her head finding its way back where it belongs, she sighs and there's no mistaking what it means.

The things I'm saying are dangerous to her. Especially given the fact of her being the only one I'm ever planning on saying them to.

Embracing the comfortable silence again, I'm unaware how much time has passed when my eyes pop open, relaxation obviously having turned into sleep, and I shift in order to look down on the woman still resting peacefully in my arms.

Giving her a once over, not wanting to startle and wake her, but acutely aware of not having much of a choice. She'd taken a hit to her head tonight. A not so friendly one. Years of concussion exams aside, the common sense approach is you don't let someone fall asleep.

Shaking her softly, attempting to rouse her gently by whispering her name, she shifts in my arms and her eyes flutter open to meet mine.

"I'm sorry, baby. We fell asleep."

Understanding in her eyes, she shifts in the bed, languidly stretching and moving into a sitting position. Eyes now wide and aware.

"How do you feel?" I ask.

"I feel a little dazed, most likely due to crashing as hard as I did, otherwise, I feel fine."

"Good," I announce, moving to a sitting position on the bed and standing up.

"Where are you going?" She asks as I make my way across to the door.

"I'm going to make us something to eat. Since the last time either of us did, we were together, I know for a fact you're overdue."

"And what about you?"

Making my way back over to her and pressing my lips to her forehead, heart rate picking up with the release of her soft breath, I nuzzle my face into the side of her neck, kissing her there all while explaining myself.

"Taking care of you *is* taking care of me. So, get comfortable, princess, because, for the next twenty-four hours, Nurse Gavin is at your service."

And with that, as her laughter fills the room, I turn and leave the room.

Chapter Twenty-Three

Gavin

Being here now, we've come full circle.

Dawson and I are back where it all began. Maybe not exactly where we began, considering we met at Johnny's, but close enough.

Standing in the doorway of Matthias and Kimber's place, where our first date went awry, it's as good as it's going to get in terms of us going back to the start. There's no way in hell I'm taking this girl back to the bar.

"Hey, Gav?" Kimber calls out.

"Yeah?"

Crossing from her place on the other side of Kemper and coming up beside me, she grins.

"You think if Dawson is on her best behavior tonight, you'll let her stay and enjoy the pie this time?"

If it was anyone else doing the ribbing, reminding me of the jackass I'd been the first time we came here, I would have cut it off at the pass, but it's Kimber. And judging by Dawson's muffled laughter as she covers her mouth with her hand, I'm okay with letting it slide.

"It's pumpkin this time, so I really want her to stick around for it."

"I don't know, Kimber. It all depends. If she can be on her best behavior, I'll think about it."

Sticking her tongue out, she slips her arm through Kimber's when it's offered and both girls head off, leaving me and Matthias alone.

"What the hell was that?" He asks after he watches them go, and I shrug. "And you told me growling was bad. Pretty sure I witnessed something even worse...Daddy."

With a quick slap to my back as he passes, he follows after the girls, leaving me to deal with the aftermath of my nonsense in peace.

Leaving behind another thing I never want to hear again.

We're *definitely* leaving the Daddy stuff to the adult film industry.

Making my way into the kitchen, following the sound of Dawson's laughter, I catch all three of them around the counter, forks in their hands. Dawson's just slipping into her mouth as I make my way to her side, a perfectly practiced moan escaping as she experiences what I can now see is the pie, sitting picked apart on the countertop.

"You started without me?"

Swallowing the bite, she smirks at Kimber before turning to me with a grin. "Don't I always?"

"Wow!" Kimber exclaims while Matthias coughs with the distinct sound of the word gross coming through.

"Nice try, princess."

Eyes crinkling, she keeps the shots coming.

"It's not my fault you're always so consumed with the finish."

With a high five to Matthias—a move I'm going to make him pay for later—I silence her when reaching over, I pluck the fork from her hand and jam it down into the pie. The aroma alone made me understand quick why the three of them jumped on it.

"Hey!" she calls out, elbowing me in the ribs. "Get your own fork."

"When it's so easy to steal yours?" I ask, mouth full of pie with no regrets.

"You're such a child."

Catching the grin on Kimber's face, I go to respond but she cuts me off.

"Wow."

Calling all eyes to her with the one word, Matthias asks the question on all of our minds.

"What is it, little one?"

There used to be a time not all that long ago, where hearing Matthias call Kimber little one, would have made my blood run cold. Especially back when we were together in the very beginning. The fake relationship later aside, his connection to her was always such a pain. Standing here in their kitchen with the eyes of my own girl on me, I liken it to when I call Dawson a princess. It has the same meaning.

"I'm sorry, Dawson." Kimber starts. "I don't want to embarrass you, especially with the way things happened last time you were here, but I think we've gotten comfortable enough with each other where I feel it is okay to admit this."

Okay, now I'm curious.

"Admit what, Kimberlee?" Dawson chimes in.

"You and Gavin, the way the two of you are with each other…"

I get it now. She's seeing the very thing I've been feeling for a while but still haven't been able to admit to the woman standing so close.

Willing her to stop before she takes the words straight from my mouth, wanting the moment I tell Dawson how I feel to be ours alone, she curiously studies me before nodding and turning back to my girl.

"It feels like you guys have known each other forever. Are you sure you only met a couple of months ago?"

Thank God.

Breathing a silent breath of relief, I look down to Dawson as her lips curve up into a smile.

"I wish I could have met Gavin before, but sadly; it wasn't meant to be. I'm really happy we met when we did, though."

Grinning wide, I waste no time bringing her into my side and pressing my lips to her head as my other arm hands over the fork I stole.

"Aww!" Kimber sighs, causing the rest of us to laugh, but what the other two don't see and that is only for me, is the depth to Dawson's eyes, the softness in them appearing with my small gesture.

Could it mean what I hope it does? Does she feel the same?

Thank you, she mouths and trying my hardest not to read anything into the look she gave me, I merely nod before turning my attention back to our hosts.

"So, now that we've ruined dinner, what's the plan?"

Expecting Kimber to answer, her being the talkative one, I'm as surprised as the rest of the room when it's Dawson.

"Actually, if its cool with the both of you, I was wondering if I could steal Matthias for a couple of minutes. Shop talk, ya know?"

Swallowing down the rise of jealousy I have at her choice of words, and even her wanting to be alone with Matthias at all, focusing on the shop talk portion of what she's asked, I give her a quick kiss before Kimber speaks for the both of us.

"Of course. While you guys do that, I'll have pretty boy here help me actually cut the pie."

Motioning with my hand when she looks to me for confirmation, I make no attempt to turn to Kimber when they both begin their exit from the kitchen. My eyes following them long after they've disappeared out of sight.

All the while my mind swimming.

What could Dawson possibly want to talk to Matthias about?

Better yet, what could she possibly need from him that I can't give her?

It doesn't matter how long I've worked around this man, spent hours locked in the same space as him, he's just as intimidating as he was the first time we met.

"I told you the last time you were here, Dawson. I don't bite."

Releasing an awkward little chuckle to match the laughter Matthias begins with, I nod and make myself comfortable on the sofa.

"Yeah, I got it. You're a real softie. I can tell by the way you hover."

"Some would say I'm protective." He admits.

"And some would say it's borderline scary. So, you'll excuse me if, for the next few minutes, I stumble over my words."

Moving around the small decorative table resting in front of the sofa, he makes his way over to the other end and like me, makes himself comfortable.

"We're not at work, so you've got even less to fear, but okay. What is it you wanted to talk to me about that you couldn't say in front of your man?"

My man.

It's got an interesting ring to it, though I don't exactly enjoy putting a label on what we have. Especially a possessive one. He's his own man.

"It's about the show next week. I know what we're supposed to go out there and do, and I've got no issues with any of it, especially since I'm still learning the ropes. I just thought we could do something a little...extra."

"I'm listening...." He says and there's no denying his interest is peaked.

Maybe I can be good at this after all.

"I know you and Gavin aren't supposed to go at each other, Bryan wanting to keep building it until the final match, but I was thinking if you were interested, I could be the one putting hands on you."

Rubbing the bridge of his nose, forehead pulled tight, he sighs.

"Putting hands on me how?"

Once he asks the question, I can see why he looks so uncomfortable. With all the research I've attempted to do since Bryan asked me to work with Gavin, all the deep dives into what other valets have done before me, both in CPW and in the bigger promotions, I know what he's thinking.

I also know it's going to be nothing like he assumes. I would never dream of doing what has been done to some of the other guys in the past. I won't insert myself into a real-life relationship.

"I was thinking maybe we could work out a move, a cheap shot I could do to take you down with. Nothing too intricate, because I mean, I'm not your opponent, and you're supposed to be one hundred percent for the match. Just something small that'll get the crowd riled enough to hate me and make you sympathetic. Well, more so."

Matthias is very over with the crowd. He has been for a long time to hear other people tell it. There's something about the realness of the man, both in his clothing choices and attitude in and out of the ring which has people flocking to him.

In a business born of fiction and make-believe, at least when it first began, he's as real as it gets. It speaks to people.

My idea is just building on the perception.

"You want to be the one to lay hands on me so your boy isn't seen breaking rules?"

"Ideally."

"Are you sure you've never worked for a wrestling promotion before?"

"No," I shake my head laughing. "I can honestly say I've never thought of it before now. Why are you asking?"

Leaning back on the sofa and slapping his hands on his legs, rubbing them up and down the fabric, he smiles.

"Honestly, I don't know how much you've learned about CPW as a promotion, and considering what you were doing before you landed here, I'm sure you wouldn't even know the half of it given the lack of superstars who appeared on your news show."

"You being the one and only," I add and he laughs.

"Yeah, and I didn't even want it. What I'm trying to say is, you would have worked well with Smith. Hell, I think if Bryan can get his head past making you a ring performer, you could easily fit in elsewhere."

He's getting all of that from my one little off the cuff idea? What?

"Writing and booking. When this whole thing with Gavin runs its course," Turning to me, his eyes serious, he stares me down as he continues. "And it will run its course, Daws, it always does...I'd talk to your cousin and Bryan. I think you'd be a good fit there. I've worked with a lot of people over the years, and never once have I had someone who wasn't an opponent, come to me and give me ideas to make a spot better."

"Really?" I'm in complete disbelief. With as open as the rest of the place seems to be to ideas, it seems odd that Matthias has never experienced it.

"Yeah. To get back to your idea, though. I'm in. Honestly, if you want crowd reaction on you, negatively speaking, there's only one thing you can do."

There's a second after I've secured his participation where my stomach bottoms out thinking of Gavin, but shaking it off, not wanting to make light of the moment I'm presented with, I ignore it.

Gavin will understand.

"What should I do?"

"The biggest cheap shot of them all. What every man loathes, but what every guy in the locker room has had to face at one time or another. Dawson, you're going to have to hit me with a crotch shot from behind."

Oh my.

I grew up with sisters, and we were sheltered. It doesn't mean I don't know what damage a move like what Matthias just mentioned can do to a guy, though. Sure, I've seen matches where it's happened since I joined HFWA, but never in my wildest dreams did I ever think I'd have a man telling me to do it to him willingly.

Can I really go through with this?

Pulled away from my thoughts by the sounds of Matthias's deep laughter, I blush and he grins.

"It's going to hurt like a bitch regardless, but I can prepare myself for it. I can protect the boys if that's what you're worried about."

In what I'm sure is an unintentional move, he looks down towards his groin and I groan. Of all the conversations I've had, this one takes the cake. The last thing I ever imagined speaking on being Matthias Kemper's package.

"Yeah, um...call them something other than your boys, and you've got a deal."

After another round of raucous laughter, he leans forward and stands from the sofa, with me quick on his heels. Meeting his outstretched hand with my own after we make our way around the little table.

"Dawson," he says as I go to slip my hand out of his. "There's one more thing I'm going to need for you to do for me."

He's agreed to let me crack him in his crown jewels. Pretty sure I'll give him almost anything he wants after that.

"Sure."

"You can't, under any circumstances, tell anyone. Not Bryan, not Reese. No one."

"Of course. I figured as much."

"Dawson, if you want this to work, you can't tell Gavin either."

I had a feeling when he said anyone, he meant Gavin, but I'll be damned if it doesn't sting when he puts an actual voice to it.

So far in our relationship, we've never lied to each other. I'm not sure how to feel about taking something I'm so incredibly proud of and ruining it.

In agreeing to Matthias's rules, could I be spelling the beginning of the end?

Gavin

"Gavin and Dawson, sitting in a tree—"

"If you finish that song, I'm revoking your pie privileges," I say, meeting her grin with a hard roll of my eyes. One I feel straight in the back of my skull from the sheer nonsense she's spewing.

"Okay, fine," Kimber says, slipping another bite of pie into her mouth and chewing. "How about this, then. You're in looooove with her."

I've always wondered why eye rolling isn't an Olympic sport. With the sheer amount of times I've done it in the kitchen today alone, ignoring the last ten years of constant rolls this business has given me, by now I would have to be the champ.

"I saw it earlier, Gavin, so don't even try to deny it. You're so head over heels for her it's almost sickening."

"Says the woman who goes around bragging about Matthias's growling."

"One time, Gav."

"Yeah," I grunt. "One time too many."

Forking up another bite of pie and filling my mouth with it, we both go silent with only the sounds of our chewing and occasional moans from Kimber to fill the time. A moment of silence I enjoy but she quickly breaks when she swallows before I do.

"I'm taking your attitude to mean you haven't told her yet."

"There's nothing to tell."

"Liar." Sticking her tongue out, she snakes it back in and smiles. "You're still the worst liar I know, Fortune."

Everything I felt earlier, it's still there. If I'm going to be getting into this with anyone, it's going to be Dawson. Not Kimber. Even knowing that for the longest time I thought it was this woman I loved, and seeing the difference now, there's no way I can let her be the first one to know.

It feels wrong.

"What the hell could they possibly have to talk about that could be taking this long?"

"Knowing Matthias," Kimber laughs. "He's probably listing all the reasons why she should run for the hills."

Shifting so fast, I almost take her head off with my arm, I glare at her.

"You're joking, right?"

"Yes, Gavin! Jesus. Settle down, lover boy. I'm sure it's just about work like Dawson said."

When I make no effort to settle, instead, letting my nervousness show as my leg begins shaking and tapping against the linoleum floor, she reaches out and rests her arm on mine.

"Trust her, Gavin."

"Easy for you to say."

"No, it's not. You were there when everything happened with Matthias. You saw how hard it was. Nothing about any of this is easy. I just had to learn to trust him, the same way I'm telling you to trust her now."

"I don't know what to do with all of this..." I stop, wanting to say more but not sure how to explain it. How do I make a previous object of my affection understand how new to me all of this is? "All of this, Kimber, it's new."

"I know. I'm also willing to bet it's pretty damn scary too. It was when I realized how I felt with Matty. I questioned everything about it. It used to eat me alive."

Maybe she does get it. I mean, she's right when she says I was there for everything that went on with them, both in CPW and since we arrived here. I saw what their feelings did to both of them. If there's anyone who might get a little of what I'm feeling, it's Kimber.

Kemper too.

"How did you sort it all out?"

"I stopped trying to run from it. Deny it. I had to trust myself. Trust in him. It's something we both still struggle with, and we've been together for a while now. Maybe we will always struggle with it, but instead of doing it apart, we're working together as a team. People don't give tag teams enough credit. They're the best."

Jokes about our business and about tag teams aside, it's sound advice she's giving me.

The advice I'm determined to take when Matthias and Dawson enter the room and she's rounding the table quickly, finding her way to my lap. Pressing her forehead to mine and smiling brightly.

"You miss me?"

"Always." I easily admit, returning her smile. Following Kimber's advice, I swallow down the fear and just enjoy the fact that it's my arms she's in. "Did you work everything out with Matthias?"

"Mmhmm." She hums but doesn't give more.

"You gonna tell me what it was about?"

"Nope." Pressing her lips to my nose, she laughs softly and instead of pressing her, I do her one better. Placing my lips to hers, I capture the words she's now speaking. "You'll see soon enough."

Silencing her altogether until a few minutes later at the sound of two clearing throats, we're brought back out of our little bubble.

"Looks like we've overstayed our welcome," Dawson whispers against my lips and I nod.

"Come home with me?"

Her final words all the proof I need that Kimber's words from before were true.

"Always."

Chapter Twenty-Four

Dawson

Okay, girl. Time to wrangle in those butterflies.

As Gavin's music hits, we let the sound overtake the auditorium, both of us in tandem moving toward the curtain and bouncing on our heels for another beat, then two, before we step through. Gavin at the ready, with a microphone in hand, ready to interrupt Matthias.

Making our way down the ramp, stopping at about halfway, Gavin brings a hand up in the air at the same time as he leans in to speak into the mic. All the while, having me, in the getup from the photoshoot, cellphone in hand, taking snaps.

"Cut my music and shut the hell up!"

His unabashed cockiness only serving to make the crowd more raucous, we continue our walk together, as Gavin continues to talk. Only this time, his words are directed solely at the man in the middle of the ring.

"Months ago, you screwed the HFWA Universe out of the chance at a real champion. Saint Kemper, he took what didn't belong to him, and what he didn't deserve!" Eyes roaming the crowd as we find ourselves just outside of the ring, Gavin turns to me and smirks when I nod in agreement, the small action setting the crowd off again.

A chorus of angry outbursts surround us, their reactions making it both hard to speak above, but also for me, hard to understand.

How a tight nod could get a rise out of these people, I'll never know.

"In two weeks at *Engage*, I'm putting an end to this, and bringing that," he pauses and points at the belt over Matthias's shoulder. "back where it belongs."

Separating and taking a flanking position, despite my strict rules not to be involved in the actual in-ring competition, Gavin walks up to the steps on one side, while I make my way around and do the same with the other.

Matthias's attention now being split down the middle and having to decide quickly which one of us he's to keep his eyes on. Which one of us is less likely to hit him with a cheap shot. A decision made without Bryan's approval before we'd come out and only Matthias and myself are aware of.

Poor Gavin. Even he's about to be in for a treat.

Maybe even a riot if the rise from this crowd is any indication.

Walking along the apron until I'm standing directly in the middle, I watch as Gavin slides through the ropes, effectively ending Matthias's eyes on me as he fully focuses on his opponent.

Staring him down, despite the rule from earlier stating neither of these guys can get physical with the other. A rule no one is aware doesn't apply to me.

As Matthias takes a step forward, his jaw ticking as he turns and greets Gavin's smile, I take my chance. Sliding through the middle rope just as Gavin begins speaking again.

"You see, Kemper, it was never supposed to be this way. You were always just a placeholder. For the title *and* for this business."

Fists clenching at his sides, he steps toward Gavin, spitting distance now between them. And much like he's done in previous matches I've watched; he doesn't back down. His stance only giving Gavin one option.

To respond in kind.

"I mean, let's be honest. It's why you were never handed the brass ring in CPW. Why no matter what you did, however many main events you were a part of, you never won the big one. It's because we all knew you weren't good enough to hold my jock."

3…2…1

It's time.

Just as Matthias reacts, his fist about to connect with Gavin's face, I'm hitting first.

Doing just as Matthias and I planned and coming up from behind, landing a cheap shot in between the man's legs, as hard as I can muster. A move Matthias only serves to sell to the crowd as his hands find their way to his crotch and he's falling down to one knee. Breathing heavy until he finally allows himself to fall all the way to the mat into a fetal position.

Even with having gotten the move off, and knowing it didn't cause nearly the amount of pain Matthias is now displaying, I'm shocked at just how well he makes the crowd believe in what I did. The moans escaping, magnified by the mini microphone clipped to his shirt, only serving to rile them more.

Gavin's eyes when I finally look up and meet them, surprised for about a millisecond before he snaps back into character and grins manically. Catching me when after jumping over the huddled mess of Matthias on the mat, I dive straight into his arms.

Our lips meeting in the second of events unplanned tonight.

"You're going to pay for your little secret later, princess." He threatens playfully once we part.

"I'm banking on it."

"Keep smirking like that and we're not going to make it to the locker room."

If I didn't know him the way I do, I'd think he had no clue what he was doing, but the awareness is there in his eyes. The blue of them flooded with a need he's never held back our entire time together. His eyes pools of desire I want nothing more than to drown in.

This plan is making us all winners.

Slipping back into his arms easily, he pulls us towards the ropes and sitting on them to allow me to slip through, he waits until I've jumped down before following suit. Our attention no longer on our competition but on heading back the way we planned, all the way to our prospective locker rooms.

Though, unbeknownst to the powers that be tonight, I won't be where I'm expected.

Tonight, I'm with him.

Gavin

"What part of me vetoing in-ring involvement did you not get?" I immediately turn and bombard her with when we've made our way into the locker room and away from the prying eyes backstage.

Swallowing down the urge to kiss the shit out of her as the side of her face flicks up, I resign myself to standing in place until she gives me an answer.

Her talk with Matthias now making perfect sense, but her silence on it, the reason she did it in the first place, still in question.

"I wasn't at risk."

"Says you."

"You can't be serious right now. God," she huffs, turning away and stalking further into the room. "You sound like Reese."

"Low blow, Daws."

"Just calling it as I see it."

There's no way it's going down like this. After everything she went through the last time she was in the ring, I shouldn't even have to spell out why this bothers me so much.

Sure, it was a simple crotch shot. Matthias the only one feeling the end result. It still doesn't change the fact that in doing it, she'd gone against her bosses *and* me.

"The only thing you should be seeing is concern."

"I can handle myself."

I'm well aware of her ability to hold her own. She's taken to this business faster than most, inserting herself in ways others before her didn't have the nerve to. It doesn't change the facts, though. She was hurt, and if she's out there with me, it's my job to protect her.

Something I can't do if she's going off half-cocked.

"I know," I admit, lowering my voice despite the overwhelming need to make her understand my position. "I'm not saying you can't."

Watching as before my eyes her body relaxes, the rigidness melting away at what I hope is what I've said, she turns and looks my way.

"Is this our first fight?" she asks.

"No," I respond easily. "It's just a guy standing in an empty locker room admitting he's a little too overprotective of his girl."

Gifting me with a smile which sets her whole face alight, she takes a step closer.

"His girl, huh?"

"Mmhmm," I murmur as she takes another step, then another, dangerously close now to breaking into my personal space. An act I silently beg her to do as my eyes follow her every move.

"You were that worried about me?"

"Always," I admit. "I always want you safe."

I feel the shift the exact second it happens. Words I give no thought to, spitting out as if they're just common knowledge, seem to awaken something within Dawson. Her softened expression more so before a storm seems to pass through and they flash.

Electrify.

And ending the minimal amount of distance in an almost desperate need to connect, bringing her into my embrace, a spark erupts between us, but instead of jolting us back, it only pushes us forward.

Closer.

As close as two people can get.

Gripping her tightly, I plant my lips on hers, her pleasurable groan awakening the beast inside of me, and before I know it, I'm taking her lips, sucking on them and biting down, driven deeper when her arms find their way around me and give back as good as I'm giving.

Fighting past the sharp reminder of where we are, even though we've got the room to ourselves, courtesy of the perks I've spent at least the last five years being slammed for, I focus my attention, mind, body, and soul on the woman in my arms now, more than ready to deliver on my promise from the ring earlier.

Making her pay in the most pleasurable way possible.

Dawson

"How did you manage to swing this?" I ask, motioning around the empty room at the exact moment he moves in, grinning mischievously. His nose brushing against my neck, his breath warm against my flesh delivering his answer.

"I'm Gavin, Fortune, baby. I get whatever—and I do mean whatever—I want."

Heated by his whispered tone, his response seemingly hitting every erogenous zone I have, I moan as I press deeper into him, his lips taking their rightful position as he takes his time, tasting me. Each kiss a caress. An intimacy that while needy, is in no rush.

"And what is it...Gavin Fortune wants?"

"Whatever you're willing to give." He huskily responds as my hands begin their descent from their place around his neck and down over his back. His muscles arched as his body presses itself into mine. His body trembling under my touch the lower my hands slip, along with his breath catching when my fingers trace over the outer lining of his wrestling tights.

"Dawson," he whispers almost reverently, his voice shaking as I slip my way inside, taking my time, prolonging his body's response as I hook and began to pull the material down. My own breath catching as my fingertips graze delicately over his ass, his hooded eyes meeting mine as his hands rest atop mine and join me in separating him from his gear.

His body, slick with sweat from our earlier altercation in the ring, glistening under the lights as he stands before me complete bared. My eyes hungry as they peruse every inch, admiring the care that has gone into his look. The definition in his chest, able to make even the most talented sculptor jealous.

A body, given the hungry look in his eye as he watches my perusal, that's all mine.

Hooking his own hands into my top, he lays waste to it as he slips it up and over my head to the floor, his desire spilling over as he cups my breasts in his hands, massaging them, eyes lost in mine as he does. My own body trembling when with the release of one hand, he slips it into the elastic of my own gear and yanks.

His body moving against mine, maintaining both the warmth and connection as he frees his other hand and moves deliciously slowly down my body, slipping them down my legs and then off.

The brush of his hands as they delicately run against my legs, up and down in repeated succession, until finally slipping his hand easily between them, brushing against my heat, has his name falling in a rush.

"Gavin...please."

Keeping his hands on my skin, he rises back to his feet, hands gripping my face as he crushes his lips down onto mine. Reading my mind when after releasing them from my face, his hands find their way to my back and he lifts me into his arms, my legs easily finding their way around him.

"Hang on tight, baby." He says, his voice deep and gravelly.

Moving with ease, my lips moving from his and making their way down over his cheek to his jaw until finally touching down on his neck, he crosses the room, his breathing laden, and into the showers.

His intent obvious, but also a first.

Of all the ways we've been together, it's never been this way. The knowledge of it, making me all the more eager, what he must notice as he releases a soft chuckle as he leans in once we've stopped and turned the knob, his lips finding their way to mine again hungrily as the water begins to cascade down over us.

Our hands exploring, guttural sounds building and then pouring out as we lose ourselves in the taste and feel. The both of us held captive to our most carnal instincts.

Desire reaching a fever pitch when after feeling the brush of his cock against my pulsing and needy heat for what feels like the hundredth time, I'm crying out and begging for him to end the torture.

Pushing me back against the wall, he licks a quick line across my bottom lip before biting down at the exact moment he lines himself up against my entrance, pushing forward at the exact second I cry out, capturing the sound as he owns my mouth again.

Makes love to me with it.

"Fuck," he curses, pausing as I tighten around him, sucking in a sharp breath as he closes his eyes. Losing himself in the feel, the sound—the absolute ecstasy—that always appears when we're together this way.

Our bodies made for one another, moving together, his mouth muffling my cries when with each move we make, he pushes deeper, burying himself inside me.

My need for release building like a slow-burning blaze, each movement, every kiss only stroking it, giving it life as he picks up in speed, my name falling from his lips through the now desperate panting, begging with me with every thrust to come.

To join him in going over the edge.

"Right there," I breathlessly whisper, guiding him in his movements, what will give him the high he's after. And as he heeds my words, his hips pushing harder, his cock driving deeper, I grip him tighter, the aching now a full-on burn as I feel myself on the edge. "Oh God, Gavin. Yes." My voice practically hissing out my affirmative response as my nails dig into the flesh of his back as wave after wave of pleasure floods its way through my body, his own release at the height of mine mere seconds later, the perfect crescendo.

A moment only made better when his lips pull from mine, his soul evident in his eyes as the darkened pools of blue stare deep into my own, and he whispers the words my heart has been desperate to hear.

"I love you, Dawson."

Held in position, wanting to stay this way forever, his last words repeating for as long as time allows us, I'm not at all prepared for the violation that comes once I've finally opened myself up and admitted my feelings in return.

No sooner does the declaration of love fall from my lips then our moment—our entire world—is turned upside down by the sound of footsteps. Followed up quickly with loud cursing, and then the very irate voice of the last person in the world I want to think about, much less deal with, after what we've just shared.

Reese.

Swallowing down the rush of panic, my eyes finding Gavin's as we stand as still as statues, his eyes closed and his forehead pulls tight as he releases a heavy breath. Pleasure depleted, and a deep seeded sense of foreboding coming to rest in its place.

"What the fuck is going on here?" Reese curses, and it's with his question, I stop trying to fight it. I finally accept the truth.

The secret's out.

We've been caught.

Chapter Twenty-Five

Dawson

"Daws," Gavin's voice, soft and soothing says, my mind recognizing his footfalls as he crosses the room. Resting his hands gently on my shoulders, I instinctively lean back. "I'm sorry."

He has nothing to apologize for. It was silly of both of us, more me than him, though, to assume we'd be able to hide in plain sight forever. The last week especially, we've tested every boundary imaginable. Our kiss in the ring before the ladder match easily springing to mind first, even with all of the others.

"We didn't do anything wrong, Gavin," I respond in kind. Soft. The opposite of what we both just experienced when Reese burst into the locker room, catching us in the shower. "It was a stupid rule, to begin with."

I mean every word. I know the firing squad I'm about to walk into when I summon up the courage to leave this room, and it changes nothing. I feel regret at having to hide my relationship with this man, but I don't regret what we were doing.

My mind is more consumed with whether or not the words he spoke so delicately as he made love to me in the shower, were real. Whether he meant them. My heart aching to ask but with the events of the last several minutes, my mind not built for the answer.

"We need to go out there and face the music, princess. Before we do, though, I need you to tell me the truth." Shifting my body and turning to face him, interested in knowing what he needs the truth about, he runs his fingers gently over my cheeks. "What you said...did you mean it?"

The very thought my mind is consumed with, it appears he is as well.

"Yes, Gavin. I meant it. Did you?"

His features softening, his lips curve up and he leans his forehead against mine.

"I've never meant anything more. I'm in love with you, Dawson."

Experiencing what I believe is the tenderest kiss we've ever shared, my heart opened wide and accepting of his declaration, I find security in his arms, in his embrace, as I admit the same.

"I love you too, Gavin. And nothing, not even the wrath of my cousin, is going to change it. No matter what happens when we walk out those doors together, I'm still in your corner. Always."

I can tell by his expression, when with one final righting of our clothes, we look to the door, prepared for battle, he thinks the worst of it is going to fall on him. I mean, it was evident in his need to apologize. What he needs to realize is, it's on both of us.

We both chose to go about things the way we did, given who my cousin is. So, what's happening now, we're going to own together as well. I meant what I said. Nothing is going to change my feelings on this man.

Especially not Reese.

Just because he can't accept who and what he is, preferring to hide behind the company, fake friendships, and alcohol, doesn't mean I have to do the same. We may be blood but that's where it ends.

"Ready to face the music, princess?"

"As I'll ever be, pretty boy."

Interlocking our fingers together, we start toward the door, Gavin stepping forward first and pulling it back, allowing me to walk through and then following after, easily finding my hand again and this time, holding on tighter.

In this together, indeed.

Focusing our attention ahead, we're met with the sunken eyes of Matthias, the nonchalance of Bryan, and finally, the tight, anger filled eyes of Reese. If any hope of distance lessening the impact was there before, the tick in his jaw says otherwise now.

"How long?" Reese demands, stepping out from behind the other two and moving toward us. A move Gavin scouts as he places his own body in front of mine, shielding me from whatever he believes Reese will do next.

"About a month and a half," I mumble. "Give or take."

Blowing out a hard breath and roughly dragging a hand through his hair, Reese's hard eyes find mine. "You've been fucking Fortune since before you two were slated to work together?" Practically seething, he turns to Gavin, leveling him with disgust and effectively cutting me off before I can even respond. "And you...the night I spoke to you in the parking lot, you were screwing her then?"

Gavin's face, which had been at peace in the locker room, is different now. It's easy to see what's taken place. He's flipped the switch he talked so openly to me about.

"Not at the exact moment, but yeah, boss. I did her that night."

Hearing the sharp intake of breath, it's only when every pair of eyes finds their way to me, I realize I did it.

The callous way he responds to Reese clearly bothering me more than I thought.

Shifting his weight, blocking me from the barrage of men across from us, his eyes softening and in their own way pleading, he leans in as close as he can, his words for only us and mouths to me.

I'm sorry.

I get it, I do. I'm aware of how easily Gavin can switch forms and become the asshole my cousin, hell, half the roster, believe him to be. It's a little harder reminding my heart of it, though.

"You see now, Dawson?" Reese interrupts our moment, when I accept Gavin's apology, narrowing his eyes. "This is exactly what I was talking about. You're just another notch to this guy!"

"Wrong again, boss." Gavin interrupts, another attempt at rectifying the damage his knee jerk response caused, and admitting just how wrong Reese's assumption is.

"He's right, Reese. You're wrong." Matthias chooses then to speak, stepping forward and pulling Reese's attention. "They're both telling the truth. I've known about it since it started."

"Great! That's just fucking great!" Reese yells now, his body moving in time with his eyes as he takes all of us in. It's only when he stops, and his entire focus is on his business partner he decides to speak again. "How long have you known?"

"I didn't."

"Bullshit!" Reese curses, taking a step toward Bryan. "You've been so gung-ho to put these two together. I'm willing to bet you knew before your boy did."

Ignoring how he belittles Matthias; Bryan shows no signs of weakness. If nothing else, his eyes seem to be growing harder the more my cousin says.

"Fine. I've known from the start. If your next question is if I care about them being together, though, the answer is no."

Say what?

Is Matthias aware of the situation, yes, but finding out Bryan knew this whole time? I don't know what to do with this information. How he reacted to us working together, the excitement there, why he wanted us to work together makes all the sense in the world now.

Our secret was out a long time ago.

"Excuse me?" Reese seethes.

"You heard me. They play well off each other, not to mention that since they've been together, there's been little to no drama in the back. Gavin's on the straight and narrow, no longer fucking anyone and everyone. And having Dawson around has brought life to the roster. Her willingness to get to know them, making them truly enjoy all the backstage shit we put them through."

If the situation were different, I'd want to reach out and hug Bryan for the things he's said, but given the high-octane emotions, and the waves of anger seemingly rolling off everyone here, it'll have to wait for another time.

Another place.

"I told you everyone loved you, princess." Gavin leans down, whispering.

I love you. I mouth, at the exact moment Reese turns his attention back to me, eyes as dark as night and cold as ice. Lips straight, body rigid. Not looking at me as the cousin he adores, but instead as something he's disgusted by. Someone he hates and wants nothing more than to be rid of.

Practically sneering, he takes a step toward us, Gavin and I, then another, until he's standing toe to toe with Gavin but his eyes are honed on me.

"Dawson Traymore, pack your shit and get out of here."

The final nail in the coffin coming when after both Matthias and Bryan call out in an attempt to understand what he's doing; he delivers the final blow.

"You're fired."

Gavin

Like fuck, I'm letting it end this way.

As she shifts, her hand beginning to slip from mine, I pull her into me, preventing her from doing it. From listening to her cousin.

"You're not going anywhere, baby."

Staring me down now, I just grin at him.

He can say or do whatever he wants to me, but if he believes for a second, I'm going to allow him to bully the cousin he claims to love, he's in for a rude awakening.

No one—least of all her family—is going to hurt my girl.

"Are you looking to join her, Fortune?"

"Reese—" Bryan starts, moving toward us in an obvious attempt to deescalate the situation.

"Nah, Bry. Let him do it. If he's willing to fire his own cousin for doing absolutely nothing wrong, I want to see the damage he'll do to me."

"You little pissant. Your ego is so huge, you truly believe you're a gift from God. When the reality is, there are a million guys out there even better than you, more than ready to step in and take your place."

It's not a lie, and despite what he believes is my ego being huge and unable to see it, I'm well aware of the number of guys nipping at my heels to take my spot. I just don't care. I've been a multiple time champion, traveled to places I could only dream of, doing things in my time in both companies, most never get the chance to. If this is where it all ends for me, so be it.

As long as, at the end of the day I'm with Dawson, I'm good.

His threats are as baseless and pointless as he is.

"Then do it, Reese. Pull rank and do what you've been dying to since I got here. Fire me."

Smirking, I purposely egg him on when I start tapping my feet, awaiting his response. What has both Bryan and Matthias both shaking their heads, and Dawson's eyes shooting between me and her cousin so fast, her head is surely about to spin off or combust.

Does he want a display of who has the bigger dick? He's picked the wrong guy.

No one controls Gavin Fortune, least of all a guy in a suit.

"You know what? I'm tired of this." Turning to Bryan, I scowl. "Is she fired?"

"Yes!" Reese yells, and Bryan remains silent, giving me more of an answer than anything he could have said ever would. He might not have backed down earlier, but it's clear he's doing it now. Falling in line with his business partner, but making it easy for me to push forward.

"Well, since she's done here, and we're in this together, I guess it means I'm done here too. But, before you go ahead and make a show of firing me, let me beat you to the punch. I quit."

"Are you insane?" Dawson hisses when after announcing my departure, I grab her and pull her into the locker room.

My adrenaline is still pumping, I'm hyped after what I've just done, and with the smile, I can feel deep into my features, I've no doubt what she's witnessing does indeed look insane.

It's not, though. It's freeing. Liberating.

A rush I haven't felt in years.

It feels amazing.

"Why'd you do it?" she asks, and focusing on the task of shoving my shit into my bag, I pause and turn just enough for her to catch it when I shrug.

How do I even begin to explain the many reasons what went down had to be the way things went?

It wasn't even about Dawson near the end. It was me not willing to take that guys shit anymore.

First, the meeting Dawson told me about that I wasn't even a part of. The way he'd done business, what would have kept me away from their promotion altogether given the almost underhanded way Smith ran CPW back in the day. The sly tactics better left to the generation before this one.

The rules he put in place aren't new, so those were fine, despite our need to break them and be together the way we were, but the enjoyment Reese got keeping Dawson and me apart, even when Bryan was doing everything he could to shove us together toward the end, is another reason I can't stick around.

Firing his cousin was just adding insult to what was already becoming a pretty big injury. Ever since she stepped into the building that first day, I realize immediately, I've had one foot out of it.

"Why'd I do what?" I asked despite having a feeling I know where this is going. "Are we talking the way I treated you when he asked if I fucked you or why I quit?"

"Both."

"It's been coming for a while." I give up once I'm done with my bag, answering the easier of the two questions. "I love you, Dawson. There's no excuse for what I said. I wanted to get a rise out of him, especially with the smug and pompous look he was sporting. Thinking he was so right. I meant what I said in the hall, though. I'm sorry. I didn't think it through."

Nodding in what I hope is acceptance or at the very least understanding of my boneheaded move, her gaze falls out around the room before finding me again and asking what's really on her mind.

"How has this been coming for a while?"

"Reese only wants to be hands-on when it's convenient for him, leaving pretty much everything else, especially the wrestling, to Bryan. It's worked well. Throwing himself in the way he did here, I had enough. I can't be a part of it."

"What about the belt?" She whispers, looking to me, her eyes tired and filled with sadness. "I know how much it means to you."

"If it's a choice between you and the godforsaken title, there's no question, princess."

Despite the heaviness of the moment, we've found ourselves in, I can tell what I've said has gotten to her. The miniscule smile rising only securing my position.

"This was your dream, though, Gavin. I don't want you to walk away because of me and later, resenting me for it."

I now understand what my old man meant when he used to tell me his wife—my mother—was too good for him. *Way above his paygrade*, I believe he'd called her. It's happening here with Dawson.

She's lost her job, and she's standing here more concerned with me.

"This," I circle my finger around, indicating the room, but also the building. "Was never my dream, Daws. Wrestling was. I can wrestle anywhere. Besides, sometimes dreams change."

"What do you mean?"

"Growing up, all I ever wanted for myself, before wrestling became my sole focus, was what my parents had. It was the first dream I ever remember wanting. You're the dream, Dawson. If I have you, wrestling is just a perk."

As if sensing the question buried deep in my statement, my insecurity at the moment apparent as I watch her, gauging her reactions and next moves, she makes her way into my arms with a content sigh escaping upon contact.

"You have me, Gavin. I just don't want you to regret it." She admits quietly, and lifting her head and meeting my eyes, she motions with a tilt of her head to the door. "You can go back out there. I know for a fact Matthias and Bryan would have your back. They won't let Reese fire you. You can still have both of your dreams."

She's telling me I can have it all. What I want in wrestling *and* what I need in her.

Dawson is the most selfless person I've ever met.

"You and me," I assure her. "is a regret I will never have. We're in this together, remember? Unless Reese is willing to hire you back and stop the tantrum he's having, I'm only going back out there by your side. Since I don't foresee that happening, we can leave."

"Are you sure?" she asks, her eyes probative.

"Absolutely. Now," I pause, doing a quick scan of the room. "Are you ready?"

"Never been more ready for anything in my life." She admits, securing her own bag around her shoulder, her hand finding and slipping into mine.

"Then let's go home."

And with those as our final words spoken, a door closing on a ten-year career and the promise of love previously unknown, we leave the room. Ignoring the eyes of all three men still standing around in the hall, not so much as offering them a scrap.

Leaving Reese, his stupid rules, and HFWA in the rear-view.

Where it belongs.

Chapter Twenty-Six

Dawson,

Roused from my position in bed by the shrill blast of the doorbell, I go to roll out of Gavin's arms in order to grab my robe, and I'm pulled back.

"Ignore it.' Gavin sleepily says, and for a split second, before it goes off again, signaling the impatience of the person on the other side, I almost do it.

It's not like we were expecting visitors.

After the events of the last twenty-four hours, we'd been blissfully alone.

As the bell hits again, I attempt to slip out and again am pulled back. "Mmm, Dawson," he moans, eyes still closed. "I've got a much better offer for you here."

"Don't I know it, pretty boy," I say as I finally shuffle out of his arms and over to my side of the bed. "It doesn't look like whoever is here got the memo, though."

Turning over with a groan, I move from the bed and sliding into my robe, tie it closed and sneak from the room. Disappointed at having to leave at all, but more than a little ready to end the incessant dinging of the bell.

Ringing off again as I finally make it down the stairs, I release a groan of my own, calling out. "Keep your pants on! I'm coming."

With a quick glance in the mirror by the door, content everything is covered, I open the door, coming face to face with the last person I expected to find on my doorstep. Though, taking him in before he realizes he no longer has to lay on the bell, he's decidedly more relaxed than the last time we saw one another.

"Dawson."

"Reese," I respond in kind, shivering from the chill present in my tone.

"Can I come in?"

My first instinct is to say no and shut the door in his face, heading back upstairs to the offer Gavin spelled out before I left the room. It's what he deserves after the stunt he pulled. I don't do it, though. Instead, moving out of the doorway and motioning him to come in.

The connection we share winning out over instinct.

"Thanks, Daws."

"What do you want, Reese? I thought you said everything the last time we spoke."

Releasing an exasperated sigh, he moves toward me and I immediately jump back. Familiarity only taking me so far when it comes to interacting with the man in my living room now.

"I repeat, what do you want?"

"What do you think I want, Daws? I came here so we can talk."

Beginning to pace back and forth, taking in what's he's said, I ask the only thing I can. The only question I want an answer to.

"Are you here to apologize for the way you acted?"

"No."

Well, alright then. Looks like I know how this is going to go.

Moving toward the door, I pause with my hand on the knob before flicking my eyes his way. "I wish I could say it was nice to see you, but if you're here to spout more of the same, I've got things to do."

"Dawson—"

"No, Reese. After the way you fired me in a hallway full of employees and friends, proceeded to then berate Matthias, and worse, your own business partner, the last thing I want to do is talk. We're done."

"Would you stop being so angry for five damn minutes and let me explain?"

"There's nothing to explain. You were crystal clear yesterday."

Ignoring my place at the door, he moves deeper into the room and throws himself down on the sofa like he belongs there. A small move only serving to anger me more.

Just who the hell does he think he is?

Family or not, he's beyond reproach with his actions. Not respecting my need for him to leave, and taking over like he used to do when we were kids.

"What part of *I don't want to talk to you* are you not getting? I snap, pulling his attention to me and the firm scowl clear across my face.

"You don't mean it."

God. What is it going to take for this guy to get a clue?

"You've told me to screw off a ton of times over the years, Daws, and not once have you ever meant it."

"When we were kids." I remind him, unable to find one instance in our adulthood where I've said those words. "Things have changed since then, Reese."

"Right."

Aware of the weight of Gavin's feet on the steps as the creak, I swallow the urge to run to him in order to keep him from walking in and seeing who is sitting nonchalantly on the sofa. Instead, resigning myself to the inevitable confrontation, I give up my own fight to get the man out and give him some rope and a little leeway.

The faster he says his piece, the faster he'll hang himself with the proverbial rope, and I can get back to enjoying the rest of my day.

"If you're not here to apologize for being an asshole, what else is there to explain?" I ask, going back to his earlier statement in an effort to end this quickly. Gavin clearing his throat as he finally hits the room, bringing both my attention and Reese's away from each other and on him.

"You should have ignored it." He states, rubbing at his eyes, and I can't help grinning. He has no idea how right he is. "What do you want, Harrison?"

"To talk to my cousin, Fortune. So, how about you fuck off and let me do it?"

Oh, hell no.

He doesn't get to come in here and talk down to yet another person I care about.

"You're the one who isn't wanted here, Reese, so how about you do what you just told Gavin to and get the fuck out."

The burn of the curse on my tongue threatens to weaken me. I've made a point of not being a spiteful and angry person, and here's Reese bringing it out of me, turning me into someone I don't even recognize.

"Aren't you two adorable? Congrats, Fortune. You've got my cousin wrapped so tightly around your finger, maybe even your dick, she's beginning to sound like you."

Driven by pure rage, I'm across the room in seconds, my hand connecting with Reese's face, the stinging sensation embraced as he jolts back from the assault. A fight I don't give up when moving in quickly, I slug him as hard as I can in the stomach.

The selfish prick is going to regret teaching me how to fight.

"Don't you dare come into *my home* and speak to the man I love that way."

Wiping a hand across his face, he gets back to his feet. This time, the anger from the hall the night before, back with a vengeance. His eyes flashing with the same fury as mine.

We're *definitely* family.

Standing my ground and stopping Gavin as he begins making his way to my side, I focus again on Reese.

"Unless the next set of words out of your mouth is an apology to Gavin, we're done here."

"You don't mean that, Dawson. If you'd stop and think about it, stop allowing yourself to be led around by the prick over there, you'd see the truth."

Oh, there's a lot of truths I'm seeing here this morning, but none of them are what he wants me to see. The only prick in the room is him.

"And what truth am I not seeing, hmm?"

"He's using you. When he's done, he'll trash you like he's done with every other woman who crossed his path."

More of the same. *Of course.* I shouldn't have expected more. It's all the same regurgitated crap I've been hearing since I started in HFWA.

All of these people thinking they know the man I'm involved with when in reality, all they know is what he spent years wanting them to see. Becoming what they expected him to. Never doing what I did and seeing what was underneath. Never giving him the chance to be anything else.

I'm so sick of it.

"You're the only one trashing things, Reese." I fume, not even attempting to hide my disdain anymore. "You've taken a relationship I treasured and spit on it. Spit on us."

It's not about Gavin anymore. It's just him and I. The relationship we had, just as I said. Something I treasured. Hell, the first night I met Gavin, he'd said it best.

"Seems like a pretty stand-up guy if he's looking out for his family."

Up until now, Gavin was right.

Those days are *clearly* over.

A fact Gavin must also come to the same conclusion about as he moves toward Reese, grabbing a hold of him and using whatever strength he's got built up this early and moving him to the door. Out of my line of sight.

"You've overstayed your welcome, Harrison. What I said the last time we saw each other, still stands. We're out. Both of us."

Pushing the door open, Gavin's final stand isn't spoken, but physical. Shoving my cousin hard in the back and not even blinking as the man stumbles and attempts to catch himself as he falls over the step, he slams the door behind him, huffing out a harsh breath before turning my way.

"I'm sorry, baby."

Huh? What could he possibly be sorry about?

He'd only done what I've been trying to do since I saw it was Reese on the other side of the door.

"For what?"

"You had it under control. I didn't need to get involved. I just, the second I saw your eyes misting, I couldn't let you deal with it anymore."

Oh. Crap. I thought I'd done a good job of not showing how affected I was. Guess not.

"It's okay, Gavin."

"No, Daws, it's not. This shouldn't be happening."

Now I know there's more he's getting at. He's looking at the situation we're in as a whole, and not just what's happening in the here and now. What after dealing with Reese, I'm not about to stand for.

"You're right. It shouldn't be happening this way. In a perfect world, Reese wouldn't be such a helicopter parent, and we could be out and open. It's not perfect, but there's also something else it isn't."

"And what's that?"

"Your fault."

Chapter Twenty-Seven

Gavin

"Thank you for meeting with me," Bryan says, shaking my hand after we've both entered the office.

"I wasn't going to. Dawson can be pretty persuasive, though."

"She's not with you?"

"Nah, man. Didn't want to risk running into that piece of shit cousin of hers."

I'll give it to the guy. He's not so much as flinching with the way I'm talking about his partner. Obviously, the guy I saw shades of in the hall a week ago is back. He's not even attempting to deny the claim I've made about Reese.

"Can't say after everything that went down, I blame her *or* you."

"Funny you should say that. I'm still wondering how it is you found out about us."

Shades of the way he'd been in the hall, the first time Reese confronted him, are present again now as he makes no move to try and shy away from what I'm asking. Taking it further when a second later, he's clearing his throat and giving me the answers I'm after.

"Matthias and I, we made a deal after the accident. He's a master at bottling things. His feelings, his thoughts, information. You name it, the man can hold onto it and let it eat him alive. I'm sure you can figure out how I found out."

Damn. I'll hand it to Kemper. I never thought he'd given us up, especially not with the little chat we had in the locker room about him holding things back from his best friend. He played me like a fiddle.

Only, where I expect to be angered by it, I'm not.

Despite the way everything went down, I'm glad we're out. The longer we had to hide, the worse it felt. Dawson should be exalted, not hidden away like some dirty little secret.

"Okay, well, tell me what this is all about, Bryan." I switch gears, making my way across the room and planting my butt in the chair across from him.

"What's it going to take to get you back?"

"As adorable as you are, you're not my type, bro. Sorry." I joke, and despite the serious stance he's trying to take here, he cracks a smile.

"Glad to hear it. Former man whores don't exactly do it for me either. No offense."

"None taken." I chuckle. "You know what it's going to take."

Sitting here in person rehashing what was already spoken about over the phone a couple of days after I walked out, isn't going to change a thing. He's aware of what needs to happen. I'm not settling for less.

"You really aren't afraid of us taking you to court?"

"Nope."

I'm not rich by any means, but I do live modestly. If I've got to go back to raw potatoes and ramen for a bit while I find my footing elsewhere, so be it. I'm not compromising what I believe in or my relationship with Dawson, for anything. Least of all this company.

"Reese won't agree to hire her back, and truthfully, given the contract she signed and her place within the company, there's cause for the dismissal. There's not much I can do there. You, on the other hand, you weren't let go."

"It's a stupid rule, Bry. You know it. The only reason it stands is that you didn't get her to sign a separate contract for her role in the ring. If you had gotten her signature then, it would have made the previous one null and void, and we wouldn't be having this conversation. None of it matters, though. All I'm wondering is if this was his plan the entire time."

"What?"

"If he planned from the start to catch her somehow and fire her. Using what he walked in on, what you all walked in on, as an easy out in order to do it."

Shaking his head vehemently, not willing or not wanting to believe there could be validity in what I'm saying, he continues to have his partners back.

"Reese is a hot head, and on occasion can be a bit of a tool but he wouldn't pull a stunt like this. Not with anyone here, least of all his family."

"She was fired on a stupid technicality, Bryan. So, unless you make him come around and bring her back in, I think we're done here. I won't come back without her."

Interrupted by the shake of the office door as it opens, we both turn at the same time and come face to face with the very person we'd been discussing.

Well, the less pretty one.

Reese, face flushed, as though he'd run a marathon before coming here, steps into the office and stalks toward us. His eyes steeling toward me the closer he gets.

"Give me the room," he demands, eyes locked on Bryan's and after a few seconds where I assume Bryan wants to fight back, he heaves a heavy breath before standing and giving the man what he's after.

"Not for nothing, but if he leaves, I'm going too. I've got nothing to say to you."

Flicking his attention to me, his face hardens.

"This meeting never should have taken place without me."

If he thinks he's getting away with a flippant remark like that, he's got another thing coming. Considering the shitty meeting he'd held without Bryan's appearance or even mine, he's got no leg to stand on here.

"Oh, you mean like the meeting you had with half the roster before Dawson even got here?"

"Excuse me?" Bryan questions, his gaze flicking rapidly between us.

"Of course! You weren't there, so naturally, you don't know anything about it. But the big man here, he knows. Go on, Harrison. Explain to your partner here why you held a meeting warning the roster off of your cousin and didn't make him a part of it."

Growling under his breath, he turns to Bryan but offers no explanations. No denials or excuses either. They're just locked in a staring contest.

"I was trying to prevent assholes like you from getting your claws into her. Clearly, I had reason to do what I did with the spell you've put on Dawson."

"Reese—" Bryan starts and Reese interrupts.

"It was none of your concern, Bry."

"Like hell, it wasn't."

There's clearly something taking place between both of these men as their stand-off continues, their attention pulled entirely off me like it's just the two of them in the room. Too bad I could care less. What I told Bryan is the truth, and not even Reese inserting himself is going to change it.

Either Dawson is rehired or I'm staying away.

Pulled away again by another knock at the door, this time the interruption coming in the form of River and Ross, they shelve their obvious issues and Bryan makes his way over to them, eventually exiting the trailer altogether, leaving Reese and me alone.

Great.

"Let me guess," Reese starts, taking Bryan's vacant seat in the chair across the desk from me. "My business partner got you in here to try valiantly to get you back."

Grunting out my response, he continues. "He is the nicer of the two of us. Me on the other hand, I could give two shits about you. I do care about this business we've created, though, and as such, I feel I need to remind you that you're under contract. And I won't hesitate to sue your ass."

"Bryan already said as much. Like I told him, I don't care. I'm not afraid of you. I'll keep you so tied up in court you'll go out of business before it's over."

There aren't too many things in my life I'm willing to bring out the Fortune level of cockiness for, but this is definitely one of them. He may be right in terms of having me locked into a contract, but the fear he's hoping to instill isn't happening.

"What if I said you wouldn't be the one going to court?"

After the view I'd gotten a week ago at Dawson's, I know he's a callous prick but what he's insinuating is a whole new level.

Threatening me with the person I love, it's a weakness I didn't expect to be exploited. Especially given their relationship. Apparently, I'd given him the credit he doesn't deserve.

"You wouldn't dare."

Smirking slyly, his sickening grin rises and expands as he takes his stand.

If he means what he's saying, there's no way I can fight it. I will not let Dawson be dragged through the mud, especially not by this piece of crap.

"Try me, Fortune. I told you, Bryan's the nice one. I'm the hardass. The Enforcer. I've spent the morning speaking with our counsel, and if I do in fact want to go after Dawson for the breach of contract, even with her being fired for said violation, I have the right. You may want to bankrupt me, but are you prepared for me to do the same to her?"

Sick bastard. He damn well knows my response.

Seconds turn into minutes, and the comeback I'm looking for—my earlier confidence— is no longer there. He's got me between a rock and a hard place, and he knows it. If only he would see it for what it means, instead of the way his sick mind has twisted it, maybe we wouldn't have to let it go this far.

The weakness he's found in me is because my feelings for his cousin are genuine.

"I've spent a lot of time with your cousin, Reese. I know how close the two of you were growing up. How much love and admiration she has for you when you're not riding her ass like a second father. The woman absolutely adores you. Loves you without question. If you even feel half of those same feelings for her, you won't put her through this."

My valiant speech seems to fall on deaf ears as he just continues to stare through me.

How did I not see this before? How can their feelings be so different from each other?

It's because Dawson's heart is pure, dumbass.

"I care a great deal for my cousin. One doesn't have anything to do with the other. I will not show favoritism. Not in business, and not in life. If I show one ounce of weakness, the boys here wouldn't hesitate to exploit it. Something you should have realized sooner. It's a shame, but if I have to take a stand against Dawson in order to get you to toe the line, so be it."

I want to fight this, argue it, and make him crumble under the weight of my dominance but I can't. When it comes to Dawson and keeping her safe, even from something like this, I'm always going to back down.

Become the little bitch he's making me out to be.

"Think about what you're saying. You know what this is going to do to her."

"I have thought about it, Fortune. So, you either come back to work and proceed as planned or the next time we'll be seeing each other will be when I take your newest conquest to court." Leaning across the table, arms folded in front of him, the twinkle in his eyes as he smiles making me sick to my stomach, he delivers his final blow. "What's it going to be, Fortune? You or her?"

Swallowing my pride, knowing the satisfaction he's going to get with what he's holding over me, I give him the answer he's after, while also making myself a solemn promise not to make it easy on either of them once I'm back.

If he wants to use Dawson against me, he'll get his way, but I'm going to make him rue the day he ever stepped into his office and did it.

Reese wants a fight, well, he better be ready. The man coming back isn't the same one who left.

And this Gavin, he fights to win.

"I'm coming back."

"Honey, I received a rather distressing call from Reese earlier. I'm concerned. Is there something going on I should know about?"

I should have seen this coming. If there's anyone closer to my parents than I am, it's Reese. He was a staple for years at Sunday dinners with the family. Seems like his style to go ahead and bring this to my parents in an effort to sway me to his side.

"Everything's fine, Mom. You know the way Reese is."

"Oh, I do, sweetheart. I also know that sometimes when it comes to matters of the heart, one can be blinded and not see the reality of the situation. With everything Reese told your father and me, I'm concerned it's what's happening here."

It's worse than I thought. Reese clearly dumping everything at my parent's doorstep.

It's taken me days to process what happened with him. To attempt separating the boy I grew up idolizing, with the cold and callous businessman he's become. Even having spent time with him in our adult years, I always just saw the boy I loved. I'm still struggling with separating the two.

Being haunted for the last three nights of dreams of us as kids. His protective nature over me, what reached a fever pitch in junior high, causing me to wake up drenched in sweat and haunted.

Though, it's not those memories that are the worst.

It's the times he made me feel better when we were little.

The way he didn't laugh at me when after running off from my parents after a fight, I'd taken to the empty field behind our house and cried because I'd crunched leaves in my haste to get away.

Yes, I know. It's pathetic, crying over a leaf being crunched, but hey, that was me.

I was concerned about everything in the world, from people to animals, and hell, even nature.

Reese, though, he'd just pulled me into his arms and soothed me. Telling me the trees wouldn't hate me because I had broken one of their own.

The absolute assault of memories like this since he fired me, also serving to make me question everything. The worst is the way I look at Gavin.

I'm ashamed to admit, I've given a lot of thought to whether or not he was right in all of this. If I am as blinded and wrapped up in a spell, the way he assumes. My mind latching onto the idea with how I reacted to Gavin's own comment in the hall.

His ability to get a rise out of someone coming at my own expense.

How easily he'd switched gears back to the man they all knew him to be, and less of the man I had gotten to know, forcing me to question things in exactly the way I'm sure Reese wants.

Also, what my mother's concern is doing now.

I'm known for being level-headed. I don't allow myself to be fooled by delusions of grandeur or worse, people who have devious motives. With how Gavin and I met, to the pull we couldn't deny and kept us close to one another, to where we stand now, together, I don't want to believe what I'm experiencing is what my mother referred to as me being blinded by love.

But could it be?

No, Dawson. You can't think this way. You can't allow him to win.

Except, as I placate my mother and end the call, throwing my body down onto the sofa and shutting my eyes, there's no denying with all these doubts now, I'm doing exactly that.

Gavin isn't here, so I should be experiencing at least a little separation, but between my mothers' call and my own mind, it's clear there's more to it.

The separation I'm feeling is like I'm trapped in a game of tug of war. I can feel my body being physically and emotionally yanked away from the man I have admitted to loving, in favor of being imprisoned with the man who to his own credit, has only ever wanted to protect me.

Roles have been reversed in a matter of days.

Where Gavin had started out as the character, and over time had grown into a man—the man—he was always destined to be. The version of Gavin I've wanted nothing more than for the entire world to see the same way I do. And as he's done it, I've shifted, until the Dawson I was when I entered into this entire arrangement with HFWA, has whittled away to nothing, and what's left is the character I've become after losing the only person who before Gavin, truly mattered to me.

I play my part to perfection when Gavin is here or when like yesterday, we were together at his place. We kiss, we cuddle, we converse, and in the end, we always end up in bed together. Making love, screwing, fucking. In those quieter moments, though, when his eyes aren't on me when I'm alone with my thoughts and my actions over the last several months, the façade is broken, and I'm just me.

The Dawson of old exists but she's lost.

I'm struggling, even now, to fight the doubts, to fight against what deep down I know to be true. Hell, to fight against my cousin, and it's just not working.

The only truth I see is, I'm the one at fault for all of this.

What Gavin is enduring, the pain I've caused Reese, worse, what I've turned him into, it's all on me. I put all of this in motion, and it's up to me to make it right.

With my career in HFWA done, there's only one thing left to do.

I've got to separate myself from Gavin.

Chapter Twenty-Eight

Gavin

I don't know how I pulled it off but this week alone, it's as though I'm still in CPW. Back in the good old days of riding the high of being a champion without having the actual belt around my waist.

After blowing Bryan off the first ten times he questioned me about how Reese coerced me into coming back, not wanting the underhanded tactics to come out for fear of reprisal against Dawson, I'm back where I was with Smith, making sure in my hunt for the title against Kemper, I'm given the world.

Only the best rental cars for events leading up to the first ever pay per view, *Engage*, have been given to me. High-end suits, watches, and other miscellaneous items, all willingly strapped around my wrist, my body, or other appendages, all in the name of feeding the fight moving forward.

Mid-card matches I'm putting on in the days leading into the fight, all of my own choosing with the end results I want. Even the altercations in the middle of the ring I've had with Kemper, all of my own design.

It's as though the Gavin Fortune of old never left.

The way I used to brag of running CPW back in the day, I can now safely say, I'm doing in HFWA. Making Reese pay exactly the way I wanted when I agreed to come back in the first place.

In the pocket.

Since clearly, family ties mean nothing to the man.

What should have me on cloud nine, though, has me wilting away, like a flower that's been plucked and left without water or a sustainable food source to stay alive. The weight of the secret

I'm keeping from Bryan, the locker room, and Dawson, slowly eating away at what's left of my self-esteem and confidence.

In protecting her, I'm ultimately wrecking the part of me I can still remotely stand.

And it's not just me suffering. It's her too. I can see it in her eyes every night when I make my way home and we fall into bed together. We exist in any way together. The deadness there, like there's a part of her that even though she has stated time and again she isn't bothered by or missing, I can see she is.

The relationship she has with her cousin is one of the strongest ones in her life. Her lack of knowledge in his true motivations still causing a loss.

She's not the same Dawson she was when we met. She's not even the same Dawson I fell in love with. Every day we're together, I can see I'm losing her more. I just don't have the first clue how to stop her from pulling away. Admitting what I'm doing and why I'm afraid will make things worse.

Sure, she'll end up realizing what a prick her cousin is, on an even grander scale, but it'll only make the loss she's suffering, not having him in her life, harder to handle.

The only thing I'm thankful for, being her not here to witness the transformation taking place. This side of me, the one I told her I secretly hated but was great at projecting, not something I want the love of my life having to witness.

If the loss of Reese doesn't make me lose her, witnessing this version of me would.

"The imported water you asked for is in your locker room." the voice of the spineless boss says, breaking me free from my thoughts.

"Good. I've been waiting so long; I almost tried the swill you all drink."

It's there, right on the edge, the urge to throw up, but I just swallow it down the way I have been for the week since I've been back. The show now only a few days away, and my act becoming even more pronounced in the days since I put it in motion.

The end is in sight.

Turning my attention to the scoff I hear about a foot away; I take in Matthias. The empty look in his eyes reminding me of the woman I left this morning scouring over job opportunities in the paper.

The loss of Dawson clearly affecting not only me but him too.

"Catering has also been given your suggestions, so you can expect them to be ready after your match tonight." Bryan rattles on, unaware of where my attention lies. Matthias's fidgeting on his feet holding me captive. His need to speak with me obvious.

"Glad to hear it. Hey, Kemper," I say, taking Bryan's focus and putting it on his buddy. "You mind if we go over a few things I want to add to the fight on Sunday??"

Grunting out an affirmative reply, thankfully Bryan gets the hint and heads off, giving us space.

"Are you ever going to explain what the hell is going on with you?" He huffs once his friend is out of earshot.

"You know what's going on."

"Right. You're acting like a petulant child because your girlfriend was fired. Got it. Except, Gavin, we both know there's more to it."

Yeah, of course, there's more, but given how fast Matthias took our relationship to Bryan after our little chat at his place, he's the last person I want to unload on.

"It's got nothing to do with Dawson, Kemper. I'm just acting like the douchebag everyone expects."

"And no one wants." He chimes in, finishing the sentiment, causing me to shake my head vehemently in denial.

"Come on, man. You've got to admit, for the last few weeks, no one knew what the hell to do with me. They want this version because it's predictable. Easy."

"Right," he laughs uncomfortably. "And we all know how Gavin Fortune loves making everyone's life easier." When he shakes his head pathetically, the weight of the secret I'm holding becomes even heavier. And instead of keeping to my word and staying silent, the next time I open my mouth, it all comes tumbling out.

"They threatened Dawson, okay? When I wouldn't come back, Reese used her against me. I figured if he was going to grab me by the balls and violate me, it was going to be on my terms. So, enter prick, Gavin. It's the only way I can come back and not want to strangle the piece of shit."

"Wait, Reese and Bryan did what?"

"Not Bryan, Kemper. He doesn't have a clue. He thinks I'm back because Reese made me an offer I couldn't refuse. Hence all of the useless stuff I've been asking for. No one knows, but Reese, me, and well, now you."

"He threatened to do what with Dawson?" Matthias fires back and I fill him in just as fast, feeling lighter having admitted the truth. "You're doing all of this to protect her?"

"Thought it was obvious. Why else would I be doing this?"

"You're in love with her." He states, and I merely nod. It's another thing I would assume would be obvious at this point. "And Kimber?"

Unable to stop it, I laugh. Hard. "Stand down, bulldog. She's my best friend."

Obviously, content with my answer, he does a quick scan of the area around us before moving in closer, his next words to me barely able to be heard even with our proximity.

"All of these stupid things you're asking for, the money you're making Reese put out, how do you feel about kicking it up a notch? Because if you're game, I think I've got a solution for both of your issues."

"What issues are those?"

"Your love for your girl, and your absolute piss poor attitude with her not here anymore."

Can't argue with those. They *are* my issues.

"Add in the need to protect her," he continues. "And well, this could be a win for everyone. Me included."

"What's the plan?"

At this point, if it solves any of the things Kemper mentioned, I'm willing to agree without hearing it. With the way it feels not having her here, the emptiness I'm experiencing since she's been gone, and the way I feel like half a man even when we're together, I'd sell my soul at this point if it would change things.

"Bryan runs the behind the scenes stuff in regards to the show, so how about me and you have a meeting with him. Give him an offer he can't refuse."

"And the offer would be?"

"We bring Dawson back for *Engage*. At some point during the match, have her come out and be in your corner. The crowd won't expect it given her absence in the last couple of weeks, I don't expect it for the same reasons, and well, neither will you."

I've got to hand it to the guy. If I didn't know all of his reasons for wanting to take a step back from the business, I'd question why HFWA is letting him walk away. His expertise at running with a story is still one of the best I've ever seen. Then and now.

Feeling the weight on my chest lifting, there's no stopping the lift to my face.

This idea of Matthias's...it's genius.

"You really think we can sell him on it?"

Not even bothering to hold himself back, he releases a boisterous laugh before slapping me on the back. "Bryan's the biggest Dawson and Gavin fanboy there is. I guarantee you he's going to be down with this idea." Leaning closer, his voice lowers as he speaks again. "But if we do this, there's one condition."

"Anything."

"By the end of the night, we're going to expose Reese to Dawson. When it's all said and done, you're leaving this place with your girl *and* the title around your waist. I won't settle for it going down any other way."

"Deal," I say, meeting his outstretched hand in the middle.

Time to make Reese Harrison pay.

It doesn't matter how much busy work I give myself; I can't stop the flow of emotion from spilling over. It's been weeks now and it never lets up.

From bawling over coffee and a bowl of cereal to breaking down and curling into a ball watching something trivial on television, my open wounds are constantly being exposed.

Appearing like a hot poker to the skin, it leaves me spent every time a new wave crashes through.

Like now, for instance.

I summon up the strength to ask Gavin to come over, promising to cook him dinner...my lame attempt at trying to shake myself free of the constriction around my heart, in order to get us back on track, and again, the tears are falling like a river down over my cheeks, the feel of them as they hit my skin, like burns. Scalding me.

He'll be here any minute and I'm standing in the kitchen, frozen in place as I wait for the oven timer to go off, falling apart.

I keep going over everything in my head, trying to figure out when the exact moment it all went wrong took place, and the only thing I can come up with was the day Reese offered me the position and I stupidly agreed.

Selfishness on my part had given me the type of relationship I wanted but, in the end, cost me the most important relationship of my life.

Well, it had been until Gavin.

Grabbing onto the counter as I feel another wave of anguish as it threatens to take me off my feet, the doorbell rings. Turning in the direction of it but still unable to move, I cry out, praying he'll hear me and let himself in.

After a few minutes pass, I hear the click of the front door and lifting my eyes, I'm met with the very concern laden eyes of the man who not once in the last week, has let a moment go by without reminding me of his true feelings.

I know he's consciously aware I'm pulling away from him. Our lovemaking almost robotic in nature compared to the way things started, but where another man would have thrown his hands in the air and washed himself of the drama, he's consistently come back.

Every single time.

"Daws…" Crossing the room in the blink of an eye, he's pulling me away from the security of the counter and into his arms. His hands in my hair, his softly spoken words soothing the waves of emotion that even now are threatening to roll over.

"Gavin, I can't…" I attempt to admit, my voice giving out before I can even finish the sentence. "I can't keep doing this."

"I know. I can't keep watching you do this to yourself."

I'm sure he can't. He's been here all week watching the slow descent into madness taking place. If I could tell him to go, if I believed he would actually leave, I'd force his hand here. I'd say whatever it took for him to distance himself from me because he's safer this way.

My reaction to a spat with my cousin, way too over the top for anyone. Least of all the man in the business of making things of that nature sell.

"I don't understand why this hurts so much. Reese and I, we've fought before. We always butt heads because we're both so damn stubborn, but this is different. There's this hole in my heart. I can physically feel it, and nothing I do seems to cover the loss. It's just there, always bleeding."

I don't have to see his face; his body stiffening is enough of an indicator of his reaction to what I've admitted. He's trying, I know he is, but he'll never truly understand how someone like me, who he always says has a pure heart, can love someone like Reese.

"I'm going to make this right, Dawson. I swear to you." His vow touching a part of my heart that over the last week has been numbed to much of anything, but also a promise I know he won't be able to keep.

"How?" I ask.

"Maybe if he's forced to be around us enough, he'll see how much I care about you and let up on whatever Daddy complex he's got going on. As much as I'm not a fan of the guy these days, he's seen more of the way I was before than he has of the way we are together."

For a brief second, Gavin's words break through the haze. Reese has had no experience with this version of Gavin. He's been saving this part of himself for me, never really letting it out when it comes to what he does for a living. Maybe there is some truth to the idea that Reese would come around.

Except, much like Reese hasn't seen this side of Gavin, Gavin doesn't know my cousin either. Just his stubbornness alone means he'll never back down in his position. In his mind, he's always right.

Only, he's not. Not this time.

Letting the waves crash over me as Gavin's grip becomes tighter, I let it all out.

"You deserve...you deserve better than this, Gavin. You told me during one of the first times we were together, you like to travel light. You've spent years creating the version of yourself who doesn't have to carry around dead weight. It's the one part of your personality I never disputed because I loved how you kept yourself free from the drama you weren't a part of creating in the ring. This," I say, pulling back just enough to run my hand around us. "This isn't light."

"Daws, when it comes to you, I don't want light and breezy. I want the heavy load. Its what relationships are supposed to be about. When things are heavy, we carry the load together."

It's no wonder I fell in love with him. He's been saying things like this our entire relationship. Capturing my heart so epically, I don't think if we weren't meant to be, I'd ever recover from him. The worst part of all being, he backs it up with actions. His stance in this kitchen right now, solid proof.

"Everything is a mess because of me, Gavin. You shouldn't have to carry something you had no part in."

Separating from me and taking a step back, his hand lifts to my face and he brings it up, aligning it with his field of vision, making sure with whatever is about to happen next, I've only got his eyes to stare into. To believe in.

"I'm not letting you do this anymore. I've put up with it for almost two weeks, and it ends now. You didn't make me talk to you the night we met. You didn't make me fuck you either. I wanted to do those things. As for everything once you were in HFWA, you didn't cause any of it. I don't know how else to make you see that my choices, they're my own. Every step I took with you, and before and after you, it's done because I want to."

"Gavin—"

"Oh no, princess." He cuts me off, resting a finger over my mouth. "You're going to let me finish. I fucking love you, Dawson. I'm always going to love you, even when, like right now, you're pushing me out the damn door. I'm going to love you when you're put together *and* when you're falling apart. Nothing and I do mean *nothing*, is ever going to change it. I own every single thing I have ever done, and I will stand on the roof yelling at the top of my lungs admitting the things we've done together. Because those are the things I cherish most. I have no regrets, and baby, you shouldn't either."

His words are like a sledgehammer to the walls I've built around myself, the ones wallowing in the pain of what is my cousins' actions and the loss of our closeness. But it's not powerful enough to break it wide open. All it seeming to do is make the waves of agony all the more powerful as they wash over me, leaving me shaking, cold, and ultimately alone.

The way I feel I deserve to be.

What Gavin deserves better than.

"I need you to hear me, Dawson."

"I do."

Releasing an awkward laugh, one definitely not humorous in nature, he releases his hold on my face and takes a step back.

"You don't, princess, but I think with some time you will. I don't want to make this worse, make the weight you're carrying around heavier. The last thing I want to do is cause you pain, and I can see, my being here, trying to get you to see the truth, it's doing it. I'm the reason you're shaking, and I can't live with myself knowing I caused it. I brought you this far."

"I just…" I pause, wanting to tell him what I need but struggling because I still don't know what it is. "I need time."

"I know you do. I've known all week. I'm going to give you the time you need, but Dawson, I'm not leaving you. Not the way you think. I'm still one hundred percent in this with you. I just won't be the cause of any more of your pain."

Nodding, the tears falling now, not ones of agony as they were before, but of relief. Giving me what I need, reminding me he's not walking away, its as though he knows better than I do what needs to be done here.

"I'm sorry, Gavin."

"For what?"

"This past week...the way I've been."

"Princess," he says, again taking my face in his hands, only this time, brushing his lips across the top of my nose first. "I'm the one who's sorry. I've known you're not here with me, and yet I've asked things of you, done things with you, that have taken advantage of what we share. I'm the one who needs to be apologizing. Not you."

No. There's no way I can let him think us being together was anything but two-sided. He didn't take advantage of my body, and he didn't take advantage of my heart either.

"You didn't take advantage. I wanted everything."

"Me too. But baby, I want you—the real you—more. I don't want you taking on a role to be who you think I want you to be. I just want you, Daws. I always will. I love you."

With a quick brush of his lips to my cheek, his back turns and closing my eyes to him, not wanting to witness him walking away, I turn back to my place at the counter.

It's only when I hear the door click closed that I allow the cord I've kept myself tightly wrapped in, to come undone.

Allow myself to fall apart.

Chapter Twenty-Nine

Gavin

How do you make someone believe they aren't responsible for anything, other than the choices they make, in any given situation? More to the point, how do I make Dawson understand her taking the job in HFWA wasn't the reason everything came to a head?

I'm not familiar with the situation I'm facing. I have no experience in how to heal a wounded heart. I've always just spent my life being the one doing the wounding.

Dawson is on this precipice, where at any given moment she could fall over, into what for her, must be murky depths below. She wants a relationship with her cousin, yet doesn't understand why it isn't the same for him.

She wants to have a relationship with me *and* her family. She's being torn apart from the inside, out. Her breakdown from the night before all the proof I need of how close to the edge she is.

Standing here, being away from her when I know how vulnerable and exposed, she's feeling, tears me up. All I want to do is forget this stupid plan of Matthias's, quit again, and go back where I belong.

With Dawson.

None of this, the wrestling, the fame, and the adoration, matters going forward if I'm doing it alone. For the first time in years, I want to share this with someone else.

"You ready for this?" Matthias asks, and with my grunted reply, he brings his fist to the door, knocking until we hear Bryan call out for us to enter.

I'm not prepared for the grin on Bryan's face when I step into the office or the way his best friend easily joins him in it before we've even taken seats across from him.

This is too easy for them. It's clear they're on the same page with this plan Kemper thought up. I just don't get why I can't bring myself to do the same.

"Matthias went ahead and filled me in on what the two of you want for your match at Engage. I have issues where Dawson is concerned given what transpired, but I'm also well aware of what a coo this would be if we brought her back. Crowd reaction alone, whether or not she involves herself, is enough for me to want to do whatever it takes to make it happen."

I have to hand it to Kemper; he was right about his friend.

"What do you think it'll take to get Dawson on board?"

Bryan's eyes immediately fall to me, with Matthias's coming a few seconds later when there's no sign of reply. This being the one aspect of the entire idea I haven't been able to nail down.

With as distraught as she's been, there's no telling what her reaction would be to this.

All I know is, I have to get her back. She belongs here. We all do.

I won't be right until she is.

I told her last night I would never walk away, no matter how far she tried pulling away, and I meant it. She told me she would always be in my corner, and now it's time for the script to flip, and for me to be in hers.

Always.

"Honestly," I lean back in the chair, sighing heavily. "I don't know what it's going to take. She's hesitant to talk about this place, let alone the matches I'm in. So much of it reminds her of her cousin, it's like she won't allow herself to go there."

"I'm sorry, Gavin," Bryan says. "I didn't stand up to Reese when I had the chance. I fell back and let him take the lead. I could have done more."

"No, see, you couldn't have. We all know the way Reese is. It's the reason it was so easy to quit. I grew up around a schoolyard of bullies. I couldn't let a grown man become one. He doesn't get to pick and choose when he wants to be my boss."

Except that's not exactly true is it? He's bullying you with what he's holding over your head.

Ignoring the voice despite being unable to admit it's wrong, I forge on. "I think if we want to get her on board, it's going to have to be you doing it, Bryan. And I can't have any part in it. Let it be her choice to come back, none of us the wiser."

"You want to lie?" Matthias cuts in, as always shoving the truth in my face.

"Yes...and no. Yes, we would be keeping this from her, which I suppose could be seen as a white lie, but the end result outweighs it. Her being back where she belongs, is the end goal. Us together. Her not doubting her place. I can make her forgive me for this one little slip."

"How you'll manage that, you're going to keep to yourself, pretty boy." Matthias laughs, turning his attention back to Bryan. "So, as much as I hate the idea of keeping secrets, I have to agree with Fortune. I think if you go to her with the offer, you'll have a better chance of getting her on board, even with the way she feels about this guy." He thumbs over to me, grinning.

"Well, alright," Bryan says, pushing back from the desk and standing. "I've got my marching orders. I'll let you know how it goes."

Moving from behind the desk, and heading toward the door, my brain finally kicks in as I realize what's going on.

"You're going to Dawson *now*?"

"Yeah," he pauses in step. "We're already behind. The match is in a few days." Having said his piece, he heads for the door and just before he steps through it, he calls out a warning. One I'm going to have no other choice but heed.

"Fortune, stay out of Reese's way. I want you in one piece when I bring your girl home."

Throwing the paper down on the table and forcing my traitorous eyes not to look over at the laptop again, I lean back in the chair, taking in the situation I've found myself in.

Reminded again how important the opportunity Reese had given me was, and chastising myself for how I'd shit on it for sex.

No. Stop it. It was about more than sex.

I shit on it for love.

A love that's not doing me a damn bit of good these days, as I'm spending my time either logged in or circling things in the paper, all in an effort to keep myself afloat.

My money situation was never horrible, and I'm sure to be fine for the next several months given my budgeting during the time I worked at LiveWire, but I still hate the way it feels not having anywhere to go every day.

I really did buy into HFWA being where I belonged.

How wrong I was.

Interrupting my pity party, I flick my attention to the door as the bell sounds. A second one quickly following it garners all of my attention but my body makes no moves in order to go answer it. Questions, the only thing I'm capable of as I continue to stare a hole in the wooden structure.

Who the hell could be on the other side?

My parents are off on a trip my father surprised my mother with, my sisters never paying me enough mind to visit, rules them out too. Gavin's at work, putting together the title match with Matthias, and Reese not even so much as breathing in my direction since he'd showed up here unannounced, also leaves them off the chopping block.

A chokehold of sadness ripping at my insides as I'm reminded again how alone I am.

After a hard knock sounds, I finally drag myself out of the chair and to the door, opening it and finding the last person I ever thought to grace my doorstep standing there.

Bryan Michaelchuk.

"Can I come in?" he questions with practiced ease, his body exuding confidence his voice isn't aligning with.

"Not sure why you'd want to, but sure." Moving back and turning from him as he takes a few quick strides in, I wave a hand around the room with faux enthusiasm. "Welcome to my humble abode."

Following closely behind until we're both standing awkwardly in the living area, he makes himself at home the same way Reese had before him, throwing his body down hard into the lounge chair.

"Thanks for having me."

"Of course," I respond flippantly, crossing to the other end of the room and occupying the seat farthest from him. "What brings you by?"

Leaning forward and resting a hand heavily down onto his leg, he rubs his hand over his head before fixing his eyes on me.

"I wanted to give you an apology. It's a little late coming, but I'm hoping you'll still accept it."

Now, considering how routine my days have become since being ceremoniously ousted on my ass, this piques my interest. There not being one thing, he should have to apologize for.

"Apologize for what?"

"In order for me to answer your question, I'm going to have to explain some things. Some private things that I'm asking for your silence on once I've said them."

"Depends what the big secret is, I suppose."

"Fair enough." He concedes, quickly moving on. "Dawson, I'm sorry for not putting up a bigger fight when everything happened with Reese. You and I are both aware you did violate your contract in being with Gavin, but I knew about it from the beginning, thanks to Matty. I went in with the knowledge of you breaking the rules, and I honestly didn't care. Still don't. The only reason you were fired being I didn't get you to sign a new contract when I shifted your position."

"Matthias told you?"

Nodding with ease, not even remotely bothered, he shifts again in the chair, this time his eyes falling from mine and focusing on the sofa between us.

"He did. It's a deal we made after his accident. I told Gavin the same earlier today. I felt he was owed the same apology."

Heart softening at the mere mention of Gavin's name, let alone the knowledge Bryan has given me in admitting fault for something he didn't have to, has the hard shell I've sheltered myself in, beginning to crack.

"You have nothing to be sorry for. Sure, I didn't get to sign a new contract. Truth is, I didn't even know there was a different contract, given I was on a probation period. It doesn't change anything. I made the choices I did, and I paid the way I should have."

"No, Dawson, you didn't." he immediately argues. "You made no mistake being with Gavin the way you were, based on the new contract rules. Sure, Reese would have still flipped his lid, but we could have easily worked around it. Gotten him to come around, at least in terms of keeping you on."

"Either way, your apology is accepted. Even if I don't agree with you."

"There's more to it, though. More I would like to explain if you'll allow me the courtesy."

It's been a really long time since I've had someone sit across from me and engage with me this way. I'm not sure how I feel about it, much less how I should be responding. He's being entirely too formal, and I haven't the first clue why.

We don't work together anymore. He's no longer my boss. Why put on a show?

"The floor is yours." I squeak out in an effort to keep playing his formalities game.

"Reese and I, we're more than business partners."

Okay, not for nothing, but duh. I already know this.

I'm not about to interrupt the man, but he has to know with as close as Reese and I were, he'd already divulged his little secret.

"We've been engaging in a sexual relationship for the last two years. It's more to me than it is for him. I'm aware of it, but we were getting to a point not too long before you showed up, where I thought we were on the same page."

Oh boy.

Reese is apparently treating everyone he loves like crap. Bryan paying as much as I have been.

"Even before Matthias came to me about you and Gavin, I'd gotten wind of it. Seen things. Especially after you arrived. One instance, in particular, searing itself into my brain, and leaving its mark because of how similar it was to Reese and myself."

Damning my curiosity at wanting to know what Bryan had seen, I shift uncomfortably in my seat, all the while following his own actions and looking anywhere but at him.

"Brady caught the two of you backstage in one of the more secluded halls. He wasn't the only one." Bryan offers up, saving me from the embarrassment of asking.

"Oh, God." I groan. "Now I'm the one who should be apologizing."

Releasing a small chuckle, he sits up straighter and his eyes find their way back to me.

"Don't be. As I said, it was a lot like the first time with Reese. I feel like you should know this about us because it explains, at least a little, why I didn't back you up that day."

"Bryan, I appreciate it, you wanting to explain yourself, but you don't have to. I already knew about you and Reese. He told me shortly after he came out to me as bisexual. He was struggling at the time. I understood the struggle because if you have any insight into his parents, you know how deeply rooted they are in religion. They aren't the most accepting of alternative lifestyles. He knew my family wasn't like that. So, he opened up."

There's so much more I can say here, tell this man in order to give him true insight into the man I can see he cares for, but it's not my place. Especially not now.

Maybe not ever.

It's up to Reese to make Bryan understand what the man means to him.

"I didn't stand up for you because I didn't want what I feel for your cousin to possibly come out and be used against me."

"I figured as much given everything you've just admitted."

"Well, tell me, oh wise woman, do you see this coming? I was wrong and I want to fix it. If you'll let me."

Nope. I can safely say I didn't see him wanting to fix anything for me.

We're both in the same boat with the cousin who shall not be named. I'm pretty sure given Bryan's earlier stance, offering me even a lifejacket on a sinking boat is a no-no.

"Can't say I did."

Shoving a hand into his jacket pocket, he pulls out a folded group of papers and getting up from the chair, tosses them down onto the coffee table across from him.

"This is the first step in rectifying things."

Getting up myself and taking them, I don't even so much as look at them, focusing my full attention on the man bringing them in order to get answers.

"What is this?"

"It's a contract. Well, it's two contracts. The one on top is the first step, though."

Finally allowing my eyes to fall to the papers now in my lap, I flip them open and take in the very contact he's speaking of. After going through each of the pages, making sure not to start on the second contract directly underneath, I see the signature line already signed on his end and also the date listed on it.

The very day I signed the original contract in their office.

"Bryan..."

"You'll need to sign with the same date of course but once you do, I'll have them fast-tracked through. Your departure from the company will be expunged, and you can come back as if you never left."

Leaving the whole aspect of fraud out of the equation for the moment, I study the contract again, one setting me up for both in-ring work and the backstage offering I was gifted with from the start. Reese's signature on the line is even more startling than everything else I'm witnessing on the pages.

"How did you get him to sign?"

Smirking, he's given me all the answer I need, but still cheekily responds anyway.

"If I tell you what powers I used in order to secure this signature, I'd have to kill you, and we all know how Gavin would react if I did that."

Again, my heart soars with the sound of Gavin's name being spoken, but this time, unlike the last, I'm also experiencing a sickening feeling.

There's no way this, what Bryan is attempting, can go through, right?

"I can see you're struggling to understand what's going on, so let me make it easier for you. I never filed the original paperwork with our lawyers, Dawson. The only contract they will have, the only legally binding one is the one in your hands. The one you'll graciously sign for me."

Bryan is giving me my job back.

I can feel the defeat from earlier slowly beginning to fade with the prospect now being presented but I still can't shake it entirely with how it's all going down.

What Bryan had to do in order to get this.

"What about Reese?"

"Let me worry about my business partner."

Right. Like I'm going to let him deal with Reese on his own.

"We deal with him together or I sign nothing."

"Fair enough." He concedes.

"What's this other contract?"

Now grinning from ear to ear, he moves from the chair across the room and plops himself down on the sofa directly to my right, leaning over and slipping the top contract out of my hand so I'm able to focus on the next one.

"Your first assignment."

Looking over the contract, the legitimacy of it, there's no disputing this one and how the line where Reese would sign, isn't there. The only signature on the document being Bryan's.

"Correct me if I'm wrong, but doesn't the first contract outline my duties? Why would I need a separate one for each assignment?"

"You don't. Only for this assignment because I'm covering all of our asses."

"What's the assignment, exactly?"

I could sit and read what my duties are but at this point, with the sheer information overload I'm beginning to experience, I'd rather get it from the horses' mouth.

"I want you at Engage in three days."

"Excuse me?"

Laughing softly, he pushes forward. "Come on now, Dawson. I know your hearing is even better than mine. You heard me. I want you at Engage. More to the point, I want you in Gavin's corner."

My stomach bottoms out the second I hear whose corner it is I'll be in. He'd had me almost to the edge until then. There's no way he's here doing this of his own volition. Gavin had to have put him up to it.

"I'm sorry, Bryan, I can't do what you want me to."

Dipping his head to the side, looking from me to the contract and back again, I'm struck by how clueless he seems to be in why I answered the way I had.

"Gavin put you up to this, didn't he?"

Scoffing, he shifts his body until he's sitting up straight.

"Gavin doesn't know anything about this. I'm here on my own, Dawson. I know how it seems; I do. I'm not here for him, though. I'm here for you. I don't have a dog in this fight. Sign the papers or don't sign. It won't matter much to me either way. This is business, pure and simple. I want you in his corner because it's where you fit best, and it's what we've already built. Changing you up now and sticking you with anyone else wouldn't make sense from a business standpoint, let alone a story one."

My ability to tell when someone is pulling the wool over my eyes is uncanny on a good day, so if Bryan didn't mean any of what he was saying, I would be able to tell. There isn't anything to be found, though. No dishonesty from this man. His earlier nervousness about the relationship with my cousin, the fidgeting he'd done, and the way he wouldn't or couldn't look me in the eye, it's not happening now.

Bryan wants me back because it's where he believes I belong.

And I'll be damned if I don't want to agree.

I do belong there. In HFWA *and* with Gavin.

"Tell me your silence means you're thinking of an inventive way to say yes."

Laughing despite the seriousness of the moment, I cast one last look down at the contract in my lap before lifting my eyes and staring him down.

Giving him what he came for.

"You've got yourself a deal, Bryan. I'm in."

Taking the pen from his outstretched hand, and meeting his grin with one of my own, I flick it open and sign on the dotted line.

Twice.

"Welcome home, Dawson. We missed you."

Chapter Thirty

Gavin

Somewhere, beyond these locker room doors, my girl is out there.

Even from my place buried away in the locker room, I can tell this is one of the most hyped up crowds we've ever performed in front of. Their cries for more punishment resounding off the walls of the place as each match goes off without a hitch.

Lighting aligned and set in all the prime locations, cameras rolling, our performances tonight not only going live on pay per view but also streaming live for any subscribers to the newly put together HFWA website.

Tonight is a game changer.

In more ways than one.

This is the night we put HFWA on the national map. Where we become more than just some independent promotion, and instead, skyrocket into the stratosphere of professional wrestling on a worldwide scale.

Despite the preparation I've done in order to get here tonight, there's no denying the butterflies I have over what happens when it's all said and done.

What Dawson will do with the information I plan on giving her. If she can withstand yet another hit to her relationship with Reese and overcome it. Swallow her fear and realize what I've known from the start.

We're forever.

Going over tonight, winning the title, it's both important, and not so. Because the HFWA Heavyweight Title won't mean anything if she's not with me on my journey with it.

Turning toward the sound of knuckles on the door, I ready myself for whoever it is on the other side. My heart leaping at the thought of it being Dawson but also aware it most likely won't be.

It can be her cousin, though. A thought that even with my promise of staying out of his way I've been keeping to for the last three days, still manages to steel me to the person stepping through.

The other boss.

"Is she here?"

Nodding, he steps through, and I see he's not alone.

"You know if you're caught on camera being in here, this could all blow up in our faces," I state, coming face to face with my opponent for the night.

"Kayfabe is as dead as Smith and his guaranteed contracts," Kemper responds, grinning.

"What are you both doing in here?"

Where I expect Matthias to give it up, it's Bryan stepping forward, his face no longer jovial.

"When were you going to tell me the only reason you're back is that Reese used Dawson as a threat?"

Looks like *that* particular cat is out of the bag.

Matthias, merely shrugging when I narrow my eyes his way, shifts from his place at the door, making his way all the way through as the door slams behind him.

"I knew I shouldn't have trusted you."

"Gavin, you should be happy he came to me about this. It was my knowledge of what Reese was holding over your head that made it easier for me to convince Dawson to come back."

"I didn't want him blindsided. It's bad enough Dawson is unaware the lengths to which Reese went in order to get you back here. It would have been even worse with Bryan." Matthias adds, and again I'm struck by the lack of fight I have to argue.

"She's still unaware?" I ask, though I already know the answer.

"Yes. We're leaving it to you to deliver that particular bombshell at the end of the night. Though, this guy," Bryan thumbs over to Matthias. "Almost told her when she walked through the doors a few hours ago."

With Bryan's admission, my heart rate picks up, and I can feel the jolt to my bloodstream. Just knowing she's here has me keyed up. I'm one step closer to bringing my girl back to me for good. Not this tug of war she's been giving me for the last two weeks.

"What has Reese had to say about her being here?"

"He's locked himself away to stew, I suppose." Bryan weakly admits, but there are obvious signs of pain flicking through his eyes. The idea of his partner being locked away clearly causing him an agony I wasn't expecting.

I'm missing something here, I know I am. The time for figuring it out, though, is long past. I've got a show to put on.

My final one as Gavin Fortune, the character.

More than a little ready to take my place as Gavin, the man.

The work is over. It's time for me to shoot now.

"Don't think you're off the hook for keeping this shit from me, but I get why you did it. Next time, though, if this partnership withstands the amount of stunts Reese has pulled over the last several months, you bring it to me first. We clear?"

"Crystal," I say though I linger on the part of his statement which speaks to what could possibly be the state of HFWA in the long term.

Could Bryan possibly walk away after what Reese pulled?

"Stop looking at me like that, Fortune. I'm not giving this puppy up without a fight. And honestly, given the man I've now got to go face down, I have no doubt it'll be a hell of a slobber knocker."

With a final wink, he turns to go, and where I expect Matthias to follow, he doesn't so much as twitch in response to his friend walking out of the room.

"After the match tonight, what are your plans for her?"

I've given this a lot of thought over the last two days of solitude. I don't want her working as a valet forever. I think after tonight, depending on what her answer is to the very big question I have is, I want her in the back. The same way Matthias wants to be.

"What would you think about having her working with you?"

"I'm not making any decisions for her. She's had more than enough of that since she arrived here, but I'd love it. I don't let just anyone give me a nut shot, remember."

If she's not out in the ring with me, I don't want her behind a microphone either. She's been doing the very same thing for over ten years. As long as I've been wrestling. If she's open to it, I want her where I can see even more of her personality shine through.

Writing and booking.

Something tells me, between her and Matthias, I'll be booked in some of the best matches of my life, and for once, it's not me being cocky. It's being secure in their skills.

"You want to bring it up with her or is this another thing you're leaving to me?" I laugh, the visual of Matthias taking the shot to his nuts in the ring still on a loop in my head.

"We'll figure that out once we get through this match. Sound good?"

"Yeah," I say, and hearing me loud and clear, he moves to the door.

"For what it's worth, Fortune, I'm proud to drop the title to this version of you. It's been a long road. I'm glad to see common sense finally won out." Throwing the door back, he flashes me a familiar grin, the same one he wore before our last match. "Let's tear the house down."

Dawson

Here goes nothing.

Knocking on the door with both names emboldened in gold across the front, I take a step back and prepare myself for the wait I know is coming.

After stalking Matthias and Bryan around for the last fifteen minutes, complete with catching them both come out at different times from the very locker room I've been avoiding like the plague since I got here, I know the person I'm looking for on the other side of the door is alone.

Just the way I want him.

If I'm going to be back here again, I'm doing it with a clear conscience.

Which means, I'm dealing with Reese.

There's no way I can go forward in HFWA having all of this baggage I'm carrying around. Believing I'm the cause for everything is starting to wear me out. I suppose, given how many people have come to tell me what happened was less about me, and more about something bigger at play, it makes sense it's wearing out its welcome.

Even if I'm not fully on the same page, I'd have to agree. So, while I have to take responsibility for some of it, so does Reese.

"How many times do I have to say leave me the hell alone before you get it?" Reese snaps, throwing back the door. Staring me down cold, but shaken in his tone as the final bit drops off.

"I was never good at leaving you alone, you know this," I respond, pushing my way into the space and breezing past him until I'm crossing the trailer and throwing my body down into the seat across from the desk.

Being here is like Déjà vu.

"I was wondering how long it was going to take for you to come crawling back." He snaps, throwing the door shut with a hard slam before making his way over to the seat across from me. The consummate professional, always.

More like the consummate control freak.

The way I'm seeing him now, turning my stomach but also reminding me of what I wasn't seeing in the days we've spent apart. The heartbreak I felt at having thrown away the closest relationship I've ever had all for naught.

Doesn't seem like it's bothering him one bit.

"That's where you're wrong. Bryan re-signed me. I didn't crawl anywhere."

"What do you want, Daws? Did your one trick pony finally throw you to the wolves, and you're here looking for another handout?"

Wow. How did I not see this before now?

"You're going to leave Gavin out of this. What's going on is between you and me."

"Right," he scoffs, adding insult to what he assumes is an injury by gifting me with a hard roll of his eyes. "If you're sitting here saying this, I'm assuming it's because he told you what I did to him."

What he did to him? Come again?

I have no idea what he's going on about, but I'm not about to let him know I'm clueless. Let him think I know it. With his cold indifference toward me, showing me a lot more in a few minutes than years of our closeness afforded me, it serves him right.

"He did. Why'd you do it, Reese?"

Bringing his hands down together on the table and leaning over, he stares me down.

"What else did you expect me to do, Dawson? You left me no choice with the way you two carried on. The spell he put you under. If you weren't going to think for yourself, I was going to have to do it for you. The both of you. So, I used the only weakness I know he has. His conquests."

Swallowing down the urge I have to react, the surprise at what he's saying shaking me even more than I'd been when I got here, I lean back in the chair and do the best impression of Gavin I can. Summoning up every ounce of confidence I've got in the process in order to pull it off.

He threatened me.

"I expected you to come to me the way we've always done in the past, and speak like an adult about this. We could have worked through a lot of this without getting anyone else involved, Reese. I'm sorry for what you walked in on, I am. I should have respected you, and the opportunity you were giving me enough, to bring the status of my relationship with Gavin to you. But the steps you've taken since haven't exactly been inspiring me to open up."

This is me being as honest as I can. I regret not bringing this to him. I'm sure it still would have turned out the same way, with his little secret meeting and all before I even arrived, but he was owed more than I gave.

Huffing out a heavy breath, he follows my own move and leans back in his seat, intimidation tactics stalled.

"From a purely business standpoint, I could have ruined you both, Daws. I didn't want to do it to you but with what Gavin was pulling, I had to do something."

"So, you thought, what? I'm going to test this guy and his feelings for my cousin by threatening her livelihood? Integrity? What, Reese? What were you hoping to gain from the stunt you pulled?"

"You away from him."

"Well, considering the way I've been treating him for the last two weeks, I'd say you got your damn wish. The funny thing about getting what you want, though. The price you end up paying usually isn't worth the cost."

As I go to stand, he's up out of his seat and grabbing my wrist in an attempt to stop me.

"What does that mean?"

"It means, I made the wrong choice. I never should have pulled away from Gavin the way I did. I was trying all this time to save a relationship that never should have been in the first place."

"You..." he chokes out, emotion finally showing. "You don't mean that."

"I mean every word, cousin. When I walk out of here, you're dead to me. And for the record, until you admitted it, I had no idea how and why Gavin agreed to return. So, thanks for the info, I guess? You've made what has to happen now so much easier."

Pulling from his hold, rubbing at my wrist as it begins to sting, I meet his eyes with the steeled coloring of my own as he again asks me what I mean.

"I'm going out there tonight. I'm going to stand in his corner, where I belong. The corner I never should have left. Goodbye, Reese. Good luck in all your future endeavors."

Fleeing from the trailer with the same ferocity as I'd had a few minutes before when I barrelled my way into it, I don't stop until I'm back in what will be my locker room for the night, able to breathe freely again.

I meant what I said to Reese. What has to happen now has never been clearer.

It's time for me to take what is rightfully mine.

Praying as I ready myself for my own private battle before even heading to the ring, I'm not too late.

Chapter Thirty-One

Gavin

Standing at the closed-circuit monitor in the back, away from the camera's for maybe a minute or two, I take in the scene as Bryan sits at the announce table, alongside Kimberlee's brother, Zach, and their special guest commentator for our Iron Man match, Brady Raines. Having held the title before, it seems only natural he's out again now. Especially with the opportunities, he'll be presented with once the title is strapped around my waist.

I pay close attention as they amp up the crowd watching at home, for the match about to take place. Our first ever main event at a pay per view. It's only when my name is called, I shake off any residual fear I've got heading into this headlining performance, and start making my way toward the ring.

Toward the cameras.

Right on cue, the person stepping in for Dawson tonight, Lauren, appears from the left calling my name and ignoring her as planned, I keep walking. It's only when I hear her heels clicking against the tile and feel her hand come out and brush against my shoulder, I come to a full stop, giving her the time of day.

"Excuse me, Gavin. You're seconds away from going one on one in a 30-minute Iron Man match against the current HFWA Heavyweight Champion, Matthias Kemper, in the third match in your best of three falls tournament. With him winning his last two matches against other opponents this past week, and with the absence of Dawson in your corner, what are your feelings going into the match?"

"My feelings, Lauren? Let me stop you right there. My feelings haven't changed. When I head out to the ring tonight, Dawson by my side or not, I'm planning on putting the final nail in Kemper's coffin. Bringing the HFWA Championship back where it belongs. Around the waist of the only man in this locker room deserving to wear it. I don't need help to put Kemper into retirement. He's going to put himself there all on his own when I'm through with him."

Continuing my walk, all eyes now back on the action at ringside, the thunderous sound of my music erupts just as I reach the curtain, and with one last quick shake to my senses, I proceed out through the curtain.

Ready to put on a show.

Matthias, after I've made my way down and through the ropes, following suit minutes later as his own music erupts, and he emerges with the belt hung around his shoulders. His body rigid, his stare deadly, as he stalks his way to the ring and enters much the same as I did before him. Handing the title over to the ref for the match, and proceeding to make his way languidly over to the corner farthest from me.

Holding the title in the air, showing the crowd in attendance, and the people at home just what we're here fighting for, I play to the crowd. Pointing at Matthias and taunting the people ringside, as I tell them exactly what I plan on doing to their God tonight in the ring.

As the bell sounds, signaling the start of the match, and we move in on one another, I smirk before my expression quickly turns to a snarl. A low growl releasing when as I get closer, Matthias makes no move to lock up, ignoring my earlier taunts and bravado.

Teasing each other, our hands never meeting for the full lock, both of us move in a circular motion around the ring, gauging each other until Matthias takes the lead and we lock up. His one arm gripped around my neck while delivering an arm drag, holding me in place as I attempt to use my ring awareness to shift and move my body over to the ropes to cause a quick break.

"Get the hell off me," I yell back to Kemper after the ref repeatedly asks him to break to no avail.

Finally allowing the break, he moves back to the center of the ring awaiting my removal from the ropes. The clock now reading 28 minutes when after I finally break free, I take a quick scan at the titantron at the top of the ramp.

Attempting to lock up again, both of us feeling each other out, I move first, going low and hooking Matthias by the leg, bringing him down. He rolls through, going for the quick pin, getting a count of one before both of us are back on our feet and staring each other down.

Locking up again, I try to take Matthias down by the legs, but he turns it around on me, twisting the move into a backslide, which I easily power my way out of before I can be counted with my shoulders down.

Smiling at each other, we both move around the ring again, our dance becoming familiar as I taunt him, begging him to come at me. To give me all he's got. And as I get what I'm after as he moves in, I catch him with a kick to the chest, unprepared for him having scouted me and catching it before it can connect fully. Holding my leg there, as I pander to him and the crowd. Shaking my head around, crazed, like a deer caught in headlights, he swiftly drops it and with the crowd egging him on, he lunges forward, goes low and takes me down into a rollup again.

My shoulders on the mat for a hard two count this time, I pick the perfect moment to kick out and jump easily back up to my feet, shifting back and leaning against the ropes. Matthias, grabbing me by the arm, swings me forward to the other end of the ring, bending over as the momentum pushes me forward, straight into him, and at the last second executing a brilliant sunset flip over his back. Coming for Kemper, grabbing him and pulling him down on top of me, he scouts me again as he leans back, snags one of my legs and hooks it for a speedy one count. Quickly turning it into a snap mare takedown, floating through, and putting my shoulders to the mat for another one count.

Acutely aware of everything and everyone, I slip out of the ring in the separation after the pin and run around the outside.

Gesturing to the crowd, grinning and taunting the people closest to ringside. Earning their ire just the way I want.

Matthias, given the breathing time with me on the outside, attempts to give back as good as I'm giving to the crowd as he begins to run circles in the ring, riling the crowd up as he moves with chants for him, even louder than some of the earlier ones he'd been gifted. His eyes once they latch on to mine on the outside, turning to stone again. All traces of humor and playfulness for the crowd done, as he awaits my re-entrance.

Making my way slowly up the ring steps, our attention is stripped away from each other as my music hits. A few seconds later, the cause of it known, as Dawson steps through the curtain. Pausing at the top of the ramp and grinning, her eyes center on the both of us. Making no move to head down to where the action is, she stands and basks in both the surprise from the crowd at her appearance, as well as the shock registering on both of our faces. Kemper as faux surprised as I am in the seconds it takes for me to register what it all means.

Slipping easily into character, my expression changes first, as I show the crowd what it means for me and my chances at the title. My own grin now mirroring her own, the two of us as in sync as always.

As if she'd never left.

Focusing back on my opponent, I move to the side of the ring and slip back in under the bottom rope before the ref has the chance to count me out, pulling Kemper's attention away from Dawson and back on me. And wasting no time, he stalks toward me once I'm to my feet, hitting me with the chops he'd prepared me for earlier in the week. One after the other in quick succession, knocking me back into the ropes and using his built-up momentum, swings me again to the other side of the ring. Knocking me down hard to the ground but capitalizing on it with an upper body shot to the face and neck once I hop back to my feet. Dropping and covering me, he gets me for a barely there one count before I kick out forcefully. Turning over, Matthias moves swiftly, grabbing me by the face, and pulling me up and into a body slam again quickly covering me for what he assumes will be an easy win.

Breaking after a two count has me kicking out, he grabs me again by the hair. Pulling me to my feet, he delivers more chops to the chest, knocking me into the corner.

Cutting my gaze away from Matthias, I watch as Dawson makes her way slowly down the ramp, the hairs on my arms rising with the pull of her closeness as she makes her way fully down and around, finally stopping, but making no move to get involved, once she's in front of the announce table.

The raised voices of both Bryan and Brady alerting me even more to just how important her being here is, for me and the match. With her mere presence breathing new life into me, I vow silently to go even harder at Kemper. Wanting to show her, both realistically and fictionally, what her being here does.

What her true influence is.

Allowing Matthias to swing me from one corner turnbuckle to the other, I brace myself for the impact as he flies from one side of the ring to the other, and using his own momentum against him, I fling him up and over my shoulders. Matthias landing as practiced, just on the outer side of the ropes, using them to his advantage as he swiftly dives up, keeping his balance on the top ropes and jumps off, at the exact second I duck underneath and he catches himself after a quick flip, just in time to meet a wicked right hand to the face, bringing him down to his knees.

Grabbing Matthias by his own hair, I pull him to his feet, twisting him around, which he flips the script on, landing me straight into the line of fire with a kick to the stomach than straight into a turnbuckle powerbomb. The move connecting as my back hits hard before I bounce back off and fall to my knees, attempting to crawl away.

What Kemper capitalizes on with a cradle pin as the ref hits the mat as my shoulders are down. Before he can even go for a count of two, I'm moving and turning it around, rolling Matthias around and hooking him up for the pin.

The first fall of the night, after an elegantly laid out dance between the two of us, officially mine.

My attention again travels to Dawson after gaining the pinfall, finding her eyes glowing as she stands ringside, dressed to the nines in one of the shortest but most elegant dresses I've ever laid eyes on, grinning from ear to ear and clapping. Making my heart soar at the sight of her, it takes everything in me not to slide out of the ring in order to act on the feelings she's inspiring in me.

Wanting to kiss her more than I even want air to breathe in order to finish the rest of this match.

Lauren from the right corner of ringside calls out my name, alerting the crowd at home too who has taken the first fall of the night. The crowd in the building reacting as expected, as a chorus of boos I'm sure can be heard from miles away, mixing with the softer yet equally as telling chants for Matthias to get his ass up in order to end me.

Not wanting to slow down the pace of the match, I go at Kemper again. Coming up from behind and shoving him into the ropes. Earning a wicked elbow to the face as he attempts to break the hold I'm maintaining. Spinning on his heels, he comes out swinging but misses as I pull him into a side slam before running to the ropes, climbing them all the way to the top at the same moment Matthias rolls out onto the outside.

Pulling on the ropes, not wanting to give Matthias an inch, I dive over, connecting my body to his and knocking him to the ground, while still maintaining balance on my feet. Grabbing onto the barricade as my legs weaken under the impact.

Dawson stalking closer, watching the action unfold, gets dangerously close to Kemper, glaring at him as I keep my focus, grabbing him by his hair and pulling him again to his feet before swinging him into the barricade.

Hearing the count from the ref, aware of what it means if I'm caught out here when he hits ten, I grab him from his place on the ground, and pulling him by his hair, smash his head off the outside portion of the ring before throwing him under the rope and shoving him in to break the count. Flashing a grin to Dawson who is stepping even closer, before slipping under the ropes myself.

Having given Matthias time to get to his feet, I'm unprepared for the assault of fists I'm met with upon my entrance back to the center of the ring. Kemper unloading shot after shot, picking me up and delivering a neck breaker before jumping straight into the cover. Earning him a two count before I forcibly kick out.

Bringing me to my feet, he attempts to deliver a suplex, but I catch him, delivering a heavy chop to his chest and pulling the momentum back in my favor as I continue delivering chops, one more dangerous than the next until again Kemper's back is hitting the ropes. His worn upper body hanging over the top rope in an attempt to catch his breath.

What I refuse to allow him to do as I grab him and swing him, only this time, as I attempt to execute the same move Kemper had earlier, bending over as he bounces back off the ropes toward me, I'm thrown off course with a sharp kick to the face stunning me momentarily, but what I quickly recover from as I fight back with another strike to his neck.

Our dance becoming more intense as I swing him forward into the corner turnbuckle, enjoying the sound of devastation I hear as his back makes contact.

A glorious symphony of sickeningly pleasurable sound.

Following it up with a forearm to the face, I'm moving again, back to the other side of the ring, wanting to repeat the forearm attack, but he catches me as he delivers a shot straight to my knee, knocking me down to the mat.

Rolling me into the pin, I turn it around before the ref can even begin, flipping it into a roll-up of my own. The ref getting a one count before Kemper turns it in his favor, getting my shoulders down on the mat for a quick two count. Using all of his strength after I've kicked out again, and lifting me up with one of my own moves, pulling me into a powerbomb and delivering me down perfectly in the middle of the ring.

Kicking out barely at the count of two and a half, my breathing labored, my body wanting nothing more than to shut down for a while, I force myself forward. Shoving Kemper off of me and turning in an effort to get myself back up to a standing position, albeit a shaky one.

Rushing to the side of the ring as Kemper turns, I hit him with a fast kick to the gut, following it up with a superkick straight to the man's face. Kicking what I hope is his teeth straight down his throat. Matthias, on cue, falls to the mat as the rowdy crowd is on their feet, their chanting even louder now as boos again fill the building.

Hooking his leg, I close my eyes and leaning back on top of the man I'm hell-bent and determined to retire in style tonight, I get another three count.

Lauren's voice shouting quicker this time, as she announces the second fall of this match again going to me.

Taking the moment, I grin, turning my attention to the titantron and the numbers flashing there, changing and blinking as they update to the tally thus far.

Gavin Fortune 2
Matthias Kemper 0

With Matthias down and out in the middle of the ring, I struggle to my feet and before I can even take in what's happening, I feel my body being pulled around until I'm face to face with an intruder to our match.

Dawson, her eyes brimming with tears and her entire face alight due to the smile she's wearing. Closing the distance, my arms find their way around her and I crush her to me, throwing all caution, thoughts of what her cousin will think, and everything that's taken place over the last two weeks, to the wind when after inhaling and exhaling deeply, I slam my lips down roughly on hers.

Meeting mine in kind as she attempts to steal the control of the moment and her lips become harsher. Hungrier. Desire mixing with the rush of the match, and the reaction from the crowd, until I'm positive we're drowning in nothing but.

"Finish him." She states once we've broken apart, and with a small wink and a smirk, she slides herself through the middle ropes, jumping down to the ground below, finding her way back to her place in front of the announce table.

The distraction giving me everything I need to keep going, a renewed sense of urgency to end this right, but what publicly ends up costing me when I turn around and Matthias is back on his feet. Like a rabid dog, aware of his need to get a fall on me, he's out of the gate, throwing lefts and rights, stunning me, and giving no wiggle room to mount an offense as I find myself falling to my knees and then the mat under the weight of Matthias's hits and his body.

Hands finding their way to my face, I attempt to block the blows from the beast he's become as he continues to thrash at me, the crowd becoming more riled—more fired up—with every blow he lands.

It's only a few seconds later when the pain stops and there's no movement from Kemper, I peek out through a slit in my hands, and I'm given the reason for it.

Standing in the ring again is Dawson, eyes locked and loaded on Matthias, smooth like a feline when she steps toward him, almost as though she's stalking her prey.

The last thought I have before finally giving my eyes the chance to rest is simple.

So much for her not getting involved anymore.

Dawson

If there was ever any doubt about where I belong, standing in the ring and staring down Matthias now, it would all become crystal clear.

The rush of the crowd, and the way both of these men have spent years feeding off of it, what has my blood pumping and damn near on fire as I stalk toward Gavin's opponent, my face a mask for my true feelings, but a dead giveaway for what has to happen.

Interfering, it'll cost Gavin, but only a little. He'll lose a fall, but it will cement him *and* me in infamy as the heels to beat within the HFWA.

Matthias, attempting to back down from what he must realize is going to be my own version of an assault, steps back, trying to create distance.

A distance I won't let him have; my two steps closer equalling one of his own until we're face to face. The slight smirk he's wearing only for me as he readies himself for what will be my hand connecting with his face.

Payback for what he'd done to me during the ladder match.

The sting in my hand as it connects only pushing me more into this transformation of mine, as once his eyes drop away, I take my open hand and bring it into a fist and continue hitting him, even as the bell sounds off around me and the ref comes to Matthias's defense, pulling me away.

Matthias may have gotten a fall, making the count 2-1, but I had gotten so much more.

The rush I'd been longing for in my entire career in entertainment.

It's right here.

In this very ring.

Gavin, now fully aware of what's taking place, gets to his feet, and as his eyes find mine, I see are filled with predicted rage, right before he starts yelling. Questioning what the hell I'm doing getting involved.

"I have this, Dawson! What the hell were you hoping to accomplish?"

Not letting my earlier grin slip, I merely shrug, and that's when everything changes. The crowd seems to go quiet, though thankfully, not eerily so, and Gavin's eyes go from angry, to the delicious hunger I'd seen in them right before he kissed me.

His smirk morphing into a full-on grin, one fully reaching his eyes as he holds me in his sights and stalks closer.

"If you would just do what I said and finish him, I wouldn't have had to get involved."

Flicking my eyes from him to his opponent who I now see is shaking off my assault and becoming aware of what is going on, I turn my back on Gavin. This time taking the ring steps down, and blowing a kiss to both men once I've reached the bottom.

And Gavin, doing as he always does, takes in the situation before him and does what I told him to.

He finishes it.

Gavin

I knew there was something I should have insisted on before sending Bryan to bring my girl back.

As ecstatic as I am with her being here, and having her involved in the match, going toe to toe with Matthias wasn't what I signed on for. I know the man wouldn't lift a hand to her, he's Saint Kemper for a reason, but good god, I couldn't break through the fear coursing through my veins as I took in what she was doing long enough to remind my brain of it.

After tonight, I'm never letting Dawson get involved again.

Focusing my attention on Kemper after Dawson's final cheeky blow kiss, we stare each other down. This, what happens now, will leave its mark on the business as a whole but even more so, set the bar to beat in HFWA.

Closing the distance, Matthias attempts to hit me with a kick to the face but scouting his move, I catch him, grabbing his foot and spinning around, I grab him by the neck and lock him into position for a sleeper hold. His body working in tandem with mine, relaxing into the move until it looks as though I've taken him out. Relinquishing it and letting the man drop to the mat in the middle of the ring, I turn my attention to the crowd and gesturing to them, puckering up my lips and blowing a Dawson inspired blow kiss of my own, I turn back and deliver the crescendo to our entire program over the last several months.

Kicking him in the side of the head, rendering him immobile, I sling his legs around my neck and lifting him up high into the air, deliver a debilitating powerbomb. What to everyone here, they know as the Fortune Found.

And dropping down to the mat and hooking his legs, delivering on my act even more by lounging lazily across him, hand straight into the air and counting as the ref hits the mat, I get the three count at the exact moment the clock on the titantron twenty feet away begins to sound throughout the space.

The crowd on their feet as I feel the arm of our ref for the evening pulling me toward him, attempting to get me up in order to declare me the winner.

The **new** HFWA Heavyweight Champion.

Allowing the referee's assistance, I pull myself to my feet, my ears ringing with the sound of the auditorium each second until the belt is handed over. The levels then becoming more muted until there's no sound at all.

This moment—my moment—doing away with all outside distractions, minus the one I can sense as she slides her way into the ring, and gracefully into my arms seconds later. Her whispered congratulations, the only sound with what we've just accomplished, I will ever want or need.

Her lips searing my skin as she kisses my cheek first then finds her way easily to my lips. Mine answering back in kind, flooding her with every emotion I'm feeling in the moment, making her understand just what all of this means.

Hopefully also showing what *she* means.

"I love you, Dawson," I whisper, those same eyes from before, spilling tears now as she mouths back the sweetest reply.

I love you more, Champ.

Releasing my hold on her as the team from the back makes its way down the ramp and over to the ringside corner where Matthias resides, I look from Dawson to the title and then out over the crowd. And that's when it happens. The change I've been waiting for.

As I lift the title above my head and roar as loud as I can be heard through the auditorium, I drop the façade once and for all.

When a man has been given everything he could ever want, there's only one thing left for him to do.

I drop the Fortune and just become Gavin.

Chapter Thirty-Two

Gavin

The first time Smith ever ran a pay per view, I was holding the Heavyweight belt, so what happens backstage once Dawson and I make our way through the curtain, is expected.

We're surrounded by people. Droves of them. Half of these people, not performers, but still people who work tirelessly to put the show together. All of them hoarding around us wanting to just reach out with a pat on the back to say congratulations.

Our business, one could argue, is a fictional one, but the responses from these individuals, it's all real. There is no feigning happiness or story to be found. This moment, in the annals of wrestling history, an important one to more than just the man or woman who struts out there in public holding the title.

I bask in the adoration and praise, not because it's expected, but because I appreciate it. If these folks didn't want the belt on me, believe in me, whether it's the bosses or a damn camera guy in the back, I wouldn't be getting the praise I am now. They wouldn't be here at all.

Dawson, though, she's like a deer caught in headlights, but holding her own. She's genuinely smiling at the hoard around us and even starting up a few little conversations with some of them. Adapting quite easily to the life I've led for the past ten years.

Almost as if she belongs here.

Just on the outskirts of the mob, I see Matthias. His eyes are hooded and serious, which I've come to learn over our time together is commonplace for him, but there's more to it. The way he looks at me once I catch his eyes, I can see happiness there. Acceptance.

And honestly, with our history, standing here able to witness it is everything I need.

If the man who dropped the belt to me believes me to be the right fit, then it means I am.

"Guys," I shift toward the crowd of onlookers, bringing Dawson close. "As much as I would love to sit here and bask in all of your adoration, I need a few minutes with my girl even more. I'm sure you can understand why." I motion to her, perusing her entire form with my eyes, both for the benefit of the crowd, and myself.

Even backstage she's a stunner.

What I don't tell the people standing around, is the real reason why I need to get her alone. The coup de grace of the evening, if you will. I want Dawson alone because even though I can easily see she wants to be by my side right now, I need to tell her the truth. Make her understand what her cousin has done and why we're even standing here, to begin with.

Snaking her way through the crowd, Kimber pushes her way past the people still milling around while others have begun taking off, and she pulls me into her arms, making sure as she clutches me close, she does her best friend duties.

"You better be taking her back to the locker room to seal the deal, Fortune. It's already been two weeks too long."

The loss of her, what I thought about earlier, the shades of it I'd seen since she was thrown unceremoniously from the building by Reese, it's there clear as day in Kimber's words. For the first time, her finding another woman she enjoys spending time with, and not wanting to give it up.

"I plan on it. And I would actually go through with the plan if a certain Women's Champion would release the chokehold she has on me."

Laughing as she lets me go, she turns to Dawson and repeats much of the same. Bringing the woman I love into the tightest embrace and saying something that by the end of it, has both women's eyes welling up with tears.

Throwing my arm around her, and using my other to hand her the belt, her being the real champion to me given everything she's faced and we've endured since our first night together, I guide her silently toward my locker room.

Pulling from my arms when we've made our way through the door, she spins around to face me, her eyes having thankfully dried up on the walk, and a smile now lifting her entire face.

"That was, god, Gavin. Being out there, the crowd's reaction to me, to you and Matthias, to us…it was surreal. I can't believe I was a part of it."

Once upon a time, when I was first starting out, my reaction was much the same as Dawson's now. The absolute innocence of it is another reminder of what she brings to the table in our relationship. During my short time with her, especially given how everything here is so new and exciting, has breathed new life into what was becoming a pretty stale work environment. In her eyes, I see wrestling in a new light.

A refreshed one.

"Does that mean you'd be interested in doing it again in the future?"

Taking one step closer she grins. "How soon are we talking? Because if you're thinking about doing it again tomorrow, I might need to stop you."

Following her lead, guided as I am by the smile still lighting her face, I take a confident step forward at the same moment she takes another one, bringing us chest to chest.

"So, tomorrow is out, but how does every other day for the rest of our lives sound?"

I stop, immediately chastising myself for jumping the gun, but my body and heart motionless when she answers.

"I was hoping you'd say that."

This, the woman standing here now, is the Dawson I've been waiting for. The one so secure in her answer, there isn't even the slightest shake or tremor in her voice or body. Her eyes practically glowing under the fluorescent ones above us with the excitement of the future together.

She's back.

Taking a step back, I head over to where my bag is stashed and tossing it on the floor take a seat. Motioning with a quick pat to the wooden slated seat beside me for her to join me.

I want to hold onto her answer, her eagerness to want to do this with me in the future, but I can't until I'm sure there's nothing else standing in our way. Which, right now, there is.

Reese is still between us.

"I need to tell you some things. Stuff I should have told you when it happened, but kept to myself. Mostly because I saw what was happening to you and I didn't want to make things worse."

"Okay…" she says, eyes concerned, body tensing but her hand still reaching out for mine. Thankfully giving me the connection to her I'll need for everything about to come.

"I told you before, I don't ever want to be the reason for your pain, princess. What I'm about to tell you, it's going to hurt, and for that, I'm sorry."

"You're not the only one with something to say, Gavin. I realized something tonight. Hell, I realized it last week but was too lost in my own misery to accept it. Something happened earlier when I got here, and it's made it so I can't deny it, even though part of me still wants to."

There's a trace of sadness in her eyes but it isn't the same as what I'd experienced over the last two weeks. It's lesser than it was, but it still makes me want to jump out and demand to know what it is, and who I have to pummel for causing it. It's only when she speaks again, I shove it down and force myself to listen.

"What is it you want to tell me, Gavin? Does it have to do with us? With the way…I've been acting?"

Shit. No.

As her eyes fall away from mine, I'm immediately pulling them back as I reach out with my free hand and touch her face.

"Yes and no, Dawson. It's not what you're thinking, but it does affect us."

"What is it?" she asks softly, this time thankfully, not looking away.

"The reason I came back after being so adamant I wasn't going to is because of Reese."

"He threatened you."

Wait...what?

"Yeah, he did. He threatened me with you, but how do you know?"

"He told me as much tonight. He didn't realize when I walked in that I wasn't there because you'd sent me, so he blurted the whole thing out."

She'd gone to see Reese?

"You went to see him?"

Nodding, her gaze falls to our hands, where she grabs a hold of mine tighter. "Yeah. I thought if I could sit down with him, face to face, just the two of us, I would be able to make him see what's happening between you and me. The feelings that even when I was trying to hard to fight them, I couldn't possibly win against. I thought if I could explain it, he would understand it and accept it. Instead, he told me this. How you chose me."

"I will always choose you, Dawson."

Eyes softening, she releases a sigh. "Oh, Gavin...You never should have been put in that position."

"Maybe not, but if I had to do it all over again, I would choose the same thing."

"What I don't get, is why you didn't tell me. I know I pulled away from you but you never left my side until a few days ago. So, why not bring this to me sooner?"

"I didn't want to hurt you more."

It's so incredibly easy, to be honest with this woman. She doesn't even have to demand it of me, the truth is just always there on the tip of my tongue ready to spill out. If she had prodded me just a little harder, I never would have been able to hold this back from her. I would have spelled it out when it happened. Even if my reasoning for holding back was still valid and important to me.

"Oh, pretty boy. Remember when you said I needed to see everyone's part in things? Well, you do too. You didn't cause this. Reese did, and I did by letting my feelings for him, for our lifetime together, overshadow what I've always known to be true. I may have been hurt to find out what he did or tried to do, but it wouldn't have been you who caused it."

I know this. I've always known it. She can handle herself. In keeping this from her and leaving it until now in order to share it, I'd taken a gigantic shit over everything I've been trying to do since she arrived. I'd stripped her of her own power. Her own voice.

"You're right. I should have told you. I'm sorry you had to find out the way you did."

"You know, I'm not." She laughs uncomfortably. "Better I heard it from the horses' mouth anyway."

Right. Her meeting with Reese.

"So, other than learning what you did, how did it go with him?"

If she's here with me now, and Reese is still off barricaded in the office where Bryan said he was earlier, its clear what way everything went, but I want to her to tell me. I want to see how she's handling it with my own eyes.

I need to know if the loss of her cousin is going to end up being a problem when we leave here tonight.

"Finding out he threatened me with a lawsuit in order to get you to comply with what he wanted, Gavin, it breaks my heart. Not in the way it did when he fired me, though. It breaks my heart because you had done something so incredibly selfless in trying to protect me, it should have been all the proof Reese needed to see how much you care about me. It should have changed things. It didn't, though."

No, it hadn't. I remember the meeting as if I'd just lived it, and all it did was make the man smugger because he'd gotten one over on me. The epitome of the billionaire businessman at play. There hadn't been a moment at all where he realized what agreeing to his terms actually meant.

Dawson's not the only one whose heart breaks over it.

If Reese could have just seen what was happening, what I did in making the choice I did, maybe things would have ended up differently, and we'd be celebrating together instead of apart.

"He was cold, Gavin. All traces of the boy I knew, the man he became, the guy who because of fear of reprisal came out to me and me alone, he was gone. There was no soul left in his eyes. It was all darkness. What you've been telling me, what Bryan explained when he came to the house with the contracts, I finally allowed the filter I've had on him to drop, and I saw it all. I saw him for who he really is. Or at least, who he is now."

"What he became," I add quietly, and as she sucks in sharply; I realize what I've done.

I'd understood Reese.

"This is what I want him to see. You, just like this. I was hoping I would have been able to do it tonight. Gotten his blessing for working this show, and also for our relationship. You of all people seem to understand him, yet for some reason, he can't see past the persona you've created, to who you really are."

I have spent years focusing on myself. Working my way up in the business, creating opportunities, very self-aware and involved in myself. Almost to my own detriment. I'd stopped giving a crap about the people around me, and in turn, forced everyone to fall in line with the version of myself I was presenting. I made it extremely difficult to like me, let alone for anyone to genuinely love me. Though, sitting here in this room with the only other person besides Kimber who has even tried, it's shedding the remainder of the character I've come to loathe.

My need to make all of this right, to force Reese's hand into accepting us, accepting his cousin for the generous and beautiful soul she is, is the strongest it's ever been. I want to make all of this better for her and it sucks knowing I can't.

That I may never be able to.

Reese is his own man, he makes his own choices, and right now, his choice is to distance himself from the only real version of love he's ever known. I know this to be true for him because it is for me.

She's my one true love.

"I wish I could make this right for you, Daws. I do. Knowing it's a choice between him or me is ridiculous because it doesn't have to be this way. Bygones and all of that. I may not like the man, but for you, I could learn to."

"That's just it, Gavin. It's not a choice. Not anymore. He made his decision. As my father likes to say, he made his bed, and now he's got to lie in it. What everyone was trying to get me to see, I do now. Crystal clear. I won't ever stop loving my cousin, but I can't allow him to own the rest of my life the way he's owned the past two weeks. It's time for me to choose, and I have."

She's choosing me.

"Gavin, the way I acted this week," she continues, her voice lowering, her body visibly shaken. "I'm sorry. I became so caught up in the loss of my cousin, it distorted my view of what was really going on. What we share. How we feel. It was all still there; it never went away, but it was buried under the weight of Reese, and what I could only see as the mess I caused."

"Dawson, you don't need to apologize to me. I was in it. We lived it together. I knew it wasn't going to get better until I took a step back and let you figure it out. I want to fix, rescue, and make right everything you face that is even remotely unpleasant, but I also realize I can't. You're your own woman. Your own person. We may be one unit together but we're still two unique people apart from it."

"So, what you're saying is...you haven't washed your hands of me?"

At first, I think her question is a joke. I'm waiting for the soft laugh to escape or the raging belly laugh that doubles her over to come, but when I take her in, all of her, I realize she's as serious as a heart attack. Coming here tonight, what she'd learned from Reese, she was truly afraid she was too late.

You can't be late for an appointment that was never set to begin with.

It's only a few seconds after I've thought it and her laughter falls, I'm made aware I said the words aloud.

"I'm not too late?" she repeats the question, and I nod, but I also end the distance between us and pull her to me. Placing my lips anywhere and everywhere she'll let me, from the top of her head straight down to her neck, burying her in kisses. In feeling.

Every single kiss filled with an answer only she will be able to hear.

She could *never* be too late.

"Dawson," I say, pulling away long enough to bend over to my bag on the floor. Grabbing the ring I tossed in there earlier and holding it out between us, I show her as I hand it over, just how serious I am. "I love you. I will always love you. Through the good days, and even more through the bad ones. It's unalterable and unwavering. I want everything with you, and I want it to start now."

"A key ring?" she questions, looking from the ring to the key dangling on it and back to me again, searching for some sort of answer. Some understanding of what this means.

"It's not exactly the ring I'm sure a girl expects, but since you're not just any girl, and I'm not some ordinary guy, I figured this is as good a place to start as any. Since we've practically been living together in two different places for months, I want what comes next."

"Gavin," she whisper-sighs. "I don't know what to say."

"I do. Say you'll move in with me."

"Are you sure?"

Silly woman. Am I sure? Pfft. Did she forget who she's talking to?

"Am I sure I want to spend every morning waking up to those breathtaking eyes? Falling asleep to your heart beating slowly over mine? Talking shop over dinner, lazily lounging around watching movies, and listening to you softly snore on the sofa when you fall asleep on me? Or maybe beginning each day making slow leisurely love to you and every night surrendering to the passion we share? Yes, Dawson Traymore, I'm beyond sure. Now, the only question left to answer is, are you?"

The silence the room is drenched in after my answer to her question is alarming. I'm aware of every move she makes. Her body as it stretches, her breath as it falls and her posture as she leans back against the wall. Every move torturing me as I sit and wait for her response. The time passing without a word starting to make me question everything until finally, she stands and turns to me.

"I'll be right back."

Rising at the exact moment she turns and bolts from the room, I start to go after her, believing I've scared her off, and desperate to make it right. But before I can even make it through the door, she's storming back through it again.

This time, holding up a key between us, and bringing it up to the key ring, she takes her time slipping it on. Her face expressionless until she's done whatever she's attempting to do, and raises her eyes to mine.

"Gavin Foster Fortune, you beat me to the punch. I was going to do this a few weeks ago, with as often as you were staying over. So, let me make it right. With this key, I just want to say, I would love for you to move in with me." A symphony of her laughter escaping when I bring her into my arms, her next words adding to the sound, like music to my ears.

To my very soul.

"Let's go home, Champ."

THE END

Acknowledgments

My children. Caleb, Noah, Raine, and Isabella. Four people that if it weren't for their very existence, their love and support, and the ways they continue to enrich my life and teach me as I attempt to do the same with them as they grow, would leave me only a shell of the woman I've become. Thank you for being the four unique individuals that you are and for listening and heeding my words when I'm not hearing them myself. For never giving up, never giving in, and for never losing your flames. I love you all and I always will.

Pamela Sparkman. Your impact, the imprint you left behind and have left behind after every book I write, it will never be forgotten or made light of. It's been a pleasure and an honor to know you. To love you. Thank you for everything.

My beta readers. All of you individually and together as a unit. You took on a book that I know for some of you, would never in a million years be what you read, and had faith in me to deliver on what I have with you in the past. Whether as readers apart from the writing process, or the ones scouring over endless chapters making sure it all worked right. You are at the very core of this book. Your words of encouragement, along with your constructive criticism through every part of this, appreciated, accepted, and treasured. Thank you so very much. I love you all.

Joey. Here we are again, guard dog extraordinaire. A journey of our own again taking place during the making of this one that even though we're nowhere near done with, I don't regret taking for a second. Thank you for being my best friend and believing in me when I don't. I love you and I always will. ANF, pretty boy.

My Autism Family. This isn't a book geared toward the lives we live the way Count on Me was when I wrote it (more specifically my life at the time), but it is one that is just as affected by what you've brought to my life in the time spent writing it. The years even before the idea presented itself. For the hours spent rejoicing over the positive moments in our lives, as well as the ones where we just held each other as we cried and admitted our fears and inadequacies, you've given me something that can never be recreated. Something so pure and so moving that I'm going to carry it with me long after my time here is done. Thank you for loving me, for supporting me, and for believing in me when a lot of times, I didn't. I love you all.

Pro-Wrestling.
From the time I was five years old, you've been a staple in my life. We break up and go our separate ways sometimes, but at the end of the day, we always come back together in the most glorious of ways. The imprint you as a whole and the superstars apart from it have left on me and my heart will never be made light of. You've changed me. Given me something over the years to believe in when much like I've said to the others above, I didn't have the strength to believe in myself. Thank you, pro-wrestling. For being what I needed you to be then, and what you've been today. Much love and respect always.

Readers, Bloggers, Book Buyers the world over.
Without you, this dream of mine, of any authors, wouldn't exist. Sure, we would still write the stories that you are all so fond of sharing with the world, but we wouldn't be able to reach the masses we do because of you. So, for that and everything else you do, from the bottom of this very humbled and honored author's heart...thank you. We appreciate every single thing you do, day in and day out, and we (me) always will. Never stop shouting your love for things that make your heart soar, and I swear to you, I won't stop shouting my love for you.

About the Author

Melyssa Winchester is a mother of four from Toronto, Ontario, Canada.

When she's not writing, you can find her curled up with Supernatural or Veronica Mars, two of her many favorite shows. And when those aren't available, curled up with a book, on the lookout for her next book boyfriend. If you want to find her, check Facebook (Melyssa Winchester) or Twitter (@AngelicDivinity), as she might have an addiction to both.

Melyssa is currently working on **Company**, the fifth novel in the ***Black and Blue*** series, as well as **Coming Undone**, the eighth book in the ***Count on Me*** series.

Books by Melyssa Winchester

Love United Series
Holding onto Heaven
No Surrender
Wanted
Stairway to Heaven
A Light in the Dark
My Heaven (Alternate Ending to Holding onto Heaven)

Count on Me Series
Count on Me
Hear Me Now
Take Me with You
All My Heart
Here & Now (with Joey Winchester)
Unbroken
What Lies Beneath
Coming Undone

Black & Blue Series
Shades of Blue
Into the Blue
Heroine
Shoot

Before the Light Series
Hold onto Me (Michael's Story)
Absence of Light (Ryan's Story)

Stand Alone Titles
The Space in Between
Remembering Sunday
Fall (with Joey Winchester)